MW01256616

About the author

Roger M. Kean has been writing for many years, but only in the past three as an author of published fiction. He has written five action tales based on a core of late-Victorian boys' adventures, available for the Kindle from Amazon and other eBook formats from Smashwords.

Having spent a stint at Hornsey College of Art studying painting, Kean attended the London Film School, where he began writing film scripts and his first attempts at full-scale novels. For eight years he edited film documentaries for the BBC before moving into full-time journalism. In the 1980s, as co-founder of magazine publisher Newsfield, he created and edited the best-selling CRASH magazine for the Spectrum home computer and then ZZAP!64 for the Commodore 64. Since then, Kean has authored several history reference titles, including the well-reviewed *The Complete Chronicle of the Emperors of Rome*. Now he spends his time inventing new scenarios to populate with characters from the imagination. He lives with his partner in the the Welsh Marches of Shropshire, England.

WINNING HIS SPURS

Roger M. Kean

RECKLESS BOOKS

First published as an ebook in Great Britain in 2011 by Reckless Books
and in the U.S.A. as a Smashwords ebook edition

First published in paperback in 2012

Typeset in Minion Pro by Reckless Books
Ludlow, Shropshire, England

Cover design and internal illustrations: Oliver Frey / http://oliverfreyart.com
Maps: Roger M. Kean

Contents

Major sites of the Third Crusade

Kingdom of Jerusalem

Central Europe, end 12th century

Chapter 1: The Failing Crusades

Central England, late July 1189

Lowering cloud pressed down on the Vale of Evesham, the purple-grey edges lost against the sharp Cotswold escarpment above the distant hamlet of Broad Way. An occasional flicker deep in the smoky billows warned of the thunderstorm to come. As the first fat drops of rain slapped against his cowl, Father Francis raised his eyes to the heavens in mild admonition and wearily turned his ambling nag toward the nearby manor house of Erstwood where he knew he would be guaranteed a warm welcome at the hearth of Dame Editha, a nobly-born Saxon member of his far-flung flock.

The overhanging trees through which he guided his old piebald mare partly deflected the rain, but its full force hit him as he rode into the open lands of Erstwood. Fortunately, the house lay just ahead. Its appearance would have told any traveler that this was a Saxon freeholding of some importance. Father Francis saw a strongly fortified building, with few outer windows, surrounded by a dry moat with a drawbridge. Erstwood looked capable of holding off anything short of a real attack.

With a sigh of relief, the damp priest dismounted in the courtyard as a groom took the reins and led his equally relieved horse to a dry stable. As anticipated, Dame Editha offered him a hearty welcome. She was a handsome woman in her late thirties, whose bearing, clothing, and flaxen hair gave away her Saxon heritage.

"Good Father Francis, how pleased I am to see you and give you shelter in this furious summer storm." She leaned closer and lowered her voice. "I'm really happy because Cuthbert is driving me mad with wanting to know all about the Crusades. Please satisfy his curiosity. You know so much about the subject."

"I'm hardly an expert, Dame Editha, but if I can…"

At that moment the subject of their discussion came running into the hall, a lad of fifteen years. His fair, curling hair and bright open face, as well as the style of his dress, spoke of a purely Saxon origin, but a keener eye would have detected the Norman blood that also ran in his veins. His figure was slimmer and lighter, his features more gracefully shaped than was common among Saxons. He wore a tight-fitting jerkin of a light-blue cloth which fell from the waist nearly to his knees. A short woolen cloak of a darker blue hung over his shoulder. In his hand he held a Saxon cap with a little heron's plume, which Father Francis knew he liked to wear jauntily on one side.

As Dame Editha went off to make arrangements for the priest's comfort, Cuthbert eagerly settled him on a window seat, uncaring of the pouring rain beyond the mullions. A distant crack of thunder signaled the approaching heart of the storm. But for Cuthbert there were only the priest's words.

"Why do you wish to know about the Crusades?"

"Father, you know I've no father to tell me, since he fell in battle in Normandy three years ago, and everyone is full of the talk that there's to be another attempt to wrest the Holy Land from the Saracens. But no one can tell me how all this happened to begin with."

Father Francis sighed deeply, took a breath and started haltingly. "To this day, my son, the Crusades have brought Europe little but distress. It began with the pilgrims. From ancient times swarms of them have gone from all parts of Europe to visit the holy shrines.

"When the followers of the Prophet Mohammed took possession of the Holy Land, they made life difficult for the pilgrims, with heavy fines and all kinds of cruel persecution. They trampled them underfoot as if they were unwelcome beetles. So terrible were the tales that reached us that men came to think it a sacred duty to seize the Holy Sepulchre of the Lord from infidel hands. Then Pope Urban boosted the movement when he preached at Clermont ninety-four years ago to a host said to number more than thirty thousand clergy, barons and princes.

"Thereafter, men flocked from all parts of France to hear him preach and when he finished the multitude, carried away by their enthusiasm, swore to win the Holy Sepulchre or die. Monks threw off their habits and took up the sword—even women and children joined the throng. The mass formed up behind a monk called Peter the Hermit, whose violent words inspired them. But what, my son, could be expected from a great army without leaders, without discipline, without tactics, without means of getting food? They visited like a plague the countries through which they passed."

"But weren't they all filled with the grace of the Holy Spirit?" Cuthbert sounded puzzled.

Father Francis shook his head. "More like Satan's spirit. In Hungary they devastated the fields. In Bulgaria the people fell on the approaching locusts with fury and the peasant crusaders died horribly. It was said that of the quarter of a million who set out, no more than a third crossed into Asia Minor. And once there, having reached only Nicaea, their fate was no better than that of those who had perished in Bulgaria. The Turks massacred the adults and enslaved the children to use their bodies—boys and girls—for their lusts... but that's not for your ears, young Cuthbert.

"Others, equally wild, misguided and unfortunate, followed. Some never reached farther than Hungary, where they were put to death for the evil deeds they had performed while crossing Germany, attacking the Jews and torturing them. Rape and plunder were the crusaders' objectives. In these irregular expeditions no less than half a million perished."

Cuthbert leaned forward. "But that wasn't the end."

"No, not at all. Godfrey of Bouillon, with his brothers the counts Eustace and Baldwin, led the first militarily organized Crusade, with many other nobles, knights and their retinues, and it was well armed and under good order. Duke Godfrey's discipline was such that the people of Hungary and Bulgaria allowed them to pass without hindrance, and though he ran into difficulties with Alexius Comnenus, the crafty Greek emperor in Constantinople, he succeeded in crossing into Asia. There he was joined by many from England, France, and other countries. Duke Robert, the son of our William the Conqueror, led a strong band of Normans to the war, as did the great princes of France and Spain. The army which crossed the narrow Bosphorus was the largest host ever seen, scores of thousands of knights, men-at-arms, and archers.

"Nicaea, scene of the massacre of the Hermit's rabble, they took after a series of desperate battles which lasted many weeks, and the crusaders afterward defeated the Turks in a great battle near the town of Dorylaeum. But success also brought conflict among the leaders, and Baldwin, the brother of Duke Godfrey, left the main army and founded his own County of Edessa in upper Mesopotamia. The rest, suffering from disease, famine, and the heat, slowly made their way south to Antioch."

"I have heard tell of Antioch." Cuthbert's eyes glimmered with excitement and Father Francis saw the boy's dreams of adventure in them.

"The crusaders besieged this important city but its massive defensive walls proved so strong that the Turks inside held out for months, and it was at last only taken by treachery. No sooner had the crusaders occupied their prize than a huge Saracen army from Persia besieged the holy warriors in their turn. During the first siege, the crusaders had seized all the food that could be taken from the region, so Antioch's storehouses stood empty. As the people came close to starving there came the discovery of the Holy Lance that had pierced Christ's side on the Cross and, inspired by this divine miracle, the Christian army dashed out won a great victory over the Turks and the Persians."

"And then they reached the Holy City?"

"Finally, lad, but only after much squabbling among the leaders and another slow progress. The crusaders' losses by then had been so great that no more than forty thousand of those who had crossed the Bosphorus reached Jerusalem itself. This fragment of an army now appeared before strong fortifications they no longer had the means of battering. There were no siege engines, no provisions or munitions of any kind. Water was also scarce and it seemed as if the crusaders had reached Jerusalem only to perish there.

"Happily, just at this time a further band of Genoese crusaders turned up at Jaffa. They had stores and the skilled workmen capable of making the war machines for the siege. On July 14 in 1099— four years after Pope Urban had called the princes of Europe to the Cross—the first assault went in. After a bitter resistance, the Saracen defenders were worn down and the mighty walls breached. But in taking the Holy City, the crusaders massacred all the inhabitants— Muslim, Jew, and Christian alike—thousands in number, and so became the bloody-handed masters of Christ's Holy Sepulchre.

"Godfrey was now chosen King of Jerusalem and his victory inspired other armies to follow his example; but badly led, they all suffered on their way, and few ever reached the Holy Land. Godfrey died in 1100, and his brother Baldwin of Edessa succeeded him."

Cuthbert hung on every word. "What happened next?" he begged.

"This was over ninety years ago, my son, and since then there have been fresh efforts to crush Mohammedan power, but so far there's been little reward for Christian efforts. Were it not for the commitment of the Knights of St. John and of the Temple—the Hospitallers and the Templars—two great companies of men who devote their lives to protecting the Sepulchre against the Mohammedan infidels, our hold on the Holy Land would have been lost.

"Bit by bit the Saracens have seized post after post from our hands. Edessa went in 1144, and in response Louis VII of France took the vow and headed a noble army. Germany joined France, but no success came of this effort either. The infidels defeated Germany's Emperor Conrad, with the loss of almost all his army, and Louis was also attacked and a large portion of his force slaughtered."

Father Francis paused. He gazed out at the vertical curtains of rain, now and then illuminated by brilliant lightning flashes, his silence framed by thunder. He gave a heartfelt sigh and turned back to Cuthbert. The raging weather clothed his words in dismal meaning.

"It was a disaster. We thought that the First Crusade had showed that our chivalrous knights and men-at-arms were irresistible, the Second on the contrary proved that the Turks were the equal of Christian knights. Gradually the Christian hold on the Holy Land was shaken. Two years ago, in 1187, at a dreadful place gloomily called the Horns Of Hattin, although fighting with extraordinary bravery, the armies of the Kingdom of Jerusalem were annihilated in a calamitous battle. The king was taken prisoner and Christian power crushed. Then the great new Saracen commander Saladin marched against Jerusalem and forced it to capitulate.

"Such, Cuthbert my boy, is the last sad news which has reached us. No wonder it has stirred the hearts of the kings of Europe, and that every effort will be made again to recapture the Holy Sepulchre and to avenge our brothers cruelly murdered by the infidels."

"But, Father, from your story it would seem that Europe has already sacrificed an enormous number of lives to take the Holy Sepulchre, and that after all the fighting, when we've taken it, it's only to lose it again."

"True, Cuthbert, but we must hope that things will be better in future. The Templars and Hospitallers have swelled their ranks enormously and have the best lances in Europe. This time when we seize the Holy Sepulchre from infidel hands the two military orders will be able to maintain it against all assaults—"

"—And those who take up the Cross now!"

Father Francis curbed the boy's enthusiasm with a stern glare. "I say that the great misfortunes which have fallen on the past crusaders have been a punishment from Heaven, because they didn't go to fight in the right spirit. It's not enough to take up sword and shield and to place a red cross on the shoulder. Those who desire to fight the Lord's battle must have clean hands but, more importantly, clean hearts, and go out in the spirit of pilgrims rather than knights."

"They should trust just in the spirit?"

Father Francis almost laughed. "No, I don't mean that, for only a fool would despise the courage, bravery, tactics, and weapons of the Saracen foe—but I mean that they should lay aside all thoughts of worldly glory, or of lands gained, or of rivalry against one another."

"And do you think that King Richard and the other kings and nobles getting ready will go with this spirit?"

Father Francis hesitated.

"My son, it's not for me to judge motives, or to speak well or ill of those who have been chosen for this great undertaking. Of all tasks it's the most praiseworthy. It's horrible to think that the holy shrines of Jerusalem should be in the hands of infidel unbelievers. It's the duty of every man, regardless of rank or station, who can bear arms to put on his armor and join the armies destined for *Outremer*."

"Over the sea," Cuthbert echoed. The Norman word fired his imagination.

"Whether success will crown the effort, or whether God wills it otherwise, is not for men to discuss. It's enough that the work is there, and it's our duty to do it."

A flash lit up the dark sky and revealed in the failing light Cuthbert's face glowing at these stirring and powerful words.

"Yes, Father! That's what I want. To take up the Cross and march to Outremer beside the Earl of Evesham and my king."

"Oh ho, I see. Of course it's natural for a lad of spirit like you to want to set about the Lord's holy business, but Cuthbert you're some way off sixteen and I think you'll find Sir Walter, your liege lord, won't take you in his retinue until you've put on some more years."

His mother's hail to announce that a meal would be ready in a few moments stifled any retort to this crushing put-down Cuthbert might have made. *In truth the boy has some reason for hope*, Father Francis thought. Before his recent death in Normandy, Cuthbert's father, Sir Stephen de Lance, had been a Norman knight of some renown, a fourth-generation descendant of one of the Conqueror's knights. In service to Sir Walter, Earl of Evesham, he had also been the earl's close friend. Sir Walter, through his marriage to Gweneth, the Saxon heiress of Evesham, owned in the king's name all the surrounding lands and forests, and in turn had permitted the marriage of his friend Sir Stephen to Gweneth's cousin Editha, whose ancestors had owned Erstwood from a time long before the Normans' conquest. So Cuthbert de Lance was distantly related to the earl.

But, as Father Francis reflected, Sir Walter, ensconced in his great castle, surrounded by all the Norman panoply of knights, men-at-arms, squires, and pages, was hardly likely to take much notice of a lowly half-Saxon relative. *Poor Cuthbert must needs console himself with one day being confirmed master of Erstwood. That will be the pinnacle of his powers.*

Father Francis said nothing of this to Cuthbert, though.

Chapter 2: The Outlaws

Evesham, August 1189

On a bright, summery morning Cuthbert, idly seated on a low stone wall, watched squad after squad of armed men riding up to the castle of the Earl of Evesham. From his costly belt hung a light short sword, while across his knees lay a crossbow, which in itself declared his Norman blood, the Saxons having always preferred the axe and the powerful English warbow. Cuthbert's brow wrinkled as he looked anxiously at yet another group of young blades riding past him toward the castle.

I would give anything to know what wind blows these knaves here. From every small castle in the Earl's fief the retainers seem to be hurrying here. Is he going, I wonder, to settle once and for all his quarrels with the Baron of Wortham?

As he pondered on this interesting possibility a jovial-looking functionary, closely followed by two large hounds at his heel, dodged past a pack of horsemen clattering into the castle and came down from the main gate. He turned to head into Evesham town. Cuthbert sprang to his feet and walked briskly to intercept Hubert the falconer before he could turn the corner of the outer ward and pass out of sight. Hubert's sudden appearance was a godsend.

"Ah, Master Cuthbert," Hubert said as he halted. His panting dogs slumped to a rest around his feet and lowered their mournful jowls on their forepaws. "What brings you so near to the castle? It's not often that you favor us with your presence."

"I'm happier in the woods, it's true, but I had an errand to run for my mother and I was on my way back, when I saw all these knights, squires, and men flocking into the castle bailey. What's Sir Walter up

15

to, I wonder?" Cuthbert was well aware of Hubert's delight in gossip and knew he thought Cuthbert a harmless listener to secrets the falconer could hardly bear to keep to himself. Nevertheless, he shook his head sagely.

"Oh, the earl keeps his own counsel."

Cuthbert just kept quiet, knowing that a pause would certainly reveal more detail.

Hubert harrumphed and then, leaning forward conspiratorially, said, "But a shrewd guess might be made about the reasons for the gathering. It was only three days ago that Sir Walter's gamekeepers were beaten back by the landless men of the forest when they caught a bunch of them cutting up a fat deer."

Cuthbert gave Hubert a wide-eyed look of outraged surprise, the better to encourage more information.

"Now you know the earl my lord is an easy man and kindly to everyone. He doesn't enjoy harassing the common Saxon people the way most of the neighboring barons do, but he's still as fanatical as the worst of them when it comes to his forest privileges. It wasn't helped by the way the gamekeepers were treated. They cut poor figures with their broken bows and draggled plumes after the hoodlums had dumped them in a stagnant pond. Sir Walter swore an oath that he would clear the forest of the outlaw bands. So I would guess that this assembly is for that purpose. On the other hand…"

Hubert stretched out both of his arms expansively to encompass infinite possibilities and Cuthbert leaned forward to encourage the falconer. "It could also be that he has finally lost his rag with that evilly disposed and treacherous bastard baron, Sir John of Wortham, who has already begun to harry some of our outlying lands, and has rustled, I hear, many head of cattle. It's a quarrel that's going to have to be fought out sooner or later, and the sooner the better, I say. You know me, Cuthbert, I'm not a warlike hawk, but I'd gladly throw on my mail shirt to help raze to the ground the keep of that robber-tyrant, Sir John of Wortham."

"Well I hope that's what it is. I should hate any harm to come to the forest men. Thanks for all that Hubert," Cuthbert said and smiled broadly. "But I can't stand around here gossiping with you all day."

Hubert's florid countenance paled somewhat. "For God's sake, Cuthbert lad, don't tell anyone that the news came from me. He may be a kindly man, but Sir Walter would have my balls struck off if he knew that my tongue had let slip any warning to the outlaws, especially if they then slipped through his fingers."

"Don't worry, Hubert, I can keep a secret when the occasion needs it. When do you reckon the knights are likely to start their war?"

Somewhat relieved by Cuthbert's airy reassurance, Hubert said, "Oh, any time soon. I left the first ones to arrive swilling beer and stuffing themselves on game pies, and from what I hear, they'll start as soon as the last ones arrive, which will be soon, unless indigestion gets them first. Whoever's their quarry, they're bound to attack before news of the call to arms leaks out."

With a wave of his hand to the falconer Cuthbert went on his way. He uncrossed his fingers. Everyone knew that you could downgrade a lie to a harmless fib by crossing the first two fingers of your left hand when giving an assurance. He disliked deceiving Hubert, but the lives of the forest men were more important. Leaving the common road, he struck across the gently undulating country dotted here and there by clumps of trees. As soon as he was out of sight from the castle walls, he ran at an easy mile-eating lope without stopping, until after half an hour he arrived home at Erstwood Manor.

On entering the gates, Cuthbert rushed up to the upper floor and the solar where his mother sewed with three of her maids.

"I need to speak to you," he gasped as he caught his breath from the run.

"What is it now?" she said. When she saw his expression she waved her hand to the girls. They quickly gathered their work and left.

"Mother," he said, when they were alone, "I'm worried that Sir Walter is about to make a raid on the outlaws. Armed men have been coming in all the morning from the manors around, and if he's not intending to attack the Baron of Wortham he must be plotting against the landless men of the forest."

"What do you want to do, Cuthbert?" His mother's tone was stern, though she appeared anxious. "It won't do your future any good to meddle in these matters. At the moment the earl looks favorably on you for the sake of your father, but still—"

"Mother, I've so many friends in the forest. What about Cnut, your own second cousin, and many others of our friends, all good honest men who are forced to find refuge through the cruel Norman laws."

"What do you plan to do?" she asked again.

"I'll take my pony and warn them of the threat."

She pursed her lips and sighed. "If you're set on going, you'd be better off on foot. I've no doubt that men will have been set to watch for any warning sent from the Saxon franklins' homesteads. You're familiar with all the paths and it's no great distance. On foot I think you can evade the spies. But one thing, Cuthbert, you must promise me—and you can uncross your fingers—that if the earl and his men meet with the outlaws you won't take any part in fighting."

Cuthbert hung his head momentarily, before looking straight into his mother's eyes. "I've no reason to argue against the castle or the forest. My blood and family are with both. I want to save bloodshed in a quarrel like this. I hope that the time will come when Saxon and Norman can fight side by side for our common cause."

A few minutes later, having changed his fashionable blue jerkin for one of much drabber hue, Cuthbert started for the great wildwood, which then stretched to within a mile of Erstwood. Much of the country was given over to forest, which provided the Norman elite preserves for the hunt. He knew it was death for a Saxon or any serf to be caught poaching, but the very policy of the Normans in preserving the woods for the chase prevented the needed increase in cultivated land, and so drove many to live outside the law merely to survive.

The trees were widely spaced at the forest's edge, but as Cuthbert ran farther into its depths the branches grew more thickly and closer together. Here and there open glades ran across each other, and in these his sharp eye, used to the ways of the forest, could often see the stags darting away at the sound of his footfalls.

After a long run Cuthbert reached the place he was aiming for, an age-old clearing created by a long-forgotten storm. Overshadowed by giant trees, men of all ages and appearances were at work. Some were occupied stripping the skin off a buck which hung from the spreading limb of a tree. Others roasted portions of the carcass of another deer. A few sat apart, some talking, the fletchers busy making arrows, while a few lay asleep on a grassy bank.

As Cuthbert ran into the clearing, several men rose to their feet. One was a giant.

"Ah, Cuthbert," he shouted, "what brings you here, lad, so early? You don't usually visit before midnight when you can sight a stag by the moonlight in your crossbow."

"No, no, cousin Cnut," Cuthbert said in a teasing tone. "You can't say I've ever broken the forest laws, although it's true that I've often watched while you have."

"I think that makes you what your Norman friends call in that ghastly Latin-French of theirs 'an accessory after the fact.'" Cnut loosed a deep belly laugh. "If the foresters caught us in the act, I doubt they would see any difference whether it was the shaft of my longbow or the quarrel from your crossbow which brought down the quarry."

By this time Cnut had walked across the clearing toward Cuthbert, and closer up realized that something was wrong. "You've been running fast, lad. Catch your breath and tell me what's afoot."

"I have, Cnut, I've not stopped once for breath since I left Erstwood. The earl's preparing for a raid."

Cnut laughed disdainfully. "He's raided before. The landless men of the forest can hold their own against a handful of Norman knights and retainers in their own home."

19

"Maybe, but this is no common raid. This morning knights and mounted men-at-arms from all the manors within miles have ridden in. At least five hundred are likely to attack today."

"Hmm." Cnut frowned. Exclamations of surprise, but not of fear, broke from those standing around. "If that's so, lad, thanks for the warning. We can slip through the fingers of ten times five hundred, but not if they took us unawares. Hemmed in, things would go badly for us. Which track will they take and what's the end-game?"

"I don't know. All I gathered was that the earl intends to sweep the forest and put an end to your law-breaking. You had best be off before Sir Walter and his men get here. Why not shift your quarters to Langholm Chase until the storm's passed?"

"Langholm!" Cnut shuddered. "Sir John of Wortham is a worse landlord by a long shot than the earl. I can't hate Sir Walter, he's a good knight and a fair lord. If only he would rid himself of that ridiculous Norman notion that the birds of the air, the beasts of the field, and the fishes of the water all belong to Normans, and that we Saxons have no share in them, I wouldn't have a quarrel with him."

A chorus of ayes met this statement.

"He doesn't grind down his people or neighbors, seems content with a fair share of the tenant farmers' produce and is a fair judge. Wortham's a fiend incarnate. He would gladly cut the throats, or burn, or drown, or hang every Saxon within twenty miles of his keep. He's a disgrace to his order, and some day when our band gets a little stronger, we'll burn his nest about his ears."

"A hard nut to crack," Cuthbert said with a grin.

"I'll crack both his Norman nuts one day. Ladders and axes will go far, lad, and the Norman men-at-arms dread the shafts of our arrows. Still, if we must be his neighbors for a time, so be it."

The preparations were simple. Bows were taken down from the branches on which they hung, quivers slung across the backs, short cloaks thrown over the shoulders. The deer was hurriedly dismembered and the joints fastened to a pole slung on the shoulders of two men. The drinking-cups, some of which were of silver, looking strangely out of place among the rough horn implements and wood platters, were bundled together, carried a short distance, and dropped among some thick bushes for safety. Then the outlaws started out for Langholm Chase and Wortham.

Cuthbert stayed for a while at the edge of the deserted clearing. Unsure which of several routes the earl's men might take in their approach, he remained motionless and listened intently.

After some time had passed he heard the distant note of a horn. It was answered from three different directions and Cuthbert, who knew every path and glade, was able accurately to work out those by which the various battles of knights and men were entering the forest. Knowing that they were still some way off, he began to run, weaving through the clustered trees directly toward them.

When he could make out distinct voices calling and the breaking of branches, he rapidly climbed a thick tree and hid himself in its boughs. From there, secure from the sharpest eye, he watched what must have been a hundred men-at-arms, led by Sir Walter himself and half a dozen of his knights, tramp beneath his feet.

As soon as they had passed, Cuthbert slipped easily down the tree and made at all speed for home. He reached it, so far as he knew without having been observed by a single passer-by.

After a brief talk with his mother, he followed her advice and started out tirelessly for Evesham. "Your appearance at the castle will divert any suspicion that you might have had a hand in warning the landless men," she'd said. "It's natural a boy your age should be curious at seeing the movements of so large an army and your being there should not raise any comment."

When he reached the castle he would chat with his acquaintances in the bailey and so make witnesses to his presence. He still felt some guilt about Hubert, but soothed his conscience by telling himself that—in addition to crossed fingers—he had used the phrase "when the occasion needs it," and this had definitely been an occasion when the falconer's secret could not be kept. Besides, he could always make his confession to Father Francis… well, at some point in the future.

That was the plan, but he never reached Evesham. When he was about a mile from the town and joining the road between Evesham and Worcester, he spied a small group ambling toward him. On a white palfrey rode Margaret, the earl's little daughter. Her nurse accompanied the girl, also riding, and two retainers on foot. He was a great favorite with Margaret, for he often brought her pets, such as voles, nests of young owlets, falcons, and other woodland creatures. So he was about to hail her, when the peace was abruptly shattered as ten mailed and mounted men burst out onto the road from a thicket of trees.

Without a word the knights rode straight at the alarmed group. Margaret's retainers were cut to the ground before they could draw a sword in their defense. One of the gang cold-bloodedly slew the nurse with a blow from his battle-axe. Margaret, snatched from her palfrey, was thrown across a saddle like a little sack, and then her abductors galloped off in a cloud of dust.

Chapter 3: A Rescue

Evesham, mid-August 1189

Cuthbert was so astounded at the sudden calamity that had befallen the Earl of Evesham's little daughter that he remained rooted to the spot where, fortunately for himself, unnoticed by the villains, he had stood when they first exploded from concealment.

He wondered frantically what to do for the best. He doubted that the earl would have left many mounted men behind at Evesham, and there appeared to be about twenty kidnappers, strong enough to beat off any rescue attempt from that direction. One thing he knew for certain, and that was the identity of the criminal band—they hadn't even bothered to hide Wortham's colors—he could see the device on their badges.

Sir Walter's main force was far off in the greenwood's depths, on a path altogether out of the line for Wortham, and there would be no chance whatever of bringing them up in time to cut off the marauders on their way back.

There remained only the outlaws, who by this time would be in the forest of Langholm Chase, perhaps within a mile or two of Wortham castle itself. The road by which the kidnappers had to travel would be far longer than the direct line across country, and Cuthbert swore to strain every sinew to reach his friends in time to get them to intercept Lady Margaret's captors before they could reach their stronghold.

For an instant he hesitated whether to run back to Erstwood to get a pony, but then decided that it would be as quick to go on foot, and easier to find the outlaws.

All these thoughts whizzed through his mind in only a few fevered moments before he broke into a sprint. He soon realized that his pace would kill him, and although there was so little time, he would be of no use to kidnapped Margaret if he collapsed through over exertion. He slowed down, but even so, had Cuthbert been running in a race, he would certainly have carried off the trophy from most boys of his age.

The distance to the forest was a bit under twelve miles, and in an hour and a half Cuthbert was deep within its shade. Unsure as to where the outlaws might be, he jammed his index fingers between his lips and gave a piercing whistle. Any of the band within hearing would recognize the signal. He thought he heard an answer, but uncertain, ran on almost as speedily as if he had just freshly set out. Five minutes later a man stepped into the forest break along which he ran. Cuthbert recognized him at once as one of Cnut's party.

"Where's the band?" he gasped.

"Half a mile or so to the north." The man pointed.

Guided by the outlaw, Cuthbert ran on until, panting and barely able to speak, he arrived at the spot where Cnut's men had gathered. In a few gasping words he explained what had happened, and although they had just been chased off by the captured child's father, there was never a moment's hesitation among the forest men in promising their aid to rescue the girl from the clutches of a baron they regarded as a far worse enemy, not only of themselves but also of the whole Saxon nation.

"No time for gossiping," Cnut declared. "They've had a good start over us, but they won't fear a quick pursuit and will avoid blowing their mounts by galloping the whole way. We may still be in time."

Sounding a long note on his horn to call in scattered outlaws, and leaving one at the meeting-place to give instructions to the rest, Cnut went off at a swinging trot through the glades toward Wortham castle. The men made their way along the edge of the trees to the point where the road from Evesham ran through the forest. The landless men only just made it in time, as there came along the beaten track a faint clatter of hoofs and the rattle of metal fittings.

"Here they come." Cuthbert calmed his nerves.

Cnut gave rapid directions, and the band took up posts behind the trees on either side of the road.

"Remember," Cnut said, "for God's sake don't hit the child, shoot the horse on which she's riding. The instant the animal collapses, rush forward. We have surprise on our side, let's use it well."

Moments later the troop of horsemen—eighteen in all—could be seen as dark, flickering shapes through the tree trunks, advancing toward the slow bend at little more than a gentle canter. They were too closely packed in formation for the watchers behind the trees to see which man had little Lady Margaret in his grip.

As they came abreast the concealed outlaws, Cnut gave a sharp whistle, and fifty arrows flew thickly from tree and bush into the passing pack. More than half their number fell instantly. Some, swords hastily drawn, tried to rush their concealed foes, while others broke into a gallop in the hope of riding through the snare into which they had fallen. Cuthbert leveled his crossbow and waited with intense anxiety for a glimpse of Margaret's brightly dyed dress. Soon he saw a horseman break away from the rest and hurtle forward at break-neck pace.

Several arrows flew by him, and one or two struck the horse on which he rode. But the destrier stoutly kept on its way.

Cuthbert lowered his crossbow onto the low arm of a tree and, as the rider came in line with him, lightly touched the trigger and the steel-pointed quarrel flew true. It struck the passing horseman just in front of his ear. He fell from his horse as though pole-axed. His mailed body crashed into the dust with a sickening thud.

True to its war training, his destrier came to an abrupt stop and turned back to its fallen master, rearing and threatening anyone who came near. Margaret, who had been held against the saddle's front horn, managed to hang on with a terrified grip. Cuthbert ran out from cover, but then slowed his pace to avoid spooking the horse. He called out soothingly to the animal and it quieted down. To his delight the girl opened her arms and cried, "Cuthbert!" She was still unharmed.

He approached the restive animal slowly, continuing to make soft cooing sounds. "There, boy, I know you're hurting, but no one else will harm you. There, there…"

The destrier gave an uncertain snort, but allowed Cuthbert to approach closely. The fight still raged fiercely farther down the road. Cuthbert pulled Margaret from the horse and ran with her into the wood. There, they lay low until the few survivors of the baron's horsemen had broken away and ridden past them toward the distant castle.

Absorbed in their individual engagements, none of the outlaws had noticed the rescue. As Cuthbert came forward with his charge, who was busy repairing the damage to her expensive hairdo and bonnet, loud shouts of joy and triumph greeted their appearance.

Cnut threw his arms around Cuthbert and almost crushed the last of his wind from his chest. When he struggled free of the giant's grip he said, "This is an ill wind that may blow some good. Surely this will make the earl a firm friend of you landless men instead of a bitter enemy. I'm sure that better days are dawning for Evesham Forest."

"Hmm," Cnut rumbled, "we'll see about that change of heart."

Three men cut some tree branches and soon made a rough litter. They perched Margaret on top and, borne on the shoulders of two stout outlaws, the band made for Evesham, Cnut and Cuthbert walking beside her. A few of the company dropped back to act as a rearguard in case the baron attempted to regain his prey. Uneasy at being so near Wortham, Cnut kept up a stiff pace. Cuthbert could scarcely drag one foot in front of the other—he had already covered more than twenty miles, most of it at his fastest speed.

"Why, lad, you're nearly out of it. We can pause and make a litter for you as well."

Cnut met Cuthbert's indignant refusal with an easy laugh. However, when they came to the hut of Wythin the miller, he borrowed his shaggy forest pony for Cuthbert to ride. It was verging on evening before they came in sight of Evesham. From the distance squadrons of men could be seen cantering toward the castle, clearly the earl's small army of outlaw hunters returning frustrated from the forest. But there was a visible air of unrest, with individual riders dashing off in different directions.

"It looks as though the theft of Lady Margaret has been discovered," Cuthbert muttered to Cnut.

A moment later one of the mounted retainers rode up to them at a fast pace. "What have you sons of bitches done with the Lady Margaret?" he shouted angrily. "She's missing."

"Here I am!" the child cried out, almost upsetting her crude conveyance in her excitement.

The horseman gave an inarticulate grunt, and without a word wheeled his horse and galloped back toward the castle, leaving the rescuers coughing in the dust raised from his horse's hoofs.

As Cuthbert and the outlaws approached the gate, Sir Walter, accompanied by two knights and his senior squire, rode out from it and came to a skittering halt in front of them. As he dismounted from his restless horse the bearers lowered the litter and the earl's daughter sprang down and leaped into his arms.

For several minutes the confusion and babble with everyone speaking at the same time prevented anyone being heard, but as soon as some sort of order was restored, Cuthbert gave the earl a concise report of the events. Sir Walter said nothing as he listened, but the color of his face altered dramatically as his levels of anger mounted, and when Cuthbert concluded, his fury erupted with the force of a mountain blowing its top.

"This, this… outrage!" he roared. "At my very gates, to steal my daughter. That knave Wortham has gone too far this time, and…" his eyes roved around at the company of landless men. "And to think that she should have been saved by the bravery and devotion of the very men against whom I have just vowed vengeance in the depths of the forest." Sir Walter, still hugging his daughter to his side, strode up to within inches of Cnut, the steely eyes in his rugged, battle-scarred face fierce with anger, his clean-shaven jaw clenched tight. The two powerfully-built men locked gaze in frank appraisal.

"This is not a time for talking or making promises," the earl rasped, "but you can be assured that from now on the deer of Evesham Chase are as free to you and your men as to me. Forest laws or no forest laws be damned, I'll not raise my hand against men to whom I owe so much." And, addressing all the assembled hunters, he said, "Come when you can to the castle, my friends, and let's discuss what can be done to undo your outlawry and restore you to honest labor again."

Cuthbert returned home tired but delighted with his day's work, and Dame Editha was as relieved to learn that her headstrong son had not crossed swords with any of the earl's men as she was surprised at his tale. The next morning he went to the castle, and heard that during a grand council held the evening before, it had been determined to attack Wortham's castle and to raze it to the ground. When he saw him, Sir Walter's seneschal crossed the inner bailey and beckoned Cuthbert forward. "The earl wants to speak with you, young de Lance."

After expressing his gratitude for the rescue of his daughter, Sir Walter asked if he would go into the forest and invite the outlaws to join forces with those of Evesham to attack the baron.

This was a task Cuthbert was only too willing to undertake since he felt this alliance could only further strengthen the position of the landless forest men. But his enthusiasm received a setback when he repeated the earl's proposal to his forest friends. It disappointed him to discover that many outlaws were skeptical about mixing themselves in the disputes of Norman nobility.

"But this is a golden opportunity to put right the wrongs you've all suffered under Norman laws. Sir Walter will keep his promises."

In the end, it was Cnut who persuaded them that, as the Baron of Wortham was an enemy and oppressor of all Saxons, it was in fact their own battle they would be fighting rather than that of the Earl of Evesham. His argument won over the waverers and the men gave in, agreeing to give their aid, and promised to be at the rendezvous outside Wortham castle soon after dawn next morning.

The bailey of Evesham was a scene of furious bustle when Cuthbert returned with the happy news for Sir Walter. Armorers worked at repairing conical helms and nasal guards, mail coifs to protect the head and neck, and mail shirts, or hauberks, sharpening swords and battle-axes, while the fletchers prepared sheaves of arrows and crossbow bolts. Close to the main gatehouse others oiled the catapults, ballistas, and other machines for hurling stones.

Everywhere, men chattered about only one thing: what were the chances of the imminent assault. "Wortham's hold is powerfully built," Hugh said when he came alongside Cuthbert. The falconer had donned his leather hauberk, but Cuthbert didn't think it made him look any more military. "It will need all and more than the machines we have available to undertake such a formidable siege." He shook his head gloomily. "Its garrison is large and made of desperate men. Be sure too, knowing what a hornets' nest he's disturbed with his outrage, he will have demanded that his feudal vassals come to his assistance."

"But his cause is damned," Cuthbert said. "He cannot win, and I shall be there to see his downfall."

"Mother, I must be there. My luck combined with quick thinking is what helped to save the Lady Margaret and I must be in at the end." Cuthbert's protests fell on resolutely deaf ears.

"I won't hear of it," she said firmly for the fifth time.

He tried his most winning smile, dimple deep. "Please give me your permission to ask the earl to let me join as a volunteer."

"Absolutely not, Cuthbert. And don't you dare sneak out and go with the outlaws."

In the end, the most that he dragged reluctantly out of her was that he might go as a spectator, with strict warnings to keep himself out of the fray, and as far as possible beyond bow-shot of the castle wall.

Early next morning some four hundred fully armed men emerged from the forest's cover at Langholm Chase to attack Wortham's castle. The force consisted of twelve knights with their retinues, amounting to about a hundred and fifty Norman men-at-arms in hauberks and surcoats bearing the badge and colors of Evesham on their chests, and a miscellaneous gathering of other retainers, two hundred strong in their padded gambeson jerkins. Eighty forest men completed the earl's army, although they were not fighting under Evesham's standard, but were there as tolerated irregulars. Because there were among the landless men real outlaws, escaped serfs, and some men guilty of bloodshed, the earl could not be seen to have these men fight for him until they had been in some way acquitted of their crimes.

It was an arrangement that suited the outlaws perfectly. Their most vital skill was in the bow, and by taking up their own position, and following their own tactics under Cnut's leadership, they would be able to do far more damage, and with less risk to themselves, than if forced to fight in the Norman fashion.

In accordance with custom, as Evesham approached Wortham a herald went forward and, after a blast on his horn, read a proclamation demanding the garrison's surrender. It called Wortham a baron by theft, a false knight, and a disgrace to his class and his king, and warned all those within the castle to stop giving him aid or obedience, and to submit themselves to Sir Walter of Evesham, earl and representative of King Richard.

A burst of taunting laughter from the walls answered the herald. Several of the men turned their bared backsides in rude defiance, and the herald had to beat a hasty withdrawal when a mocking flight of arrows followed him back to his ranks and showed that the besieged were perfectly ready for a good scrap.

"The baron has not been idle," Cnut told Cuthbert. "We've heard tell from a cottager. Aware that this dispute has come to such a point that hostilities are certain sooner or later, he has for some time been quietly accumulating a large store of provisions and munitions. He's also strengthened his hold's defenses in every way. See, the moat is freshly cleaned and filled to the brim with river water. Look at the great quantities of heavy stones they've collected and piled on the most exposed points of the battlements, ready to hurl down on anyone trying to scale the wall."

"Yes, I see many sheaves of arrows and piles of crossbow bolts are to hand at all points. Your cottager is right. The miserable worm has been preparing for a siege for weeks."

After a word with Father Francis the evening before, Cuthbert understood the background to the coming battle. Only the previous year the crown of England, Normandy, and Anjou came to grace the head of Richard Plantagenet. A popular choice for king with the commoners and many of the nobility he might be, but there still remained a powerful faction which thought the young king's rebellious past made him unfit to rule and wanted his brother Prince John in his stead. "Their reasoning is self-seeking. It is well known that John will bow to the pressure of his ambitious barons, whereas Richard spurns any unless they can stand up to his brash but forthright manner," Father Francis said.

"The Baron of Wortham is one of those who wants Prince John on the throne, and he has many fellow supporters to call on when threatened. Messengers have been sent in all directions—to Stafford, Nottingham, Gloucester, Hereford, and even Oxford to petition the baron's friends to march to his assistance. He boasts he can defend his hold for many weeks, but from behind his walls he cannot break the power of Sir Walter, who he calls a braggart earl."

"Surely no one will support such a dastardly cur?" Cuthbert said indignantly.

The priest looked grave. "I fear many have already complied with his demand, while he expects those at a distance to respond later. You must understand, Cuthbert, that there are many among the Norman nobility who consider the Earl of Evesham's mildness toward the Saxons under his rule to be a mistake. The Norman lords and their feudal retainers are few and we conquered Saxons are many. They may not approve Wortham's tyranny and yet still look on his cause as their own."

As the outlaws moved off to their assigned position, Cuthbert gave the castle a last look before bowing to his mother's warning. The hold stood on slightly elevated ground. From the edge of the moat the walls rose high, with strong flanking mural towers and battlements. In the middle of the castle bailey rose the stout tower keep, or *donjon* in Norman Frankish. From its upper battlements archers and catapults commanded the whole circuit of defense. A strong outwork on the nearside bank of the moat guarded the drawbridge. This, he knew, was to be the first target of the assault.

Cuthbert—keeping faith with his mother's instructions by settling himself high up in a lofty tree from where he had a fine view of the proceedings—wondered how on earth they were going to succeed. *Winning the outwork should be straightforward but after that I can't see how we're to assault the castle itself.*

A songbird settled on a nearby branch and regarded Cuthbert curiously. It gave a trill of sweet notes at odds with the desperate work about to begin. Cuthbert addressed his little black companion. "You see, the earl's siege engines aren't powerful enough to damage such strong walls. Ladders are useless if you can't plant them, and if the garrison's as brave as the castle is strong, I reckon Sir Walter's embarked on a task that'll keep us here until next spring."

The blackbird cocked its head at his words, but offered no comforting advice before it flew off.

The men of the forest skirmished to within bowshot, and then, taking advantage of every hollow in the ground, of every bush and tuft of grass, worked up close to the moat, and let loose a heavy fire with their bows against the defenders on the battlements to prevent their using the catapults against Evesham's main force advancing on the outwork.

This structure was stoutly defended. But the earl's impetuosity, backed as it was by the boldness of his knights, carried all obstacles. Men-at-arms speedily filled the narrow offshoot channel of the main moat which encircled the outwork with the bundles of brushwood they had prepared the previous night. Across these the attackers rushed. Some thundered at the gate with their battle-axes, while others placed ladders by which they finally succeeded in gaining a footing on the wall.

Once there, the combat was virtually over. The defenders were either cut down or taken prisoner, and in two hours since the assault had begun the outwork of Wortham castle was in Evesham's hands.

As Cuthbert had correctly observed, this was only the beginning of a daunting task, and it had already cost more than twenty lives. They were now little nearer to capturing the castle than they had been before.

The moat was too wide and deep for the brushwood trick to work again. The drawbridge had been lifted at the instant the first man-at-arms gained a footing on the wall. And now that the outwork was in Evesham's hands, a storm of arrows, stones, and other missiles poured into it from the castle walls, making it certain death for anyone to show themselves above its parapets.

Seeing that any sudden attack was impossible, the earl now directed a strong work gang to go and cut down trees in order to construct a pontoon which might be thrown across the moat.

This was the work of at least two to three days, so in the meantime Cuthbert returned to Erstwood in a depressed mood. As he related the turn of events to Dame Editha, she clucked her tongue sympathetically, but had no more immediate words of consolation than had the blackbird.

Cuthbert flung himself away and crossed the solar to stare

miserably out the window into the quiet courtyard below. Addressing the air more than his mother, he said, "They're never going to break in. The evil baron has too much strength, and in only a few more days many of his allies will arrive and raise a counter-siege. Our kinsmen will die, mother, and there's nothing we can do."

"Don't be too cast down, my son. There may be something that could be done. Come here to me and let me explain."

Chapter 4: Wortham's Evil Secret

Near Evesham, mid-August 1189

Gurth was impossibly old, older than any other man in the Vale of Evesham. Some even joked that he had fought with Harold against the Conqueror, but obviously that was not possible. Even Gurth no longer remembered when he was born, but there were few other holes in his sprightly memory.

As Cuthbert picked his way gingerly between strutting hens, he pondered on the revelation his mother had shown him. He had always thought that Gurth was little more than a common cottar, picking out a precarious living on his small-holding, but instead the bent old fellow, his mother insisted, had once in his youth been a great and famous stone mason; the reason, now, for Cuthbert's visit.

Gurth, who had few visitors, was pleased to see Cuthbert and asked him to sit for a bit on a wooden trestle bench that stood outside in the small yard. Cuthbert, with the impatience of youth, had no time for any pleasantries and got straight to the point.

"My mother tells me, Gurth, that you helped to build Wortham's castle."

Gurth pushed his head back and gave vent to a loud, toothless huffing guffaw. "Oh no, no, young sir," he chortled. "Old as I am, I were only a child when that castle were built." He hawked and spat on the dusty ground, and then added darkly, "In fact my father worked on it and it cost him, and several others, his life."

"Oh. How was that?"

"He were killed by the Norman baron, the grandfather of the present bugger, as soon as the work were finished."

"But why were they all killed?"

"We were only Saxon swine," Gurth mouthed bitterly. "Even more so in them days and to a bastard Norman a few of us more or less didn't matter much. We were just his serfs. But my mother fled with me when she heard the news of my father's murder. For years we remained far away, with some distant relatives in the forest near Oxford. Then she pined for her native air, came back, and took service with the franklin of Erstwood."

"But why should your mother have taken you away?"

"She always believed, Master Cuthbert, that my father were killed by the baron to prevent him telling anyone the secrets of the castle. He and some others had been kept in the thickness of the walls for many months making secret passages."

"Gurth, that's what my mother told me to ask you. She's heard something of this story before, and now that we're attacking the castle, and the earl has sworn to level it to the ground, it's vital to find out whether any of the secret passages lead outside the castle, and if so, where. As any boy knows, almost all castles have an exit by which the garrison can make sorties or escape through. I thought that maybe you might know enough to give us a clue as to the existence of such a passage at Wortham."

The old man thought for some time in silence, and then said, "I may be mistaken, but why don't you try searching in the copse near the sharp bend in the river. There you might find the mouth of a tunnel."

"Why do you think that?"

"I went with my mother to take some clean clothes to my father. It were the last time I ever saw him. As we neared the castle I saw my pa and three other workmen, together with the baron, coming down from the castle toward that place. My mother didn't want to be seen by the baron, so we stood behind the trees at the edge of the wood and watched what they were up to."

Gurth gurgled deep in his throat and snorted powerfully before ejecting another gob of phlegm from between pursed lips. Cuthbert watched it join the first splat.

"The baron came with them down to the bushes, and then they crossed the river. One of them cut some willows, peeled them, and erected the white staves in a line toward the castle. They walked for a bit on each side and seemed to be making calculations. Then they went back into the castle, and I never saw my pa again."

"I'm sorry, Gurth. I know what it's like to lose a father."

The old man nodded. "The baron had a suspicious and evil mind. The castle were already finished, and most of the masons discharged. But there were a party of serfs kept at work and two masons, and rumor had it that they were engaged in cutting the secret passages. Whether true or not, I don't know, but I do know that none of them ever left the castle alive. We were told that a bad fever had killed them all, but no one believed it."

He looked at Cuthbert from beneath bushy eyebrows, eyes pained with the distant memory. "The report went about, and I always believed it, that they were all killed to preserve the secret of the passage."

At daybreak next morning, not wishing to lose any time in making use of the information, Cuthbert rode his pony hard for Langholm Chase. He did not wish the earl or his followers to know the facts that he had learned until they were proved, so he made his way around the camp of the besiegers until he was challenged by an outlaw sentry. "Ah, it's you, young lad, gave me a start you did."

"Where's Cnut?"

"With a load of 'em making ladders for the earl's men."

"Can you fetch him here without making any fuss about it? I've something important to tell him."

Cnut arrived shortly, curious to hear what Cuthbert had to say. His dour expression brightened as he listened to what Cuthbert told him.

"This could be just what we need right now," the big Saxon said enthusiastically. "Although many years have passed and your copse may seem very different. Still, let's go and find out. I'll get two of my trusted lads with axes and billhooks to clear away the brushwood. For the moment the less that know about this interesting possibility the better."

The river—more a stream really—ran in its own little valley, some twenty or thirty feet deep. An extensive coppice grew on the curving bank not far from the castle, and it was in this that Cuthbert hoped to find Gurth's secret passage entrance.

The trees and undergrowth clustered thickly. Cnut grunted his dissatisfaction. "If a tunnel ever existed it's been unused for many years."

Cnut's two axemen had to chop down a tangle of briars wrapped around well-established young saplings to make their way up from the water toward the steeper part of the bank. The little wood stretched some fifty yards in length, and as none of them knew at which point the passage—if it were there—was supposed to emerge, it required a very close search.

"What do you think it would be like, Cnut?"

"Something like a rabbit-hole perhaps, or more likely still there wouldn't be a hole at all. We must look for moss and ferns because it's likely that they would have used that kind of plant to conceal the door from any passer-by, yet allowing anyone from inside to cut their way out through it without difficulty."

After a fruitless two hours, Cnut decided that the only place in which it was likely that an entrance could be hidden was a patch where ivy and trailing plants thickly covered a slight gully.

"It looks level enough with the rest," Cuthbert said.

"Hmm, maybe, but try probing there."

One of the outlaws thrust the end of his staff into the clustered ivy. For some time he met solid ground, but suddenly the staff's point passed through freely, pitching him on his head, amid a suppressed snigger from his comrade.

Cnut gave a satisfied grunt. "Here it is, if anywhere."

With their billhooks they quickly cleared away the overgrown creepers. A few minutes' work revealed that the gully deepened into a narrow cut an outstretched arm's span in width, at the end of which stood a low door.

"Here it is," breathed Cnut, with triumph. "And the castle is ours. Thanks, Cuthbert, you're cleverer than you look." Cuthbert didn't deign a retort. "It's not been used lately, that's clear," Cnut went on. "These creepers haven't been moved for years. Shall we go and tell the earl what we've found? What do you think?"

"Better not," Cuthbert replied quickly. "We might not succeed in getting all the way through—the tunnel may have fallen in farther along. I'd rather that we knew what we're up against, but I'll speak to him and tell him that we've something up our sleeves which may alter his battle plans for tomorrow."

Cuthbert made his way to the earl, who had taken possession of a small cottage a short distance from the castle.

"What can I do for you, young Cuthbert?" Sir Walter rasped, wearily looking up from a parchment.

"I want to ask you, sir, not to attack the castle tomorrow until you see a white flag waved from the top of the *donjon*."

The earl glared back in irritated puzzlement. "How on earth is anyone going to raise a white flag from the enemy's keep?" he growled.

"It may be," Cuthbert said cautiously, "that I have some friends inside who will be able to make a diversion to our advantage. Sir, it can do no harm if you will wait till then, and may save many lives. May I ask when you intend to attack?"

"The bridges and all other preparations to get us across the moat will be ready by tonight. We'll advance under cover of darkness and, as soon as we can after dawn, make a concentrated assault."

"Very well, my lord. I trust that before the echo of your war horns has faded, the white flag will appear on the keep, but it can't do so until after the offensive's properly under way or—better still—at least the pretense of an attack."

Some two hours before daylight Cuthbert, Cnut, and twenty-five picked outlaws made their way to the copse. In addition to their swords and warbows, each carried an iron crowbar and an axe. For his own possible defense, Cuthbert carried his short sword and a quarterstaff. He thought a crossbow would prove cumbersome and of little use in close quarters combat. Not, of course, that he had any intention of becoming involved in any fighting in keeping with his promise. Using the crowbars, the door was soon prised loose. It opened silently and without a creak.

"Well, well," Cnut observed, "we're right that the door's not been used in an age, but it's certain," and he placed his torch to the hinges, "that it's been well greased within the last day or so." He stooped forward and sniffed. "Yes… pig fat. No doubt the baron intended to escape this way if things went badly for him—now we can make absolutely sure they do. I think we'd better wait here quietly until it's light."

Cuthbert agreed. "The earl will have the horns sounded as a signal for the advance. It will take a bit of time before they're fully engaged, and that should be enough for us to break open any doors there may be between us here and the castle, and force our way inside."

Daybreak seemed a long time coming and it felt still longer before the huddled group heard the earl's battle signals. Cnut signed to the three most powerfully built of his men to follow as he ducked under the low lintel and entered the secret passage.

Cuthbert now faced a dilemma. There was no real question of his remaining behind in the coppice, on the other hand he'd promised his mother to take no part in the fighting. He thought about it long and hard for a breath, and then followed the others into the dark passageway. Obviously, in going with Cnut's men he was not obeying the letter of her instructions. At the same time he felt sure that the effect of a surprise would be complete and crushing, and that the party would gain the top of the keep without any serious resistance.

In which case the risk was so small as to justify him in going along.

After some yards of crawling the tunnel opened up so that they could just about stand with bent heads, but only wide enough for a single file. Dank and moldy smelling near the entrance, after a few moments the walls and floor became dry, dusty and—save the footprints going and returning, doubtless those of whoever had recently silenced the hinges—the passage appeared to have been unused from the time of its unfortunate builders.

After about five hundred paces the tunnel widened out and they came to another strong oak door. This, like the last, yielded to the efforts of the outlaws' crowbars, and the stealthy advance continued. Within a further twenty paces they reached a steep, narrow flight of steps leading upward.

"We must be under the keep," Cnut said. "In fact, I can hear battle noises."

Mounting the steps, they came to a third door, thickly studded with iron and dauntingly stout. Fortunately the locking system had evidently been designed to operate from either side, although the hefty clanking it made caused Cnut to stop for a moment, fearing that the noise must alert anyone on the other side. They all waited, breathing stilled, but it seemed that the castle's occupants were fully engaged in defending themselves.

The door opened behind a thick hanging of tapestry. Cnut pushed this aside cautiously, glanced around, and then quickly stepped into a small room still in the thickness of the keep's wall. It contained the merest slit for light, and was clearly unused. Another door led into a larger apartment, also unoccupied. Now the cries of the besiegers, muffled by the walls, grew louder and the orders frantically shouted on the battlements above clearer. The thwack of mangonel ropes snapping out, the earthquake crunch of landing boulders from the other side, and the ding of iron as arrows struck against helm and mail added to the din.

"Just as well they're in the thick of it," whispered Cuthbert, mother's promise forgotten, "no one's heard us. We're in the heart of the *donjon* and this spiral stair should take us up to the battlements."

Cnut nodded curtly as he swiftly crossed to the indicated stairway. "They'll be so surprised, that we should be able to knock them aside like rabbits caught in a gamekeeper's trap. Now let's go."

So saying Cnut led the way upstairs, followed by the forest men. Cuthbert, as before, remembered to let five or six of them intervene between him and Cnut to keep his conscience clear.

After mounting fifty or sixty steps, they issued onto the keep's roof. Here, some forty men were engaged in shooting crossbows and working engines to hurl javelins, stones, and other artillery over their own lower outer walls at the besiegers. Without exception, their attention was so focused on their work that they remained unaware of the addition to their numbers until all the outlaw band had all clambered up and, at Cnut's sharp order, suddenly fell on them with a loud war cry.

Taken utterly by surprise by men who seemed to have risen from the bowels of the keep as if by magic, the Baron of Wortham's soldiers offered only a feeble resistance. Some were tossed over the battlemented edge, others cut down by killing sword slashes that spilled their guts on the blood-splashed stones. Cuthbert fastened a small white flag he had prepared to his quarterstaff and waved it above the battlements.

Even now the defenders on the castle's outer wall were ignorant of what had happened behind them in the keep. It was not until the surviving fugitives, running out through the unbarred doorway and down into the bailey, shouted that the *donjon* had fallen to the enemy that the besieged became aware of the imminent danger in their rear.

To that point the battle had been going well for the Wortham garrison. In fact, the baron was surprised at the assault's feebleness. The arrows which had fallen in clouds on the first day's attack were now comparatively few and ineffective. The besiegers scarcely appeared to push forward their bridges with any urgency, and it seemed to him that some disagreement must have arisen, completely crippling the energy of the attack.

When he heard the words shouted from the bailey below where he directed the defense—and even contemplating making a sortie against his apparently unwilling enemy—he could not believe his ears. That the *donjon* behind should have been carried by the enemy was impossible. With a bellow he called on the bravest of his men to follow, tore down from the wall, and rushed across the expanse toward the keep's outer steps.

Cuthbert's signal had been seen, and the earl, who had given instructions to his army to make a mere feint of attacking, now blew the signal for the real onslaught. The bridges were rapidly run across the moat, ladders were planted, and the garrison, paralyzed and confused by the attack in their rear, as well as hindered by the arrows which now rained down on them from the keep above, offered only a paltry resistance. The men of Evesham, led by Sir Walter himself, clambered up their wooden towers and streamed over the walls.

There followed a scene of murderous chaos and desperate strife. The baron had just gained the top of the keep's outer stairs, and was engaged in a fierce battle with the outlaws, when the news reached him that the wall had been taken. With an explosion of obscenities he again turned and rushed down, hoping by a furious effort to rally his men and hurl the foe to hell.

But it was all too late. His men-at-arms, disheartened and frightened, fought without method or order in scattered groups of threes and fours. They made their last stand in corners and passages. As they knew there was no hope of mercy from the landless Saxon forest men, they fought to the last against them. But many of the baron's retainers offered a less determined resistance to any Norman knight or man-at-arms. They threw down their weapons and surrendered for ransom.

The Baron of Wortham continued fighting viciously until he was slain by an arrow fired from the keep above, and with his fall the last resistance ceased. A short time was spent in searching the castle, binding the prisoners, and carrying off the valuables that the baron had collected in his raids. Then sappers set light set to the internal timbers, fired the granaries, and in a few minutes thick smoke wreathed out of the various loopholes and openings to inform the country around that they were free from the oppressor at last.

The masons waited for the flames to destroy the timber parts before they could start the work of slighting the castle's stonework.

Chapter 5: Preparations for Holy War

Fall 1189 to Spring 1190

The earl called all the landless men and outlaws living in his forests to gather around him on the field of battle where, behind him, masons were already beginning the work of dismantling the walls of Wortham's hold as the flames died down. There and then he bestowed freedom on any of them who might have been his serfs, and called on all his knights and neighbors to do the same, in return for the good service which they had rendered.

"And what can I do for you, Cuthbert?" Sir Walter asked, as they rode toward Evesham. "I'm indebted to you now on several counts."

"Thank you, my lord." Cuthbert stroked his pony's neck and gave the offer hard thought. "At the moment I can't think of anything I need, but if you go off to fight the king's wars or if you take up the Cross and go on the Crusade to Outremer, could you take me as a page, in the hope that I might one day win my spurs as a knight? Are you thinking of going to the war, Sir Walter?"

"I don't know yet, my boy. Much depends on the king's mood. King Richard is determined to take up the Cross, and if he calls on his nobles to join him in the effort to free again the Holy Sepulchre from the infidel horde, I shall feel bound to go. Myself, I don't care as much as some do about this question of the Holy Land. There's been enough blood shed already to drown it, and we're no nearer than when the first pilgrims made their way there. I doubt whether the minds of the people are quite prepared, but I hear that there's been a lot of preaching by hedge priests, friars, and monks in some parts, and that many are eager to join in the war."

* * *

"Do you think, father, that it will do England good?" It was the week following Cuthbert's talk with Sir Walter and he seized the opportunity to press Father Francis again on the subject of the Holy Crusade as the priest stopped for refreshment on his way to Evesham.

"In spite of the terrible loss of life on the first crusades, I think— whether we regain the Holy Land or not—that it will be good for the nation that Saxon and Norman should fight together under the sign of the Cross. So far the races have been too much apart, and we've only seen each other's bad qualities. Fighting side by side on the soil of the Holy Land, and shouting together for England, will bind everyone and make them feel that they're Englishmen, no longer Normans and Saxons."

He laid a hand on Cuthbert's shoulder.

"I'm giving a sermon at Evesham next Sunday morning on this subject, and as I know you're in touch with the forest men, I would like it, Cuthbert, if you could persuade them to come and hear me. Now that even the runaway serfs may find gainful employment, thanks to Sir Walter, this will be a great opportunity for them. They're valiant men, and the fact that they enjoy a joint of royal venison as much as any noble doesn't make them worse Christians. If they agree to take the vow, they would make a good band of archers and footmen to accompany the earl."

"Has Sir Walter decided to go?" "Oh, I don't know that for certain," Father Francis said hurriedly at Cuthbert's eagerness, "but his chaplain tells me that he's coming around to the notion of it as his duty."

"Oh I do hope so, because if he goes, I'll be going too. He promised to take me as his page the first time he went to war."

Father Francis shook his head. "Cuthbert," he chided gently, "this is far from the spirit in which we agreed a while ago that men should go to the holy war."

Cuthbert hung his head a little. "Yes, Father, men. But I'm a boy," he added slyly, "and after all, boys are fond of adventure for adventure's sake. But," he finished, with a winning smile, "no doubt your eloquence on the green will make me see the error of my ways."

"Get on with your work," Father Francis said with a smile. "You're an impudent devil. I will do my best on Sunday to turn you to a better frame of mind."

It was a large crowd that gathered. People came from miles around. The forest men in their green gambesons mingled with the congregation of cottars, serfs, men-at-arms, squires, and goodwives, every face attentive and serious but full of anticipation. The news of the Holy Sepulchre's loss had been a profound shock and concentrated the minds of people everywhere on the means of retaking the shrine and the city of which it was an integral part. The thought of the holy places in the hands of infidel Saracens affected everyone with a feeling of shame as well as of almost incomprehensible grief.

Knowledge that Father Francis was not the only advertised preacher heightened the palpable sense of excitement running through the gathering. A friar who had returned recently from Outremer was to speak of the cruelties which pilgrims suffered at Saracen hands.

Cuthbert was surprised to hear Father Francis, at ordinary times a quiet sermoniser, thunder as loud as the storm they had shared weeks before. He did not hide from his audience the trial of the task ahead—the peril, disease, heat, hunger, and thirst, as well as Turkish and Arab swords. But he spoke of the great nature of the work and of the glory which awaited those who joined this Third Crusade, whether they lived and returned or whether they died in the Holy Land.

His words—spoken first in English for the benefit of the majority and then in Norman-Frankish—had a powerful effect on the crowd, which included many Norman retainers from the nearby manors, and several knights with the ladies of their families standing a little apart from the common people. But the friar's following address roused the congregation to a pitch of fervor that amounted to hysteria.

The mendicant Friar Eudes' appearance was not encouraging. Weedy and pale, with the worn, anxious face of one who has suffered a great deal, his voice once he got going turned into a powerhouse of ferocious inspiration. Eudes stepped forward onto the green holding aloft two pieces of wood from the Mount of Olives tied together in the form of a cross, and from there he harangued the crowd. His words poured out in a fiery stream, kindling the hearts, and stirring at once the devotion and the anger of his listeners.

He told of the holy places and the men who had died for them. He spoke passionately of the knights and infantry, each of whom proved himself again and again a match for a score of Saracen infidels. He spoke of the holy women, who, as fearless and brave as any knight, had borne their share in the horrors of the siege.

Then he turned up the pitch, not to hurl insults at the infidels but to hold up to scrutiny the lukewarm hearts of all Christians. He told his rapt listeners that the loss of Jerusalem was a misfortune brought about by a lackluster attitude.

"Does it matter," he fulminated, "if the few knights who remained to defend the Holy Sepulchre were heroes? A few heroes cannot stand against an army. Christendom made a mighty effort to capture the Holy Sepulchre and having done so, sat down, relaxed, and then came home, saying 'Job well done.' And so the vast expenditure of blood was wasted. The Crusade is not a work in which a quick-fix of spiritual fervency will bring about success! No! Bravery at first, yes, but endurance afterward is needed. You men must not only help to seize the Holy Sepulchre from the hands of the heretics, but also give your lives, if necessary, to hold onto it.

"Men with wives and families won't take this view, and I don't expect it of them. But there are single men, men with no ties, third and fourth sons with no future here, men who can devote their whole lives, as did the knights of the Military Orders, to this great battle. I'm speaking out to the humble and common as well as to the nobles—all must bind themselves to take and defend to death the Holy Sepulchre."

So, gradually raising the pitch of his speech, Friar Eudes continued, his face now transformed, shining as though with an inner light, until by his intensity, his wild gesticulations, his impassioned words, he drew his listeners along with him. When he stopped, a mighty shout of "To the Holy Land!" burst spontaneously from every mouth.

All around the green men fell to their knees and begged him to give them the sign of the Cross, and bless their swords and their efforts.

With foresight, Father Francis had prepared a large number of small white crosses of cloth. These he now fastened to the shoulders of the men and boys as they crowded up to receive them. They held hands high, kissed the Mount of Olives cross that Friar Eudes extended to them, and swore to give their lives, if need be, to rescue the holy shrines from the infidels.

When he had handed out the last cloth cross, Father Francis stepped up the low bank and again addressed the gathering. "Think carefully about the oath that you have sworn. When King Richard sets out, it may be that you are not called on to go, even though you have today sworn. That's because the king knows that England's green land must be tilled, planted, and harvested. There must be protectors here for the women and children. This England of ours must flourish. We can't give up all her sons, however willing they might be to take the Cross. Some must go and some must stay—these are matters to be decided later. For now, return to your homes. You will hear soon enough when the hour for action is at hand."

Two weeks later the castle echoed to hustle, bustle, and flurry. The Earl of Evesham had just made the five-day return journey to London and brought with him a royal authority to raise a full levy for the holy war.

Father Francis was pleased to tell him that the forest men—outlaws no longer—were clamoring to be included, and he had drawn up a list of names of those he considered suitable. Sir Walter was happy to hear that the ranks of heavily-armed retainers he planned to take with him would be stiffened by the addition of a hundred archers skilled in the fearsome warbow.

The priest had another immediate duty, that of diffusing a potentially explosive argument between Cuthbert and Dame Editha. "Please talk sense to her, father," Cuthbert pleaded. "I am old enough and capable enough to share in the perils of the expedition." And then he paced up and down the courtyard while Father Francis spoke to his mother locked away in the solar. When they came out, she gazed at him with a stern mien, but one mixed with barely contained distress.

"The good father has persuaded me of your cause, Cuthbert." She wrung her hands and then scooped him into her arms, unable to contain her sobs.

Cuthbert was not long in asking for an interview with the earl.

"Certainly, Cuthbert," Sir Walter responded graciously, "I will take you with me, first, because I promised you I would. Second, because of the quick wit and cleverness you displayed in saving my daughter and in the attack on Wortham. For these reasons you will be a valuable addition to my contingent. Third, I will do so for my friendship with your father, Sir Stephen de Lance, and your mother, Dame Editha… though I doubt she will thank me for it."

With heartfelt gratitude, Cuthbert assumed his new duties as a page at once. And he found plenty to do: to see that the earl's orders—and those of Tybalt, his most senior squire—were properly carried out; to carry messages to Evesham's knights at their various smaller castles, manors, and holdings; to work under the seneschal in accounting the stores of arms and missiles which would be necessary for the expedition.

For almost all of these functions, Cuthbert was well equipped. He was already for his age well trained in weaponry. Many of the veteran soldiers of the castle garrison, who had known and admired his father, had always been ready to give him lessons. He was well able to wield the Norman battle-axe and the flange mace as well as short sword, long sword, and the curved falchion sword, and was enthusiastic in his desire to prove as good a knight as his father had been.

His friends the outlaws had taught him the warbow and the quarterstaff—a mean defensive weapon in talented hands. Cuthbert, who possessed a wiry strength and the stamina of a long-distance runner, was well-built for his age and had attained a considerable amount of skill with both sword and crossbow, as well as with the type of slim dagger known as a Misericorde that he always carried.

He could also read and write to a degree unusual for a petty noble, although this particular skill had not been acquired so cheerfully as had the martial arts. After all, if a knight had a firm seat in his saddle, a strong arm, a keen eye, and high courage, literacy was irrelevant other than for making his mark on a document. In fact, Cuthbert tried to hide his ability from the other men, who otherwise would make fun of him and tease him about "wearing the petticoats of an unmanly cleric."

Cuthbert had protested with all his might against the edict forced on him by his mother and Father Francis to teach him the knowledge of his letters and a neat, tidy hand—skills he felt more suited to the cloisters of a monastery than a battlefield. In the end he had given in most unwillingly to her pleading. Now, while he might still cover up his shameful secret from his peers, his reading and writing skills greatly pleased Sir Walter, and Cuthbert could thank Father Francis—under his breath, of course—for bullying him.

The preparations were at last complete, and the gallant little army assembled at the castle ready to start on the ten-day journey to Hamtun. Owing their feudal service to the Earl of Evesham were some two hundred men-at-arms, six knights, the hundred archers dressed in their forest green, with quilted gambesons to dull the enemy's arrows, and a bevy of squires and pages. All the country from around gathered to see them depart. Dame Editha was there, and by her side stood the earl's little daughter Margaret. The earl glittered bravely in his full mail armor and beside him rode Tybalt his personal squire, with Cuthbert following in the bright clothes of a page.

Just at that moment, however, his face did not match his costume, for although he tried his best to look bright and smiling, he was struggling to prevent the tears from filling his eyes at leaving his mother. For her part, the Dame cried unrestrainedly, and Margaret joined in the deluge. The crowded mob cheered loudly, the horns blew a brash fanfare, and Tybalt raised Evesham's standard to blow out in the brisk westerly breeze.

Everyone setting out so bravely knew that no pleasure trip lay ahead, and that, of the preceding crusades, not one in ten of those who left had ever returned. But even this stark fact failed to dampen spirits. While some set out strong in their holy duty, a fervor fanned by the preaching of the hedge priests and mendicant monks, by far and away the most were looking forward to the adventure, the glory, and the booty.

Above all, they were delighted, like schoolboys, to be away from the monotony of garrison life. These were men full of a combative spirit and they wanted to exercise their warlike nature—if it were in a good cause, well so much the better.

Cuthbert knew Father Francis wouldn't have approved.

The Earl of Evesham's detachment marched through England to Hamtun on the Solent without incident, and from there sailed to Havre in the English possession of the Duchy of Normandy. The varying scenes through which they passed delighted Cuthbert. The towns were a source of wonder, for he had never visited anything bigger than Worcester. He had been for a festival, the religious significance of which he could no longer remember, and because his mother's cousin was the Abbess of St. Anne's Convent in the town. As its French name, Havre—Harbor—suggested, it was an important port, full of bustle and excitement. Every day more ships brought in nobles, their retinues, and camp followers from England.

King Richard was there—he counted his Norman and Angevin estates as more his home than England—and as each corps landed he had it march down to join the main assembly outside Vézelay, a small town well south of Paris in the French Royal Domain. Leaving Havre, the levies began to taste the hardships which lay ahead. Since the English troops were marching through friendly territory, pillage was strictly forbidden, but while some of the crusader leaders paid for all they had, there were many who took what they required without recompense to the local peasants.

The route was thinly populated and the movement of so large a number of men along the same road rapidly exhausted all the resources. In weeks, the country looked eaten up. Although willing to pay for what his men needed, the Earl of Evesham himself often lay down on the turf on an empty stomach.

"If this is what it's like now," he grumbled in Cuthbert's hearing, "what will it be like when we join the French army? I have a feeling that we're more likely to starve before we sail, let alone perish in battle in the Holy Land."

After a long succession of marches they arrived in sight of the great camp at Vézelay, although "canvas city" described it better. Here were gathered a hundred thousand. The pavilions of the leaders, nobles, and other knights rose in regular lines to form streets and squares.

It was less cozy for the great mass of troops, who had to sleep in the open air since the difficulties of carriage were so great that only the elite could afford to take along tents. In front of each pavilion stood the lance and banner of its owner, and side by side in the middle of the camp rose the proud royal pavilions of Philip II of France, called Augustus, and Richard I of England, already glorying in the nickname Lionheart. Around them were the bright gonfalons suspended from crosses of all the nobles of western Europe.

The Evesham contingent was rather late in arriving, and the great body of the host had already assembled. Cuthbert gazed with delight at the varied colors, the nobles' extravagant clothes, the martial knights, and the air of discipline and order which reigned everywhere—although he was soon to discover that this orderliness ran only skin deep. They were met by a squire of the camp-marshal, who conducted them to the lines allotted them.

The earl's tent soon went up, with four or five grouped around it for his knights and one set aside for the knights' squires and pages. When this was done, Cuthbert found time to stroll away to take in the sights. A temporary town it might have been, but it attracted every conceivable type of camp follower. The country folk flocked in with their goods, smiths and armorers set up their forges, fletchers offered church-blessed arrows for sale, knights rode about on their brightly caparisoned horses. The daughters and goodwives of the vicinity avoided the encampment, but their fellow women of lesser repute quickly set up shop and the bordellos soon attracted lines of willing, panting customers, among them several of the foresters. One of them, a lad known by all as Gilly, a year older than Cuthbert, took him in hand. "Come, Cuthbert. Let's have some fun."

Cuthbert hesitated, but the heat in his loins at the thought drew him along and in turn they were admitted. One of the maids within, a mite prettier than most, took one look at comely Cuthbert and dragged him away into a dark corner. She quickly realized his inexperience and took control. "It's not just for pissing," she crowed at his embarrassment, and he soon learned that she was correct.

After, he wandered about in something of a daze, sure he'd committed a terrible sin, one he could never confess to Father Francis, but one he suspected he might well wish to suffer again. Players and jesters were the cause of merry laughter, while minstrels and troubadours, dressed like exotic birds, sang of former battles and raised the spirits of the coarse soldiers with amusing songs of love and romance—some less romantic than others.

Sometimes there was a break in the jollity as loud shouts and fierce oaths rose up. Then the loose ladies would run off like startled fawns, and men rush to the spot to see what was up. Often, the quarrel was purely private, but when it broke out between the retainers of two nobles, their friends were sure to pile in, and serious fights quickly got out of hand before the camp marshal and his posse could intervene. Sometimes such incidents led to words between the principals and bad feelings which frustrated the aims of the great enterprise they were supposed to be engaged in.

Several times in the course of his walk Cuthbert witnessed arguments which were only prevented from becoming physically violent by someone in authority turning up in time. Every time, these broke out between the Anglo-Normans and the French. Between the Saxons and the French there were no disputes for the simple reason that neither understood the other's language, but that was not the case between the French and King Richard's Normans who—with slight variation—shared the common Frankish tongue.

Cuthbert watched narrowly what was going on and decided that the degree of bad feelings between the men of the different armies so early in the campaign promised little hope for the final success of the expedition.

When he returned to the tent he shared with the squires and other pages, a summons awaited. Sir Walter was keen to listen to Cuthbert's thoughts on the camp and questioned him as to what he had seen. Cuthbert frankly acknowledged that there seemed to be great tension between the followers of the two armies.

"How will it be, I wonder, when we also mingle with Italians, Spanish, and Germans?"

Beneath his heavy brows, the earl's flinty eyes held Cuthbert's. "I've been," he said gravely, "to the royal camp, and from what I hear there are reasons for what you say. King Richard is the most loyal and gallant of kings, but he's haughty, and in speech his quick tongue often gets the better of his brain. As a prince he made promises to Philip which as a king he has taken back for the noblest of reasons, but it means the barons of France have no love for Normans, who also see us as interlopers in their territory, even though Normandy is our homeland.

"The breach between the kings has been healed by the common cause of the Holy Land. It must be hoped that this bad feeling will die away, and that we'll copy each other in our deeds on the battlefield… but I do wonder…?"

Chapter 6: Turning Over a New Page

Vézelay, March and April 1190

On the third day after the arrival of the Evesham levy at Vézelay, Philip of France gave a banquet for King Richard and his principal nobles. The two kings, brought up in each other's company and once the best of friends (some rumoured that as young men they shared a bed as lovers), had squabbled over territories in France but had partly mended relations when Richard promised to marry Philip's sister Alys, and for the sake of the Crusade they maintained the appearance of being on good terms.

The Earl of Evesham was invited and chose as his page Cuthbert to accompany him to the royal pavilion to wait on his needs. Here, at the far end from the entryway, Philip Augustus sat on a raised dais surrounded by his courtiers. The Earl of Evesham paid his compliments to the French king, and in return received a welcome of flattering words, before an usher showed him his place toward the end of the high table. A long blast on a herald's horn announced the arrival of Richard, accompanied by his royal retinue.

For the first time Cuthbert saw his king. In strode a man of regal stature and enormous strength. Cuthbert was pleasantly surprised that in some respects he looked more Saxon than Norman with his light hair and a clear, bright complexion. In the height of fashion, he wore a mustache and neatly trimmed pointed beard. Although his expression was generally open and good humored, Cuthbert also observed in his quick motions and piercing glances signs of the hasty temper and turbulent behavior for which he was known after rebellions against his father Henry II and his princely brothers Henry and Geoffrey.

The Earl of Evesham sat next to a French knight, Sir Joscelín Barras, Count of Brabant, a great thug of a man who gave Sir Walter a sour glance. Cuthbert took his place behind his lord to serve him with wine and food and next to the count's page, who looked to be some five years older than Cuthbert and considerably taller.

As the banquet progressed the buzz of Frankish conversation grew fast and furious. From the very first, Cuthbert noticed that Sir Joscelín was generally rude and offensive, no doubt because of the amount of wine he drank, usually a whole goblet at a gulp. Perhaps, thought Cuthbert, he was accustomed to live alone with his crude retainers, which made his manners coarse. Either that, or he disliked the English. At any rate, his remarks were calculated to anger Sir Walter.

He began his conversation by wondering how a Norman noble could live in a country like England, inhabited by a race little more than pigs. Cuthbert bridled at the remark and so too did the earl. Sir Walter angrily retorted that the Saxons were every bit as civilized, and in some respects superior, to the Normans or French. This poor start went farther downhill as the feast dragged on. The French count continued to spit out innuendoes and snide attacks on the English, and to talk with a vague boastfulness, which Cuthbert could see irritated Sir Walter.

As Cuthbert was about to refill his master's cup of wine in the second hour, Sir Jocelín's tall page suddenly jolted his elbow and almost caused Cuthbert to spill wine on his master. His swift recovery meant that the wine went all over his own tunic instead.

"What a clumsy child," the Brabant page scoffed.

"You're a rough and ill-mannered lout," Cuthbert spat back angrily. "If we were anywhere else I'd give you what for, as you deserve."

The tall page burst into a mocking laugh. "Ooh, I'm frightened. Why, I could stuff you in my pocket you little pip-squeak."

"I think," said Sir Joscelín to the earl—for the boys had raised their voices—"you had better send that brat of yours home and order him to be whipped."

"Sir count," the earl growled, "your manners are boorish, and if we were not starting a crusade, I would be more than happy to teach you a lesson on that score."

The dispute's volume rose higher, until some angry word caught the royal ear.

Amid the general hubbub King Philip rose, and saying something to King Richard, left the table, at which signal the banquet began to break up. A page of the French court came up and told Sir Walter and Sir Joscelín that both kings wanted to see them in Philip's pavilion. The two nobles strode through the milling nobles and senior knights, regarding each other like two dogs eager to fly at the other's throat. Cuthbert and the Brabant page stood silently just outside the pavilion's inner chamber, where they clearly heard what passed within.

"My lords, my lords," remonstrated Philip. "This is against all law and reason. How dare you brawl at my table. If this is how we start out, I've no high hopes for the future of our enterprise."

"Your Majesty," the Earl of Evesham said, "I regret what has happened. But it seemed, from the time we sat down, that this lord wanted to pick a quarrel with me, and now I ask your Majesty's permission for us to settle our differences in the lists."

Richard gave a grunt of approval and happily assented.

The French king disagreed forcefully. "Don't forget our mission for which we've assembled here. You've all taken a solemn oath to forget private quarrels and feuds until the Holy Sepulchre has been recovered. Are you going to show that the oath is a mere form of words? No, sirs, you must lay aside your feuds, and must promise me and my good brother here that you will keep the peace between you until this war is over. It doesn't matter whose fault it was."

"The quarrel, sire," Sir Joscelín said, "was between our pages, who were almost coming to blows in your Majesty's presence. All I suggested was that the earl might curb the insolence of his page, and instead of doing anything he met my remarks with scorn."

By swaying slightly, Cuthbert could just see a little of the room beyond and the four men in there. Sir Walter was about to dispute this lie, but before he could open his mouth King Richard leaped in.

"Pooh, pooh, gentlemen. Nobles shouldn't interfere in the squabbles of boys. Let 'em fight—it won't harm anyone. By the way, your grace," he said, turning to Philip with a laugh, "if the masters may not fight, there's no reason in the world why the ruffians shouldn't. We're lacking amusement. Let's have a list tomorrow, and let the pages fight it out for the good name of their masters and their nations. How's that, gentlemen?"

Sir Joscelín of Brabant agreed with alacrity, saying that he was sure his page would be glad to fight. Sir Walter gave his assent with some reluctance.

"That's agreed, then," King Richard said, happily clapping his hands and rubbing them together in anticipation. "I'll have a piece of ground marked out tomorrow morning and my footmen will keep it clear. We kings will judge. Fight on foot or on horseback?"

"On foot, on foot," said the King of France. "I don't want the chivalrous sport of knights brought into disrepute by any failure on their part riding noble steeds. On foot at least it will be a fair struggle."

"What weapons?" Brabant asked.

"Oh, swords and battle-axes, of course," replied King Richard with another deep laugh.

Cuthbert kept his silence as he accompanied Sir Walter to his pavilion. "This has not been well done," the earl finally spat out as he ducked through the opening.

"Well, my lord," Cuthbert said, "I'm glad. That's how it should be. He insulted me without cause, other than envy at still being a page at his advanced age."

"Age? What do you mean? What's he like? I never bothered to look at the cur," the earl asked in an alarmed tone. By the time they left the two kings, the count and his tall page had already gone.

"He must be approaching or gone past twenty and well past his time even if he were a squire."

"That won't make for a fair match!" Sir Walter grated, now looking thoroughly concerned.

"You know, sir, that I've trained well and I can hold my own against any of your men with light weapons, so I've no fear that this gawky idiot will disgrace me or discredit you or England."

"Hmm, well, if you're sure. But you'll need some mail. Mine won't fit. I'll get the armorer to check around and see if there's anyone who will fit, and a simple cap. The lighter the better, you'll need to be nimble. Will you want a light sword and battle-axe?"

"No," Cuthbert said, "I'm strong and practiced enough to use those of the men-at-arms. I could wield my father's sword, and that was a heavy one."

The morning dawned to an immediate buzz of excitement. News of a fight to take place between an English and a French page, by the permission of the kings of England and France, and that their Majesties were to judge, caused a stir of from one end to the other of the vast encampment.

In a meadow just outside the campground a crew of King Richard's men marked off an oval space of about an acre. Serfs pitched a pavilion on one side of this and a small tent at each end for the combatants. Around the enclosure men-at-arms formed a ring, and behind them a dense scrum of spectators eagerly gathered.

At the appointed hour, the two kings arrived together. As Sir Walter could see, Richard was in an exuberant mood, but then, he preferred the clash of arms, the mêlée joust, and the sight of combat of any kind to any other pleasure.

Philip, on the other hand, looked somber. He was a far wiser and more politic king than Richard, and although he had consented to the sudden proposal, his expression suggested that in his heart he felt the contest was a foolish one. As he took his chair next to Richard, Sir Walter heard him mutter, "I trust this will not create more bad feeling among the men of our nations, whichever way it goes."

All knew that he had reserved the right to stop the fight before either page was likely to sustain any deadly injury.

When the monarchs had taken their places the heralds sounded their horns, and the two combatants advanced on foot from their ends of the lists. A murmur of surprise and dissatisfaction broke from the crowd.

"My Lord of Evesham," Richard said angrily to the earl, "you should have said that the difference between the two is too great to allow the combat to be fair. The Frenchman looks big enough to tuck your page under his arm and walk off with him."

The difference was striking. Arrayed in a full suit of knightly mail—a knee-length haubergeon, mail chausses on his legs, with a mail coif and gloves—and with his helmet and lofty plume of feathers, the French champion towered above Cuthbert, who, in his close-fitting steel cap and link armor, seemed a very dwarf alongside his opponent.

"It's not size, sire, but muscle and pluck that wins in a rumpus like this," Sir Walter murmured in Richard's ear. "Remember David and Goliath. Your Majesty needn't be afraid that my page will disgrace us. He's distantly of my blood, of mixed Saxon and Norman descent, and will, believe me, do credit to both."

The king's brow cleared. "Brother Philip," he said, turning to his royal companion, "I'll bet my gold chain against yours on the short-shanks."

"It's simple robbery to take your wager. The difference between their bulk is quite incredible. However…" Philip gave a brief smile, "My chain against yours."

According to the rules the fight commenced with swords. Cuthbert was a match in strength for his opponent, although he was a good head shorter. Constant exercise, however, had hardened him and he'd been taught by the best the Vale of Evesham could supply. Nevertheless his adversary's superior height allowed the French page to rain blows down from a difficult angle to block. Cuthbert managed with difficulty, but as soon as the first fury of his rival's assault slowed, he took to the offensive and drove the Frenchman back step by step.

The French armor proved superior to Cuthbert's sword and it resisted several dangerous looking cuts no matter the power he put behind the swing. And then disaster struck. The Frenchman's sword whanged down across the flat of Cuthbert's blade close to the guard and struck the weapon from his hands. Even through his gloves, the blow left his hands singing. The packed French *gens d'armes* cheered loudly, encouraging their champion, who gave a shout of triumph as he advanced threateningly.

As Cuthbert backed off, shaking his hands to get some feeling back in his fingers he saw from the corner of his eye King Philip stand. The move struck him with fear that the king would stop the match as threatened. There was no way he would let the long streak of French piss get the better of him. Cuthbert seized his axe and made such an athletic display with it that his foe dropped his own sword and took to the same weapon.

Now his superior height and weight gave him an even greater advantage than with the sword. Cuthbert instantly realized this and pushed himself to the limits of his strength and speed to dodge the lethal swipes aimed at him. He managed to place one or two slashes of his own, always aiming at the same spot, the hip where his opponent's mail skirt flew up during violent movement, revealing a patch of less protective hose above the mail chausses.

The spectators quieted down. The tension became tangible. In the hush the whirring of air rushing past razor-sharp axe blades was clearly heard, punctuated by the harsh breathing of the combatants.

At last the Frenchman struck Cuthbert so percussive a blow that it beat down his guard and struck the steel cap from his head, bringing him to one knee.

In spite of the loud ringing in his ears from the shock to his head, he was up in an instant, and before his foe could retrieve his guard, Cuthbert aimed again at his momentarily exposed hip. But the Frenchman had now seen this weakness in his defense and anticipated Cuthbert's move by blocking with the haft of his axe. Reacting to his feint was exactly what Cuthbert hoped he would do. In a flash he made a complete revolution on one heel and brought all his strength behind the axe as it struck the unguarded side of the other's helm.

The impact split the metal and the French page dropped to the ground as if someone had pulled the tendons from his limbs. As he lay on the churned-up grass senseless, a great deafening roar broke from the English half of the soldiery. Cuthbert leaned over his prostrate opponent and, receiving no answer to the question "Do you yield?" rose to his feet, and raised the axe above his head.

The Norman and English contingent as one hailed his victory in a cacophony of shouting and gloating.

King Richard ordered the summoner to lead Cuthbert to the royal enclosure and he walked from the arena to continual cheers of approval. Although the French soldiers were downhearted, many also applauded his brave performance.

"Well, aren't you a happy surprise!" King Richard beamed. He strode forward to greet Cuthbert as the champion came—a bit unsteadily—into the enclosure behind the royal pavilion. "Brave, courageous, bold, *and* short. You handled that fight as well as many a knight would have done. If you were older, I'd knight you on the spot. Hah! I don't doubt that the occasion will come when you embrace the Saracens as you did that long-shanked opponent of yours."

"Thank you, sire," Cuthbert managed.

The king pulled the gold chain of office from around his neck. "Do you object, brother?" he asked Philip, who merely shook his head with a slight smile.

"Here's a gold chain. Take it as proof that the King of England says you have sustained the honor of his country." He leaned forward to bring his head level with Cuthbert's and added confidentially, "If at any time you require a boon, bring or send me that chain and you shall have it. Sir Walter," he said, straightening up and turning to the earl, "in this bold youth you have a worthy champion, and I trust you'll give him every chance to distinguish himself. Tell me when you think he's ready for the knightly rank and I'll administer the rites myself."

After his interview with the king, two men carried Cuthbert shoulder-high to his tent amid the hearty plaudits of the English soldiers. His own comrades flocked around him—the men of the greenwood headed by Cnut, were especially jubilant over his victory.

"Who would've thought that the child of such a short time ago, should now have held up our country's honor?" Cnut crowed happily. "We're all proud of you, Cuthbert, and if one day you ever need us to follow—just lead us to glory, and we'll show that the men of Evesham are as valiant as any under King Richard's rule."

"You must be wary, Cuthbert," the earl said to him that evening. "Believe me when I tell you that both of us have made an enemy, who—although he hasn't the power—certainly has the will to harm us... maybe even attempt to kill us. I kept one eye on Count Joscelín during the fight, and again when you were led up to the king. Hatred and fury lit his eyes. The page too, I hear, is his own nephew, and he's now the laughing-stock of the French camp at having been conquered by one so much younger than himself."

"He brought it down on his own head, my lord."

"So he did, but that won't make him any more reasonable and it would be sensible to take precautions against his vengeance. Be on your guard, and don't go out at night unattended. Keep Cnut near you—he's as faithful as a watch-dog, and if the need arose, I'm sure he would give his life for you. I shall be also on my guard. After all, his quarrel with me hasn't gone away at all, so the fury of this fierce and ill-restrained knight will be aimed at both of us."

"What's his problem?" Cuthbert asked, shaking his head in puzzlement.

"You've seen how the Baron of Wortham was, a man with a mean streak as wide as the sea we crossed to get here. There are just some knights about like that. I've had a poor account of Joscelín from some of his fellow nobles. They say he's one of those men who disgraces the calling of knight, who are nothing more than a mixture of robber and soldier. He harries all the lands in his fief and he's now only joined the Crusade to avoid being tried by his overlord, who has been unable to ignore the cries of the oppressed people under Joscelín's heavy hand."

As Sir William prepared to dismiss Cuthbert, he rasped darkly, "There are those who say he has no Christian right to be here, but the choice was given him to be outlawed, or to join the Crusade with all the strength he could raise. Naturally he chose the second course. But his are the instincts of a robber and he surrounds himself with violent men of low character, and he will try to get back at us at every chance. Be on your guard."

Chapter 7: A Cur's Revenge

April 1190

Two days later the crusader host broke camp and began the long southward march. After a week's tramping down the Saône and Rhône valleys the army earned a three-day halt at Montélimar and encamped nearby in order to collect provisions for the next stage. Here the armies were to separate, the French to march to Genoa, the English to Marseilles, the port at which they would embark on a hired fleet.

One evening the earl sent Cuthbert with a message to another English lord, who had accommodation in the town at the bishop's palace. Cnut accompanied Cuthbert, for he now made a point of seldom letting him out of his sight. It was light when they reached the bishop's palace, but here they were delayed for some time, and night had fallen by the time they started back.

"The town shuts down quickly," Cnut observed with a chuckle. "The good citizens keep off the streets and lock themselves indoors, frightened that such a large army sits outside their town. They are wise, soldiers are never be trusted to behave well."

To avoid any trouble the two kings had issued stringent orders that no French *gens d'armes* or English men-at-arms were to leave the camp after nightfall. As a result of this curfew, and that self-imposed by Montélimar's inhabitants, the streets were already hushed and quiet.

Cnut and Cuthbert proceeded along the lanes unmolested for some distance. Occasionally a solitary passer-by, hidden under a hooded cape, hurried past. The half-moon's faint luminance relieved some of the gloom in the unlighted streets, which were so pocked and rubbish strewn that anyone without a flaming brand was likely to cause themselves severe injury through falling into a hidden pothole or an open sewer.

Here and there, in the tradition of that part of southern France, occasional wayside shrines were built into the sides of dwellings or walls, in front of which the two Englishmen paused briefly to cross themselves. Just after they had passed by one such altar a shout split the night. A party of ten men jumped them from a side alley. Cnut recovered from the surprise quickly and drew his sword. Cuthbert snatched out his Misericorde and they laid about them furiously, but the armored bushwhackers were too many. The big Saxon took a mighty blow from the flat of a sword and fell partly stunned to the muddy cobbles. Cuthbert, armed only with the little dagger saw that further effort was hopeless so he took to his heels and ran for his life. He bled copiously from two wounds, but although deep gashes nothing was broken and they did not disable him at first.

Speed alone saved him as he flew along the darkened streets and he strove to keep ahead of his pursuers. They, weighed down by weapons and mail, were unable to keep up with the flying footsteps of one clothed in the light uniform of a page, but the pursuit persisted. *If I don't find refuge soon the blood I'm losing will weaken me fast and I'll fall to the thugs.*

His breathing grew ragged and his knees ached from pounding on uneven cobbles. He began to think that the end was at hand and that Sir Joscelín's henchmen—for surely they were—would soon avenge their master's humiliation. Then he saw a cowled figure standing at a door a little way ahead. Just as he staggered up, the door opened and the sudden glow of light from inside falling on the road revealed the individual crossing the threshold to be a monk.

Without a moment's hesitation Cuthbert rushed through the still gaping portal. He cried out, "Sanctuary!" and sank almost fainting on the floor.

The porter swiftly slammed the solid door shut and barred it securely. In a moment there was a rush and clatter of feet and then a furious hammering of fists against the timbers. One of the monks uncovered a latticed opening in the portal. "What do you mean by this affront? This is the Monastery of St. John and it is sacrilege to lay the hand of violence even against its gateway. Go away or the abbot will lodge a complaint before the mayor tomorrow."

The hammering stopped, and after some indistinct muttering and clearer expletives from the other side, the band of hoodlums retired.

Two of the brothers lifted Cuthbert and carried him up to a cell just off the monks' dortoir, where the monk-infirmarian speedily examined his wounds, and pronounced, that although his life was not in danger, the loss of blood had weakened him gravely. "One cut is serious," he said. "It will be some time before you fully recover from it, my son."

Cuthbert thanked him weakly. The physician made up a potion and helped Cuthbert to drink it to the dregs. He pulled a face.

"I know. Horrible taste, but it will make you sleep deeply and aid in healing your wounds. When you wake will be soon enough to tell us why those men were chasing you. Sleep now."

Some time passed before he felt sufficiently recovered to sit up and talk. "How long have I lain here?"

"Two days, my son."

Cuthbert groaned at the delay. "I must let my lord know. Can you send a messenger to the tents of the Earl of Evesham?"

At his words the kindly infirmarian's expression turned grave. "My son, I'm sorry to tell you the army moved away yesterday, and is now probably some twenty-five miles away. There's nothing for you but to be patient. When you're well again you can follow the army and rejoin your master before he embarks at Marseilles. But tell me, what's a youngster like you done to attract murderers—they obviously weren't just robbing you?"

Cuthbert told the monk of his suspicions about the Count of Brabant and his fears for Cnut. It turned out that the brothers of

St. John had heard of his victory in the tourney and immediately understood the danger he faced.

"I know nothing of this Cnut, but your enemy knows where you've taken refuge and if he's determined to get his own back, he'll no doubt have some of his ruffians watching the monastery. I'll have a word with the prior to detail a watch. But it will be another two weeks at least before you'll be fit enough to continue your journey."

Cuthbert's frustration was no match for his weakened condition and he resigned himself to his incarceration with ill grace. However, he regained strength more rapidly than the monks expected. They fed him generously, and this and his good constitution soon enabled him to recuperate. At the end of the first week he said he would like to be on his way.

The infirmarian disagreed. "You might be well enough to perform a page's lightest duties, but the hardships of a long and lonely journey are a different matter. There will be all sorts of hazards to face. You may have to trust to speed and endurance for your life if you're still being followed. It would be madness to go until you're fully fit."

Cuthbert sighed, but the monk's next words made him uneasy.

"Besides, we've seen beyond doubt that the monastery is under close scrutiny. The town's full of ruffians and camp-followers. Some are retainers of lazy knights, but most are those who follow any army to buy plunder from the soldiers, and to rob and murder should there be a hope of getting hold of gold. That means if Brabant needs more hands, he won't have to look far to hire them. We could appeal to the mayor, but his protection extends only to the town walls. If we can think of a means of smuggling you out, after that you must rely on your own strength and cleverness to avoid any traps that may be laid for you. You needn't worry about missing your countrymen, they will be delayed for a long time at Marseilles."

Given this reasoning, Cuthbert agreed to remain for another week, by which time he felt absolutely restored to strength again, and capable of as much exertion as before the attack. But getting safely out of the town still posed a serious problem. He spoke at length with the prior, who told him the use of a disguise would not work.

"Every monk who has gone out has been checked, and some of the shorter ones have even been jostled in the streets to throw back their cowls for a sight of their faces. No, whatever we do it must be as clever as possible."

Cuthbert thought about this for a moment before saying, "Whatever scheme you might come up with to get me clear of the walls without being seen, once in the country I wouldn't have a horse or armor. That would make it a perilous trip, even if none of my enemies were on my tail. What I propose is to go to the mayor, and claim the means and an escort. If he will just give me a few men-at-arms for one day's ride, I can choose my own route and take my chance of finding my way down to Marseilles."

Protected by a cohort of the brethren, Cuthbert was soon delivered safely to the door of Sir John de Cahors, the mayor—who was not best pleased to meet him.

"So you're the young pest. You've caused me no end of trouble and stress. Couriers have flown to and fro concerning you with angry messages from your fiery king. When in the morning a tall, stalwart Saxon dressed in green was found, slashed about in various places, lying on the street, the townsmen, not knowing who he was, but finding him still breathing, carried him to the English camp where he was claimed as a follower of the Earl of Evesham."

At this news, Cuthbert gave a deep sigh of relief. "You found Cnut alive."

Sir John treated Cuthbert to a severe frown for the interruption. "As may be, young man. There was great anger over this, and soon the big earl himself came down in a high dudgeon to tell me his page was missing, and had probably been murdered. The rest of the army had moved off, and the earl only remained because of his missing liegeman. I assured the fuming noble that I would have a thorough search made in the town. Although in no way satisfied, he rode off after his king with all his force, carrying with him the Saxon man we picked up."

Cuthbert opened his mouth to speak, but the indignant mayor shouted him down.

"If that wasn't enough, two days later King Richard sent a message saying that unless this missing page was found, or if we discovered he had been killed and his murderers were not brought to justice and punished, he would damned well burn the town down around our ears on his return from the Holy Land."

Cuthbert succeeded admirably in suppressing a grin at this.

"Your king's not a man to mince words—even though threats are empty from men starting out on a quest from which they may not return. Still, I had a search made for you even though I became convinced that your body had been flung into the river. So I'm glad that you're alive—your master obviously thinks highly of you. The earl left in my charge your horse, in case we should hear from you. Also a purse of money and the chain mail which he said you wore at a tournament lately."

Cuthbert gave an exclamation of pleasure. He hadn't the money to purchase a mount, and no protection beyond his Misericorde, so the difficulties of the journey to Marseilles had confounded him. But with his good horse under him and mail on his back he knew he would survive any dangers which might arise.

"Sir John," the prior said, "we know spies have been watching the monastery."

"If I could find them, I'd hang them over the gates of the town," the knight said wrathfully. "But right now there are as many thieves as honest men in the place. I'd have to hang a lot of men to ensure getting hold of the right ones. Besides, I'd lay money that they're more likely lurking on the roads between here and the sea." He turned to Cuthbert. "If I had the men to spare, I'd send an escort with you, but what's left after the Crusade has taken the rest, I need to keep order here."

"I thought, sir, that if you could loan me the use of four men-at-arms to ride with me for the first day, I could look after myself after that, especially if you could find me one honest man to act as guide and companion."

He outlined his plan to first head west for the first day's travel before finding a road going south, thus avoiding any traps set for him on the direct route to Marseilles.

The mayor thought about it briefly, and then agreed.

Chapter 8: A Long and Winding Road

May to October 1190

All day they rode in a westerly direction and before nightfall had covered over thirty miles before entering a small village. Cuthbert gave the men-at-arms a small bonus for their help, released them, and paid for a bed at the only inn. The man the Sir John of Cahors picked out to act as a guide looked after the two horses.

The mayor's choice pleased Cuthbert. Twenty-three and with an honest face, he told Cuthbert his father had a small farm near Avignon. He himself had a yen to go into a good trade and had been apprenticed to a master smith at Montélimar. Having served his apprenticeship, he found that he had mistaken his vocation, and now intended to return to his family's vineyards.

Cuthbert calculated that he would make at least four days' in a southerly direction before encountering any dangers. His exit from the monastery would soon be discovered—if it hadn't been at the time he left it—and the moment the gates of the city opened a spy would rush south to warn his comrades. These, he calculated, would doubtless take a road which at some point intercepted his own route. As they rode fast and made a good distance each day, he hoped to succeed in beating them.

On the third day his horse cast a shoe and forced him to slow their pace. On the fifth day after leaving Montélimar they arrived at a small town where a smith agreed to shoe his horse for a fair fee.

The next morning as he prepared to continue the journey, Cuthbert failed to find his guide. He made hurried inquiries of the innkeeper, who told him that the young man had gone out the evening before and not returned. Extremely uneasy at this circumstance, Cuthbert went to the town guard in case his guide might have been brought in after a drunken spree. But there was no news there. He was returning to the inn along a narrow street when he spotted a familiar shoe lying in the gutter of a greasy side alley. A sick feeling assailed his stomach. The guide wore one exactly like it. He recognized the buckle.

With great caution, Cuthbert sidled into the narrow alley, more of a sewer between the lodgings. Refuse littered its sides, and behind one larger pile of rubbish he saw a shoeless foot sticking out.. The young man of Avignon would no more make wine with his family. He lay sprawled on his side. Flies buzzed noisily where they gathered around the gaping slash in his throat. Cuthbert leaned weakly against a wall. They hadn't known each other long enough for grief to be overwhelming, but he still felt a deep sadness at the waste... and anger. *My enemies linger nearby. But they shall pay for this, I swear it.*

As the church bell chimed twelve, Cuthbert rode out on the southern road.

A shiver ran down his spine. *Will they have now overtaken me?* He kept his eyes alert and his senses finely attuned. He pressed his horse hard and carefully avoided all copses and small woods through which the road ran. Several times he circled a thicket and returned to the track after passing it. His three-year-old horse was a fine one and, with Cuthbert's light weight, capable of a great burst of speed if he needed it.

At length he approached an extensive forest, which stretched for miles on either side. *No detour this time.* Half a mile before he reached it the track divided. He slowed the horse to a walk in order to conserve its strength and wind. *This is the perfect spot for an ambush.* At the point where the track branched and the leading edge of the forest came right to the verge of the road sat a man in the bedraggled garb of a mendicant hedge priest. He held out his hands, palms up.

"Good sir, in the name of our Holy Savior grant me some small favor."

Cuthbert's skin prickled with a nameless dread, but he threw the man a small coin. As he did so, he could swear he heard a rustling in the bushes behind the priest. His thoughts raced. *They're here. What to do?* And then he squared up to the beggar-priest and spoke in a deliberately loud voice.

"Which is the fastest and best route to Avignon?"

"The right-hand track is the best and shortest," the priest indicated. "The other makes a long circuit and leads through several marshes, which your excellency will find it hard to pass."

Cuthbert thanked him, and moved forward, still at a walk, along the indicated right fork in the road. When he had gone about a furlong, and was hidden from the sight of the hedge priest, he reined in and waited quietly. As he expected, he soon heard the sound of horses' hoofs coming on at full gallop along the other track as it gently diverged from the one he was on. He smiled grimly and gentled his mount with a rub behind its ears.

Your evil master must think me young indeed to try and catch me with such a transparent trick. I don't suppose that blasted page has more than eleven men with him, and put five on each road. It was clear that the fake priest's task was simply to see which road he took. *I heard his horse in the bushes back there and that's him now riding to tell the ambushers on the other road that I've taken this one. Even now they'll be cutting across to join their fellows farther down this way.*

Cuthbert cautiously retraced his steps to the junction and turned down the left-hand route which, as he had correctly anticipated, was now clear. He encountered none of the advertised marshes and he traveled through the forested landscape without incident to arrive safely that night at a village, having seen no further signs of his pursuers.

The next day he started again early and rode until midday, when he halted at a small town and, in urgent need of food, stopped outside its only inn. A sixth sense warned Cuthbert not to stay too long so he declined the groom's offer to stable and take care of his horse. "Hold him outside the door for me and give him a light brush down, some water, and a few handfuls of grain," he commanded the groom as he handed the lad a coin.

He downed a surprisingly good stew. And then, dropping another coin on the table, he made for the doorway. As he appeared in the opening he saw several men loitering close by. Danger screamed at him. The thugs spotted Cuthbert leave the inn and ran at him.

With two running steps and a single bound Cuthbert sprang up into the saddle just as the nearest man reached out and tried to drag him from his mount. Cuthbert whipped the wicked little Misericorde from his belt and plunged it into his attacker's throat. The man fell back, gurgling helplessly as Sir Joscelín's page leaped forward, broadsword held back over his shoulder ready to strike out.

 Cuthbert seized the short mace which hung at the saddle bow and hurled it with all his force full in the face of his enemy. The unexpected move took the Brabant page by surprise. The heavy weapon struck him on the brow fair and square between the eyes, and with a cry the lanky hoodlum fell back, his face completely smashed in by the blow which had pulverized his brain. The uplifted sword flew from his nerveless hand to sail backward harmlessly through the air.

Even before his foe's corpse hit the ground, Cuthbert drew his long sword and dug his heels into his horse's flanks. The animal shot forward as Cuthbert struck out with his blade at two men who made a snatch at the reins. One ducked but the other took the keen edge of the sword across the side of his head and Cuthbert had the satisfaction of seeing his ear fly off. In another minute he was galloping out of the village, convinced that he had killed the leader of his enemies, and that he was safe now to continue on to Marseilles.

So it turned out. Without further incident, he arrived at the great seaport and soon discovered the Evesham contingent's camp. As he entered the enclosure an inarticulate shout of wild joy greeted Cuthbert, and Cnut ran forward to grab him out of the saddle in a giant bear hug.

"My dear Cuthbert, my dear, dear Cuthbert! You escaped. We'd all given you up. If you hadn't survived I should never have forgiven myself, believing that I might have somehow done better and have saved you from the cutthroats who attacked us."

"Thanks, thanks, Cnut," Cuthbert gasped between hugs. His feet scrabbled for a hold on the ground, but the huge Saxon swung him about. "I've struggled with my conscience. I feel bad that I abandoned you. When he hit you it sounded like the blow of a smith's hammer on the anvil."

"Think nothing of it. You did the sensible thing, lad. Fortunately, my steel cap saved my head somewhat." Cnut replied. He lowered Cuthbert to the ground.

"Hah, and yes, his skull is as thick as they come, too," one of the archers taunted with a good-natured laugh.

Cnut made a rude gesture with his right hand. "Well, now you're safely back, I'll recover quicker. I think that fretting over you has kept me back more than the inflammation from the wound itself—but there's the earl at the flap of his tent wondering what's happening."

Sir Walter seemed to be really affected by his page's sudden reappearance. As Cuthbert walked up he awkwardly held out both arms and embraced him as a father might.

"Well, Cuthbert," he mumbled gruffly. "I've been so anxious for you. Had you been my own son, I could not have felt your loss more. We didn't doubt for an instant that you'd fallen into the hands of that villainous count's retainers. From all we could learn, and from the absence of any corpse by the side of Cnut, I imagined he must have had you carried off. Of course, he denied any involvement, and has now disappeared to Genoa. But we'll meet again on the shores of Sicily, and there I shall have satisfaction."

As Sir John of Cahors had anticipated, the crusaders settled in for a weary delay at Marseilles. The English fleet, commanded to be there on the army's arrival, had failed to keep the schedule. King Richard, impatient as ever of delay, at last lost his temper and embarked on a cog with a few of his chosen knights, and set sail for Sicily, the point at which the two armies of the expedition were to reunite. A few days later the fleet arrived.

The word "English" did not accurately describe this navy. Cuthbert and Cnut spent some time examining the vessels with great interest. The ships were mostly unfamiliar looking oared galleys of the maritime nations of Italy—Venice, Genoa, and Pisa—for England owned few vessels suited to the Mediterranean. Some northern round-bellied cogs turned up, but their sails needed stronger winds than usually prevailed on the middle sea. One English salt they spoke to turned his nose up at what he called "rowing boats."

"Our canvas may flap if God don't give us a bit of breeze, but I knows this sea, and when she's so inclined the Mediterranean is capable of violent tempests. See, it's quite shallow in many places, so the wind throws up huge waves, for which our cogs is built, whereas those long row-boats is often swamped and destroyed."

As there were insufficient vessels to carry the entire army, a portion of the English host embarked immediately and sailed after their king. The remainder followed as soon as the fleet had come back to Marseilles to collect them.

The cogs and galleys were so tightly packed that none of the men could walk about. Every man slept where he sat, and in fact considered himself lucky if he could find the room to stretch out full length. Most slept sitting against bulwarks or other supports. In the cabins, where the knights, their pages, and squires were housed, the crowding was less excessive, but in the close confines the air soon grew disgustingly stale, and there was no chance of getting onto the crammed deck for some fresh air. Many of the men suffered sea sickness and within hours of leaving port the stench of shit and vomit was enough to make those unassailed by the ships' motion fell ill.

Fortunately, within two days they approached the straits between Sicily and the mainland to put in at Messina. The French army, which had sailed the shorter distance from Genoa, had already arrived.

"But where is King Richard?" Cuthbert asked of a page who had come with the first wave.

He shrugged. "No one knows and everyone is afeared for his life."

The king turned up some days later, and the explanation for his disappearance soon became widely known, to some amusement. Even Sir Walter, normally of a serious nature, cracked a craggy grin when Cuthbert helped him dress one morning. "Impetuous majesty, his ship was driven from its course by a violent storm, which proves the saying: more haste, less speed."

Three weeks later, all the crusaders were assembled around Messina, where it was intended to remain some time before starting out on the treacherous sea voyage to the Holy Land. The nobles' squires and pages were kept busy in the festival atmosphere as the kings and their barons vied with each other in entertainments, jousts, and other tournaments. The Italian knights also made a brave show, and anyone would have been forgiven for thinking that this huge army of men had gathered there simply for the purpose of amusement and feasting. To add to the jollity many nobles and their ladies came to visit from the mainland, among them the Queen of Navarre and her beautiful daughter, Princess Berengaria.

This development did not please the Earl of Evesham over much, as Cuthbert overheard one evening while he served food and drink to Sir Walter and Tybalt.

"Rumor has it that this visit is at Queen Eleanor's instigation. That indomitable woman has her eye firmly fixed on adding Navarre to adjacent Aquitaine, the country she had brought to Henry II on her marriage to him. She has plans to marry her son to Berengaria for the purpose, and King Richard all too often does as his mother demands."

Sir Walter quaffed his goblet and held it out to Cuthbert for a refill, itself a sign of his discomfort for the earl usually took drink in only small quantities.

"She's going to be trouble," he grumbled. He addressed the remark at Tybalt, but Cuthbert couldn't help butting in on the conversation. "Sire, in what way?" He had been struck with the lady's exquisite beauty and wondered what problems so fair a maiden could cause.

The knight glanced up in some surprise at the interruption, but the ticking off Cuthbert expected didn't materialize. "Have you noticed the way our good lord, the king, gazes at her. It's not just that in marrying her he gains the country of Navarre to add to his collection—he's become obsessed by her. But in long promise to King Philip he's betrothed to Alys of France. If he reneges on the marriage, all hell will break loose. Berengaria is the damsel of our distress, mark my words."

As day after day passed, it became evident to all that the King of England was indeed infatuated by the princess. All sorts of gossip now became camp currency. Agitated quarrels between the two kings were bruited abroad and these were quickly reflected in bad feeling between the French and English knights. Soon the fun turned to fuming, squabbles, and outright violence. The great enterprise became bogged down in a tidal wave of passions on the rocky shores of Sicily.

Chapter 9: Princess Berengaria

Messina, Winter 1190-91

Returning late to the English bivouac from a mission for Sir Walter, his path took Cuthbert through a section where the French were encamped. The day had been leaden and now rain lashed down in cascades. Cuthbert realized that he was completely lost in the vast, sodden canvas town. He was also on his own because Cnut had been unavoidably detained by his duties.

In his confusion Cuthbert almost tripped over a guy rope and ran up against the wall of a tent. It seemed like a good idea to ask directions, since the torrential rain had kept all sensible people dry under their awnings, so he made his way to the entrance. As he was about to draw aside the hangings, he heard a passionate voice ring out from inside, and the words caused him to withdraw his hand suddenly.

"I tell you, I would rather drive a dagger into her heart, than allow our own princess to be insulted and pawed by this hot-headed island dog."

"It's sad indeed, my sons," said another, but in a calmer and smoother tone, "that the success of a great expedition like this, sent to recover the Holy Sepulchre from the infidels, should be wrecked by the headstrong fancies of one man. We should remember the words of the old Greek poet who told us how Princess Helen caused a great war between peoples of that nation."

Cuthbert heard a third, gruffer, voice. "I know fuck all of either of Helen or the Greeks, or of their blasted poets. They're a shifty race at the best of times, and I believe everything bad that's said of them. But as to the Princess of Navarre, I agree with our friend—to slip a stiletto between her ribs would be a righteous act because it would remove the cause of dispute between the two kings, and prevent a war between the nations. Never forget, his insult to our Princess Alys is more than we, as French knights, can bear. If King Philip gives the word, every knight in the army will be ready to turn his sword against the English curs, Holy Crusade or no."

Then Cuthbert heard the calm second voice again.

"It would be hot-headed to shed blood. This Helen must be removed, but not, as our friend the count has suggested, by a dagger. There are scores of religious houses where we may put this bird in a gilded cage without anyone knowing where she is. And it would be poetic justice—she would be in the right place to pray for forgiveness for having almost caused the failure of an enterprise in which all the Christian world has a hand."

The strengthening wind gusted rain against the tent, and its hammering on the canvas drowned out the voices. As Cuthbert strained to listen, he heard footsteps squelching through the quagmire toward his position, so he slipped away into the darkness. Eventually, drenched through, he managed to find a recognizable landmark and was soon back within the safe confines of the English camp, where he went straight to the Earl of Evesham's pavilion and told him what he had overheard.

"This is serious indeed," Sir Walter said. A thunderous look settled on his heavy brow. "It promises nothing but danger. I said she'd be the cause of strife for us all. It's true that the king's unbridled love for Berengaria will wreck the Crusade through the anger which it's roused in the French king's breast—and his nobles are incensed. I knew something like this would happen. But, the disappearance of the princess would be just as fatal to the expedition because Richard will live up to his sobriquet and act like a raging lion. He wouldn't make a single step toward the Holy Land until he'd exhausted every avenue to trace his lost lady love. Could you point out the tent where this overheard conversation took place?"

"I'm sorry, my lord, but no," Cuthbert answered glumly. "In the darkness and the terrible rain one tent is like another. I'm sure I'd recognize the three voices again. In fact I'm certain that I did know one of them. It was the Count of Brabant."

"Are you sure?" The earl arched an eyebrow.

"Yes, Sir Walter. I'll never forget what he sounds like as long as I live."

"Well, that's good," the earl said through gritted teeth. "At least it gives us one person to watch. It would never do to tell the king what you overheard, though. In the first place, his anger would be so great that it would burst all bounds, and would cause, likely enough, an instant battle between the two armies. In the second, Brabant would of course deny the charge and assert that you were lying, that you were making it all up to discredit him with the king, because you wanted to settle the old score. No, if we're to succeed in preventing harm happening to the princess and an open break between the two monarchs, it must be done by keeping a secret guard over Berengaria, and ourselves frustrating any attempt on her."

"Good grief, what a pile. How on earth anyone thinks a handful of undercover archers can keep a watch over that, I don't know."

Cnut was right, Cuthbert mused. The apple of Richard's eye lodged in the Bishop of Messina's palace, which the good prelate had put at the disposal of the Queen of Navarre and her court. The bishop had removed his retinue to the—frankly—cozier former monastery attached to one side of the sprawling palace (a convent clung like a limpet to the other side).

The two Englishmen had wandered casually into the town in the morning—its streets sparkled fresh and bright under a warm sun after the night's rainstorm—to reconnoiter the position and appearance of the building. It was huge, irregular, and joined at different levels with several other substantial structures, including the two monasteries lying alongside.

Cuthbert cleared his throat and spat a gobbet of phlegm on the grassy verge, a habit he'd picked up from Gorth. "It's clearly going to be difficult to keep up a complete surveillance on the exterior of so large an palace. There look to be so many ways in which the princess might be captured and carried off by unscrupulous men."

Cuthbert pounded his brain in vain to think how they could possibly safeguard her.

"You're right there," Cnut agreed mournfully. "There seem so many opportunities for the bastard of Brabant to succeed in snatching her."

"Hmm. Well, we can rule out anything taking place in the course of the daily round of entertainments. The queen and the princess always have an escort of knights, and no attempt could be successful except at the cost of a public uproar and much loss of blood. No, it will be this crumbling structure of stone and brick where an attempt will be easiest."

The fact that one of the speakers in the tent had used the words "my sons," indicated to Cuthbert that a priest, or monk at least, had a hand in the plot. He mentioned this to Cnut. The Saxon shook his head wearily.

"Might it be that this man has some power in one of the monasteries?" He raised an eyebrow at Cuthbert. "Or he might be an agent of the bishop?"

Cuthbert gave his big friend startled look. "That would certainly put the lion among the doves. The king, Sir Walter says, has little fondness for prelates, especially this bishop." He sighed heavily. "Conjecture gets us nowhere, Cnut. The problem is more the location than the possible plotters. Look how easy it would be in the night for a party from one or other of the monasteries to enter the palace on the inside, and carry off the princess without the slightest alarm being given. Once within the walls of the convent, she could be either hidden in the dungeons or secret places, which buildings of that kind always have, or quickly carried out by some quiet exit and taken into the country, or transferred to some other building in the town."

Cuthbert held his head in his hands in frustration.

When he made his report to Sir William, the earl agreed with Cuthbert's judgment that they lacked essential intelligence.

"After all, lad, what you overheard Brabant and his cronies discussing sounds more like an intention than a well-formed plan of action. Indeed, it may have been no more than idle boasting, but that's not a risk we can afford to take. If we assume they are serious, we must maintain as close a watch as we can on our old enemy, Sir Joscelín, either to hear more or to find out if he's in the habit of regularly visiting his co-conspirators or receiving them in his tent. That way we'll discover the identity of those you overheard."

Discovering the location of the Count of Brabant's pavilion proved simple and in daylight Cuthbert confirmed his familiarity with the tent. He explained to Cnut what was required.

The Saxon hummed and hahed. "I see no way we can keep up a watch during the day, but after dark—I've got several in my band who can track a deer and will be able to follow the count without being seen."

"That should do the trick, Cnut, for I doubt the conspirators will dare to get together so openly during the day."

"I'll detail little Jack to the task. He's no bigger than a boy of twelve, although he can hold his own against the best man in the troop and his night-sight is the best. He'll keep such sharp watch that no one will go in or leave without his knowing where they go. On a dark night he'll be able to slip among the tents, and to move here and there without being seen. He can creep on his stomach without moving a leaf, and trust me the eyes of these *gens d'armes* won't glimpse him."

"Cnut, all I want to know at the moment is whether the other conspirators visit his tent, or whether he goes to theirs, and their identities—nothing more, no getting involved in any rough stuff."

"I understand," Cnut said. "I'll go tell Jack."

Three days later Cnut informed Cuthbert that each night after dark a party of five men met in Sir Joscelín's tent, and that one of the five always came out when they had assembled and stood guard at the entrance.

Cuthbert smiled. "Locking the stable door after the horse has bolted."

"What do we do now?"

"I'll talk to Tybalt first, Cnut. This matter's too serious for me to take a step without consulting him or the earl."

Tybalt pronounced himself ready to take a party of men and deal with the count in no uncertain terms, but Sir Walter quickly dissuaded him of any hasty action. The earl was pleased, at least, to hear that their suspicions about the Count of Brabant had proved correct and that the venue of the meetings suggested his role as the ringleader.

"Should we now go to the king? Cuthbert wondered. Sir Walter remained unconvinced.

"If I denounce Sir Joscelín Barras it will look like petty revenge for his insults. The ill-will between us is already too well known—not just the dispute at the banquet, but when we arrived here, the king told Philip about his conduct in connection with the suspected assassination attempt on you by his page at Montélimar. Sir Joscelín, of course, denied any connection to the matter. He had, he said, sacked his nephew after your tournament, and knew nothing further whatever of his movements. It was obvious to all that the Brabant page could not have afforded from his own pocket the services of the mercenaries who helped him. Clearly, they were either the count's liegemen or ruffians hired with his money. But because there was no direct proof, Philip dropped the matter.

"So you see, Cuthbert, that for me to go to the king now with an even more serious accusation based on the evidence of my page—who would have a good reason to smear the count's name—would look like an attempt to damage the character of a brother knight. No, we must stick to our plan. The only chance we have to foil this dastardly plot is to keep a constant eye on his movements, and also to have three or four of the toughest of Cnut's band on watch under cover each time that the princess is in the palace."

Feeling that nothing more could be done until they knew more, Sir Walter left the business entirely in Cuthbert's hands. "Take as many men-at-arms or archers as you choose and use them in my name."

Tybalt remonstrated and claimed the role as his to perform, but the earl remained adamant. "I need you at my side," he said firmly. "It is Cuthbert who uncovered this conspiracy and his to see through to its conclusion."

Cuthbert speedily outlined his plans to Cnut and then left it to the Saxon to draw up a roster of the archers so that six of them would always be on duty to keep an eye on the palace every night—day ruled out as being too risky for the plotters to make a move.

"That should give us enough to observe the various entrances of the palace and the adjoining buildings. They must conceal themselves under an arch, or maybe lie down and pretend to be drunk—that shouldn't be difficult, there are plenty of drunks about in this port."

During his discussion with Sir Walter, Cuthbert had wondered where they would take the princess, and the earl had suggested that Sicily had too few hiding-places so the conspirators might steal away in a ship to the mainland. As this seemed to Cuthbert a likely scenario, he arranged with the owner of a small fishing smack for ten of the archers to sleep on board every night, and paid extra to the owner for the crew to be always on hand. Cuthbert decided to station himself with this shipboard party.

Night after night passed, and so long a time went by that Cuthbert began to think the coup must have been postponed, or even abandoned. However, he was determined to relax none of his vigilance during the remaining time that the expedition might be in Sicily.

The gathered host sullenly put aside its differences for the brief days of the Christmas feast and celebrated the start of the year of the

Lord, 1191. Even so, Cuthbert's vigil continued. So it was in the first days of January, three weeks after the first watch had been set, when one of the archers spying on the entrance to one of the monasteries, jumped on board the craft and shook Cuthbert by the shoulder.

"A band of men, maybe five or more, has just left the monastery carrying a large, long bundle between them—I can't see what. They're making their way in this direction. I whistled to Dick, who was next to me in the lane. He's following them, and I came on ahead to warn you."

The pitch-dark night made it hard to see anyone moving much beyond the prow of the boat. Three streets led down toward the sea from the bishop's palace complex, which stood at the top of the town. The schemers might take any of these, depending on where the vessel they were headed for was docked.

Cuthbert thought quickly and then sent six of his men, with instructions to keep silent, along the line of the wharf, to bring him word should anyone come down and board a boat, or should they hear any disturbance in the town.

He, with his four remaining archers and the sailors, loosed the ropes which fastened the boat to the jetty, got out the oars, and prepared to put out at a moment's notice. Of course, there was no guarantee that the abductors intended sailing away. They might prefer to hide their prisoner in one of Messina's convents, but Cuthbert remained convinced that they would leave Sicily urgently. They must know that in his almighty anger King Richard would burn down the city, and search every convent and every mansion from top to bottom for the princess.

They waited.

Soon the man he had sent furthest to the south came running up with the news that a boat had pushed off at the far end, with a gang of some ten men on board. As he came along he'd warned the others, and shortly they were collected in the smack, numbering in all ten of Cuthbert's men—including Cnut—and six sailors, Cuthbert making the seventeenth.

The boatmen told Cuthbert that their quarry would no doubt row out to a galley anchored in the roads, and since there were only three such vessels offshore as night fell, the choice was happily narrowed. They rowed in the direction in which the other craft would have gone, but it in the dark they were quite unable to see it.

The boatmen all laid on their oars, and everyone listened intently. Then the creaking of a pulley sounded in the still night at a distance of a few hundred yards. "A ship is getting up sail," Cnut hissed.

Cuthbert judged the vessel's bearing from the noise. "Turn the prow farther out to sea," he ordered. The crew rowed steadily but quietly until the tall mast of a galley became faintly silhouetted against the starry sky. At that moment a cry of alarm came from on board the galley. "We're seen! Row flat out," Cuthbert shouted. With the element of surprise gone there was no more point in being stealthy.

The rowers bent to their work and in a minute the boat ran alongside the large craft. As Cuthbert and his sixteen men scrambled up onto the deck the crew, who were stood nearest the boarding, attacked with nothing more than marlinspikes.

The conspirators had no expectation of being caught and have no plan of defense in place, Cuthbert thought with some glee. His sword rasped from its scabbard and he plunged headlong into the fray.

It wasn't until the last of the boarders had gained a footing and were beginning to fight their way along the vessel, that from below four men-at-arms ran up on deck. One, in a tone of authority, demanded what was going on. The clash of swords and the shouts of combat answered him and he swiftly took his men to join the obstinate fight that exploded over the deck.

The boarders were all lightly clad, and this on the deck of a ship lumbered with ropes and gear, and in the dark, proved a great advantage, for the mailed men-at-arms frequently tripped, stumbled, and fell. The fight lasted several minutes. Cuthbert ducked just in time to avoid a swing from one sailor's staff which would have cracked him on the head and took the man in the guts with a sword thrust.

He squealed in agony and fell heavily, hands clutched to the gaping wound when Cuthbert yanked his bloodied blade back.

Cnut, armed with a heavy mace, struck out with great sweeping blows which broke down the guard of his opponents, and generally leveled them out on the deck, stunned or dead.

As they saw the battle going against them, the galley's crew quickly lost heart—after all, it wasn't really their fight. On the other hand, the men-at-arms and the eight pikemen who lumbered onto the upper deck after them, fought stubbornly and well.

Cuthbert recognized the voice of the man at their head. It belonged to his arch-foe Sir Joscelín Barras. The count fought with extreme bravery, and when almost all his followers were cut down or beaten overboard where the weight of their mail dragged them to the depths, he resisted staunchly and well. With a heavy two-handed sword Sir Joscelín cleaved himself a space at the galley's bow and kept the whole of Cuthbert's party at bay, until Cnut, who had just finished off the last of the pikemen, came forward and engaged him.

Cnut's lack of armor gave the count an enormous advantage, but it also proved his downfall when his mailed foot slipped on the bloody gore slopping on the deck and his hurriedly donned casque fell off. Before he could recover, Cnut brought his formidable mace down with a terrible force on the count's unprotected head. Without a further word or a cry Sir Joscelín fell forward on the deck, killed like a pole-axed ox. Blood and brains leaked from his split skull to mingle with that of his slaughtered liegemen.

It was only as the cacophony of conflict died out that a woman's cries of distress could be heard coming from below. Cuthbert looked in some surprise at Cnut, still in a daze from the fury of killing, and then suddenly the reason for the entire escapade flooded back into his addled head.

"My God, Cnut, the princess…"

Hastily sheathing his carmined sword, Cuthbert ran and skidded across the slippery deck to a staircase and, followed closely by Cnut, more fell than ran down to the galley's under-deck.

At the bottom they found a man-at-arms placed at the door of a cabin. In spite of the commotion overhead, he bravely had a go at challenging them as they both dropped the last three steps in one go to a ready crouch.

"Oh, c'mon man," Cuthbert snarled. "Do you really want to join your comrades, stretched out on the deck, or drowned in the bay?"

He didn't. If the sounds of battle from above had not convinced him earlier, Cuthbert's steely countenance, despite his obvious youth, seemed to do the trick. He laid down his wavering sword.

"You'd better go in alone Master Cuthbert," Cnut said, taking out a surprisingly clean handkerchief to wipe some bloody smears from Cuthbert's cheek. "The lady's less likely to be frightened by your appearance than by mine, for she must wonder what's going on."

He pushed open the door, suddenly unaccountably nervous. The princess he knew so well by sight, though never at such close proximity before, stood at the other end of the cabin. In the glimmering light of a single oil lamp, he could see her deathly pale face staring out. Her robes were torn and disarranged, and she wore a look at once of grave alarm and surprise on seeing a handsomely dressed—albeit battle battered—page enter with a deep reverence.

"What is the meaning of this outrage, sir? Whoever you are, I warn you now that the King of England will punish this indignity most severely."

"Your H-Highness," Cuthbert stammered. "Please be calm. There's no further reason for alarm. The schemers who kidnapped you and brought you aboard this ship are all killed or surrendered. I am Cuthbert, page to the Earl of Evesham, and devoted servant of King Richard."

Cuthbert hastily filled in the details of their suspicions, their surveillance, and the three-week long watch to foil the plot, as well as their failure to prevent her being carried on board.

"But by good fortune we arrived here in time. A few minutes later, and the scoundrels would have succeeded in their object, as the sails were already being hoisted and the vessel making way when we boarded. Her head is now turned toward the shore, and I hope in a short time to have the honor of escorting you back to the bishop's palace."

The princess, a touch of warmth returning to her cheeks, sank onto a couch with a sigh of satisfaction and relief.

"I'm indebted to you, young sir," she said. "Believe me, the Princess Berengaria is not ungrateful, and should it be ever in her power to do anything for your lord, or for yourself, or for those who have accompanied you to rescue her, believe me that she will do it."

Ignoring her irritatingly haughty use of the third person in referring to herself, Cuthbert dropped to one knee before her. "May I be so bold as to ask a favor?"

"It is granted at once, whatever it be, if in my power."

"My request is, lady..." He hesitated, before continuing uncertainly looking for the right words. "That you will do your best to deflect the natural anger which King Richard will feel at this violent attempt. Clearly, he must be told, but much depends on the telling, and I'm sure that, at your request, the king would be restrained in his reaction. Otherwise, I'm afraid that his anger will bring the two armies to blows, and destroy for ever all hope of a successful outcome for our joint Holy expedition."

The princess regarded Cuthbert coolly for a long pause, then gave him a faint smile. "You are a wise and good youth," she said finally. She held out her hand to him, which, as duty demanded, he placed to his lips. "Your request is sensible and most thoughtful. I will use any poor influence which I may possess to persuade the king to allow this matter to pass over. There's no reason why he should take up the case. I'm no more under his protection than under that of the King of France, and it is to the latter I should appeal because were they not his subjects?"

"The conspirators' leader was Sir Joscelín Barras, Count of Brabant, with whom my master has an old feud, and who now lies dead at the hands of Cnut, leader of our men-at-arms. The others who were most active in the plot have also perished. I think it's doubtful now that we'll find any clues to lead us to any others who may have been in league with them. The only man in this party who's still alive was placed as a sentry at your door. He's only a man-at-arms, so I'm sure he doesn't know any details of the plot, and he's simply carried out the orders of his master."

By the time this interview was concluded, the galley had pulled in close to the wharf. They waited until the pale light of dawn stained the eastern horizon before getting off the galley, and soon after dawn the princess was safely back in the palace from which she had been stolen a few hours previously.

"That went well," Cnut observed dryly.

Cuthbert shook his head slowly. "Phew, she's quite a woman, that Berengaria, but my God, these Navarians—or whatever you call them—are really stuck up."

"Nah, Cuthbert lad, that's just nobles for you."

Chapter 10: Off the Corsair Coast

Lent and April 1191

King Richard rarely sat around in idle relaxation, but there was one person who could calm and entertain him—the young minstrel from Picardy whose bright hair gave him his sobriquet of Blondel. The French *trouvère*, who had only arrived in Messina to join the king shortly before Christmas, had a skill with the lute that matched his silvery voice, but although he sang lays of chivalry and romance, the king also treasured his troubadour for the bawdy songs he also knew which lightened the mood of many an otherwise dreary evening. Richard himself had a fine baritone voice and, knowing much of Blondel's filthier repertoire, often joined in alternate verses.

And that's how the duty herald found them, quietly separate from others of the court, enjoying a rather rude sing-song-along. The arrival's breathless words changed everything. In an instant the young king was on his feet, thundering orders left, right, and center, demanding his horse, his pages, his squires, his swords, and his barons.

Long before all these worthies could assemble, the king was mounted and galloping toward the bishop's palace. In moments he disappeared behind closed doors, alone with the Queen of Navarre, Berengaria, and their ladies in waiting. Those outside in the corridors just stood and cringed at the furious explosions of passion made incomprehensible by the thick walls, but even more terrifying because of that. Richard remained there until the afternoon, when he sent for his principal lords, who had been waiting in their pavilions on tenterhooks, half-knowing and fearing what they thought they knew.

When they arrived, they found the king standing in the principal hall of the palace, where he proclaimed Princess Berengaria of

Navarre as his wife to be. The wedding, he told them, would take place shortly.

The announcement caused a tremendous stir in both camps, uproar in fact. To Cuthbert, still flush with the success of his plan, it all seemed a tempest in an ale jar. He said as much to Tybalt, with whom he enjoyed a relationship that fell well short of friendship but at least amounted to toleration on the squire's part. Tybalt had escaped the life dedicated to Holy Orders his father intended for his youngest son when Sir Walter offered him a place as a page, but he'd been given a clerical education which made him a self-professed expert on matters political. Tybalt filled Cuthbert in.

"The Norman-English nobility have never backed the alliance with King Philip's sister Alys, so it's no surprise they're pleased to hear that this is now absolutely broken off." For a moment, he stared into space, his face radiant. "And we are well content that Princess Berengaria should be our future queen, for her beauty, high spirit, and kindness has won all hearts." He sighed deeply. Cuthbert thought he was putting it on a bit thick with clasped hands at his breast. And then his canny face sharpened up. "And, of course, Navarre is a satisfactory territorial addition to Aquitaine, already held by the English crown."

"And the French?"

"Ah, well, that's different. Naturally, the French barons will be deeply indignant, insulted, furious even. It may look as though war will be the inevitable outcome of our king's proclamation. And I'm sure King Philip is enraged, but he has probably resigned himself to this outcome for some time. I'm sure, young Cuthbert, that he is politic enough to forestall any open outbreak. He knows that a dispute will not only put an immediate stop to the Crusade, but that it might lead to more serious consequences at home."

Cuthbert frowned in concentration. "What troubles does a great king have at home?"

"It's not so simple, my dear boy. The French barons are not easy neighbors and, unlike in England, hold strongly to their rights. Philip is the first French king to successfully exercise control over his nobles, but in usurping the powers of his barons and bending them to his will he has also made enemies of many who would prefer a weaker man on the French throne. So the last thing he needs is a war to destabilize his still shaky hold over those who theoretically owe him allegiance. Of course the French also hate us Anglo-Normans for holding great swathes of territory the largely independent French barons regard as their own."

"Thank you, Tybalt. That was most instructive." *And stop calling me "my dear boy."*

So, no war, but the coldness between the battalions increased, their camps were moved farther apart to prevent trouble brewing, and during the time that they remained in Sicily, there was almost no further contact between the two armies.

As winter gave way to spring, the French monarch broke up his camp, and in March sailed for the Holy Land. The English had hoped that their king would wed his princess quickly before they left Sicily, but this was not the case because Lent overtook them—a period when no marriage could take place. Instead there were jousting tournaments and fetes in the name of the princess. Two weeks after the French departed, the English army embarked and the fleet sailed for Acre.

Cuthbert's rescue of the princess had repercussions—good ones. King Richard sent for the Earl of Evesham after he'd returned from the bishop's palace and his announcement of engagement to Berengaria, from whom he learned the details of the plot and its discoverer.

Cuthbert awaited his lord's return from the audience in a fever of nervousness. He feared the princess might have taken against his brashness, in spite of her kind words to him. When he finally returned, Sir Walter's expression calmed him down somewhat.

"You have made a sound impression," the earl began. "King Richard said that he was indebted to me for the rescue of the princess. I told him his praise should go to my page, the lad, I said, whom you may remember as having fought and vanquished the French page at Montélimar, and who you praised for his courage and bravery at the time. You may also remember that through his own shrewdness he escaped murder at the hands of the Count of Brabant's minions, and your Majesty was good enough to complain about it to King Philip. Then I explained everything that you uncovered and how you had finally intervened to save the princess. And I did not leave out Cnut's part."

"Thank you, my lord," Cuthbert said with as much humility as he could manage in his excited state.

"But before it goes entirely to your head, the king also said that although you appear brave and wise for your age and he would make you a knight here and now, he didn't think it would be good for you to become celebrated so young. It would attract the envy of others."

"I–I understand, sire. I—"

Sir Walter slapped a hand on Cuthbert's shoulder and smiled. "He has given his promise to raise you to the ranks of chivalry when you can demonstrate your skill and bravery against the infidels in the Holy Land."

In a whirl, and to his embarrassment, Cuthbert found himself the center of the royal circle on the following morn. The king expressed his gratitude graciously, patted him on the shoulder, and said that he would be one day one of the best and bravest of his knights. The royalty of Navarre gave him their hands to kiss.

Cnut too received his reward, a gold chain in token of the king's pleasure, and a heavy purse to distribute among the men who had followed him.

When the English fleet of two hundred ships set sail from Sicily, it made a grand sight. From the myriad masts flew the banners of

England and those of the lords who commanded; while the pennons of the knights, the bright plumes and mantles, the flash of armor and arms, made the decks alive with light and glowing hues.

The king's cog sailed in the vanguard, and around him clustered those vessels carrying his principal barons. The Queen of Navarre and Princess Berengaria also went with the fleet, on a ship separate from the king since it was inappropriate for the betrothed to be together in such intimately packed conditions. Strains of music rose from the waters as the fleet of galleys and deep-hulled sailing ships left port. The picturesque image was as far removed from the horrors of war as could be imagined.

For two days the expedition sailed on, and then a change of a sudden and disastrous kind took place.

"What's all the bustle about?" Cuthbert asked Cnut. "The sailors are clambering up the ropes, and it all seems very confused... are you all right?"

Cnut, normally the picture of health, looked green about the gills.

"I'm fine, really, but I don't think I was made for a life afloat. My stomach rolls the opposite way to the ship no matter how much I try to stop it—and now I think there's a storm coming. An hour ago it was wall-to-wall blue sky, but look at that bank of cloud over there— it's risen half-way up. The signs which pass us landlubbers by have no doubt been screaming at the sailors for some time."

At speed, the sails came down across the fleet, and in the blink of an eye its whole aspect changed. But as quickly as the sailors went about their work, the storm rolled in even more rapidly. Some of the ships whose crews were slower or less skilful than the others were caught by the gale before they could get their sails snug, and the great sheets of white canvas were blown from the mast ropes as if made of paper. In a moment an almost tangible blackness covered the sea and the only light came off the frothing waters.

There was no longer any thought of order. Each ship had to shift for herself and each captain had to do his best to save those souls under his charge, without thought of what might be happening to the others.

In the *Rose of England*, the cog carrying the Earl of Evesham's contingent, order and discipline prevailed. The earl's harsh voice had been heard at the first puff of wind, shouting to the men to go below, except for a few who might be of use to help haul at ropes. His standard was lowered, the bright flags removed from the sides of the ship, the shields hanging over the castles at fore and aft were hurriedly taken below, and when the gale struck the ship was trimmed in readiness to receive it. The captain—a Genoese of great experience, even of the tempestuous northern seas—had thought it prudent to leave a few square yards of sail for steerage and this tiny area soon had the cog tearing along through the waters at a tremendous speed.

His greatest fear was that in the hours of darkness they might run into one of their fellow ships. Even in the war of the elements they could hear from time to time crashes as one ship rammed another, with shouts and despairing cries. Once or twice other vessels loomed from the darkness threatening the *Rose*, close on one hand or the other, but the captain's steadiness in each case saved the plunging ship from collision.

As the storm continued, glimpses of other ships became rarer. The *Rose* was a solid vessel and with the little sail out her captain began to hope that he was now clear ahead of the rest of the flotilla. He tried lying-to, but the ship's high-sided fighting castles acted like sails, and there was little more to do than run before the squalling fury, cresting each wave in a spume of wind-blown spray before dropping into the watery valley gaping below.

After two days and nights the wind dropped to a bluster, the seas began to calm. The earl asked the captain where he thought they were.

"I can't be certain, signor. The wind's shifted several times. I'd hoped to gain the shelter of Rhodes, but a change in the wind's direction pushed us away, so I'm afraid that—from our current direction—we must be very soon off the coast of Africa."

"Damn and blast!" the earl swore. "That would certainly put a speedy end to our Crusade. These Moors are pirates and cutthroats to a man, so even if we avoid being dashed to pieces on the rocks, we'll end up enslaved to one of these infidels."

Three hours later, the captain's gloomy prophecy turned out right. Breakers became visible at various points ahead of them, and although the storm's fury had abated, it was still too strong to fight the wind. With the greatest difficulty the steersmen got the *Rose* through an opening between the reefs, but in another few moments she struck heavily. The main mast cracked explosively and went over the side. When disaster seemed inevitable, a fortunate swell carried the vessel over a low sandbank to become wedged between two rocks, and this acted as a barrier, reducing the power of the incoming breakers. Although occasionally some waves still struck her with considerable force, the captain hoped that the *Rose* would not break up.

Darkness came on. The storm calmed down further. As there was no longer any immediate danger, and passengers as well as crew were exhausted by the tossing which they had received during the last forty-eight hours, the crew of the *Rose* slept soundly.

The sun rose brilliantly and there was no sign of the great storm which had scattered the fleet of England. Half way to the horizon, about four miles away, a hazy buff-colored line marked the shore, low and sandy, with higher hills in the distance. On the shore a white town with minarets and domes shimmered in the pale morning light.

"Know where we are?" the earl asked, Tybalt and Cuthbert at his side.

"As far as I can tell, signor," the captain answered, "we've been driven up the bay called the Little Syrtis—a place full of shoals and shallows, and alive with pirates of the worst kind."

"Can we get the ship off?"

"First we'll have to survey what damage—"

"I don't think we're going to have time for that, sirs," said Cuthbert quietly. He was peering toward the shore under a hand raised to shield his sharp eyes against the water glare. "Those two galleys putting out from that town will have something to say to that."

"It's true," the captain said wearily. "Those are the galleys of the Moorish corsairs. They have thirty to forty oars, a shallow draft and move like the wind."

Sir Walter asked, "What do you advise? Our poop-mounted ballistas only face forward, so they won't be much use against boats that can row around us, and are no doubt equipped with heavy catapults. They must already know, given our situation, that we're aground and defenseless, and will be able to plump their bolts into us until they've knocked the *Rose* to pieces. However, we'll fight to the last. I won't have it said that infidel dogs captured the Earl of Evesham and sold him into slavery. Not without striking a blow in his name, I won't."

Cuthbert narrowed his eyes against the glare and watched the corsair vessels row toward them at frightening speed.

"My lord," he ventured. "We might yet trick them."

"Not another clever scheme," Tybalt said in a dismissive tone.

"Let him speak. How, Cuthbert?" the earl said. "I would hear your tactics."

"I think, sire, that if we sent all the men-at-arms and the archers below, leaving only the ship's crew on deck, the pirates might take us for a vulnerable merchantman. It might make them careless on their approach. To look realistic, the men on deck could fire off a couple of stones with the ballistas, but that wouldn't stop the infidels coming alongside."

"It could work," the captain said.

"And when they're alongside, what them genius?" The sneer in Tybalt's voice did not put Cuthbert off his stride..

"Once they're alongside, we can fasten one or both to our side with grapnels, and then up comes everyone and English lance, sword, and bow will give them something to think about. Even better if we can take one of the Moorish craft by force, drive the pirates overboard and beat off the other. Then we take the most valuable stores from the *Rose*, and make our way as best we can to the north with oars and sail."

The earl turned to his squire. "Tybalt?"

"I suppose as a plan it promises some hope," he said reluctantly.

"What do you think, captain?"

"The sailors of Genoa never give up without a fight, signor, and this is a brave idea that promises every success—or at least the clean death of us all. The Corsairs have grown fat and lazy with easy pickings in recent years. It could work. Send your men below before the pirates can see us well. Have them armed and in readiness for the signal, but those with mail should not don it. Were they to fall overboard, the weight of the mail would drag them to their deaths by drowning. My crew will prepare grapnels and ropes. We'll lash the bastards so securely to the *Rose* that they'll not get away."

These preparations were soon made.

The soldiers, initially apprehensive at the thought of slavery, suddenly bucked up at the prospect of a struggle ending in possible escape. Cnut—somewhat recovered now that the ship was holding steady—had the Saxon archers prepare their bows and arrows. The men-at-arms grasped their pikes and swords, while above their heads the sailors moved about as if making preparations for defense, but in reality getting ready the grapnels and ropes.

One of the pirates made a faster speed than the other, and soon came within range. Immediately, its fighting occupants sent flights of javelins and stones down on the *Rose* from powerful catapults carried on the bow.

The crew of the *Rose* replied with their crossbows and arrows from the fore castle.

The corsair sheered off at the last moment to row around the grounded ship, all the while loosing arrows and hurling javelins. After one circuit, the corsair *rais*, satisfied that no precaution was needed with a feebly-manned ship in so great a strait as the *Rose*, set up a wild cry of "Allah!" and his crew rowed toward her. Cuthbert, sheltered behind the shattered stump of mast had never seen such a fierce band of cutthroats before.

As the sleek galley's hull bumped the *Rose* the sailors cast grapnels into the corsair's rigging, and fastened her to the *Rose*. And then a loud shout of "Hurrah for England!" erupted from below decks. The side ports opened and a volley of arrows flew down as thick as winter rain on the astonished corsairs. The Moors were thrown back into their vessel, and a platoon of heavily armed men leaped down from the ship on top of them. The men who rowed the galley uttered the most piercing cries of terror as the battle raged above their heads. They were unable to take any part in it because they were all slaves and chained to the oars.

Taken by surprise, and indeed outnumbered, the resistance of the corsairs was slight. In a close fierce combat like this the lightly armed Moors had little chance against the English, whose heavy swords and axes destroyed their defenses at a blow. The fight lasted less than three minutes, and then Cnut's men tossed the last of the corpses over the side.

When the second galley arrived on the scene, seeing what had befallen his consort, the *rais* called out to his oarsmen, who at once turned the galley's head. Followed by the jeers and cheers of the Englishmen the corsair ship rowed back rapidly to the town from which she had come.

Cuthbert quickly understood the jubilation among the galley-slaves at the outcome because, to his shock, many were Europeans. Before long their shackles were struck off. The slaves were of all nationalities, but Italians and Spaniards, French and Greeks formed the majority. There was no time, however, to be lost. The arms and munitions of war were swiftly removed from the *Rose*, together with the most valuable of her stores.

The galley-slaves took their places again at the oars, and this time willingly, the places of the weakest being filled by English soldiers, whose lack of skill was made up by the alacrity with which they threw their strength into the work. In an hour from the time that the pirates had attacked, the former corsair vessel was heading north, and with sixty oars she was rowed at all speed for the mouth of the bay.

Chapter 11: Outremer!

May to August 1191

Rhodes, sitting at the corner of the Mediterranean and the Aegean seas, was an island with one foot in Europe and the other in Asia. Its position made it an important harbor in the Greek Byzantine Empire ruled from Constantinople, and it was a logical haven on the long route between southern Europe and the Levantine lands of Syria and Palestine. Always busy, on the morning that the corsair galley shot into its calm waters the port absolutely heaved with crusader shipping.

Sir Walter had correctly predicted that the greater portion of the fleet scattered by the tempest would rendezvous there and everyone on board the *Rose of England II*, as they had named the corsair galley, expressed relief at seeing a forest of masts and rigging, showing that at least the majority of the fleet had survived the terrible battering.

Cuthbert could imagine the mixture of astonishment and alarm on the shore at the first sighting of the swift galley. "They must be trying to guess what message a Moorish pirate could be bringing," he said to Cnut. "There can be no mistaking the appearance of a long, dangerous-looking craft like this."

Any puzzlement turned to amazement when suddenly the standard of the Earl of Evesham was run out on the bowsprit. A great shout of welcome arose from the whole fleet, which brought King Richard to the deck of the royal flagship. When he saw who had arrived, he hailed the earl and shouted across the water to come on board and tell him what the masquerade was all about.

The Genoese captain brought the corsair close and dropped anchor as Sir Walter climbed into a small lighter, with Tybalt and Cuthbert to row him over.

The king listened with unvarnished interest to the adventures of the *Rose*, and when the Earl of Evesham said that it had been Cuthbert de Lance who thought up the clever trick by which they captured the pirate galley, the king slapped Cuthbert on the back with such force as to nearly hurl him overboard.

"By Saint George!" Richard bellowed, "it seems you are fated to wear the gold spurs of a knight. Regardless of your age, I swear the next time your name is brought before me I'll call a chapter of knights to agree on making an exception in your case. You'll miss your page, Sir Walter, but I'm sure you won't grudge him his knighthood."

"No, no, sire," said the earl. "The lad, as I've told my lord is a relative of mine—distant, it's true, but one of the closest I have—and it will give me the greatest pleasure to see him rise so rapidly. I already feel as proud of him as if he were my own son."

As they rowed back, Tybalt glowered at Cuthbert and spoke in a harsh whisper so Sir Walter would not hear. "Don't think you can take my place, you little squirt. I'll have your balls off before I see you knighted."

Cuthbert breathed heavily as he rowed in tandem with the enraged squire. "I have no wish to dispossess you, Tybalt, only to serve the earl as best I may. We have to work together, Can we not be friends?"

Tybalt grimaced and bared his teeth. "I think that unlikely, *page.*"

The English fleet remained in refit for some three weeks at Rhodes. Many of the ships, particularly the galleys, had suffered damage, but the cogs had lost masts, had fore and aft castles smashed, bulwarks battered, sails ripped, and sprung strakes that needed replacing and caulking. One ship, however, had not yet sailed into port, and that one had King Richard in a fever of anxiety because it carried the fair Berengaria and—just as importantly—the king's war treasury.

The Evesham crew and rescued slaves were not the last to arrive, and several stragglers sailed in during the following week. One day a solitary vessel entered the port, a Greek merchant come from Cyprus.

Her captain went on board the flagship, and delivered a message to the king, to the effect that two of the fleet had been wrecked on the coast of Cyprus. They had been plundered by the locals, and the crews and passengers ill-treated, and made prisoners by the island's despot. The royal Navarres were among them.

This roused King Richard into one of his furies.

"I won't sail a league nearer the Holy Land until this insolent king is brought to his knees. Make the signal to all vessels to be ready to weigh anchor at daybreak tomorrow."

"Oh no, another adventure," Sir Walter groaned in frustration, "although—in spite of the king's threat—it is at least in the right direction for Outremer."

"Isn't Cyprus a Christian land, though?" Cuthbert asked. "Why would the king of the island seize the princess?"

"I don't know his reasons, but in truth this king is only a governor of Manuel Comnenus, the Byzantine emperor, and in fact a distant relative of his. Still, that's not going to stand in King Richard's way."

The English fleet sailed to Cyprus on the following morning and formed up to anchor off Famagusta. King Richard sent to Isaac Comnenus, the island's tyrant, ordering him to release the prisoners. He also demanded that ample compensation be paid to them and two ships placed at their disposal equal to those which had been destroyed. And he wanted his royal war chest given back.

The answer became common knowledge and caused Sir Walter to fume in irritation. "This Comnenus is an insolent and haughty ruler, who thinks rather a lot more of himself than perhaps he should to send back only defiance."

Within the day, the English fleet sailed into Famagusta's harbor and archers began the fight by sending flight after flight of arrows over the walls into the town. A shower of stones and darts promptly answered this action. Undeterred, the leading ships ran in fast to the rocky wharves and, regardless of the blizzard of artillery poured down on them, the English soldiers jumped ashore.

Thanks to its sleek build, the first vessel to touch was the Earl of Evesham's corsair *Rose II*. Cnut and his men acted in concert with the archers packing the other ships to keep up a relentless rain of shafts against the battlements so that the defenders dared not show themselves above the parapet for an instant.

Under this effective cover, men-at-arms raised assault ladders against the walls, and as quickly climbed. As they reached the top, the English archers ceased shooting, and the men jumped between the merlons onto their foes cowering on the rampart. Cuthbert followed close on the heels of his lord as the men-at-arms swept aside all opposition and streamed into the town. The despot's Greek soldiers offered no real resistance, and Comnenus himself fled from the palace into the hilly hinterland.

As the English looted Famagusta, the Queen of Navarre and Berengaria were rescued, along with the other imprisoned sailors and soldiers. Over the next few weeks King Richard chased Comnenus right across Cyprus until the tyrant sued for peace when his last troops deserted. When he asked not to be chained in irons, Richard chivalrously agreed, and had silver fetters made instead. Comnenus was then banished from the island, which Richard claimed as an English possession by conquest. He also got his hands not only on his treasure, but also the great wealth Isaac had gathered over the years, which pleased the king enormously.

By this time the army itched to get at the infidels, so it came as an unhappy surprise when Richard announced his intention of marrying Princess Berengaria right there and then in the great church of Limassol. The troops grumbled quietly among themselves—as they said, they had waited nearly six months in Sicily, and the king might as well have married there before Lent, instead of causing another delay when they were so near their destination.

The Lionheart, of course, had his own way.

A glittering scene met Cuthbert's eyes. Among the assembled congregation were all the principal barons of England, Normandy,

Anjou, and Aquitaine together with a great number of Cypriot nobles, happily released from their former feckless despot. At the altar stood one of the strongest and bravest men of his time with one of the loveliest young women of her generation on his sturdy arm. For the last two weeks of May the town was given up to pleasure—tournaments, jousts, banquets succeeded each other day after day.

Everyone came down to earth with a bump when Guy of Lusignan sailed into Limassol. The dispossessed King of Jerusalem, who had been freed by the great Saracen leader Saladin, was busy coordinating the defenses of the remaining crusader strongholds. For two years he had laid siege to Acre, but victory had eluded the small force left to him after the disastrous battle at Hattin on the shores of the Sea of Galilee.

"He begged the king to bring his fleet immediately with him to Acre to join with King Philip's recently arrived army," Sir Walter informed his staff.

"Which is what we want, after all…" a knight said.

"Yes indeed, but our crafty Richard made out that he would have to think it over, and then agreed to sail as long as King Guy knelt and swore fealty to him, which he did, making Richard Jerusalem's overlord."

Two days' sailing brought the huge fleet within sight of Acre's massive white walls on June 8, 1191. When they landed on the shore nearby, jubilation met the English crusaders from every quarter. "No pen can sufficiently describe the joy of the people on the night of the King's arrival," the chronicler Ambroise wrote.

It was quickly apparent why. Even the might of the French army under Philip Augustus had failed to turn the scale. The inhabitants of Acre defended themselves with desperate courage. A half-hearted attack on the walls had been repulsed with immense slaughter—and not far away Saladin, with a large army, calmly watched the progress of the siege and bided his time.

Cnut's disgust at the French boiled over. "You'd have thought that after his dispute with King Richard he would have gladly done everything in his power to take Acre before his great rival turned up," he told Cuthbert, spitting into the dust. "But then, I never had time for the French."

"That attitude won't get us very far, Cnut," Cuthbert chided his friend. "There's already been enough friction between the armies. Be content that the French soldiery are cheering King Richard as hard as anyone. I know from talking to a French page that many men were disappointed when King Philip declared that he would make no full assault until Richard turned up. It's surely sensible to storm the walls in great force rather than with half the needed men. But he couldn't have known when he said it that there would be such a delay in our getting here."

Now that the English had finally joined the campaign, preparations for a real attack began. For the moment the two monarchs banished any dissent between them and their armies imitated the example of their sovereigns. French and English worked alongside in throwing up trenches against the walls, in building movable towers for the attack, and in getting ready for the great onslaught.

The French were the first to finish their preparations, and they delivered a tremendous effort. But the infidel defenders never lost heart, and with the greatest fortitude repulsed every attempt. They threw down scaling ladders, destroyed towers with flaming naphtha, and hurled down boiling oil on the men who advanced under the shelter of portable mantles to undermine the walls. Those who weren't cooked outright suffered appallingly only to die in agony in a short time. The French fell back after hours of desperate fighting, baffled and beaten.

Cnut gave Cuthbert an "I told you so" look when they were told of the French debacle. But any quiet glee in the English lines at the French humiliation and the confident belief that a better fortune would crown their own efforts, were bitterly dispelled.

With their preparations completed, the English attacked with splendid heroism. They were fighting under the eyes of their king, and in sight of the French army, and if courage and devotion could have carried the walls of Acre, King Richard's men would have done it. Alas, they fared no better than the French, who had the dubious consolation of watching the English fall back to camp with vast losses and King Richard raging like a wounded lion.

Many of his barons died in the offensive, and the pikemen and men-at-arms suffered heavily. The Earl of Evesham received a wound, which Cuthbert looked after. As a page, he had not taken part in the assault, although he had fumed with impatience as he watched the earl and Tybalt ride out.

However, he had not entirely missed the action. Sir Walter had permitted him to accompany Cnut and the bowmen, who did a terrific job in keeping down the Saracens on the wall and so throwing off their aim. This saved the Earl of Evesham's troop and those fighting near him from suffering nearly as heavy losses as some of those engaged in other quarters.

Before the appearance of the French and English fleets, King Guy of Jerusalem had been unable to prevent Acre with its massively fortified harbor being resupplied from the sea. Now the crusader ships blockaded the city and placed Acre beyond outside help. Despite their brave resistance, Acre's garrison and inhabitants were now nearly at the end of their resources. Saladin, although he had an army of two hundred thousand men, feared to attack the besiegers because they had thrown up strong entrenchments all around their lines to prevent the siege being disturbed by outside forces.

The leading citizens of Acre, seeing no sign of a rescuing force, their provisions being utterly exhausted, and with epidemics raging, at last surrendered. In one sense they were fortunate—King Richard, who was inclined to sack the city and put its inhabitants to the sword, lay prostrate with a fever. King Philip was kinder.

He promised to prevent the horrors of a full sack as long as Acre's elite persuaded Saladin to release fifteen hundred Christian prisoners he held and hand back the True Cross, which the First Crusade had discovered at Jerusalem, and which Saladin had taken from King Guy at the Horns of Hattin four years ago. In addition, either the citizens or Saladin were to pay a ransom of two hundred thousand gold pieces. If the payment was not forthcoming within forty days, three thousand citizens, now under guard, would be put to death.

On these terms, Acre surrendered peacefully. No word came from Saladin's camp as to the deal.

All of Christendom hailed Acre's conquest as a triumph of the highest degree and Cuthbert thrilled to have been a small part of it. "This will open again the gates of the Holy Land to pilgrims and ignite the crusaders with renewed fervor," he said to Cnut. His face glowed with youthful excitement.

What actually happened was that old divisions arose again and threatened to split Outremer anew.

The jealousy of Philip Augustus rose to new levels at the widespread enthusiasm of the combined armies for England's valiant king, and by the authority which Richard wielded in the councils as Jerusalem's titular overlord. This, combined with the effect of several debilitating bouts of illness, made the French king decide to return to France. His announcement at first caused consternation in the crusaders' ranks, but he eased their alarm by leaving behind ten thousand of the French army, under the command of Hugh, Duke of Burgundy.

The Earl of Evesham was, on the whole, pleased with this turn of events. As he told his retinue, "Although there has been a reduction of our total fighting force, the fact that the army's now under King Richard's supreme command more than makes up for the loss of a portion of the French army." A frown creased his face. "On the other hand, Philip will no doubt stir up trouble against the king when he's back in France, and in his zeal to capture Jerusalem, Richard will overlook this until it is too late, I fear."

Politics and the matters of princes did not much occupy Cuthbert. He had another interest. "Who's the young man in the gaudy garb who always accompanies the king?" he asked Sir Walter one morning as he accompanied his lord to a council meeting.

"The minstrel? That's Blondel, the king's troubadour. He has a fine voice and clever hands on the lute and soothes the king's brute force. Don't be fooled by the fancy appearance, though, I'm told Blondel is a fiend with the small sword."

As he strode along beside the earl, Cuthbert could not avoid the sin of pride. He dressed no longer as a mere page but wore the clothes of a full esquire. This promotion, while fully deserved, he thought, had nevertheless come about as a result of Tybalt falling ill with a raging fever, which looked likely to hold him prisoner in Acre for many weeks, if he recovered at all. Cuthbert pushed the uncharitable thought aside as they entered the guarded circle where the Crusade's leaders waited for the king to begin the council. As the lords and knight-commanders began the parley, Cuthbert introduced himself to Blondel with whom he sensed an affinity because of the similarity in their ages—Blondel, he thought, couldn't be more than three years his senior.

"I'm surprised we haven't spoken before," Blondel said. "The king has kept me busy at his side, otherwise I intended writing a ballad in celebration of your victory at Vézelay."

Cuthbert flushed with pride and embarrassment. "I am sure you have worthier subjects."

"On the contrary. The daring deeds of youth make the best lays. And speaking of which, I have discovered the most amusing house of ill repute in the town. You must let me take you there one evening… ah, they're breaking up already, which bodes ill."

The meeting broke up in disagreement, but King Richard carried the day. Always more a man of action than talk, tired of the Christian-Muslim diplomatic discussions, and fed up with Saladin's temporizing over the surrender demands, he wanted the ransom threat carried out. Only after that could the army get on toward Jerusalem. Saladin's time limit had passed, and on the morning of August 20, Richard had the three thousand of Acre's leading citizens led out to a place in full sight of the Muslim army's encampment, and there had their heads struck off, one after the other.

Cuthbert thanked God he had no hand in dragging the screaming men, women, and children to their awful deaths. The sight sickened him to the core, and he was not alone in his feelings. This act horrified Richard's critics among the leading crusaders and sullied his reputation as a chivalrous knight—but it left him free to fight Saladin.

The allied army set out four days after slaughtering the hostages and marched south, hugging the coast to remain in close contact with the fleet, which cruised along near them. The countryside, largely laid to waste, could not supply the army so all its needs had to come from the ships. Yet, in spite of the ships' proximity, the toll on the marching men was terrible. Roads scarcely existed through the rough and broken terrain. Fatigue under the hot sun soon set in as each had to keep his place in the tight formations—Saracen light horse soon picked off stragglers.

By midday the burning sun bore down with appalling force, turning the land into an inferno. Born in the gentle climes of middle England, nothing had prepared Cuthbert for the daily torture. On horseback, his lot was only a little better than those on foot. Dust from underfoot smothered him, clogged his mouth and throat, bloated his parched tongue. None had containers and so water was only available from barrel wagons at the halts, and then precious little for the army's wants. In front, on the flanks and in the rear swarms of Saladin's light cavalry hovered, opportunists with bow and arrow.

At times the king sent out squadrons of his knights to drive off the irritants. But it was the chase of a lion after a hare. The knights in their heavy mail and powerful destrier horses were left behind by the fleet Saracens on their desert coursers, as if the Franks stood still.

The pursuers, exhausted, sweaty, and worn out, were always glad to regain the ranks of the army. Rare successes came when one of the Turkish *ghazis*—holy warriors—risked an attack from the seaward flank. Then they were easily cut off and forced over the edge of the rocky cliffs or speared on a lance.

The enemy horse not only menaced and cut out infantry stragglers, at times when they saw an opening, they dashed in and attacked the column. In most cases the exhausted soldiers beat them off, but occasionally the Saracens gained a brief advantage, killing and wounding infantrymen before galloping away again into the haze.

On the second day out of Acre, King Richard ordered a change of tactics, and Cnut's men, like all the other bowmen, found themselves posted to march outside the mounted knights. When the enemy's horse approached within bowshot they opened up with volleys of arrows to drive them off. If this failed to deter them and they persisted in charging, the archers had to dodge nimbly between hoofs to take refuge behind the line of mounted knights.

Day after day passed in harassing skirmishes, but the enemy never offered a proper battle. Under the sun, chain-mailed knights and men-at-arms began to sizzle as the heat in the iron rings began literally to cook them. Even those footmen wearing quilted gambesons began to find them hot to wear. To remove them risked injury from a random arrow. The distance trudged each day was very small, not much better on some days than four miles, in order to avoid marching in the worst heat of the afternoon. Nevertheless, the sufferings of the men from thirst, heat, foot sores, fatigue, and—at night—the attack of swarms of tarantula spiders, was enormous.

Cuthbert now appreciated the tales he had heard of great armies simply melting away, for already men began to succumb in large numbers to the terrible heat, and the corpses of those who had fallen victim to sunstroke littered the path in the army's rear like discarded sacks. Not even nightfall brought relief. The Muslim cavalry kept up hit-and-run attacks which forced the harassed Christians to keep under arms a substantial number of men to repel the assaults—they, at least, were not crawled over and bitten by the giant spiders.

Having taken fifteen days to cover barely sixty miles, the crusaders approached the town of Arsuf on September 7, and there, to universal delight, they beheld the whole force of Saladin, about eighty thousand strong, barring their way. Had it not been for Richard's stern discipline, the knights of England and France would have repeated the mistake which brought about the extermination of the Christian force at the Horns of Hattin, and would have leveled their lances and charged recklessly into the mass of their enemies. But the king, riding around the flanks and in front of the army, gave his orders brutally.

"Any man who breaks from the ranks, I'll kill him with my own hand."

The king's peers and leading nobles gathered around him to hear him insist on fighting on the same principles as they had done on the march. The archers were to stand outside the knights to dampen the advancing force's enthusiasm with a cloud of arrows until the last moment, and then retire behind the cavalry, only to sally out again as the Saracens fell back from the steel wall of horsemen.

Cuthbert now donned his full chain mail for the first time to confront a real enemy, and rode behind the Earl of Evesham as his squire, feeling mean for thanking the heavens for the chance of the fever which had condemned Tybalt to a sweaty bed in Acre.

Father Francis would not have approved.

Chapter 12: Accolade at Arsuf

September 7, 1191

It was the first time that Cuthbert, and indeed the great proportion of those present in the Christian host, had seen the enemy in force, and they eagerly watched the vast array. If it were not for the danger of the situation, the crusaders could have thought they were about to attend a festival rather than a bloodbath. The variety and brightness of color exceeded that of the Christian army, itself no drab, with its flashing standards and heraldic surcoats. But if in banners and pennons the Christians made a brave show, the floating robes of the Saracens showed a far brighter mass of colors than the chain mail of the Christians.

As they pressed forward, so they prepared for battle, in a square, the nearness of the sea and the offshore fleet protecting that flank. King Richard placed the Knights Templar in the vanguard, along with his own Angevin and Breton troops. Behind them came Guy of Lusignan, King of Jerusalem, with the Poitevins. Next came the Anglo-Normans including Sir Walter's troops, with a contingent of Flemish pikemen. After them the French and finally in the rear the Knights Hospitaller.

Facing them were men drawn from widely separated parts of Saladin's dominions. Here were Nubians from the upper Nile, tall and powerful men, jet black in skin, with lines of red and white paint on their faces, giving them a frighteningly wild appearance. On their shoulders they wore the skins of lions and other wild animals. They carried short bows and heavy clubs studded with iron. At their side the mounted Bedouin *askari* skirmishers were light, sinewy men, brown as berries, with white turbans and garments. Next to them were the cavalry of several Turkish states from Syria and the plains of Assyria—wild horsemen with semi-barbarous armor and scarlet trappings. Here were the solid lines of the Egyptian infantry, steady troops, on whom Saladin relied heavily.

Gathered from afar were other tribes, each distinguished by its own particular marks. While the crusaders clanked and rattled in their lines, the vast array confronting them viewed their foes in complete silence, a phenomenon that unnerved men used to the noise of pre-battle shouting and cursing. The quiet didn't last long.

Suddenly a strange din of discordant music from hundreds of strange instruments—conches, sistrums, sour strings, horns, cymbals, and drums arose in a savage confusion. Shouts of defiance in a dozen tongues and from eighty thousand throats rose wild and shrill on the air, while clear above all the din the Christians heard the ululating chant of the warriors from the Egyptian highlands.

"You would think," Cnut said with a grim smile, "that the infidels consider us a flock of deer to be frightened by that noise. They'd do better to save their breath for future use. They'll need it soon enough when we get in among them. Who would have thought that a number of men could make such a foul sound?"

Cuthbert laughed. "Everyone fights according to his own method, Cnut. And truth be said, the obscene cussing of our force has nothing on the Muslims there. That noise curdles my blood and I'm sure my bowels would give way if it weren't that I know how tough and brave our knights and footmen are."

Cnut gave a snort of derision. "It doesn't frighten me, any more than the cry of wild fowl when you surprise them suddenly on a lake in winter. It means no more than that. Pah! Bunch of shrieking women. I reckon they're trying to encourage themselves as much as to frighten us. However, we'll soon see if they've got the cock on them to fight as well as they scream like girls."

He turned back to his archers. "Now, the heathens are about to have a go at us. Keep steady. Don't fire until you're sure they're in range. Pay no attention to their noise. Keep steady until you can see the whites of their eyes. Loose and retire behind the line of knights unless you still have clear shots and a safe distance."

Cnut with his archers formed part of the line outside the array of English knights, and the arrows of the English bowmen fell fast as bands of Bedouin horse circled around. "He tries to tempt us to break ranks and attack," Sir Walter observed.

For some time Saladin persisted in these tactics as the Christian army continued to press slowly forward.

"With his superiority of force—what are they? About three times our number—he reckons that if he appeals to the code of chivalry the knights will not be able to resist the urge to charge." Sir Walter eased his helm and wiped a hand over his sweaty brow. "Curse this heat. The king is right, Cuthbert. If we break ranks the victory Saladin so easily gained at Galilee will be repeated."

Hemmed in by numbers, borne down by the weight of mail and the effects of the glowering sun, the men succumbed as much to heatstroke as to the impetus of their foes. Many were the knights champing to rush out in single combat, but King Richard's orders were well obeyed, and at last the Muslim leader—Salah ad-Din Yusuf ibn Ayyub, to give him his full Kurdish name, the Sultan of Egypt and Syria—urged by the entreaties of his leading emirs, ashamed that they should hesitate to attack a force so inferior in numbers— decided to take the initiative. Forming his troops in a semicircle encompassing the Christian army, he launched his horsemen to the attack. The instant they came within range, a haze of arrows from the English archers momentarily darkened the sun to fall among them. But the light desert horses covered the ground at such a speed it was impossible for the bowmen to loose more than one or two shafts before the enemy were on them.

Quickly as they slipped back and found refuge under the knights' lances, many left it too late and were cut down. The survivors crept into the rear between the restive destriers, several receiving hard hoof kicks for their pains, and there prepared to dash out again as soon as the enemy retired. The knights sat like a solid wall on their destriers, lances pointed, and courageous as the Bedouin horsemen were, they were unable to break this steel line.

Cuthbert sat astride his mount at the hindquarters of Sir Walter's horse, like all the other knights' squires, with extra spears and arms ready to hand to his master. The Saracens charged well up to the points of the lances, and one chopped with his scimitar, severing the earl's steel lance blade from its ash pole. Pulling up hard, the Muslim turned to slash again, this time at Sir Walter's unguarded face. Cuthbert smoothly slid a heavy mace with cruelly spiked ends into his master's outstretched hand and, with one mighty swing, the earl took the lightly clad horseman surgically in the head and he went down like a reed, his shattered face exploding blood.

Hour after hour the Arab horsemen persisted in their attacks, suffering, but determined to conquer the Christian host, which still proceeded in a slow but orderly manner toward Arsuf. Saladin, seeing that the arrows of his *askaris* were not killing sufficient numbers of the enemy's chargers, ordered them to dismount to take more accurate aim at the animals. Several frustrated Hospitaller knights mistook this action as a retreat and, unable to hold themselves back any longer, broke ranks and charged.

Caught by surprise and off their horses, the infidels' early resistance was comparatively slight. The mass of the heavy cavalry, lances down at head height, swept through the *askari* ranks, trampling them down like weeds beneath their screaming destriers' fighting hoofs—but with every foot gained the resistance became more stubborn. The breakout exasperated King Richard, but he knew that his knights had already shown more patience than he could have expected. He ordered the general charge.

Saladin, expecting that the Franks would sooner or later go on the offensive, had placed his infantry in many lines behind the front ranks, and as the force of the crusaders' charge slowed, so the number of foes in their front multiplied. At the same time, massed Bedouin cavalry closed in to harass the exposed landward flank and soon the crusaders' forward momentum became bogged down. Their spears, no use in close combat, were thrown down, and with axe, mace, and sword each knight fought for himself.

The Earl of Evesham was one of a group of knights whom the king had kept close to him, and the Evesham mounted contingent hurtled into the heart of the battle behind Richard as he charged out. Saladin, aware of the king's extreme personal valor and warlike qualities, set great store on his death or capture, and had ordered a large number of his best Kurdish troops to concentrate on the English ruler. They had no problem in identifying their target from the royal standard carried behind the king. A multitude of Saracens swept down on his position and in spite of his great strength the pressure made it increasingly difficult to keep his enemies at bay.

Now that Sir Walter's lance had been abandoned for a battle-axe, Cuthbert began to take an active part in the struggle. His duties consisted mainly in guarding his master's back, and preventing his being unhorsed by any sudden attack on the flank or from behind.

King Richard, bent not only on defending himself but also on directing the general course of the battle, kept bursting through the ring of foes to ride from point to point on the field to call his knights together into close order and exhort the infantry to steadiness. Surrounded by his trusty retinue he dashed hither and thither to restore the fight where its fortunes seemed doubtful. At one point his impetuous nature led him into great danger. He erupted through the enemy surrounding him, but they made it easy so that they could close ranks immediately, cutting him off from his retinue. The maneuver worked. The rush of infidel horsemen carried away the Christian knights, and only his standard bearer followed the king.

Amid the wild confusion that raged, where each man fought for his own life, few noticed that the king had been isolated from help. Sir

Walter himself was engaged fiercely in a struggle with four Bedouins who surrounded him, when Cuthbert shouted. "The king, Sir Walter. The king. He's surrounded. For heaven's sake ride to him. The royal standard is down."

With a roar the earl turned, brained one of his opponents with a sweep of his heavy axe and hastened to Richard's assistance, closely followed by Cuthbert. The weight of his mail and heavily caparisoned horse cleft a path through the struggling mass, and in a brief space he crashed through to the king's side. Cuthbert rode hard on his master's heels. One Saracen, turning to spear his mount, fell with a strangled cry as Cuthbert's war horse kicked out, splitting the warrior's head like a ripe water melon.

In the space of an eye blink Cuthbert saw that the king's standard bearer lay dead in a spreading stain of blood from a gaping stomach wound. And then he was fighting for his own life. Just as they reached the king a Kurd who had been struck from his horse crawled beneath Richard's charger and drove his scimitar deep into its bowels. The animal reared high in its sudden pain, and then collapsed. Richard, unable to disengage himself quickly enough, fell half under the animal.

In an instant the Earl of Evesham jumped to the ground and with his broad triangular shield extended, covered his lord from the infidels pressing in on all sides. Cuthbert imitated the earl and strove with all his might to defend his own master from attacks at his back. For a moment or two the sweep of the earl's bloodied axe and Cuthbert's circling sword kept back the Muslim warriors.

"My lord, we can't keep this up for much longer."

"Is there any way of freeing the king?" Sir Walter grunted, as the blade of his axe cut deeply into another leg and its owner collapsed in a gout of gore.

The king struggled vainly to pull his pinioned leg out from under his destrier. Cuthbert suddenly realized that the poor beast still lived, and with a sudden slash of his sword he struck it on its hindquarter.

Goaded by the pain the noble animal made a last effort to rise, only to fall back. But the brief convulsion freed the king, who snatched his leg from under the dying beast, and with his heavy battle-axe in hand, rose with an oath to stand by the side of Sir Walter and Cuthbert.

The fight intensified as Kurdish foot and mounted Bedouins and Turks assayed to cut down and overpower the three Christians. Some urged their horses to ride over them. With each sweep of his axe the king either dismounted a foe or split the head of his steed, and the wall of slain piling up around them testified to the tremendous power of their arms. Still, even such warriors as these could not long sustain the conflict. The earl had already received two wounds, and the king bled freely from some severe gashes.

Cuthbert had taken several cuts about his cheeks but suffered more from blows his mail had deflected but did nothing to prevent bruising. Driven to his knees, he knew only that he was about to die at his king's side, when a shout of "St. George!" cut through the fray, and a battle of English knights drove mercilessly through the throng of Saracens to reach Richard's side. Fast behind pressed a close-formed mass of English footmen with billhooks and pikes. The Saracens gave way foot by foot before their steady discipline.

Leaping into the saddle of a riderless horse, the king rallied his troops for one more great and final charge. The effect was irresistible. Appalled by the slaughter which they had suffered, and by the tremendous strength and energy of the Christian host, the Saracens broke and fled. Saladin's last reserves gave way as the king, shouting the crusaders' war-cry of *Sanctum sepulchrum adjuva*—"Help us, Holy Sepulchre"—fell on them. The Saracens finally turned to escape certain slaughter, and the crusaders' victory was complete.

A makeshift camp soon sprang up around Arsuf and the crusaders set about licking their injuries. Sir Walter gruffly insisted on a page first tending to Cuthbert's "scratches," as he called them, before taking a stool and allowing his squire to attend his own more severe wounds.

As Cuthbert bathed a gash on his arm, the earl grimly reflected on the nature of the battle just finished.

"It was a victory, Cuthbert, but I wonder what it served us? However thorough our victories, the Saracens seem to recover very quickly. A Christian defeat is crushing, our knights dying where they stand. Defeat means annihilation for us. On the other hand, when the Saracens sense they'll be unsuccessful they feel no shame or humiliation in scattering like sheep."

He looked up at Cuthbert. "You see, the infidels have unlimited resources. Saladin can call on reinforcements at any time, whereas our manpower is limited to those we brought with us. As we run out through loss on the battlefield, the Saracens will surely win the day," he rasped.

"Don't be gloomy, my lord. We at least are victors of this battle of Arsuf. Perhaps Saladin will retreat now."

On his return from the field, the king assembled his fellow leaders and principal knights and summoned the Earl of Evesham, with the message that he was to bring his squire with him. As they approached the royal pavilion, Richard's voice boomed out.

"My lords, I had a narrow escape from death today. Separated from you in the battle, I was surrounded by Saracens. I should doubtless have fought my way through the infidel mongrels, but a foul peasant stabbed my charger from below. In another moment and my nephew Arthur would have been your king, if my good Earl of Evesham here, attended by this brave lad, had not appeared. I've seen plenty of fighting, but I've never witnessed a braver stand than they made above me. Your king thanks you, Sir Walter.

"But while I might expect such courage from one of my bravest knights, I'm not accustomed to expect it from one who has been a squire for only a few weeks. It's not the first time that I've been under a debt of gratitude to him. I promised him then that the first time he distinguished himself against the infidels he would win his spurs.

I think that you will agree with me, my lords, that he has done so, and that Cuthbert, son of the fine Norman knight Sir Stephen de Lance, has shown the courage that fits him to receive the honor of knighthood."

A chorus of approval rose from the assembled nobles and the king, bidding Cuthbert kneel before him, drew his great sword, barely cleaned of Saracen blood, laid it across shoulders Cuthbert held rigid to prevent them shaking, and dubbed him Sir Cuthbert de Lance. When he had risen, the great barons of England pressed in close to shake his hand, and Cuthbert blushed at the recognition he had received. He knew well that the usual ceremonies and penances which young knights had to undergo before admission into the body of chivalry—and which were severe—were omitted when a knighthood was bestowed in the field.

The king ordered his armorer to make Cuthbert his golden spurs and to take his shield and paint on it the device of a sword raising a royal crown from the ground, in token of his courageous deed.

In such an encampment few secrets are kept for long, and on returning to their quarters, Sir Walter's retinue fairly fell on the embarrassed lad from Erstwood until he could hardly breathe. The greatest crush came from the Saxon foresters, led by Cnut. These humble friends were delighted at his success, for they felt that they owed him so much. As Cnut proclaimed, Cuthbert was their mascot, not only because of his youth, but for his kindness, willingness to undertake any task, no matter how menial, and for his readiness to smile even during the hardships they had undergone.

Cuthbert now took rank among the knights who followed the earl's banner. A modest tent was put up for him, a page and a squire assigned him. As he entered his new abode he felt bemused at the change which had taken place in one short day—that he, at the age of sixteen, should have won his spurs, and the approval of the King of England, Aquitaine, Anjou, and Normandy. He wondered what his mother would say should the news reach her in her quiet Saxon home.

If the English hoped that victory would buy immunity from Saracen attacks, they soon found otherwise. The army which had barred their way had broken up, but contingents remained all around and the harassing stabs recommenced. In fact, the crusaders only occupied the ground on which they stood. It was death to venture a hundred yards from the camp, unless in force. Every effort to forage in the locality met fierce resistance. At least the fleet still stood offshore, able for the time being to resupply the army. Otherwise the only consolation to the dreary routine was the fact of winning the battle of Arsuf.

Chapter 13: In Saracen Hands

September to December 1191

After one pitched battle and a victory, it had been reckoned that the Crusade would advance on Jerusalem, but back in Sicily no one had counted on the climate and illness. Geography also played a part in preventing a speedy march toward their hearts' desire.

Although unconquered in the battle, the crusader army became so weakened that it was effectively at a standstill. Even King Richard, with all his hot-headedness, dared not leave the seashore to march directly on the Holy City. All knew it could not be taken without a long siege, and that raised many problems.

It could only be undertaken by an army strong enough, not only to carry out the task, but to meet and defeat the armies which Saladin would bring up to the relief. There had to be sufficient soldiers to keep open communications with Jaffa, twelve miles south of Arsuf, the only harbor where provisions and siege engines could be landed. So the war resolved into a series of expeditions and sporadic fights.

Many of the footmen were put to thoroughly fortifying the town. Detachments of knights rode out to engage the Saracens in skirmishes, with varying success. On one occasion a squire came galloping in on his lathered palfrey with the news that a forage party of footmen, guarded by a squadron of knights, had been attacked and forced to seek refuge behind the walls of a small town, some four miles inland. He had been keeping watch on a low hill and managed to get away safely. King Richard himself decided to go to their assistance and called together a large company of knights, including Sir Walter and Cuthbert, and men-at-arms.

When they arrived in the vicinity, the enemy, completely absorbed in battering down the town's flimsy gate, failed to see the threat until the relief column fell on them with the force of a thunderbolt and scattered them.

After a short pause to gather breath and wits, the enlarged group prepared to cut its way through and return to the Christian camp. A problem became immediately apparent. The men-at-arms on foot were unable to keep up with the knights' rapid pace through the reforming enemy ranks. The knights not only had to break open a path but also to keep it clear for those following. The king and the greater number of his knights led the way, with the footmen behind them. A small number of knights, Cuthbert among them, formed a rearguard.

The Saracens followed their usual tactics, and this time with great success. As the king with his knights charged them, they parted and let the Christians through with only slight resistance, and then closed in on their track. At the same time another and still more numerous body fell on the footmen and their mounted guard. Again and again the knights charged through the ranks of the Muslims, while the men-at-arms did their best to keep in close formation and resist the onslaughts of the enemy's cavalry.

In spite of their fortitude, the continual rain of arrows thinned their ranks with terrible rapidity. Charging up to the very point of the spears, the wild horsemen loosed their shafts point blank into the faces of their foe, and although numbers of them fell beneath the more formidable missiles fired by the English archers, their numbers were so overwhelming that the little band melted away. The knights of the rearguard also fell steadily. The Saracens when dismounted or wounded still fought on foot, stabbing their enemies' horses to dismount the riders.

The king's retinue made desperate efforts to return to the assistance of the rearguard, but were thwarted by the Saracens' resistance and sheer numbers. The position of those in the rear fast became hopeless. One by one the gallant little band of knights died, and a sea of turbans closed over the fluttering plumes.

Cuthbert defended himself vehemently for such a long time that he felt as if his arms were coming loose in their sockets. But eventually he was separated from the remainder of his comrades and a huge Nubian soldier knocked him senseless to the ground with a heavy blow to the back of the head from a mace.

For a moment, he thought himself still in the thick of battle, the shouts and war-cries of the crusaders, the wild yells of the Muslims echoed in his mind. Then the pain crashed in like a wave. His head felt split in half by an agony he'd never before experienced, and the horror all came flooding in… and then, mercifully, faded back into oblivion.

When he recovered consciousness again, the first impression was stillness after the din of battle. In its place a quiet chatter in many unknown tongues, and the sound of laughter and feasting came to his ears. He opened his eyes, then cursed under the unbearable dazzle of the sun. Gingerly raising his still throbbing head and looking around, Cuthbert saw that he and ten of his comrades were lying together in the middle of a Saracen camp, their ankles tethered by ropes and to pegs driven into the dry ground.

He felt the back of his head and winced as his hand encountered a lump at the base of his skull the size of a goose egg. The sun hammered down with a physical force. There was no shelter. Cuthbert saw that a few of his fellow prisoners were also conscious and like him parched with thirst. Two made signs, pointing to their mouths, begging water, but the nearest Saracens laughed in their faces, and made a dismissive gesture that suggested it was scarcely worth the trouble to drink when they were likely to be put to death soon.

He judged it late in the afternoon by the sun's position before a change came over the camp's relaxed pace. Cuthbert observed a stir as men ran to their horses, leaped on their backs, and with wild cries started off at full speed to greet a small dust cloud that had appeared on the low horizon.

Evidently someone important drew near. Cuthbert didn't doubt the prisoners' fate would be decided soon. The men exchanged a few words in Frankish from time to time, each urging the other to keep up the spirit in defiance of the infidels. Two had succumbed to their wounds during the afternoon, and now only eight were able to get to their knees when ordered by gestures and kicks to do so. One of the guards then showed the rest what to do by brutally slamming the prisoner nearest him into a position of obeisance, with his face pressed into the sand.

Soon the shouts of the horsemen and other sounds announced that the great chief was near at hand. The sand djinn resolved into a long dusty trail, then mounted figures materialized from the cloud. Among the cries of greeting, Cuthbert could make out the name of Saladin. From his position at the end of the line of captives, he risked a sideways squint and saw a bodyguard of splendidly-dressed Kurdish attendants. The sultan, however, was plainly attired. He reined his horse in front of the line of prostrate prisoners.

"You are English," he said, in passable Frankish, with only a hint of exotic pronunciation. Since the First Crusade the old German-French had become the main means of communication between the various races in Outremer as well as the Greeks of Constantinople.

"You are brave warriors, and I hear that before you were taken you slaughtered many of my people. They did wrong to capture you and bring you here to be killed. Your cruel king gives no mercy to those who fall into his hands. You must not expect it here, you who without a pretense of right invade my country, slay my people, and attack my armies. Your king's murder of the prisoners of Acre has closed my heart to all mercy. Your king put prisoners to death in cold blood because the money for the ransom he demanded had not arrived. We Arabs do not carry huge masses of gold about with us. Although I could have had it brought from Egypt, I did not think that so brave a monarch as Richard of England could have committed so cruel an action in cold blood."

One of the Christians who had looked up at this quiet tirade had his head harshly kicked for his trouble. The sultan went on.

"When we are fresh from battle, and our wounds are warm, and our hearts are full of fury, we kill our prisoners. But to do so days after a battle is contrary to the laws alike of your religion and of ours. However, it is King Richard who has sealed your doom, not I. You are the warriors of your Christ, and I do not insult you with the offer of turning from your religion and joining me. Should any wish to save his life on these conditions, I will, however, promise him a place of position and authority among us. You may now look me in the eye."

All raised their heads, but none of the knights moved to accept the offer. Each man, as Saladin ran his hawk-like eyes along the line, answered with a glare of contempt and hatred. Saladin waved his hand, and one by one the captives were led aside. They walked—according to their wounds—as proudly to their doom as if they had been going to a feast. Each wrung the hand of the one next to him as he turned, and then without a word followed his captors. There was a sickeningly wet swish-crack, like the sound of a melon being cleaved in half, followed by a dull thud, and one by one Christian heads rolled in the sand.

Since the executions began at the other end from where he still knelt, Cuthbert was the last in line to be roughly hauled to his feet by his executioners. As he stood, the sultan's eyebrows rose in surprise. He held his hand up to stop his men dragging Cuthbert off and dismounted from his horse to look more closely at his prisoner.

"By the Prophet's beard, you're nothing but a boy," he breathed, wonderingly.

Cuthbert instantly stiffened his posture in defiance.

"All the Franks who have so far fallen into my hands have been men of strength and power—how is it that I see a mere youth among their ranks, and wearing the spurs of knighthood?"

"King Richard himself made me a knight," Cuthbert growled proudly, "after having stood across him when his steed had been foully stabbed during the battle at Arsuf, and the whole host of Islam surrounded him."

"Ah." The sultan's coal-black pupils gleamed with interest. "You were one of the two who defended the king against his enemies. Hmm… I find it hard to kill so brave a youth. I have no doubt that you are as determined to die a Christian as those whose heads now lie in the sand? But time may change you." The sultan's penetrating gaze held Cuthbert for a moment. Then he stepped smartly back. The hint of amusement that had played on his lips vanished. "At any rate for now your doom is postponed."

He snapped his fingers and turned to a gorgeously caparisoned noble next to him, and spoke rapidly in Arabic. The man listened then bowed and touched a hand to his forehead.

Saladin's glittering eyes returned to Cuthbert. He reverted to Frankish. "This emir's brother, Ben Abin, is my governor of Jerusalem. You will go with the emir and he will hand you to Ben Abin. I give you to him as a gift. To you I give your life, but in all else Ben Abin will be your master."

Cuthbert heard without emotion the words which commuted his fate from death to slavery. Many, he knew, who were captured in these wars were carried off as slaves to different parts of Asia, and it did not seem to him that the change was in any way a gift. However, life is precious to its owner, and it was only natural that his heart should leap with hope that soon either the crusaders might recapture Jerusalem or that he might find some way to escape.

Saladin turned away, remounted with an easy swing into the saddle, and cantered off surrounded by his brightly garbed bodyguard. The dead were swiftly stripped of their armor and left for the carrion birds already circling overhead in anticipation of a feast. Two Saracens forcibly removed his own. He watched miserably as his gold spurs disappeared into a leather bag. Collecting the discarded mail, helmets, and shields, they mounted Cuthbert on a splay-legged, bare-backed mare. Four Bedouins, their long lances held at high point, rode beside him and followed their emir toward Jerusalem.

* * *

133

Bitterness filled his mind. This was not how he'd imagined first seeing the Holy City. There he stood with his comrades, proud and delighted at their successes, confident in the righteousness of their cause that Jerusalem would soon fall and the infidels be swept away. Instead, he was a slave, perhaps never again to set eyes on a white face, unless it was another wretch like himself.

Even in his dull state, Cuthbert could not help gazing in some awe at the city before him as they crested the hill above the Valley of Gihon. The dilapidated state caused by decades of war could not detract from the walls, magnificent in height and strength, mighty in their deep battlements, which rose on the edge of the valley. There was the church built by the first crusaders; there the mighty Masjid Qubbat As-Sakhrah—the Dome of the Rock—built on the site of the Temple of Solomon.

Far away on a projecting ridge, he made out the great building known as the Tomb of Moses. On the right beyond the houses rose the towers on the Roman walls, hiding from his view the Pool of Bethsaida lying in its hollow behind, and in the center the cupolas of the Church of the Holy Sepulchre—the very reason for the Crusade of which he had been a part.

After a few brief moments spent in looking at the city the Arabs continued their way down into the Valley of Gihon. After crossing the dip they ascended the steep road to the walls with brandished lances and yells of triumph. Under the towering walls two riders came close on either side to protect Cuthbert from any fanatic who might be tempted to strike him. And then they passed under David's Gate into the city.

The narrow streets were thronged and the news brought by the horsemen that many Christian invaders had been defeated, passed from mouth to mouth with excitement and shouts of exultation. Curses delivered with furious fist shaking were heaped on Cuthbert, who rode along with an air as quiet and composed as if he were the center of an ovation instead of an outburst of public hatred. It wasn't how he felt inside, but he refused to give any satisfaction to the jeering infidels.

At one point the mob pressed in so hard that he would have been torn from his guards, had not the emir in the lead shouted that he was placed in their hands by Saladin himself. The sultan's name acted as a talisman, and his escort continued without hindrance to the palace.

Governor Ben Abin turned out to be a stern and grave-looking man, as befitted his important position. He sat cross-legged on a divan surrounded by officers and attendants, and heard in silence the account given him by his brother. He bowed his head at the commands of Saladin and, without addressing a word to Cuthbert, waved two armed men to remove him. They led him to a small windowless room and placed unleavened bread, some dates, and a jar of water on the floor of his cell. The door closed behind them and he heard the bar lock into its socket.

Well, at least I'm not meant to starve. But what, I wonder, is in store for me?

In the morning a black slave led him through long corridors and out into a garden surrounded by a high wall. Large in size, full of trees and flowers, it was far more beautiful than any garden that Cuthbert had seen before. A variety of slaves worked in every corner. An Arab, who appeared to be the head of the gardeners, assigned Cuthbert a patch to work and used hand gestures to indicate the nature of his task. During his long night of thinking, Cuthbert had made up his mind to give his captors no cause for ill-treatment or complaint, to work as willingly at the chores assigned to him as cheerfully as was in his power, and to seize the first opportunity to make his escape, regardless of the risk to his life.

One glance around assured him that escape from this paradise was not an option. A wide walkway ran along the top of the wall, from which several guards, with small-bows and spears, kept a vigilant watch on the gardeners below. For the present, patience would have to suffice. He set to work with a will. He liked flowers and soon became so absorbed in his work he almost forgot his slavery. It was not laborious—digging, planting, pruning, and training the plants, and watering them from a large fountain in the middle of the garden.

The slaves were not allowed to talk to each other. At the end of the day's work guards marched them off to separate cells and an unvarying diet of dried dates, flat bread, and water. But in truth Cuthbert had little to complain of. The garden slaves of the governor's house at Jerusalem were indulged, if they worked hard. Ben Abin, absorbed in the cares of the city, took little note of his slaves, least of all to bother himself with punishments, and the head gardener was a man of unusual humanity.

Sometimes in the course of the day, veiled ladies of the harem would come out in groups, attended by tall black eunuchs brandishing wide, curved blades. They passed where the slaves labored, all of whom were forbidden on pain of death to look up or even to approach the *konak*, the shady pavilion where the women threw aside their veils and enjoyed the scent and sight of the flowers, the splash of murmuring waters, and the strains of music played by skilled hand-maidens.

Although Cuthbert was intensely curious as to what these strange wrapped-up figures might look like when their faces were unveiled, he cared more about retaining his manhood, so far only employed for its purpose that one day in France and one snatched night with Blondel in Acre. He had his hand and imagination, but for a lusty youth in the first flower of his urges nothing matched that first expenditure of seed in the company of another.

I'll need all the parts of it one day soon, hopefully, so I'm not going to run any risk of joining the ranks of the eunuchs by drawing the guards' anger on myself.

So, no glancing up or even looking up at the palace, which was also forbidden. From the lattice casements during the day the strains of music and merriment often wafted down on scented air into the garden; but this only added to the bitterness of his position, by reminding Cuthbert that he was shut off for life from ever hearing the laughter of the loved ones he had left behind.

After a month he began to think that there never would be a chance of escape, never anything more than the gilded confines of this cage, never again freedom.

Chapter 14: No Way Out

Winter 1191–92

Almost resigned to an eternity of slavery, Cuthbert could only hope that the crusaders would capture the city. Every night, back in his cell, he prayed that something would save him, quickly remembering the admonitions of Father Francis and hurriedly adding that he knew he was not worthy of heavenly attention.

Either through the power of prayer or because of his commendable humility—even if nudged by the memory of his priest—he was certainly worthy of someone's attention. One night, long after slumber had quieted the palace, the opening of his cell door startled Cuthbert. Crouching in alarm, he saw one of the frighteningly big Nubian eunuchs enter, and an old woman beside him. She astonished him by whispering in broken Frankish.

"My mistress, the governor's best wife, has sent me to ask your story. She like to know why you are only boy, yet already knight? How you come be slave? Saladin, Prophet bless his name, himself sent you to her lord. How this happen? She is kindest lady, and your… yes, your youth touches her heart."

Cuthbert briefly related the events which had led to his captivity. The old woman placed a basket containing some choice fruit and white bread down on the floor, and then withdrew with the Nubian as silently as she had come, leaving Cuthbert nonplussed.

Hope suddenly filled his heart. "Is it possible, he breathed out loud to the enclosing walls, "that I'll hear again and that this lady's pity might provide some means of escape?" And then, "I wonder how she looks?"

All the day long he thought of nothing but the old woman and her mistress. His delight when she turned up on the following night knew no bounds, and then again every night for a week. On the eighth night, she bade him follow her. She held a finger to her lips to sign caution, and took him to a door into the harem. Passing through several passages, they arrived at a chamber where a lady—Cuthbert assessed behind her veil—of some thirty years was seated, surrounded by several younger women.

Cuthbert made a deep bow. She began speaking in a tongue he could not understand, but after a lapse, the old woman translated and startled Cuthbert by revealing that her mistress was aware of many things: his feats of bravery, his knighting at the hands of the great warrior Richard of England, to mention a few.

"What my mistress wish to know from your lips is what is it stir up the heart of infidel world that they send armies against us, who wish but to be left alone, and who have no grudge against them? This city holy to us as you, yet here we live and all country for thousands of leagues is ours. Why should we allow it be taken from us by pale strangers from an unknowable distance?"

Cuthbert reported the circumstances of the fight at Arsuf and tried to explain the feelings which had given rise to the Crusade. This prompted curiosity about his voyage out, and of his life in England. The lady seemed more interested in this than anything, since these fierce Christian warriors were a mystery to her.

The old servant listened intently as her mistress spoke urgently and then turned to Cuthbert and asked, "You think some way to lighten your captivity?" Then she glanced down modestly before adding, "Your extreme youth, your countenance, and your bravery has greatly pleased her."

"Kind lady, nothing but freedom could satisfy my longings. I'm comfortable and not overworked, but I pine to be back again with my friends and countrymen."

Another hurried consultation took place.

"My mistress say, she willing grant you liberty, but as you come from Saladin, it cannot be done openly. It is suggest if you see plan to escape, she will help, but it must not be known that harem help, for my lord's anger would be terrible."

On the next night, when the servant came to his cell, he told her that he could think of no plan whatever for escaping from the palace. Even should he manage to scale the walls, he would only find himself in Jerusalem beyond, and his escape from that would be altogether hopeless. "Only," he told her, "if I were moved to some country residence could I ever have a chance of getting away."

Two more nights, torn between hope and despair, passed before the go-between reappeared. She told him her mistress agreed that he could only escape in the way he had suggested. He must be patient. In three days she would ask her husband for permission to pay a visit to his palace near Bethlehem—he would be too busy to go with her—and she would take several gardeners—among them Cuthbert—to beautify the place. Cuthbert returned heartfelt thanks to his patroness for her kind intentions, and hope beat rapidly in his heart.

Barely daring to think about the future, Cuthbert continued behaving as he always had in the garden. He had no idea how long after making her request Ben Abin would grant it. Four days had already passed as, with nightfall, the slaves were returned to their cells.

When the door of his cell softly opened, he sat up in anticipation of the old servant with news of his liberty, but to his shock four men rushed in and seized him by the arms. They gagged him, tied him hand and foot, wrapped a thick burnous around his head and body, and half-carried, half-dragged him out. By the change in the atmosphere and the sound of their feet on the ground he guessed they were carrying him through the garden. Then a door opened and closed. He was flung face down across—by its height—a mule like a bale of goods and a rope cruelly bound him in that position. He felt the animal put in motion, and heard by the tramp of feet that a considerable number of horsemen surrounded him.

It was hard to breathe through the gag and even harder to think in his painfully cramped position. But amid the bewilderment of his rapid seizure, Cuthbert tried to work out what could have happened. The only thing his dazed mind could come up with was that through the jealous politics of the harem, some eunuch must have got wind of the governor's wife paying attention to a Christian slave and told his master. Perhaps the Nubian guards heard something of their mistress's intentions and, fearing Ben Abin's anger should Cuthbert make his escape, warned him. Whichever, he had been thrown from the frying pan into the fire, without any doubt.

For some time they passed over rough, uneven city streets, every bump crushing his ribcage against the mule's hard back. Then came a pause and exchange of watchword and countersign, a creaking of doors, and the hollow echoing of shod hoofs over a wooden bridge. The sounds of the city dwindled as the band went out into open country. They had not gone very far when Cuthbert heard a guttural command and the company halted. Hands roughly pulled Cuthbert from the mule. Disoriented from the ride, he fell to the stony ground. Someone ripped the burnous from him.

He blinked dust from his eyes and looked warily around. He lay in the middle of ten Bedouin guards from the governor's palace garrison, but they had no further interest in their prisoner and handed him over to a band of Arabs which loomed out of the night, mounted on camels. His bonds were swiftly cut and a jabbering Arab forced a spare camel to its knees and gestured him to mount the saddle. His hands were then retied behind the rear horn of the saddle, as an Arab driver, with lance and bows, took his seat on the animal's neck. Groaning, the beast lurched up and with scarcely another word the caravan marched off, faces turned to the south.

It was the stuff of a nightmare. Only hours before he had been thrilled by the hope of freedom. Now he faced a slavery immeasurably worse than he had so far suffered. He could not understand his new captors, but one name stood out: El Kahira—Cairo! He was being sent to Egypt. No doubt the governor of Jerusalem, fearing that he might escape, and dreading the sultan's fury, had decided to transfer his troublesome slave to a more secure position.

Cuthbert had heard from old hands among the Templars that the Egyptians turned captured foreign youths into *mamluks*, their slave-warriors. He didn't think he could stand that.

The caravan journeyed for three days until they left behind the fertile lowlands of Palestine, and their faces turned from south to west. They were entering the sandy waste that stretched across the top of Sinai between the southern corner of Palestine and Egypt. The only habitation Cuthbert saw was a small town, which his captors detoured around at some distance. He saw one point at the dwellings and call the settlement Saraka.

Cuthbert had been closely guarded at first, but now in the desert the Arabs seemed to think an escape attempt would be futile and untied his hands so he could better prevent himself from toppling off the camel whenever it stumbled. Cuthbert had followed his previous instinct and behaved obediently and with some cheer. He showed himself pleased and grateful for the dates which formed the staple of their meals. He assumed so innocent and quiet an appearance that the Arabs marveled among themselves. One man had some words of Frankish and he thought he understood his meaning. They had concluded a mistake must have been made by the governor's guard when they said the prisoner was one of dreaded King Richard's most terrible knights.

Cuthbert's cuteness matched nothing inwardly, where his iron conviction was that he would escape, and soon. He didn't have any idea how far ahead Egypt lay, but he knew once he reached Cairo all hope of freedom would end. He had kept his wits—returned to him after the shock of his second capture—about him and noticed which camel appeared to be the fastest. It had a lighter build than the others, and its rider had difficulty in holding its pace down to the rest. Cuthbert saw that from the pains its rider took with it, by the constant patting and the care in watering and feeding the animal, he was extremely proud of the beast.

If I'm to escape their clutches, that camel is the means by which I must do it.

At the end of each day's journey the camels were allowed to browse at will, haltered by a short cord tied between one hind and one fore foot. The Arabs then set to work to collect kindling for a fire, not for cooking—their only food was dried dates and some black bread, which they brought with them—but for warmth, as the nights grew chilly.

Each day he had pretended great tiredness from the camel's motion, and had, after hastily eating his dates, thrown himself down, covered himself with the long, dark-blue cloak one of the men had given and feigned instant sleep. After three days of this behavior his captors had come to look on his presence sleeping close to them as a matter of course.

The second day after entering the desert Cuthbert threw himself down by the side of an uprooted shrub of small size and about his own length. He covered himself as usual with his cloak and pretended to go to sleep. But his eyes were on the alert through an aperture beneath his burnous and he noted the direction in which his escape-camel wandered into the scrub bushes to graze. The darkness came on quickly after they halted, and when the Arabs settled round their fire, Cuthbert very quietly shifted the robe from himself to the long low bush near him, and then crawled stealthily off into the darkness.

The camels moved off about a hundred yards from the camp fire and found some succulent bushes on which to graze. The soft sand muffled Cuthbert's cautious footsteps as he picked his way toward the selected camel. In his hands he carried one of the Arabs' spears, bow and arrows, and a bag of dates, stolen from where the man had left them on dismounting. The beast was restive at his unfamiliarity, but it made no movement when he swiftly undid the halter rope. It was not so easy, however, to climb into the high wooden saddle, and Cuthbert tried several times in vain. Then he repeated in a sharp tone the words which he'd heard the Arabs use to order their camels to kneel, striking the animal at the same moment behind the fore-legs with one of the arrows.

The camel immediately obeyed the order and knelt down, making as it did so the angry grumble which camels consider indispensable when ordered to do anything. Fortunately they made the noise so frequently, and herd camels always bickered among themselves, that although in the still air it might have been heard by the Arabs dozing a short distance away, it attracted no notice. Cuthbert climbed into the seat, shook the rope that served as a rein, and the animal rose. He turned its head and set off at a smooth, steady gait in the opposite direction to which they had arrived earlier.

Once away from the camp site, Cuthbert increased the camel's speed to a long shuffling trot, and the Arabs' fire soon faded into the distant darkness behind. Already dressed in Eastern garb and sunburnt, he doubted anyone at a distance would think him a Frank.

He steered by the stars and rode all night without stopping. He reckoned on having at least three hours' start, for the Arabs were sure to have dozed that time around the fires before going out to bring in their camels from their grazing for the night. Even then they would suppose for some time that the missing animal had strayed farther than usual. So the first alarm would be when they discovered his ruse with the robe, which might not be for a long time.

He hoped to reach cultivated land long before being overtaken, after which he should be able to journey onward without attracting attention. He already knew the regular Muslim greeting of "May Allah protect you."

In the morning light Cuthbert paused on top of a hill and looked back. He could see no sign of pursuit in the vast stretch of desert behind him. In front, the ground was already dotted here and there with vegetation, and in the distance he could see the walls of Saraka

144

again—which he too avoided. In a few hours' ride he should be back in cultivated country.

Cuthbert reached Palestine when the sun stood high overhead. Villages dotted the plain, solitary traders alternated with passing caravans, farmers rode donkeys, and women drew water from wells. Cuthbert arranged his burnous carefully to cover his head in Arab fashion, slung the long spear across his shoulders, and went boldly forward at a swinging trot like any other Arab bent on some rapid journey. He soon found his hopes justified. Several times he met groups of men who scarcely raised their eyes as he trotted by them, giving the greeting.

He rode all day, avoiding villages as far as possible, stopping only at a stream to give his camel water, until nightfall. Then he halted, haltered the animal to feed on some young foliage and, wrapping himself in his burnous, soon fell asleep. He had little fear of being overtaken by his captors, and it was improbable that they would hit on the exact line which he had taken.

A rough shaking rudely awakened Cuthbert. Still sleep-mazed, he realized it was already daylight. He looked up in alarm to find himself surrounded by a cluster of Arabs who questioned him as to where he came from, and what he was doing there. A glance told him they were not the bunch from which he'd escaped. As he got to his feet he pointed to his lips to sign his dumbness. The Arabs threw him suspicious looks and examined the camel, and then the person of their captive.

One grabbed Cuthbert by the arm and swiftly rolled up the long arms of his burnous. The paleness of his skin gave away his disguise, and without more ado or questioning, they tied him hand and foot and flung him face down across his camel. In moments they were on their way.

Cuthbert, dizzyingly watching the grains of sand passing below him as his mount swung along in the caravan, reflected on the nature of hope. He was beginning to get righteously pissed off with being captured and slung unceremoniously over the backs of pack animals.

Somewhat idly, he noticed from the sun's position that they now headed due east, which meant Jerusalem was not their destination. A long day's journeying, which to Cuthbert seemed interminable, brought them to a low spit of sand running along a huge mass of water. Behind, lofty cliffs rose almost vertically, but a deep gorge cleft through the mountain had afforded access to the lakeside.

Cuthbert was pulled down unceremoniously and his bonds cut. This time the barrenness they had traveled through really was a disincentive to escape. He saw at once that his newest captors belonged to some deep desert tribe over whom the sultan's authority must be weak. *They might rally to his armies when summoned and fight for a short time, but at the first disaster, or whenever they become bored with the discipline and regularity of army life, they mount their camels and return to the desert.* He suspected men such as these would happily rustle either a horse, some cattle, or other animals to pay for their conscription.

Wood cast on the shore of the sea—for it was too vast to be called a lake—was soon gathered and a fire lighted under an earthenware pot filled with water from a skin, to which the cook added some grain. Cuthbert's geography of this land was as hazy as anyone's but recalling his bible he assumed he now gazed out over the waters of the Dead Sea. It looked appealing, and since he ached in every limb from the position in which he had been placed on the camel, he signed for permission to bathe.

This he was granted, apparently—judging by the Arabs' reactions—from curiosity, for very few Arabs were able to swim, and these tribesmen, it seemed, had never before seen a naked white youth. One particularly vicious looking specimen with a gouge of a scar which ran from his jaw at an angle to his blind eye, took a great interest as Cuthbert stripped to his scanty slave's loincloth. Cuthbert didn't like the look in the one seeing eye, or the salacious licking of his puffy lips, He recalled with a shudder the words of a infantryman who claimed many Saracens liked to treat male youths like women for their lust.

I have to get away as soon as possible, but first a swim.

Cuthbert was amazed and baffled to find that instead of wading in it up to the neck before starting to swim, as he was accustomed to do at home, he had barely reached waist deep when the water took him off his feet. With a startled gasp of surprise, he found himself floating on top of rather than in the water. This was so unnatural that with a cry of disgust he scrambled onto his feet and struggled to shore. By this time the Arabs were rolling about with laughter and slapping their sides in amusement at his antics.

Goaded by the raucous barks of merriment, he stubbornly waded as best he could back into the strange sea, which for some reason beyond his understanding refused to allow him to sink in it.

This time he swam a little—more of a flounder along the surface—and, in spite of the water's horrible saltiness, felt a little refreshed. When he returned to the shore he dressed hurriedly again in his Bedouin clothes before Scarface could press his suit, and seated himself a little distance from the Arabs as they ate their gruel. One made a gesture that he might scrape out the bottom of the pot. They hadn't left much, but better than nothing after his cruel ride on a very empty stomach.

The Arabs soon wrapped themselves in their burnouses, and feeling confident that their prisoner could not escape from them in this remote and lifeless place, paid him no further attention beyond motioning to him to lie down at their side.

Cuthbert was now more determined than ever to attain his freedom. Although utterly ignorant of the place where he was, or of the way back, he thought that anything would be better than to be carried into helpless slavery in the savage and mysterious country beyond Jordan… or become the sex slave of someone like Scarface. He allowed enough time for the Arabs to fall fast asleep and then carefully and silently got to his feet.

Having already made up his mind to ignore the camels, which would only be aroused to annoyance if he tried getting one up, he struck up into the hills on foot. All night he wandered about in the wilderness and in the morning found himself at the edge of a ravine through which ran a muddy rivulet in braids. Cuthbert observed with some curiosity that on both sides caves honeycombed the cliffs.

Keeping along the cliff edge for a considerable distance, he came to a spot where a natural path wound down to the river bank. Here, he was delighted and relieved to find the shallow water on the sweet side of brackish. Dry almost beyond endurance, he nevertheless spent time taking tiny sips to prevent stomach cramps, before indulging in a long drink. Then he set off to explore the caves perforating the cliffs.

Seeing that lush fruiting bushes and many edible plants lined the river bank, Cuthbert decided to take refuge in a cave. Now that he no longer feared starving, he resolved to stay awhile to rest before making any arduous attempt to rejoin the Christian army. He picked out a cave some fifty feet up the rock face. Its low and narrow entrance opened into a much larger area inside. Then he went back down and collected a large bundle of grass and rushes for his bed.

For three days his solitariness pleased Cuthbert. He felt his mind repairing as well as his strength returning. He was busy gathering berries, quietly humming a tune he remembered Blondel playing, when a bony claw suddenly descended on his shoulder. With a startled half turn, the brave young knight just yelped at the apparition standing over him.

Chapter 15: A Hermit's Tale

Spring 1192

For a moment, Cuthbert's heart stopped beating as he stared at the hair-raising phantasm confronting him. He staggered back, gaping, and then noticed that his own reaction had caused the wild-looking figure to cower fearfully. The terrifying specter was in reality an ancient man, with an extremely long white beard flowing to his waist. His utterly unkempt hair fell to the same point so that he resembled a wild and furry nun in her gray habit. He was thin to an extraordinary extent and Cuthbert wondered how anyone could have been reduced to such a state of emaciation and live—and with a plentiful supply of fruit and berries to hand.

The old man gazed intently, and then made the sign of the Cross. Cuthbert started uncertainly and repeated the sign. The old man at once straightened up and gave him a strangely satisfied look, and then beckoned with scrawny arms to follow him.

He scrabbled up the rocky cliff after the scarecrow figure and soon found himself in a cave very similar to his own. It was a place of austerity. A sleeping-place made of large stones stood in one corner, and Cuthbert, thinking of the comforts of his own grassy couch, shuddered at the thought of the intense discomfort of such a bed. Another corner held a crude altar, signified by the rough crucifix which stood on it, and to this the hermit went to kneel in prayer. Cuthbert followed his example. Rising again, the hermit motioned to him to sit down, and made a series of inarticulate croaks.

It was so long since the old man had spoken to any living being, that he had almost lost the use of his tongue. But gradually Cuthbert recognized some of the words—and they were in Frankish.

"Are you a Christian truly... and if so, from where have you come?"

Cuthbert explained that he was with King Richard's army but had been taken prisoner, and had managed to escape (although he skated over the embarrassment of saying how many times...). He also told the old man that he had sojurned for the last four days in a cave higher up the stream.

"I... I don't know this King Richard."

Cuthbert gave him a brief account of recent events.

The hermit's sentences were slow and ill-formed. However, Cuthbert understood his words, and he seemed to get the drift of what Cuthbert told him.

"So the world is no better a place than when I first came here."

The old man then showed him, that by touching a stone in the corner of his cave the apparently solid rock opened, and revealed an entrance to an inner cavern, lit by a ray of light penetrating from above.

"This was made an age ago, and was intended as a refuge from the persecutors of that day. The caves were then almost all inhabited by anchorites, as the hermits called themselves. Many didn't care for their lives, and were quite ready to meet death through the knife of the infidel, but others clung to existence, and preferred to pass many years of penance on earth to atone for their sins before called on to appear before our Maker.

"If you are pursued, it will be safer for you to take up your abode here. I'm known to all the inhabitants of this country, who think me mad, and respect me accordingly. None ever interferes with me, the remains of what was once almost an army, who now alone survive. I can offer you no hospitality beyond that of a refuge, but there is water in the river below, fruits and berries on the shrubs. What would you have more?"

Cuthbert accepted the invitation with thanks, for he hoped that even at the worst the holy man's presence would protect him from Arabs who might discover him.

For three or four days he lived with the hermit, who, although he stretched his long lean body on the hard stones of his bed, and passed most hours of the night kneeling on the stone floor in front of his altar, had no objection to Cuthbert making himself as comfortable as he could under the circumstances.

At the end of the fourth day Cuthbert asked him how long he had been there, and how he came to take up his abode in so desolate a place. The hermit crouched in silence for so long a time Cuthbert thought he'd forgotten the question. And then said, "It is long indeed since my thoughts have gone back to the day when I was of the world. It might be sinful to recall them, but I will think the matter over tonight, and if it appears to me that you may derive good from my story, I will tell it to you."

Cuthbert did not renew his request the next day, thinking that his companion would speak if he thought fit and when he was ready. It was not until the evening that he alluded to the subject. He squatted down on a bank near the edge of the river and motioned to Cuthbert to sit beside him.

My father was a peer of France, and I was brought up at the court. Although it may seem strange to you, looking at this withered frame, sixty-five years back I was as bold and handsome a knight as rode in the train of the king—it was Louis VI, the one they called the Fat, and in your country I think it was the first Henry. I am now past ninety, and for sixty years I've lived here. I was a favorite of the king, and he loaded me with wealth and honor. I joined with him in the mad drinking bouts of the court. I was as wild and as wicked as all those around me, I thought little of God, and feared neither Him nor any man.

It happened that one of the barons of Dauphiny, whose castle lay in the same province as that of my father, had a lovely daughter, who, being an only child, would be his heiress. She was considered one of the best matches in France, and reports of her exceeding beauty had reached the court. Although my allowance from my father, and from the estates which the king had given me personally, should have been more than enough to live on, gambling, drinking, and whoring swallowed up my revenue faster than it came in, and I was constantly deeply in debt.

Talking one night at supper with some companions about what we could do to restore our wasted fortunes, one joked that the best plan would be for one of us to marry the beauty of Dauphiny. I at once said that I would be the man to do it—the idea was a mad one, and a roar of laughter greeted my words. Her father was a stern and rigid man, and he would never consent to give his daughter to a spendthrift young noble like myself. When the laughter had subsided I repeated my intention gravely, and offered to bet large sums with all around the table that I would succeed.

In the morning I packed up a few of my belongings, put in my chest the dress of a wandering troubadour, and taking with me only a trusty servant, started for Dauphiny. I won't bore you by describing all the means to which I resorted to obtain the affections of the heiress. I was well taught in music, played the lute, and knew by heart large numbers of ballads. As a troubadour I arrived at the gate of the castle, and asked to entertain its occupants. Troubadours were in high esteem then as I expect they are today, and I was quickly made to feel at home.

Days passed, and weeks; still I lingered at the castle, my heart being now as much interested as my pride in the wager I'd undertaken. Suffice it to say that my songs, and perhaps my appearance (everyone said I looked like one of those Greek heroes of old and every wench would prefer me as undressed as they were), won my way to her heart. Troubadours were given a great degree of license, and even in her father's presence there was nothing improper in my singing love songs. While he took them as the mere compliments of a troubadour, the lady, I saw, read them as I intended, which is to say, seriously. For in spite of my trickery I was in love.

It was only occasionally that we met alone. But before long she confessed that she loved me. Without telling her my real name, I disclosed to her that I was of her own rank, and that I had entered disguised as I was in order to win her love. She had a romantic heart and was flattered by my devotion. I owned up to a wild and reckless life, and she told me that her father had engaged her when she was still a baby to marry the son of an old friend of his. She didn't love this man, in fact she had never seen him.

She trembled when I proposed our running away together, but I assured her that I was certain of the king's protection and that he would, when the marriage was once celebrated, use his influence with her father to obtain his forgiveness."

The preparations for her elopement were not long in making. I purchased a fast horse in addition to my own, and ordered my servant to bring it to a point a short distance from the castle gate. I had procured a long rope with which to lower her down from her window to the moat below, which was at present dry, intending to slide down after her. The night chosen was one when I knew that the count would have guests and so there would be less fear of any watch being kept.

The guests arrived just at nightfall. I feigned illness, and kept to my room. From time to time I heard through the windows of the banqueting hall bursts of laughter. These gradually ceased, and at last, when it was still, I slipped out of my room with my rope in my hand to her apartment. She answered my tapped signal at the door immediately and I found her ready cloaked and prepared for the adventure.

She trembled from head to foot, but I cheered her to the best of my ability, and at last she was in readiness to be lowered. The window was at a considerable height from the ground, but the rope was a long one, and I had no fear of its reaching the bottom. Fastening it around her waist, I began to lower her from the window.

The night was windy, and like a pendulum she swung from left to right and back again as she went down. I had examined the rope carefully for any faults and found none but in swaying to and fro so wildly it may have caught a sharp stone. Mayhap it was a punishment from Heaven on me for robbing a father of his child—but suddenly I felt no longer a weight on my arms. A fearful shriek rang through the air and, looking out, I saw far below a white figure stretched senseless in the mud!

For a minute I stood paralyzed. But the cry had aroused others. Spinning around, I was confronted by a man at the door, his sword drawn. I was wild with grief and despair. I didn't think of getting away or of concealing my actions, I only wanted to rush without delay to the body of my lover. But this figure stood in my way, so I drew my sword, and like a madman rushed at him. A brief but furious fight ensued and, revved up by my despair, I broke his guard and ran him through the heart. As he fell back, his face came into the full light of the moon, and to my utter horror and bewilderment I saw I had killed my own father, who had been a guest at the feast.

I don't really remember what happened next. I think that I made my escape and ran wildly across the country. When I came to my senses months had passed, and I was the inmate of an asylum for men bereaved of their senses, kept by noble monks. Here for two years I remained, the world believing me dead. None knew that the troubadour whose love had cost the lady her life, who had slain the guest of her father, and had then disappeared, was the unhappy son of that guest.

I confessed to the monks, who were shocked, but consoled me in my despair by assuring me that however greatly I had sinned, the lady's death was an accident, and that if I had killed my father it was at least unintentionally.

My repentance was deep and sincere. After a while, under another name, I came to Outremer to expiate my sin by warring for the Holy Sepulchre. I fought as a man who didn't care whether he lived or not, but while all around me fell by sword and disease, death eluded me. When the Crusade had failed I determined to turn for ever from the world, and to devote my life to prayer and penance; and so, casting aside my armor, I made my way here, and took up my abode in a cave in this valley.

At that time there were many hundreds of other hermits—for the Muslims, while they fined the pilgrims who came to Jerusalem, and fought stoutly against those who wanted to capture the city, were in the main tolerant, and after some years offered no further hindrance to the community of men whom they looked on as mad as fakirs.

Here, my son, for more than sixty years I've prayed, fasted, and made penance. I trust now that the end is nearly at hand, that my long life of mortification will have obliterated the evil deeds of my youth. Let my fate be a warning to you. Walk steadily in the right way. Do not indulge in feasting and evil companionship. And above all, don't commit evil deeds, the end of which no man can see.

The hermit fell silent and stared fixedly at the passing water. Cuthbert wandered away, and left him sitting by the riverside.

In the morning the hermit broached the subject of Cuthbert's immediate future. "You have been here with me for many days now and I presume, my son, you don't want to remain here as a hermit? I think we should make arrangements for your return to the Christian host, who will, I hope, before long be at the gates of Jerusalem."

"I should like nothing better," Cuthbert said. "But I don't know the country and it seems impossible to travel through terrain infested with infidel war bands to reach the camp of King Richard."

"It won't be easy and not without danger," the hermit admitted. "As to the nature of the country, my dealings with the natives have been few and simple, so I know little about the land in between. Still, several Christian communities exist among the heathens. They're poor, and their faith may be suspected by their neighbors, but as they do no one any harm and carry on their worship in secret they're not much interfered with. There's one community among the hills between here and Jerusalem, and I have directions for finding it, together with a token which will secure you hospitality there. They will no doubt do their best to forward you to another station. When you approach the flat country where the armies are maneuvering you will have to trust to yourself."

Cuthbert became excited at the prospect of returning to an active life and the next evening, with many thanks for his kindness, he knelt before the aged hermit to receive his blessing.

With the instructions given him he had no difficulty in making his way through the barren mountains, until after some five hours' walk he found himself at a little village situated in a narrow valley. Going to the door of the largest hovel, he knocked and waited in some trepidation. A face wizened by decades of work under the harsh sun appeared hesitantly in the partly opened door. Bright brown eyes gazed in mild suspicion at Cuthbert. "I…" he began, and then fumbled for the rosette of peculiar beads the hermit had given him. He held it out.

The man's eyes widened in surprise and recognition. He said something unintelligible and then made a gesture of apology and switched to a creaky form of Frankish. "You are sent…?"

"From the hermit."

"Yes, come in, quickly now."

He didn't seem to need any explanation. "You seek a way to your people, yes? I help. In the morning. Now, come share some humble food."

In the morning the kindly man furnished Cuthbert with the sheepskin and short tunic which formed the dress of a shepherd, and dyed his exposed limbs and face a deep brown. Cuthbert went with his host, who journeyed with him to the next Christian community. The small hamlet consisted of only four huts built almost on the summit of a mountain. The inhabitants lived partly on the milk and cheese of their goats, and partly on the scanty vegetables which grew around the huts.

His welcome was as cordial as that of the night before, and the next morning, his former guide taking his leave, the peasant in whose house he had slept conducted him onward to a third place. This was the last station, and stood in a narrow gorge on the face of the hills looking down over the plain, beyond which Cuthbert could see in the far distance a faint line of dark blue sea.

This village was far more prosperous and well-to-do than the previous ones. Ghassan, the headman, seemed to be someone of local importance within the Muslim administration, while nevertheless clinging in secret to his Christian faith. He owned extensive vineyards and olive orchards, and three fine horses. He also spoke Frankish with some degree of fluency.

At considerable length Ghassan explained the state of the crusader army, which had moved some distance along the coast since Cuthbert had left it.

"It is exposed to constant attacks by the Saracens, who harass it in every way and permit the men no rest."

"But how go things?"

Ghassan shook his head sadly. "The high hopes raised by the defeat of Saladin's army at Arsuf are now deflated. It saddens me to say, but few now imagine that the Christians can force their way forward to Jerusalem."

A frown creased Cuthbert's brow. "As you say, hopes were high."

"After the great battle, your king left Jaffa in October to advance on the Holy City, but Saladin fortified the mountain passes and Richard had insufficient men to force his way through. It seemed that the French contingent would not support him in a frontal assault, although some say it was the nobles of Outremer—shame on their souls—who refused to save their own land. Instead the English retreated to Jaffa, then moved south to Ascalon and began rebuilding its defenses. There too, I have heard rumors that a great quarrel broke out between your king and the Archduke of Austria. You Franks," Ghassan rebuked sternly, "are a very fractious people."

"So what's happening right now?"

"It is said that King Richard has abandoned Jerusalem. The great portion of the crusaders' animals have died, the country is so eaten up by Saladin's hosts, and an advance on Jerusalem without a large baggage train would be next to impossible. Indeed, if the Christians were to get there, they would not be able to do anything without the aid of the heavy siege engines necessary for battering the walls or effecting an escalade. And these they do not have."

Cuthbert was aghast to hear of the probable failure of the Crusade, but the news only made him burn more strongly with eagerness to take his part again in the dangers and difficulties which beset the crusaders. Ghassan pointed out to him the extreme difficulty and danger of his crossing the enemy's lines, but at the same time offered to do all in his power to help him.

After two days' stay at the village, and discussing the pros and cons of all possible plans, he and his host agreed that his best chance would be in making a bold effort. Ghassan placed at his disposal one of his horses, together with clothes that would enable him to ride as an Arab emir of rank and station. To complete the picture Ghassan gave Cuthbert a spear—not as long as the Arabs' lances "but it will pass at a distance"— a short but very heavy mace, and a straight sword. A bag of dates hung at the saddle-bow. With the sincerest thanks to his protector, and with a promise that should the Christian host ever win their way to Jerusalem he would return Ghassan's beautiful Arabian stallion with ample payment, Cuthbert started on his perilous journey.

In keeping with its fine ancestry the horse, its glossy coat as black as charcoal, was a spirited one, and once he had descended the rocky paths of the coastal mountains to the plains below, Cuthbert rode along, exulting in his freedom and in once again possessing arms to defend himself should it be needed. His appearance was so similar to that of the horsemen who he continually passed that he attracted no attention to himself.

Through villages, and even through army bivouacs, Cuthbert rode fearlessly and arrived, without having once been accosted, near the main frontline camp of the Saracens. This extended for miles parallel to the sea. But at a distance of some three leagues beyond, he could see the white tents of the Christian army, and Cuthbert felt that the time of trial was now at hand.

He dismounted for an hour to allow his steed a rest, fed it with dates from his wallet, and gave it a drink of water at a small stream. With both man and beast refreshed, he remounted and rode briskly on as before. He passed unchallenged into the ranks of Saracen troops. Some rested under awnings, others trained in arms and reminded Cuthbert uncomfortably of Norman military disciplines. Astonishingly, he attracted no more notice than if he had been walking down a crowded street. He held his breath, but it seemed as though he would get away with it.

Without hesitation he passed through the tents and crossed the front perimeter as though on an important mission and with every right, and started across the open country. He saw bands of light cavalry here and there, some going, and some coming from the direction of the Christian camp. The Bedouin horse must have assumed that he was on his way to join some other band advancing on the crusaders. In any case, the passage of the solitary horseman excited no comment until he approached within about two leagues of the Christian camp.

There were now, so far as he could see, no enemies between him and the point he so longed to reach. *I've made it! Just one low-rising dune to pass—*

At the instant he rounded the low hillock he ran headlong into a squadron of Arab horsemen apparently spying for any movement in the Christian camp.

Cuthbert did not need to understand the Arabic shout—its command was universal.

"Halt!"

Chapter 16: Fight of Heroes

June to July 1192

Without hesitation Cuthbert dug his spurs in and the Arabian leapt forward like an arrow from an English longbow. Up to this point he had ridden at a gentle canter, but at the challenge the stallion made across the plain flat out. The startled Arabs whirled around in angry pursuit with wild yells of outrage.

They galloped at first some two hundred yards to his right—having surprised them as much as they alarmed him, he benefited from a considerable head start. For half a mile his pursuers failed to gain much, riding as they were parallel to his path. But now they closed in behind, and the nearest had made up some fifty yards. At his next snatched backward glance two of the better mounted had halved that gap.

His horse was now straining to its limit, and he felt that he could ask no more of the animal. He readied himself for a desperate fight should his pursuers overtake him. In another quarter of a mile they were breathing down his neck and an arrow whizzed by his ear. Half a mile ahead he saw riding toward him a squadron of Christian knights. *But they're still too far off for me to reach them in time.*

Cuthbert's only chance now was to turn and meet his pursuers. Most were bunched up and still about two hundred long paces behind, but not a great distance at galloping speed—which left him very little time to shake off the two chasers immediately on his tail.

A sharp sting in his calf from a wild arrow told him that time had run out and, checking his horse, he wheeled suddenly around. The leading Arabs were on him instantly, their wicked lances dipped for the kill. With the instinct born of training, Cuthbert reached for the short heavy mace hanging at his saddle-bow, and with a smoothly executed movement, whipped it up and threw it with all his force at the chest of the Arab approaching on his right.

The spear point was feet from his breast as he hurled the mace, but his aim went true and it struck the Saracen with the power to throw the man from his horse as if struck by a thunderbolt. At the same instant Cuthbert threw himself flat and buried his face in the stallion's lashing mane. The lance of the Arab attacking on his left passed harmlessly between his shoulders, tearing his clothes as it went. In an instant he wheeled in pursuit, and before the other could turn his own horse Cuthbert unsheathed his sword, spurred up behind the Arab, and ran him clean through above the hip.

The action had taken no more than a few breaths, but a desperate look back showed him that the rest of his foes were closing fast, almost obscured in the sandstorm of their dust trails. Wisdom being the better part of valor, Cuthbert turned and continued his flight toward the knights galloping his way. Seeing their quarry virtually in the arms of the Christian knights, the fight went out of the Saracens and a moment later they wheeled through a quarter-turn and rode away into the haze.

With a gasp of relief Cuthbert slowed down as he neared the line of charging knights. He saw bewilderment in their expressions at a conflict between what appeared to be three infidels. Then Cuthbert hullooed with excitement when he recognized the burly man at the head of the column, who had just drawn his long sword to defend himself from the mad emir galloping at him.

Cuthbert cried out. "My lord, my lord. Thank heaven I am safe with you again."

The Earl of Evesham lowered his blade.

"Am I mad," he rasped in astonishment, "or dreaming, or is this really Sir Cuthbert?"

"It is, sure enough," Cuthbert said. "Though I look more like a Bedouin than a Christian knight."

"My dear boy." The earl cantered up to his side and, with a long reach, he clasped a mailed hand around Cuthbert's neck. "We thought you dead. This is wonderful. How in heaven's name did you get away?"

Still struggling to get his breath back, Cuthbert filled in Sir Walter on the gist of his adventures, in between gasps and receiving congratulations from the assembled knights. Longer explanations had to wait. Approaching dust clouds announced a strong force of Turkish heavy cavalry bearing down on their exposed position.

"We have ventured too far from our lines to investigate the mystery now revealed. King Richard's strict orders are to avoid skirmishes except by his command." He reluctantly signed the others to return swiftly to the camp.

As delighted as he was to see his young protégé safely returned, the earl's joy was completely eclipsed by Cnut's reaction at seeing the dead come back to life in the guise of an Arab chieftain. Having ripped the lad he loved so well from his saddle it took several equally overjoyed archers to rescue Cuthbert from almost certain strangulation in the big Saxon's bear hug.

Order was only restored when the earl summoned the young knight to his tent, and a squire led off the fine Arabian stallion that had so bravely returned Cuthbert to the ranks of the Christian army.

"It's as though I've been one of the dead anyway because I haven't heard anything whatever of what's been going on in these months other than what Ghassan, my kind Christian host of the last three days, was able to tell me. And none of that sounded good, my lord."

"Nothing could have gone worse," the earl growled gloomily. "We've had nothing but disputes, arguments, and quarrels. First, the king fell out with Archduke Leopold of Austria."

"Ah, that Ghassan had heard, but not why. How did that happen?"

"For once the king was wholly in the wrong," Sir Walter said wryly. "We'd just taken Ascalon, and were hard at work fortifying the place. King Richard with his usual zeal, wanting to encourage the army, grabbed up some heavy stones and put them in place himself. The Archduke stood nearby with some of his knights. I wasn't actually present, but those who were say that haughty Leopold looked superciliously at Richard, laboring like a common serf. 'Why don't you get off your lazy ass and make a show of helping?' King Richard said in his usually robust but not particularly diplomatic language. Putting down his stones, he went up to the snooty Austrian and said, 'It would encourage the men, and show that this important work—which we're all engaged on—can be undertaken by all of us without putting us down.' To this the Archduke replied: 'Unlike you, I am not the son of a stonemason.'

"At which Richard, whose blood was no doubt boiling with rage at his arrogance, backhanded Leopold across the face. The swords on both sides came out faster than the whores at a May festival. Had hotter heads prevailed, there would have been a bloodbath there and then that would have delighted Saladin. As it was, some handy French nobles and Hospitallers calmed everyone down, and the Austrians simply withdrew from our camp. They sailed the next day for Acre, and presumably from there back to the Adriatic, but Richard has certainly made a very bad enemy there."

Sir Walter sighed and regarded Cuthbert from under furrowed brows in a stern countenance. "Next, the very complex politics of this kingdom created a situation. I can't get my poor Norman head around the wiles of Jerusalem. The maneuvering for power here makes the machinations of the Greek emperor's Byzantine court look like a ladies' sewing group by comparison. You may not know, but King Guy—a Lusignan—had only a thin cause by reason of marriage to call himself king. There are also Montforts, Champagnes, and Montferrats, all with claims. Since everyone considered Guy a spent force and wanted him gone—and Richard needed to make peace with at least some of his allies—he agreed to remove Guy from the throne. You remember, Guy had sworn fealty to Richard in Cyprus, so our king had the right.

"He then conferred the crown of Jerusalem on Conrad of Montferrat, Princess Isabella's second husband—oh, she's the daughter of the former King of Jerusalem, Almaric of Anjou, or Amaury, or whatever... are you following this?" Sir Walter asked suspiciously.

Cuthbert, chin cupped in his hands, nodded blithely and smiled encouragingly at his master.

"Hmm... well, no sooner had Richard done this than Conrad was mysteriously murdered before his coronation. He died from a draught of poison. No one's taken responsibility, or knows who did it. Some say he was assassinated by the men of Pisa because Conrad was allied to Genoa and had threatened to remove the Pisans' trading rights with Outremer. Others blame Henry of Champagne, who immediately married Isabella himself and became the new king. Still others say it was the jealousy of some of the knights of the Holy Orders. But be that as it may, Conrad of Montferrat lay dead, and the French, ever jealous of Richard's great popularity with the men, joined with the Germans and Austrians in accusing the king of ordering the murder.

"You can imagine that when this monstrous accusation—made by the French spokesman, Hugh of Burgundy, who had before this been an ally of the king's—came to the Lionheart's ears, he had hot words with him. And who could blame him? It's beyond all reason that a man whose faults stem from being too open should resort to stealth to free himself of the man he had just made king only a day or two before. Still, the consequences of his righteous outburst were unhappy, for Hugh upped sticks and returned to Acre with his Frenchmen... and we were left alone.

"Before this we had marched on Jerusalem. But the weather was so bad, and our train so insufficient to carry any siege engines, that we were forced to fall back again. King Richard advanced a second time, and struggled as far as the village of Bethany."

"Why, I passed through there, and it's only three miles from Jerusalem."

"I know," the earl muttered, "and many of us, climbing the hill in front, saw Jerusalem. But even then it was clear that we would have to retreat, and when we asked King Richard to come to the top of the hill to see the Holy City, he refused to do so, saying, 'No—those who are not worthy of conquering Jerusalem should not look at her.' Now we prepare to retrace our steps to Acre, and the king is negotiating a peace with Saladin."

"Then," Cuthbert said sadly, "all our hopes and efforts were in vain. We shed all this blood for nothing, and the great powers of Europe which started off so bravely to rescue the Holy Sepulchre have been thwarted, and must fall back before the army of the infidels."

"Partly before them, yes, and partly as the result of our own jealousies and passions. Had King Richard been a lesser man than he is, we might have conquered Jerusalem. But he's so extraordinary a warrior that his glory throws all others into the shade. He's a good general, perhaps the best in Europe, and if all he had done was lead men into battle, we would have surely secured the final victory. But unfortunately the man is also a knight-errant. Wherever there's danger, Richard plunges in. There are brave men in all the armies, but none who compares. He's the idol of the soldiers of every nation, as ready to rush to the rescue of a French or Austrian knight when pressed as to that of his own men. But the devotion which the whole army felt for him was as bitter as wormwood to the haughty Austrian and the indolent Frenchman. I was in the wrong months ago—King Philip's running off, which left Richard in supreme command, was in every way unfortunate."

On the day following this desultory conversation the English army departed Jaffa, leaving behind the Military Orders of Hospitallers and Templars to hold the coastal fragments of Outremer, still called— though quite erroneously—the Kingdom of Jerusalem. Cuthbert could hardly fail to notice the difference, not only in number but in bearing, from the splendid array which had left Acre months before.

Little glory could he discern in pennon or banner; the bright helms and shields were dinted, the chain mail rusted, and no one cared anything for a show of bravery.

The knights and men-at-arms were burned to chestnut by the sun and thin. Some seemed half the weight that they had been when they landed. Fatigue, hardship, and the heat had done their work. Disease had swept off vast numbers, far more than had the Saracens. But the remnant was still sufficiently formidable that the Saracens, although following at a distance in large numbers, dared not risk an attack in force on the column.

Some days after reaching Acre, the fleet admiral pronounced the ships ready and the king gave orders to embark the troops. Just as the lines of men were shuffling slowly forward onto the stone-laid wharf ready to board the ships, a small vessel entered the harbor in haste. It drew up to the shore, and a knight jumped down, shouting for King Richard. He was found superintending the loading of his horses, alongside the Earl of Evesham and his retinue.

"The Saracens, sire! The Saracens are besieging Jaffa, and the place will be lost unless assistance arrives immediately."

Typically, Richard started shouting orders, called for his squires and weapons, commandeered the nearest vessel, and leaped aboard. He shouted orders to his own knights, sergeants, and troops to follow him. As the seamen raised the sail, he was still leaning over the rail yelling orders to other commanders to bring down the troops with all possible speed, not to waste a moment. Within five hundred heartbeats of receiving the news he was en route for Jaffa.

The breathless speed with which Cuthbert found himself once again at sea had given him a new energy, which Richard wound up further. "Ah, my gallant young knight. I am very glad to see you with me. We'll have more fighting before we're done, and I know that suits your mood as well as my own."

The king's ship was far in advance of any others, when early the following morning it arrived off Jaffa.

"Your eyes are better than mine," the king said to Cuthbert. "Tell me what's the flag flying over the town."

"Sire, it is the crescent. We've arrived too late."

"By the Holy Cross, I won't allow it. If the place is taken, we will retake it."

As the vessel neared the beach a monk waded out into the water up to his shoulders to tell the king that the citadel still held out, and that even now the Saracens might be driven back. Richard immediately jumped overboard, followed by the knights and men-at-arms. The group rapidly waded ashore, and dashed dripping up to the open gate. Without pause, he threw himself on the infidels inside, who busy plundering, had failed to notice the ship's arrival.

The war cry of "St. George! St. George!" struck panic into the Saracens, and although no more than five knights and a handful of soldiers followed the king, they put to flight three thousand of the enemy. The men cut down any stragglers on the spot to leave tangled bloody bundles all over the city's cobbled streets. The king chased the Saracens out on to the plain and herded them before him like a wolf driving a flock of sheep. And then he returned triumphant to the city.

The day after this extraordinary recovery of Jaffa, more ships anchored and unloaded their troops. Combined with the city garrison, the English mustered about two thousand, a sufficient number to man the extensive walls. Saracen attacks in force began almost immediately and assaults on the walls were continuous and desperate.

King Richard loved battle in the open and hated being penned behind walls where all he could do was direct the operations of others. In the end impatience got the better of him and he announced a sortie. Only ten horses remained in the town, and Richard, mounting one, called for nine knights to ride with him. The little band of ten warriors charged down on the Saracen host and swept all before them. It was a stirring sight to see so small a group of horsemen slashing through a throng of infantry and cavalry, laying about them as though without a care in the world.

It was also foolhardy. At first beaten back in surprise, Saladin's men soon rallied, and the Christians had great difficulty in fighting their way back to the town. As the brave band neared the walls they turned to make a stand, and eight knights on foot sallied out from the town to join the hard-pressed mounted men. Cuthbert was among them, for his master the Earl of Evesham was one of the ten mounted knights with the king. The Saracen charge was so fierce it threatened to overwhelm the crusaders. The king ordered the riders to dismount, and with their horses in the center, the little cluster knelt with their lances braced on the ground, pointing out. Repeatedly the wild Muslim cavalry swept down on the hedgehog of sharp points but were unable to break their ranks. At last the king, seeing that the enemy were losing heart, ordered the knights to mount again and ride down their demoralized foes.

While this had been going on, another body of Saracens had made their way into Jaffa through another gate, and had begun to butcher the hapless inhabitants. Without an instant's delay Richard flew to their aid, with only two knights and a few archers, the rest too exhausted to move. Even these enemies were driven out from the town, with the king in furious pursuit.

One emir, distinguished by his stature and strength, dared to match himself against the king, and galloped at him. But with one blow Richard cleaved his great sword clean through the Arab's torso, severing his head, still attached to his right shoulder and arm, from his neck.

Then—having routed the Saracens single-handed—he galloped back through their scatter to the aid of the clustered knights who had remained on the defensive at the first gate. These were sinking with fatigue and wounds, but King Richard opened a way around them by slaying numbers of the enemy, and then charged magnificently alone into the midst of the Muslim host until he was lost to the sight of his companions. There was not one Christian who thought to ever see their king again, but then a great eruption of men revealed him laying the enemy to waste as king and horse, streaming gore, but themselves unharmed, returned.

This extraordinary feat of arms broke the heart of the Saracen attack, and Saladin withdrew as the day came to a close.

Cuthbert marveled at the sight of Richard's hand glued with blood to the handle of his battle-axe. All heard the retreating cries of the Saracens. "*Malek-Rik*," they shouted—"terrible king."

The success was glorious. The aftermath was not. Many were wounded, some mortally, and among their number, to Cuthbert's terrible grief, was his friend and patron, Sir Walter, the Earl of Evesham. After removing his hauberk, the king hurried to his tent.

"The glory of this day is marred for me," he said to the wounded knight, "if I am to lose you, Sir Walter."

"I fear I've not long, sire." The dying earl's words grated through hard-fought for breaths. "But I'm glad to have seen this day, for I never thought to witness such feats as your Majesty performed. I... know the Holy Sepulchre remains in infidel hands, but surely no disgrace has fallen on English arms... indeed, we have accrued great glory. Whatever may be said of the Great Crusade, it will be said by all men and for all time that had the princes and soldiers of other nations done... as your Majesty and your followers have done, Jerusalem would have fallen into our hands within a month of our putting foot to soil of the Holy Land."

Sir Walter gave a shallow hacking cough, and Cuthbert, kneeling at his side, wiped the blood-smeared spittle from the corner of the earl's lips.

"Sire," the earl went on weakly, "I have a favor to beg."

"You have but to name it, Sir Walter, and it is yours."

"Sir Cuthbert is like a son to me... by affection it's as close as though he were my own. I have no male heirs, my daughter is still young and will now be a royal ward. I ask your Majesty to give her in marriage, when the time comes, to Sir Cuthbert de Lance. They knew each other as children, and the union will bring happiness to both, as well as strength and protection to her... And one last... if it might be, I should be grateful if you would gift to him... my title, my dignity, and my fief."

"I will do so," the king said. "When your eyes are closed, Sir Walter, Sir Cuthbert de Lance shall be Earl of Evesham and, when the time comes, husband of your daughter."

Cuthbert was too overwhelmed with grief to feel a shadow of exaltation at the king's gracious promise. Although, even then, a thought of future happiness in the care of the fair young lady Margaret crossed his mind. For the last time the king gave his hand to his faithful servant, who pressed it to his lips, and a few minutes afterward gruff Sir Walter, who had so helped change Cuthbert's life, breathed his last.

Chapter 17: Blowing Up a Storm

October to December 1192

Saladin's courage in battle matched that of his great enemy, and his chivalry was no less than that expected of a Christian knight. From his Muslim foe, King Richard received more kindness than he had found among some of his fellow Crusade leaders. His tremendous exertions had taken their toll, and he suffered from fevers at short intervals and his illnesses, among other matters, speeded up negotiations with the sultan.

"I can't continue a Holy Crusade alone. England can't carry this burden with the slender means we now have at our disposal," he told his council of barons and knights. "And there are other pressing concerns." He waved a parchment in the air. "My mother urges me to return to prevent my brother John usurping my throne."

There was a combined gasp from those present, but Richard waved them down impatiently.

"Come now, sirs, we all know how the Regent thinks of me and it's no secret how I feel about the loathsome little turd. He's conspiring against me with Philip of France and has already assumed all but the title of king. Saladin wants peace. His wild troops want, for the most part, to return to their homes as much as we do. Now's the moment to make a peace that will benefit both sides."

It was true. *Malek-Rik*'s miraculous powers had lowered their spirit and made them eager to be away—Turks, Moors, Bedouins, Nubians, Arabs, Syrian Saracens, and Egyptian *mamluk* slave-soldiers, all desired at least a period of peace. Therefore Saladin consented to the terms Richard proposed. By these, the Christians would surrender Ascalon, but were to keep Jaffa, Tyre, and the fortresses and land along the coast in between. All hostilities were to be suspended on both sides for the space of three years, three months, three weeks, and three days.

As Cuthbert observed, between the sultan and the king admiration, even a cautious friendship, had developed. The two valiant leaders recognized each other's great qualities. Several times during the campaign, when either had been ill, the other had sent gifts of medicine and fruit.

At a final audience Richard promised Saladin to return after the truce with a larger army and accomplish the rescue of Jerusalem. The sultan responded that it appeared that valor alone was not sufficient to conquer in the Holy Land, but that if Jerusalem were to fall into the hands of the Christians, it could fall into no worthier hands than those of *Malek-Rik*.

On October 9, 1192, Richard Coeur de Lion left Palestine. Two weeks after sailing, a storm suddenly blew up and scattered the fleet in various directions. The ship with Queen Berengaria aboard was carried to the foot of Italy and arrived safely in Sicily, but that in which King Richard sailed went missing, and none of his fellow-voyagers knew what had become of him. Along with the king, Sir Cuthbert was also lost.

The tempest drove their cog up into the Ionian Sea. As the storm abated, the ship was blown onto the island of Corfu. All reached the shore safely with little but their dignity damaged, and King Richard then hired a small vessel to take his reduced party farther up the Dalmatian coast to Zadar. This was the port from which the Austrian crusaders had sailed—and returned—and lay under Austrian dominion, so it was no safe place for Englishmen.

The king had with him now only two of his knights, Baldwin of Béthune and Cuthbert of Evesham. Cnut was with his feudal lord—which, as Earl of Evesham, Cuthbert had become—and four of the English archers.

In a miserable little room of an inn at Zadar Richard addressed his reduced retinue. "My lords, men, I'm in deep trouble. I'm surrounded by enemies and my brother's scheming to take my place on the throne of England. Philip, whose twisted mind is far better at intrigue than at leading armies in the field, is certainly in league with him."

He paused briefly to draw a breath. "And let's not forget that the German Emperor Henry has laid claim to the south of Italy, so there's no safe haven for me there. He's closely related to both the Archduke Leopold—who hates me for that unwise but oh so satisfying blow to his face at Ascalon—and Conrad of Montferrat, who I made King of Jerusalem before his murder. That ought to be enough, but no… Conrad's numerous friends among the petty nobles of Austria and Germany spread far and wide the lie that it was by my hand that Conrad was murdered."

Cuthbert had never seen his king brought so low.

"Never has a poor king had so many enemies, and few have ever had so small a following as I have now. What do you think I should do? If I can reach Saxony, my brother-in-law Duke Henry will help me for the sake of his wife, my sister Matilda—not to mention that he loathes Philip of France. But it's a hell of a journey through enemy country. I've no funds to hire a ship, and if I did, with the seas so full of my enemies' vessels, it wouldn't be a safe voyage. No, it must be overland."

"Surely," Cuthbert protested, "no ruler would shame themselves by detaining your Majesty on your way from the Holy Land. You are under the Pope's protection. If I were in your place, I would proclaim myself loudly, mount my horse, unfurl my banner, and ride openly on."

At least twice Cuthbert's age, Sir Baldwin spoke up gently. "With respect, Sir Cuthbert, I think that you overrate the chivalry of his Majesty's adversaries. If we'd landed in France, Philip—perhaps— would hesitate to seize the King, but these petty Austrian and German princelings have no idea of true honor. They're coarse, brutal, and though they may adopt the trappings of knighthood, its real spirit has never sunk in. If friends of Leopold or Conrad get their hands on the King, they'll make capital of the advantage to the end degree."

Cuthbert frowned. "But Henry's the Holy Roman Emperor. He must uphold the sacred trust of the Crusade and Pope Celestine's promise of free travel for those who took up the cross?"

"Pah!" the usually mild-manned Sir Baldwin spat, "I wouldn't trust even their emperor. He's in league with Philip of France. No, young Sir Cuthbert, the course you advise is perfectly in tune with the King's spirit, but it would be madness to judge other people's nobility by his own. I should recommend, if I may sire, that you assume a false identity, and that we travel in small groups so as not to attract attention, each of us making our way to England as best as we can."

Silence fell for a while as everyone digested this advice, and then Richard sighed. "You're right, Sir Baldwin. There's little or no chivalry among these swinish lords. You accompany me. Not that I place your loyalty and friendship any lower than Sir Baldwin's, Sir Cuthbert," he observed kindly, noticing a look of disappointment Cuthbert could not keep from his face, "but he is the elder and the more versed in European travel."

He stood finally, and going to Cuthbert, placed a hand on his shoulder. "You will be facing dangers enough of your own, especially because your brave follower, Cnut, speaks no other language than his own, and your archers will be hard to pass as any other than what they are. You, Sir Cuthbert, must be my messenger to England, if you get there before me. Tell Queen Eleanor and Queen Berengaria where you left me, and that if I don't come home I've fallen into the hands of one or other of my bitter foes. You must rouse them to hold England for me against my brother John, and, if needs be, to move the Pope and the sovereigns of Europe to free me from the hands of my enemies. Should a ransom be needed, I'm sure the people of England won't begrudge me their goods for my release.

"Meanwhile," he added, removing from his neck a gold chain and breaking it with his strong fingers into five fragments, "that's for you, Cnut and for your four archers, in remembrance of King Richard." He smiled briefly. "Spend it wisely—it's my last."

Once Richard and Sir Baldwin had departed, Cuthbert spoke to his followers.

"We'd better hang around here for a few days. If we're arrested, the news that some Englishmen have been captured making their way north from Zadar will spread rapidly, and may cause the king's enemies to be on the lookout for him. The news that he's missing is bound to spread rapidly throughout Europe, and will alert those who bear him a grudge to search for him."

They waited ten days at Zadar before hiring a small boat to take them thirty miles farther along the coast. Cnut garbed himself as a palmer—a pilgrim returning from the Holy Land, complete with his piece of desiccated palm frond—hoping that no one would bother questioning him because of his holy vow of silence. On his surcoat and shield Cuthbert changed the English white cross on a red square for the red cross of a French knight. The archers grumblingly followed suit.

"Right," Cuthbert informed the others, "we cross Istria and make our way to Verona, from there we go via Trent and the Brenner Pass through the Tyrol into Bavaria. From there on we're in friendly territory and should find help from Saxony to reach Brabant. I'm going to need a horse to make the bluff work, but I can sell some of the jewels I collected at the storming of Acre, and use the proceeds to purchase a destrier."

"But if your story is that you're a French knight, wouldn't you just cross Italy and enter France directly?"

"You make a sound point, Cnut. I shall say I'm a noble crusader of Hainault. That's well to the north, so it's logical that I would travel through Austria as the shortest way home, and besides, we definitely don't want to enter France at any cost."

With a little care with his accent, he hoped his Norman-French would fit in with the fiction. The greatest difficulty would be with the archers… but he saw no way around that problem.

The little group set off and made easy stages up into Istria and around the top of the Adriatic toward Verona. They had little fear of any trouble in passing through the north of Italy, for this was neutral ground, where knights of all nations met, and where, neither as an English nor a French crusader, would he and his retinue attract attention.

The journey across the plains north of the Po valley took many days at the walking pace of the men. The archers continued to complain at the change in the color of the cross on their jerkins but Cnut put a stop to their grumbles. "Would you prefer to run a greater risk under our true colors than to pretend we belong to any other nationality?"

On their way they stopped at Padua. In looking at the splendor of this Italian city Cuthbert felt that by the polite manners of its people and the wonder of its university, which was even then famous, how far in advance were those stately cities of Italy to anything he knew in England.

From Padua they went on to Verona, marveling at the richness of the country, but the Saxon archers found something else to moan about. The flatness of the plain made it as bad as marching in the Holy Land, they claimed. On their right the slopes of the Alps, thickly clad with forests, reached down nearly to the road, and Cuthbert assured them that before long they would have plenty of climbing to do. At Verona they tarried again, and stared open-mouthed at the massive ancient Roman buildings, including the great amphitheater.

At Verona, they turned their back on the flatlands of Lombardy, and entered the valley of the Adige.

So far, so good. No one had stopped them, or become curious, which was not surprising. So many crusaders were on their way home, many in a tattered condition, that the somewhat shabby Englishmen passed by unnoticed. But they were now leaving Italy and entering a country where German was spoken. Trent was an important city, the meeting place of Italy and Austria-Germany. Both tongues were spoken there, but while Italian was most common, the customs, manners, and mode of thought of the people belonged to those of the mountaineers of the Tyrol, rather than of the plains.

"You are choosing a stormy time," the landlord of the hostelry where they put up told Cuthbert. "Winter's coming on and storms sweep across the passes with terrible violence. At the last village you come to up the valley—Barbiano—you'd better hire a guide. Believe me, if a blizzard blows in when you're on the passes, the path will vanish under snow, and nothing will remain but a miserable death. By daylight the road's good. It's been cut with much trouble and loaded mules can pass over without difficulty. Poles stick up at short distances to mark the way when the snow covers it. But when the snowstorms sweep across the mountains, it's impossible to see ten paces ahead. Leave the path and you're lost."

Cuthbert sipped with pleasure at a fine Veneto. Wine supplies had run out long ago in Outremer. "But I suppose that even in winter travelers cross the pass?"

"They do, sir. The road's open in winter as in summer, although, of course, the dangers are greater—like the wolves. You'll find it hard work to defend your lives against a pack. Still, it's vital to trade in these parts, so a lot's been done to make the way as safe as possible. That's why you'll come across stone shelters at every league where wayfarers can find protection from storm or wolf packs… or bears, for there are also plenty of those in the forests."

Thanking the man for his advice, Cuthbert acted on other useful hints for stragglers returning from the heat of Outremer and bought goat-skin cloaks with hoods to pull over their heads to shield them from the cold.

After two days' journey they noticed how the road's steepness slowed their pace and it wound in increasingly serpentine bends.

Three further days' trudging and they arrived at the village the innkeeper in Trent had mentioned. Here Cuthbert secured the services of a guide.

Now the ascent was long and difficult, and in spite of what the innkeeper had said about the road's quality, it really was little more than a path. In places the way became so precipitous Cuthbert had to dismount and lead his horse, whose hoofs slipped on the smooth rock. On occasion a false step would have thrown them down many hundreds of feet into the valley below, so Cuthbert judged it safer to trust himself to his own feet. By nightfall of the first day they had reached a very considerable height, and stopped at one of the small refuges.

The guide only spoke a strange dialect of north Italian, which Cuthbert could not follow, but the man's gestures on the following morning were eloquent enough for him to understand, "I don't like the look of the weather either," he agreed. The man's expression matched that of the lowering dawn sky. Cuthbert, feeling his own powerlessness in a situation so novel to him, felt serious misgivings at the prospect.

As they continued to climb, the scenery grew more barren and wild. On all sides crags and mountain tops covered with snow glistened in the sun that had banished the earlier thick cloud. The woods near the path were free of snow, but higher up they rose black above the white ground. The wind blew keenly and everyone was thankful for their warm cloaks, although even with the protection of these they found the cold bitter during the nights.

"I don't like this country," Cnut grumbled. "We moaned about the heat of Palestine, but I'd rather march across the sand there than in this inhospitable frozen region. The woods look as if they might contain ghosts. There's a silence which seems unnatural, and my courage, like the warmth of my body, is oozing out through my fingers, my ears, and my nose."

Cuthbert laughed. "I've no doubt that your courage will return much quicker than the warmth. A brisk walk will set you right again and banish the heebie-jeebies. Tonight we'll be at the highest point and tomorrow begin the descent into the Tyrol and Austria."

All day the men walked steadily on. The guide kept looking up apprehensively at the sky and—although in the earlier part of the day Cuthbert's inexperienced eye saw nothing to cause any concern—toward the afternoon the scene changed. Light clouds gathered to shut the mountain peaks from view. Wind moaned between the gorges and occasionally forceful gusts made it hard to keep their feet under them. The sky became overcast and tiny specks of hard snow, driven along on the blast, made their faces smart by the force with which they struck the bare skin.

"It hardly needs our guide's expression," Cuthbert muttered to himself, "to tell us that a storm is imminent, and he's worried." He turned to a miserable looking Cnut. "I don't know about you, but I feel better now the wind is blowing and the silence is broken, than at the dead stillness we had this morning."

Cnut sounded unconvinced. "Really?"

"After all, I can't see why a snowstorm should be more terrible than a sandstorm, and we've faced those before now."

Cnut just grunted.

The snow fell thicker and faster, until at last the whole air seemed full of it, and it was with difficulty that they could stagger forward. Where the path led across open places the wind swept away the snow as fast as it fell, but in the hollows it covered the track thigh deep. Cuthbert began to understand the emphasis his host in Trent had placed on the danger of losing the road. The party plodded along in sullen silence, each saving his breath for walking.

The guide kept in the lead. He used the greatest caution wherever the path vanished under the snow and sometimes even sounded with his iron-shod staff to be sure that they were on the level rock. In spite of his warm cloak Cuthbert was chilled to the bone and his horse struggled to stay safely on its feet. Cnut and the archers lagged behind.

"You must keep together, lads," Cuthbert shouted. "I've heard that in these mountains when sleepiness overpowers the journeyer, death soon follows."

At times the gale's violence forced them to shelter under rock overhangs until the fury of the gusts eased. At every dragging footstep Cuthbert eagerly looked out for the next refuge. At last they reached one. The guide went straight in. He had hoped to get to one father on but it would have been madness to attempt to go on in the face of the blizzard.

The last merchants to use the shelter had left some wood, but not enough to last the night, so Cnut and the archers, feeling that life depended on a good fire being kept up, set to with a will to cut down shrubs and branches growing in the vicinity. In half an hour a huge fire blazed in the refuge and, as the warmth thawed their limbs, their tongues loosened up, and a profound feeling of comfort prevailed.

"If this is mountaineering, my lord," Cnut said, "I can do without it. I trust that it will never be my misfortune to go into the hills again. How long do the storms last here? I've bellyached all the way up at the load of provisions the guide insisted we each carry. If it were only a three-day journey before we reached a village on the other side, I wondered why he insisted on our taking food enough to last us for at least a week, if not two."

"You're pleased now, Cnut." Cuthbert clapped his friend's back.

"I am. If this storm goes on, we're going to be stuck here for so long as it continues."

Cuthbert led his horse inside for the night. "It will be death for it to remain outside."

With the warmth soaking blissfully into their bones, all the company began to doze.

"What was that?" Cnut said, suddenly raising his head from his knees, all thought of sleep banished.

They all looked up with heads cocked. A second distant howl

echoed eerily between lulls in the storm. The guide muttered some word, which meant nothing to Cuthbert. He said to Cnut, "I think that's a wolf. Just as well we're safe in here. It's good solid stone and I doubt even the most ravenous beasts could get in."

Cnut spat contemptuously. "Wolves are no bigger than dogs. I've heard my grandfather say that his father shot one in the forest, and that it was no bigger than a hound. We ought to make short work of them."

"I don't know." Cuthbert frowned. "I've also heard tales of these beasts and they sound like formidable opponents. They hunt in packs, and are so ferocious that they will attack parties of travelers. Many have perished miserably, horses and men, and nothing but their swords and portions of their saddles have remained to tell where the battle was fought."

Before long, a much closer baying lament rang out, and soon the keening of great numbers of animals succeeded the solitary call. From the sound, these speedily surrounded the hut, and so fierce were their cries that Cnut changed his opinion as to the ease with which they could be defeated.

"Saracens hold no fear for you, yet you cower at a pack of 'big dogs,' Cnut?"

The Saxon snorted. "I allow that I'd rather face an army of Saracens than a troop of these ill-tempered beasts."

The horse trembled in every limb at the sound of the wolves' hunger and a lather of fear soon covered his coat. Cnut ducked violently in reaction when there came a trampling on the stone shingles of the roof. Through the open slits of the windows, which some travelers before them had stuffed with straw, they could hear the fierce breathing and snorting of the savage creatures, who scratched and tore to make an entrance.

The Saxons all turned their faces fearfully in Cuthbert's direction. "What, my lord, do we do now? I could bite my tongue for what I said earlier. These spawn of Satan are going to get in."

Chapter 18: Sentenced to Death

Austria, December 1192

Groans from the roof timbers indicated the weight of wolves on the roof was about to bring it down.

"Men, to your bows," Cuthbert said with urgency. "Cnut, shoot through the loopholes. If we can't drive them back before that lot caves in, we'll be finished."

The storm had quieted down and even though the night was dark, the black, bristly bodies were visible against the white snow and the archers shot several. To everyone's disgust, their comrades immediately pounced on those killed and tore the corpses to pieces. This savagery only added to the horror which those inside felt, though it did bring down the wolves from the shelter's roof to join in the feral feast, which was a relief.

"But there are too many," Cnut observed. "They'll soon return their attention to us."

Suddenly there was a pause in the baying around the hut. Cnut peered through a narrow window slit. "Well, I'll be damned. The pack's hared off along the path back the way we came."

Cuthbert scrunched his eyebrows together. "What's got into them, I wonder?"

The answer came almost immediately—a loud shout echoed along the pass, followed by a frenzy of snarls.

"My God! Someone else is under attack. We can't stay in here while another man is torn to pieces by these horrors. Follow me."

In spite of the guide's angry entreaties at this mad knight's impetuosity, Cuthbert flung the door open and his men rushed out into the night after their leader. With the slightly improved visibility they had no difficulty in making their way back along the track toward the first bend in the path. And there, on rounding the projecting rock, Cuthbert and Cnut saw a seething mass of wolves almost smothering a figure who stood with his back to the rock face.

The archers loosed two or three arrows apiece as they covered the ground toward the pack and then, slinging bows, drew swords, while Cuthbert took up his heavy battle-axe. With a shout of encouragement the Englishmen sprang forward, and in a few moments were in the thick of the savage animals, who quick as a flick of the head turned their rage against them. However, the power of the archers' charge carried them through to the figure of a knight in full mail, leaning exhausted against the rock. A few paces back, his horse whinnied in terror. Wolves surrounded the poor animal, leapt at its throat, snapped at its legs, and began to rend and tear it apart.

The archers' thick cloaks stood them in good stead against the animals' razor teeth. They stood in a tight group, backs to the rock, and hewed and cut vigorously at their assailants. But no matter how many covered the snow at their feet, heads cleaved in by axe and sword blows, their numbers never seemed to reduce. As fast as those in front fell, fresh ones sprang forward. Cuthbert saw that in spite of the bravery and strength of his men, their situation was becoming hazardous. They were all slumping, as exhausted as the knight they had come to rescue. There could only be one possible outcome to the unequal battle. The nonstop snarling, barking, howling, snapping jaws, slavering needle-pointed teeth set in pulled back snouts, and the evil red eyes of the wolves became almost mesmerizing.

Amid this chaos no one felt the great tremor that ran through the mountain. Their ravenous opponents did though. For a moment the attack hesitated and a gust of wind, stronger than they had yet experienced, swept along the gorge. The wolves had to crouch on their stomachs to prevent themselves being hurled by its fury into the ravine below. Then, even above the rising storm, a deep roar hammered at their ears. It boomed monstrously and grew in

183

volume. The rock beneath and behind them began to shudder like a live animal in its death throes. The wolves, now struck with terror, scattered either way along the path as fast as they could run.

"What's this?" Cnut shouted. "The earth quakes!"

"Press back against the rock face," Cuthbert cried.

A moment later, from above, a mighty mass of rock and snow poured over in a cascade, with a roaring so loud it stunned the senses. For a seeming age the deluge continued. Then, as suddenly as it had begun, it ceased, and a deathly silence reigned over the pass.

Cuthbert was the first to stand. "I think it's safe to get up. The innkeeper at Trent said these cataclysmic falls are called avalanches. The overhanging rock here saved us. We've had a narrow escape indeed."

By this time the knight whom they had rescued had recovered enough to speak and offered his deepest thanks to those who had come in the nick of time.

"I was about done in," he said. "It was only my finest Milan mail and leggings that saved me, though I feel dreadfully bruised underneath it."

"The refuge is near at hand," Cuthbert said. "It's as well we heard your voice. I'm sorry that your horse has been killed. Come on, shelter from the wind is just around this corner… that is, if it's still there."

Apart from a newly narrowed piece about four feet wide, the whole of the road had been carried away. Looking upward, they saw that the forest had been scrubbed clear. Not a tree remained in a wide swathe as far as could be seen. The great boulders which had strewn the mountainside, some as large as houses, had been swept away like straws before the rush of snow, and for a moment Cuthbert feared that the refuge had also been destroyed.

Turning the corner, however, he saw with relief that the limits of the avalanche had not extended so far. As the still-fuming guide later conveyed, the refuges were so placed as to be sheltered by overhanging cliffs from any catastrophe of this kind. They found their man on his knees, muttering his prayers in front of a cross on the floor he had made from two sticks intended for the fire laid crosswise. He could hardly believe his eyes when they entered, so convinced was he that they had all been eaten.

The rescued knight removed helm and mail coif to reveal a darkly handsome man of about twenty-five years. In a Germanic-sounding Frankish, he introduced himself to his rescuers. "I am Count Ernst von Kornstein. To whom do I owe my life?"

Cuthbert also pulled off his coif, shook the tangles from his hair and decided on the spot to trust a knight found in such dire circumstances. "In spite of my red cross I am Sir Cuthbert, Earl of Evesham."

The count's eyebrows popped up in surprise. "An Englishman."

"I'm returning from the Crusade with my followers and we were wrecked off Dalmatia. With no alternative but this route, we thought it best to go in disguise. But I instinctively felt I could tell you the truth."

"You're right," the young knight replied. "The people of these parts dislike your countrymen. But you saved my life when I'd given myself up for lost. My sword and life are at your disposal."

Von Kornstein now took in Cuthbert's appearance more closely, and again expressed his surprise. "You're very young to have gained an earldom. You scarcely look eighteen, although, obviously, you are older."

"No," Cuthbert answered with a smile, "I'm a month short of eighteen, but I've had the good fortune to attract the notice of King Richard, and to have received the knighthood from his sword."

"Well, that's something indeed," von Kornstein said, looking suitably impressed. "King Richard, who resembles the heroes of romance rather than a Christian king, is the worthiest knight in Christendom… even though he is less than popular in these parts."

"He's my lord and master," Cuthbert replied hotly. "I would give my life for his. He's the kindest and best of masters. It's true that he can't stomach opposition, but only because his own bravery and eagerness make him hateful to the laziness and cowardice of others."

The Austrian raised hands in his defense before backing to the wall and squatting down beside one of the archers. "Peace," he said with a broad smile. "Now I think I could sleep for a week."

For four days the gale raged, imprisoning the company in the refuge. On the fifth, the wind's force dropped, and the snow stopped falling. They were forced to take the door—which swung outward—off its hinges to open it, for the snow had piled up so high that the chimney alone of the hut remained above its pristine surface.

The archers set to work and with great difficulty cleared a way out. With the guide taking the lead, they started out, first climbing for an hour before cresting the top of the pass and commencing the long downward slope. The air was still and cold, the sky a deep indigo blue, which seemed even darker in contrast with the snow's whiteness. At times they had to struggle chest-deep through drifts, but in many places the wind had swept the path clear. Where the snow lay deepest, the tops of the posts still showed and directed their way. The party was obliged to travel slowly so another three days passed before they gained the first hamlet clinging to the northern slopes of the mountains.

"What are your plans?" von Kornstein asked Cuthbert that night, as they sat by the fire of the tiny hostelry. "I must warn you that Innsbruck—the first major town you'll come to—is specially hostile to the English. Its master is closely related to Conrad of Montferrat, who was killed by order of your king."

"Sir Ernst that's a lie," Cuthbert hissed angrily. "King Richard made Conrad King of Jerusalem on the publicly stated grounds that—even though he didn't like the man—he thought him the fittest of the candidates to rule well. Anyway, Richard would never be so cowardly as to have a man secretly murdered—he'd take off his head in open battle if he wanted him dead."

"I don't doubt you, since you tell me," the knight said quickly. "But the people here have it in their minds that he did, and it will be hard to get them to change their opinion, however faulty it might be. So, you must remain as a French knight while passing through the region. Another week's travel will get you into Saxony's sphere of influence and there, as you know, you'll be safe. But I couldn't answer for your life if anyone here discovers you are English."

"Can you help us?"

"Certainly, my dear Sir Cuthbert, I will go with you into Innsbruck, where I'm well known, and introduce you as a French knight to divert any suspicion. If you wish, I'll accompany you to the borders of Bavaria."

"That's kind of you, but I must find a means of replenishing the travel purse. I still have some jewels taken at Acre—"

"No, no, you can't try to exchange your booty, it will attract too much interest. You must let me fill your pocket. I know that when you return home, you will hand over the sum I give you to a holy shrine in my name, and so pay me back that way."

Cuthbert accepted the offer and they went on their way the following morning. He gave the reins of his horse to one of the archers so he could walk alongside Sir Ernst to exchange adventures. Another long day's march brought them down to Innsbruck.

Cuthbert wanted to leave as soon as possible, but Sir Ernst cautioned him to wait until after a big festival in two days' time. "A great fete is planned to celebrate the marriage of Baron Friedrich von Habsburg's daughter. As I said, he is—or was—related to Conrad of Montferrat. As the master of Innsbruck he has made it known that it will be an insult to his honor if any recently arrived should be caught leaving before the ceremony. Attention I'm sure you want to avoid."

Enormous preparations had been made—masques and pageants of various kinds invented, and the whole townspeople, dressed in their Tyrolean holiday attire, gathered in the streets. In spite of the wisdom of remaining quietly inside their large inn, Cuthbert agreed to go out with his little band of retainers to watch the passing carnival.

At the cavalcade's head marched a large detachment of knights and mounted men-at-arms, with banners bright and their horse trappings agleam. Then rode the bridegroom, with the bride carried in a litter by his side. After this came several allegorical carnival floats. One of these featured the figure of a knight bearing Austria's arms. Underneath his feet, on the car, lay a prone man clad in a banner with the three lions representing England, Normandy, and Aquitaine clearly visible. The Austrian knight stood with his foot on this vanquished figure.

This piece of satire greatly pleased the huge crowd who burst into spontaneous cheers and hand clapping. But the representation of England being dishonored by Austria had a very different effect on the returning crusaders. Cuthbert clenched his teeth and grasped his sword hilt angrily, but had the sense to calm down and ignore the insult. Not so Cnut. Furious at the slur to his royal master's standard, he thrust through the ranks of the crowd, jumped onto the car and, with a huge blow of his fist, knocked the figure representing Austria into the road. He lifted the flag of England and held it aloft.

A massed shout of indignation erupted as the infuriated crowd rushed forward. Cnut nimbly jumped down, rejoined his comrades, and pushed through those who barred their way. In a flash, the English archers darted down a side street and disappeared.

Cuthbert, a bit stunned for a moment by Cnut's understandable but undesirable action, had by then drawn his sword to join the archers. In the milling crowd, however, he became separated from his men, and before he could tear himself from the hands of the citizens who grabbed hold of him, the men-at-arms accompanying the procession surrounded him. They dragged him away to the castle. Even as Cuthbert felt satisfaction that his followers had escaped, he feared that alone, and unfamiliar with the language, they would find it difficult to escape. For himself, he had little hope. What could he expect from a baron who hated the English even before this massive insult to his dignity and his daughter's wedding?

His worst expectations were fulfilled.

"Who the hell are you, sir?" the Austrian noble shouted in a spray of spittle. "Who dares to disturb the marriage procession and to insult the standard of Henry, the emperor my master?"

"The Earl of Evesham," Cuthbert retorted stoutly. *The die is cast. I'll be damned if cower in front of this jumped up pig.* "I am returning home from the Holy Land. As a crusader I am—at the Pope's word—protected from all interruption. My retainer's actions may have been rash, but he was justified by the insult offered to England and my king. Not a knight gathered here would have acted differently if England had offered such an insult to Austria. I'm ready to do battle in the lists with any man who chooses to say that the deed was a foul or improper one. In the Holy Land, Austrians and English fought side by side, so it's outrageous to me that on my return, a guest in the country of the archduke and emperor, I should find myself treated as an enemy, and see the insignia of King Richard exposed to insult and derision by the burghers of this city."

As Cuthbert spoke, he threw down his mailed glove and several of the knights present stepped forward to pick it up. The baron, however, waved them back.

"There's no question of honorable combat. This is a follower of the murderer of my good cousin of Montferrat, who died under the hands of assassins set on him by Richard of England."

"It is false," Cuthbert shouted. "That's a foul lie, and I will maintain that it is with my life."

The baron stared back icily through eyes narrowed to slits. "Your life is already forfeit, both by your connection with Richard of England and as the insulter of Austria's arms. Tomorrow at noon you will be beheaded in the great square in front of my castle."

"A coward's answer—"

"Take him away!"

Without another word Cuthbert was dragged off to a cell and thrown roughly to the floor to brood moodily over the events of the day, until nightfall. He had no doubt that his sentence would be carried out, but his anxiety was rather for his followers than for himself. He feared that the hotheads would try something stupid and die doing so, without the possibility of assisting him.

Cuthbert blinked at the sun's wintry glare after the darkness of his cell. The main gate of the castle formed the back of the square, with a wing of the fortress closing the second side. Opposite, a wall of the city formed the third side, and the fourth opened onto a city street. Citizens densely packed this side of the square, buzzing their excitement, while men-at-arms and knights slowly gathered behind a platform erected in the middle. On this sat a beheading block, and by its side stood the headsman, leaning nonchalantly on the long handle of his axe.

A thrill of pleasure ran through the massed crowd at the first sight of Cuthbert, all eagerly anticipating the moment when the executioner's blade would separate the young Englishman's head from his insolent body. Cuthbert thought only of his men, and was pleased to see no sign of them, hoping that this meant they had avoided capture during the night.

As Cuthbert was led forward, Ernst von Kornstein confronted the baron and begged for the young earl's life. He related how the Englishman had saved him on the Brenner Pass.

The baron frowned heavily. "I wouldn't care if he had saved the life of every noble in Austria," he roared, "he would still die. Every Englishman who falls into my hands will pay for the murder of my cousin."

"My lord baron," said Sir Ernst, drawing himself up, "I renounce all allegiance to you, and will lay the case before the emperor. This is an outrage. This noble youth has thrown down the glove and challenged your knights, and I'm equally ready to do battle in his cause."

Von Habsburg hissed in fury and went purple in the face. He stepped up until his nose almost touched Sir Ernst's. He lowered his snarling voice, but Cuthbert heard his words. "You think because you're well-connected to many of my nobles and a popular figure with the people that you can deter me. Do so, and I'll have you executed as well. For treason."

He stepped back and raised his voice. "Take the cur to the block."

Cuthbert briefly smiled his thanks to Sir Ernst and then climbed the few steps to the platform. He stood with outward calm while the executioner removed his coif and mail shirt. Inwardly, he was quailing, not so much with fear at what was to come since he had faced death now innumerable times, but at the indignity of this cold killing, and at the loss of his future which had once looked so bright. But he sternly refused to give the Austrian peasants a performance and stood there impassively facing the gurgling crowd dressed only in a simple tunic.

He looked around and, holding up his hand, conveyed alike a farewell and a command to his men to remain concealed. His deepest regrets were never again to see Evesham and his young wife to be, Lady Margaret, nor to fulfill his vow to Sir Walter to preserve the castle and keep his daughter from harm. Turning to his executioner, Sir Cuthbert de Lance indicated by a gesture that he was ready and stepped forward to kneel down, and place his head on the execution block.

Chapter 19: Outlaws versus Bandits

December 1192 to February 1193

At the very instant Cuthbert bent his knee, an arrow from the wall above slapped with a sickeningly wet thunk into the executioner's brain, and he fell dead in a clattering heap. A bawl of astonishment and anger burst from the packed mob. On the city wall at this point a small mural tower projected, and on this vantage five figures could be seen. The wall itself was otherwise deserted, and for the moment the strange bowmen were its masters.

"Seize those insolent varlets," the baron shouted, shaking his sword with an impotent gesture of fury.

His words were savagely arrested as a second shaft struck him in the throat. Its bloodied head stuck out from the back of his thick neck. The Austrian baron fell into the arms of those around him.

Quickly now the arrows of the English archers flew into the courtyard. The pandemonium which reigned was indescribable. With cries of alarm, the spectators, finding themselves a part of the spectacle, took to their heels. The men-at-arms were powerless against the rain of projectiles and trapped in the panicking crowd, while the knights, hastily donning their helms, shouted contradictory orders, which no one could obey.

In the muddle no one noticed the prisoner. Seizing a moment when everyone's attention was fixed on the wall, he leaped down from the platform and made his way unnoticed through the excited crowd. He darted down a narrow lane that divided the castle from the city wall and ran along until he came to a flight of steps to the battlements. Running lightly up, he kept along the wall until he reached the tower.

"Thanks, my noble Cnut, and you, my brave fellows. But I fear you've thrown away your lives. There's no escape from here. In a breath they'll recover and attack us from both ends."

The big Saxon slapped Cuthbert on the shoulder with what would otherwise have been a gesture of disrespect and smugly announced, "We've prepared for that. This here rope's hanging down into the moat."

Glancing over the battlement, Cuthbert looked down and saw that the moat held no water. After a final discharge of arrows into the crowd, the six men slid one after another down the hawser and made their way at a run from the city. Cuthbert, certain of pursuit, quickly turned off the obvious escape route to the north and swept around the town at a distance. When they reached the southern side facing the mountains, the escapees plunged into the woods on the lower slopes of the hills.

"They will," he said, as they halted breathless from their run, "follow the road toward the north to prevent us reaching the borders of Bavaria and Saxony, and scour the country for a while before it occurs to their thick skulls that we've doubled back on our tracks."

"You should punish me, my lord," Cnut gasped, as he held his side to ease the stitch.

Cuthbert managed a breathy laugh. "You never were that tactful with foreigners. But if you got me into it, Cnut, at least you got me out again. Now, let's waste no time in talk. We must keep to the foothills and make our way as far as we can to the west. Eventually we should reach the country of the Swabian people, who I've heard tell hate the Austrians as much as we do, so surely they'll give us asylum."

By nightfall they had already walked many leagues. They stopped in a small clearing and made a small brushwood fire, clothed in the depths of the forest. As they sat and warmed their hands around its blaze, Cnut told Cuthbert what happened to them on the previous day. They had not realized that Cuthbert had joined in and been captured, but after spending the night safely hidden in the loft of a stables, there was no doubt about the outcome.

193

"The whole town was buzzing, and although we didn't know what anyone was saying, the sight of a scaffold in the big square made me suspicious that you might have fallen into the hands of these dogs. Fortunately for us, they want for training and discipline. They had no guards set on the walls."

"The Innsbruck garrison must be complacent, secure in its position in the heart of the empire," Cuthbert said.

"Well, we quickly found a good position to see what was going on. Then I slipped back to our night's hiding place and took a long rope the carters use for fastening their loads to the wagons. The rest, my lord, you know. We saw the knights coming out of the castle, with that fat swine at their head. We saw the block, the headsman, and you being led out, and that was that. I hoped fervently that you would find the way up to our tower. If you were stopped from joining us, we would have remained there and fought them to the last. After all, we couldn't let you die here alone, and besides, how would we get home when we can't speak a word of Frankish, let alone their gibberish?"

Food posed no problems for the fugitives. The forest held plenty of game and, as Cnut said, it was easy to believe that they were back in their own greenwood near Evesham. To Cnut and the archers, indeed, it was a better time than any which they had passed since leaving England, and they marched along happily, only a little cautious of any pursuit.

On the sixth day since escaping they came to a rude village, and here Cuthbert learned from the people—with much pantomime, for neither understood a word spoken by the other—that they were now in one of the Swabian valleys, and therefore secure from pursuit by the Austrians. Cuthbert engaged one of the young villagers to act as their guide to Basel, and here, after four days' traveling, they arrived, weary but safe.

At an audience with the burgomeister, who spoke passable Frankish, Cuthbert explained what had taken place at Innsbruck.

He found that the mayor and his council were quite indifferent to the misfortunes of the Austrian baron, and that on the contrary they were willing to help a crusader on his way. Cuthbert offered to part with the gold chain King Richard had given him in payment for a charger and new armor, but the burgomeister refused to take it.

"The city of Basel is not so poor that it needs to take your king's gift. The arms and horse you require will be ready in a few hours. You may pay its value in London to a Jewish merchant there who has relations here. They pass bills of exchange between them regularly."

The burgomeister also helped with travel advice, that to avoid the chaotic petty German states they should follow the Rhine's left bank through Lorraine to Saxony. The same afternoon the promised horse and weapons were provided, and Cuthbert, delighted to be saddled up again, thanked the Baselers for their kindness, and started with his followers on the journey north. They, too, had been provided with new clothes suitable to a knight's retinue, and made a better show than they had done since leaving Acre.

While the burgomeister's advice kept them safe from German nobles on the other side of the great river, it posed other problems. After Basel the countryside of the left bank was in disarray because of the demobbing and return of many troops from the Crusade. These soldiers of fortune, their previous occupations gone, gathered in organized bands of robbers. The freebooters harassed the wild country between the land owned by Basel and the Duchy of Lorraine from the neighboring Vosges mountains, which offered the bandits concealment from the Duke of Lorraine's troops. It was on the evening of the third day that the party reached a small inn standing in a lonely position in the heart of Lorraine near the foot of the mountains. Cuthbert shuddered involuntarily.

"I like not the look of this place, but it must be some distance to anywhere else we might rest, so we'll have to make the best of it."

The innkeeper received them with a fawning civility, which somehow felt all wrong coming from his ferrety face. He offered them a rough meal and rude accommodation, a cramped room on the upper floor, its boards thinly littered with stale-smelling straw. In a sort of alcove at the end sat the only furnishing, a couch with a rough straw-filled mattress and threadbare coverlet. This Cuthbert took possession of with deep misgivings, while his followers stretched themselves out on the moldy hay.

"I think that we'd better keep watch at the door," Cnut stated. "I don't trust that bean-pole innkeeper."

Toward morning the archer on guard reported that he could hear the sound of many approaching footfalls.

Springing to their feet, the rest grabbed up their weapons and crowded up behind Cuthbert at the room's only window. Outside, in the light of the false dawn, a large party of vagabond men was gathered. Their ragamuffin appearance suggested that they were disbanded soldiers and, therefore, effectively armed robbers. Cnut barred the door with Cuthbert's truckle bed. Cuthbert then leaned out the casement, and demanded in Frankish what they wanted. One, who appeared to be the leader, replied in a guttural version of the same language that they had better surrender immediately. He leered up as he spoke.

"I promise you all good treatment, sirs. We only wants sufficient to pay this worshipful company present for the trouble to which we've gone in waiting upon you, sir knight. If you have insufficient valuables on you, we can consider a ransom."

Shouts of laughter from his comrades greeted this little speech.

"I am devastated to inform you, good sirs, that I have no valuables on me," Cuthbert replied quietly. "Worse still, I can think of no one who would pay as much as a silver mark for me, let alone the others of my company. But I can promise you one thing—sharp arrows and heavy blows."

A scowl replaced the bandit leader's grin. "You talk bravely, young sir," he growled threateningly, "but you have to do with men who care nothing either for knocks or for arrows. We've gone through the

Crusade. What's more, the Pope hisself has told us we are absolved of all sin for having taken part in the holy war. That's all sin, sir, including the cutting of your very pretty throat."

"Ah hah," Cuthbert retorted. "But we've also gone through the Crusade, which means our persons are sacred and I don't think the slitting of our throats would receive the absolution on which you rely. But on our arrows, you may."

"We know most of those who have served in the Holy Land," the man said more respectfully. "Who are you?"

"I'm an Englishman, and a follower of King Richard. I am Sir Cuthbert of Evesham. You may have heard of me—I was the youngest among the knights who fought for the Holy Sepulchre."

The bandit peered up in the growing dawn light, and his eyes widened. "Well, well, well—the Baby Knight, if my eyes don't deceive. What's happened to bring you here to these lonely and... very dangerous parts?"

Cuthbert leaned farther out and gave a brief account of their misadventures to that point. "So you see, I have, as you may well suppose, neither silver nor gold, and certainly John, Regent of England, would not want to ransom one of King Richard's followers."

The brigands spoke for awhile among themselves, and then the leader said, "We believe you Sir Cuthbert. And as you've proved in Outremer to be generous in handing out blows—and I'm sure your Saxon archers are as accurate and as fast as the rest of their bloody race—we'll let you go on your way. Your position is not much different to our own, and dog shouldn't rob dog."

The brigands shouted an adieu, and left for the mountains, leaving Cuthbert baffled but pleased at having headed off a fight with a doubtful outcome.

Journeying on without further adventure, they passed from Lorraine into Saxony and went to Nancy, where Henry, the Duke of Saxony, King Richard's brother-in-law by marriage to Matilda, Richard's sister, received them kindly. But the lack of news disturbed Cuthbert—the duke had so far heard nothing of the king since he had sailed from Palestine.

"This is strange," Cuthbert said, "because we've been slow and delayed by events. King Richard should have reached here by now, or at least the safety of your son Otto farther to the east. I'm worried that something awful has happened. On our way, we found how bitter those related to Conrad of Montferrat are toward him. And Conrad's cousin Archduke Leopold is still smarting from King Richard's fist at Ascalon. But surely they would not be so bold as to detain a great champion of Christendom on his way home?"

"Leopold is crafty and treacherous," the duke said. "The German Emperor is an ally of Philip of France, so he's naturally an enemy of Richard's and will uphold the accusation of Conrad's murder. You tell me that the king was going under an assumed name, but his lordly manner, majestic stature, and famously short fuse are hardly going to be well concealed under a merchant's garb."

Cuthbert could see the distress on Matilda's face as she tried to look on the bright side. "I'm happy to hear that my previous fears, that he had been drowned in a storm or captured by Moorish corsairs, are unfounded."

"Lady, as I've been so long on the road from Zadar, it's very possible that the king has been similarly delayed without falling into any danger, and I find it hard to believe that if a man as important as the King of England were to be detained or injured, the news wouldn't be shouted aloud. Perhaps hearing nothing is a happy sign?"

Cuthbert agreed to wait as a guest of the Duke of Saxony until any news of Richard came.

At the end of the month a messenger arrived from Normandy. He came from Sir Baldwin of Béthune, who was on his way back to England via Havre, bearing the news that the king had been arrested not far from Vienna—that he had been recognized, and immediately seized. Sir Baldwin had been allowed to leave without harm so that the people of England should know of their king's captivity—though not his whereabouts—and to wait for the ransom demand.

Sir Baldwin could not be absolutely certain, but he believed that Richard had fallen into the hands of Archduke Leopold. This reliable information, although sad in itself, was in some degree reassuring to Henry and Matilda, for they felt that while the vassals of Conrad of Montferrat would not hesitate to execute King Richard, Leopold himself would shrink from the deed, fearing the indignation of all Europe by such treatment of his royal captive.

"I need to leave at once," Cuthbert told his hosts. "I must go to Sir Baldwin to see what steps are being taken for the king's release and also to claim my fief of Evesham."

"Watch out for Prince John, Sir Cuthbert," Duke Henry warned. "Now he knows his brother's out of the picture, he will do anything to gain the throne, and any supporter of King Richard will be in desperate danger."

Chapter 20: Under the Greenwood

Central England, Spring 1193

Duke Henry provided letters of introduction to the dukes of Cleves and Brabant, princes through whose lands Cuthbert had to travel to reach a port. Thanks to these passports, he and his retinue of archers swiftly reached the mouth of the Scheldt without interruption. There they managed to find a ship sailing for London. The elderly cog was not in the best of condition, foul, leaky, and barely seaworthy, and the passage was long and stormy. Several times in the force of the gale every soul on board, including the captain, gave up hope.

At last the tedious and dangerous voyage ended as they entered the Thames estuary, and rising up with the tide they reached London eight days after setting out. The noble charger which the Duke of Saxony had given to Cuthbert had suffered badly, and he thought more than once that the poor animal would die on the storm-tossed ship. However, in the estuary's smoother seas it recovered, and after landing near the Tower the animal was able to support his weight.

Cnut and the archers were, like Cuthbert, delighted to have their feet again on English soil, and the pleasure of being able almost to understand the chatter of those around—the London accent sounded funny—made the poor fellows almost beside themselves with joy. After some of the grand cities they had seen, London struck Cuthbert as small, cramped, shabby, and the stink of rotting vegetables, horse dung, and human waste compared unfavorably with Outremer's waft of oriental spices. Still, it was home.

After securing two rooms at an alehouse in the Strand, Cuthbert asked the landlord whether Sir Baldwin of Béthune was in London, or whether away on his estates.

"I've no idea, m'lord," the man grumbled. "There's few nobles at court and I've never known London bein' so dull before as it is now. 'Ow's an 'onest man to make a groat? The regent, that John Lackland, frightens off most of the gentry and nobles what's returned from the 'Oly Land or as stayed behind to look after the king's interests."

Cuthbert didn't want to prolong the conversation, aware that even walls had ears in London, and words said against Prince John might be a trap to lead him into saying something that would get him accused of treason. Besides, he was unwilling to alert the prince to his presence in England until he was ready. Instead, he sent Cnut to the Tower to make discreet enquiries of some of the gate soldiery whether Sir Baldwin was about. Cnut soon returned.

"It seems his lordship never visited the prince's court since his return from the Holy Land, which had roused Prince John's anger. It's presumed he's living at his castle down in Dorsetshire."

Cuthbert thought this over for a moment. "It's a long way to go, but Sir Baldwin is bound to know more than me about what's been happening here, so after we've rested up, off we go."

A week later, Sir Baldwin received him with immense joy, not having heard of him since their parting at Zadar.

"My dear boy, I've been thinking of you and worrying that you must have suffered a similar fate to our liege lord. Have you heard anything new of the king's state?"

Cuthbert shook his head sadly. "Nothing. I'm sure I know less than you do. In fact I'd hoped to learn something from you about his situation."

"I was separated from him at Gortz, and while he was taken a prisoner to the bastard archduke, I was allowed to continue on my way. Mind, there were many difficulties on the way and I faced several dangerous situations. I sent a man to find the king's brother-in-law, Henry of Saxony, and tell him the dire story."

"I was there with the duke, which is why I decided to return quickly and come to you."

"When I got back I learned I was the first person with any definite news concerning him since the day he sailed from Acre. So this you don't know, young Cuthbert. Three weeks ago news came that Leopold has sold Richard to the German Emperor for a part of the ransom they've demanded. But where they've imprisoned him, no one knows. It's an outrage that a Christian sovereign should hold another in captivity. Still more so, when the one seized was returning through his dominions as a crusader coming from the Holy Land, when his person should be safe, even to his deadliest enemy."

"At Zardar, you were indeed right about the treachery of the Austrian and German nobles."

Sir Baldwin snorted contemptuously. "The news has caused outrage in England, and in our French possessions and those parts of Italy not under the emperor's boot. Everyone has pledged their treasures in order to collect the ransom which the Un-Holy Roman Emperor has placed on the king. Most of Christendom had suspected that he was in the emperor's hands and the feeling of indignation has been strong, but now the truth is out, I hope the sense of anger will be stronger than ever."

"But, now that we do know," Cuthbert insisted, "there won't be any delay in ransoming the king."

"There won't be any delay in raising the funds, but the kingdom has been impoverished by the costs of the Crusade and made worse by the demands Prince John has made on the people through his small but powerful coven of lackeys." Sir Baldwin scowled at the thought, then sighed. "No, I don't doubt that most English nobles will begrudge their silver flagons and vessels to melt down to make the total required… but some will. And whether King Richard will be freed as soon as the money's raised is another matter. Prince John's been longing for the throne for an age. He's exercised the real, if not the nominal, power of a king and he's in cahoots with Pope Celestine and Philip of France for their support for his seizing the crown. He'll throw every obstacle in the way, as we can be sure will Philip. With

Richard out of the game and that weak-kneed toad on the throne of England, Philip knows he'll be able to grab our hereditary Norman and Angevin lands to add to those of his kingdom. Talking of the toad, have you seen Prince John?"

"No," Cuthbert answered, "I thought it better to find out the lay of the land and come down to ask you to advise me how things are before I attempted to see him."

"You did well," Sir Baldwin said emphatically. "When I arrived, I found that the court officials had followed King Richard's instructions and drawn up papers conferring on you the lands and title of Earl of Evesham, before leaving Acre. Several of the nobles who acted as witnesses to the document and who returned safely, swore that this was the king's desire…"

Sir Baldwin hesitated. Cuthbert raised his chin. "And?"

"John repudiated the papers. He said that as Richard's royal powers had ceased to exist before he placed his seal on it he would give the earldom to whoever he chose."

Cuthbert flushed angrily. "Who did it go to?"

"One of his creatures, of course, Sir Fulk Fleming of Eresby, a Norman knight, or so he calls himself—actually he's a Flemish robber posing as a jumped-up Norman noble. John has also, I hear, promised him the young Lady Margaret when she flowers enough to marry."

Sir Baldwin looked sympathetically at Cuthbert. "Unclench your fists. She's safe for the moment, placed in the convent of St. Anne's in Worcester. The abbess was a relative of Sir Walter, and he arranged for Margaret to stay there before leaving England."

"But a convent is no castle, Sir Baldwin."

"That's true, but the abbess is something of a firebrand. When ordered to give up her charge to Sir Fulk's guardianship she refused, saying that it would be improper for a young lady to be under the roof of a bachelor knight without a lady at the head of his house. Prince John, I hear, had a tantrum when he heard, but he didn't dare provoke the Church by ordering the convent's violation—after all, he needs the Pope on his side—and that's an uneasy relationship as it is. Besides, many of the great nobles would also have taken the convent's part, and among King Richard's many friends there's a strong feeling of anger at your having been deprived of the earldom."

"But did no one stand up for me?"

Sir Baldwin shook his head sadly. "It wasn't worth anyone's while to involve himself unnecessarily with the prince on such a subject when it was uncertain whether you would ever return to claim your rights. God knows, there are enough disputes between John and the English barons without making any fresh ones. The whole kingdom's in a state of disorder. There have been several risings against John's authority—especially in the deeply forested areas like Evesham and Nottingham—but these have been suppressed… so far."

"The king will sort it out when he's returned," Cuthbert said hotly.

"We can hope for King Richard's return before very long. It's probable that peace will be maintained, but should treachery win, and his return be prevented, you may be sure that John won't get the throne without a fight. Many nobles fear his weakness against Philip. Since he was a princeling, the French king has always bent John around his little finger."

Cuthbert frowned before asking, "But isn't Arthur of Brittany successor to the throne? He's the son of the king's dead brother Geoffrey. By blood he has the greater right to succeed his uncle, who has anyway stated it should be so. While Arthur lives John can't pretend to the throne."

"Ah, Cuthbert, don't mix chivalry with naivety. We live in an England where might is right. You can bet that at King Richard's death, whenever that may be, Prince John will seize the throne. And, aided as he will be by the Pope and by Philip of France—each for their own greedy aims—his chances are better than those of a child like Arthur."

Cuthbert shook his head sadly. "What a state this England has fallen to. Lackland is not better than the robbers I encountered in Lorraine."

Sir Baldwin huffed out a deep breath. "Enough of politics, Cuthbert, how about a feast? It's long since we two dined together, not that meals in the Holy Land were ever a joy. A boar's head and a good roasted capon are worth all the strange dishes that we had there. I was always suspicious of the meat, which—no matter what the cooks did with it—seemed to have the flavors liked by the Jews or the Saracens. A cup of English ale, too, is worth all the Cyprus wines, half full of the sand blown from the desert."

The morning dawned bright and chill. Sir Baldwin suggested they ride around his Dorset lands for some fresh air, but the concerns of the day weighed on both their minds.

"In the present situation, it would be unwise for you to attempt to regain your position if Prince John refuses to recognize you—which I'm sure he will."

"I can't—I won't just sit back and do nothing," Cuthbert insisted.

"You're very young yet, so you can afford to wait, at any rate until King Richard returns. When he does, he'll see all these wrongs are righted. How old is the Lady Margaret, by the way?"

"She's fifteen, three years younger than me."

"Hmm, pity not younger. At fifteen she's not of proper age to marry, but men can stretch points when they choose. I'm worried that the news of your coming will speed up the prince and Fulk to strengthen the claim to Evesham by marriage to its heiress. The Lady Margaret and her friends will claim that she's a royal ward, and only the king can give away her person and estates. But, unfortunately, force overrides argument and possession is nine points of the law... if you can call anything in this land lawful anymore."

When a hare startled his bay mare, Cuthbert gentled her without thinking about it. "I worry about this convent, in spite of a firebrand mother superior. Would they dare to take her by force from the convent in Worcester?"

Sir Baldwin shrugged. "England rides on the very edge of chaos and Worcester's close to Evesham. With a bunch of twenty spears, Sir Fulk could easily break in, carry her off, and marry her by force."

"In that case, I can't wait for the king's safe return. Sir Fulk Fleming of Eresby—and now by treachery, of Evesham—won't wait until Margaret is seventeen and legal and risk the king reappearing in the meantime. But it won't help me if Prince John knows I'm back in England. It won't get my lands and title back and it will put him on his guard, then he's bound to urge his minions to kidnap Lady Margaret. On the other hand, where's the harm in maintaining my silence?"

"None I can see. It's best if your enemies think you're either dead or in some Tyrolean dungeon. What will you do then?"

"Return to my old home—not my mother's manor—the forest. I've no doubt there are many good men I can trust living in the woods. And others will join when they hear that Cnut is back, and that they're needed to strike a blow for my rights. I'll bide my time, watch the castle and the convent at Worcester, try to talk to the abbess, and persuade her that her charge is in danger.

"If Margaret's still willing to fulfill her father's promise and King Richard's will, in marrying me when the time comes, I'll take her from the convent in secrecy. There are plenty of snug cottages in the forest where she can remain hidden in the care of some good farmer's wife for months, and we'll be on hand to guard her."

Cuthbert turned to look at his host and gave Sir Baldwin a grin.

"I haven't seen that wolfish expression on your youthful face before. It makes you older than your years. Perhaps you should practice it more to convince those set against you that your have already witnessed and taken part in more dangerous situations than many a man twice your age."

"Hmm, I shall try to remember the muscle positions. With the aid of the forest men, Sir Walter took Wortham castle. Although Evesham is a far grander pile than that, I think it could be carried by a sudden attack. And as you say, we know more of war now than we did then."

"I'd be cautious there," Sir Baldwin replied. "You might capture the castle with the aid of your outlaws, but you couldn't hold it. The prince has already captured stronger holds than Evesham with the aid of his lackeys and his foreign mercenaries. If you turn his puppet earl out, you'd have a swarm of hornets on you that even the walls of Evesham couldn't keep out. Besides, it would give him what now he has no excuse for, a reason for putting a price on your head—and cutting it off if he ever got the opportunity."

The dispossessed Evesham party, Cuthbert, Cnut, and the four archers, left Dorset and progressed by easy stages through Wiltshire, Gloucestershire, and up to Worcester. Sir Baldwin had supplied Cuthbert with suitable clothing for himself and the archers, and now he rode as a simple unattached knight, without a heraldic device. All the crosses and other crusading insignia that they had become so accustomed to had vanished so there was nothing to tell anyone where their allegiances lay. Cuthbert wanted to go straight to St. Anne's convent as soon as the walls of Worcester came into view, but Cnut's wisdom prevailed.

"Don't you think that Sir Fulk will have spies posted to keep a watch over the place? He'd want to know if there was any attempt to remove her secretly to some hiding place, and the appearance of a knight knocking on its doors would arouse suspicion."

Cuthbert reluctantly agreed, and they cut off before the city, going straight to the forest, where he had so often roamed with Cnut and the outlaws in more carefree days. Here he found that things had hardly changed since he was last there. Many of those who had fought with him in the Holy Land, and who had returned by sea, had taken to the forest again, joined by many new men driven into revolt by Sir Fulk's grinding taxes. The elation with which the men of the greenwood greeted Cnut was obvious, and when he presented Cuthbert to them as the rightful heir of Evesham and the well-known friend of the outlaws, their welcome grew tumultuous. It was well known that Cuthbert had been involved in obtaining the forest band's pardon from Sir Walter, and his role in the battle for Wortham castle was already a local legend. One by one they came forward to accept him as their lord, and swore oaths to obey his orders and to lay down their lives in his cause if it were to be required of them.

Cuthbert fought back unexpected tears at the report that his mother was in good health, although she had been in mourning for several months over his supposed death, which nevertheless she refused to accept. Cuthbert hesitated to go immediately to see her, worried that the shock of his sudden appearance might be too much for her.

"Let me go instead," Cnut offered. "I can break the news to her gently, and arrange for a time when she can meet you at some place away from the house so as not to create any excitement among her servants, which might trickle back as gossip to Evesham."

Cnut was absent for the remainder of that day, and on his return told Cuthbert that he had seen Dame Editha, and that her joy on seeing her cousin safely returned from the Crusade and hearing of her son's safe arrival had caused her no harm, but rather the reverse.

"You should have seen her face when I told her that King Richard had given her son the title and lands of Evesham. She was astonished and then alarmed for your safety because of the character of the pretending earl."

"It's the foul Fleming, Eresby, who will need to be alarmed… when his time comes," Cuthbert remarked.

"Her plan for the morning is to announce that she would make a pilgrimage to the holy shrine of St. Dunstan, which lies at the edge of the forest, to pray for the safety of her missing son," Cnut said. "She will insist on no fuss and take only the four most trusted thegns of her household with her. Even these she will ask to leave her in peace when they come to the shrine, and then…"

Cuthbert had already concealed himself inside the tiny cave-like space that formed the main part of the saint's shrine when she arrived. Her first sight of his mother was a dark silhouette against the light of the narrow doorway. He heard her indrawn breath and the next moment they were in each other's arms.

Her joy was so deep it left her speechless. Eventually, she pulled slightly away to take in his face. "I last saw a boy of fifteen. Now you return a young man of eighteen, stout and strong beyond your age. Come more into the light." He stood quietly while Dame Editha examined his face, head cocked this way then that. "You appear older than you are," she said wonderingly.

"Mother, it's the effect of the hot sun of Palestine and of the privations which we have suffered."

"Was it terrible?"

Cuthbert shuffled uncomfortably. *Awful beyond imagination.* "Not so bad. Worst was the monotony of our diet." *Moldy bread and maggots washed down by the stench of decaying flesh.* "And the heat, of course."

She clasped him to her bosom again. "I'm glad you found it not so hard. Sir Walter promised me before you left that you would win your knight's spurs at the first opportunity, and I've never doubted that you would one day reach your father's rank. But in my wildest imagining I never thought you would return to me a belted earl."

To preserve the secrecy of Cuthbert's presence, their meeting was necessarily a short one. He gave her only a slight and heavily edited outline of what had happened since they parted. He omitted the monstrous spiders, the slaughter of friends and foes, his kidnap, enslavement, and near-ravishment at the hands of Arabs; in fact most things he left out. The conversation then turned on the present position and on the steps which had best be taken.

"I fear your danger is as great here as when you were fighting the infidels in the Holy Land," she said. "In the short time Sir Fulk's been here, he's proved himself a cruel and ruthless master. He's driven out many of the old tenants and handed their lands to his own retainers. He sticks to the severest letter of the law when it comes to the forest, and has hanged several men who were caught infringing them. He's laid such heavy burdens on all the remaining tenants that they're effectively ruined. If he stays here long he will rule over a desert as barren as that which you have left behind."

She reached out and stroked Cuthbert's tear-dampened cheek. "If he even dreamed you were here, he would burn down the forest to get you. It's sad to think that such a worthless brigand should be a pet of England's regent. But everyone says he is. Even if you did conquer and kill him, you would have to contend with Prince John—and he spares no one, man, woman, or child, who stands in his way."

Promising to write to her cousin, the Abbess of St. Anne's, to ask if Cuthbert might speak to the Lady Margaret, Dame Editha slipped out, rejoined her thegns, and returned home.

Three days later, an urchin from Erstwood employed as a messenger by Dame Editha brought a sealed note to Cuthbert. It said that the abbess would be glad to receive a visit from Cuthbert.

"Come, Cnut. There's clandestine business afoot. We must sneak our way unobserved into Worcester and see what we can do to keep my future wife out of the evil clutches of Prince John's hunting hound."

Chapter 21: Convent Clash

Spring 1193

Dressed in the drab garb of a citizen, Cuthbert entered Worcester humbly on foot, with Cnut at his side. The Saxon woodsman was on his best behavior, the consequences of his own impetuosity in the Tyrol fresh in his mind. As they approached the precincts of St. Anne's, Cnut took up position in the shade of a house, from where he could keep an eye on anyone who looked like they might be watching Cuthbert.

The convent door opened at Cuthbert's ring and a nun showed him into the parlor where, a few moments later, the lady abbess joined him. As a youngster he had twice accompanied his mother here and the abbess greeted him kindly.

"My, I certainly wouldn't have recognized the child who used to come here with my cousin, in the brave young knight I see now. You are very changed."

"For the better, I hope," Cuthbert laughed even as he bowed to her.

"Indeed. Who would think that my gossip Editha's son would come to be the Earl of Evesham. The Lady Margaret is eager to see you, but first, aren't you exaggerating the dangers to her? I can't think that even a minion of Prince John would dare to violate the sanctity of a holy convent."

Cuthbert shuddered inwardly at the nun's unworldly conviction, but refrained from saying anything to upset her. *How to find the words?* "I'm afraid, good mother, that when ambition and greed are in one scale, reverence for the Holy Church won't weigh much in the other. Sir Fulk Fleming of Eresby cannot—and will not—wait, in case

King Richard should return. When that happy event becomes the case, Fulk may lose the estate he's stolen from me, but if he's already married to the heiress of Evesham his claim to retain much of the lands will stand. You will, unless I'm greatly mistaken, hear from him before long."

At this the abbess looked suddenly grave. She hesitated uncertainly, and then spoke quietly. "I have already heard. Only yesterday I received a note from Sir Fulk, urging that now the Lady Margaret is almost sixteen, and may be considered marriageable in another year, the will of the prince should be obeyed. He wants her removed to the care of Lady Clara Boulger…"

"And who is she?"

"The wife of a friend and associate of Sir Fulk. I responded by return saying, that perhaps in another year it would be time to think about such matters. I said that Lady Margaret is receiving an education suitable to her rank and that she is happy here. I added that I would not surrender her into any hands whatsoever, unless I received the commands of her lawful guardian, King Richard."

Cuthbert nodded thoughtfully. "That was well said, holy mother, but you see the hawks scent the distant danger, and are moving uneasily already. Don't you think it would be safer to send Margaret somewhere hidden away from Sir Fulk?"

"It's very difficult for a young lady of rank to be hidden away from such sharp agents as Sir Fulk would be certain to place on the scent. And I can't agree to her taking refuge in the house of some small franklin near the forest. In the first place, it would demean her, and in the second we could never be sure that the report of her being there might not reach the ears of Sir Fulk. Then she would be more vulnerable than she would be here. Only as a last resort, perhaps, would such a step be justifiable. Now I'll call Lady Margaret in."

The young girl entered with an air of frank gladness, but looked startled at the alteration which had taken place in her former playfellow. She hesitated and glanced at the abbess, as if inquiring whether this could really be the boy she had known who brought her small gifts. Cuthbert was struck by how much younger than her years Lady Margaret looked. *The seclusion of the convent has kept from her the maturity she would have gained living as an earl's daughter in the stir and bustle of a castle*, he thought.

The abbess came to Lady Margaret's rescue. "This really is Sir Cuthbert, your childhood friend, and the husband destined for you by your father and by the will of the king."

Struck with a new timidity, the girl advanced and shyly offered her cheek to be kissed. Cuthbert was almost as bashful, and alarmed at the stirring he felt in his stomach and loins.

"I feel, Lady Margaret," he stammered nervously, "a deep sense of my own unworthiness of the honor which your father offered me."

"I always liked you, Cuthbert," the girl said frankly, "better than any one else after my father, and I'm happy to bend to his will. These are troubled times," she said anxiously, "and our holy mother tells me you're concerned that I'm in danger."

"I hope it's not imminent," Cuthbert answered carefully. "But knowing the unscrupulous nature of the false Earl of Evesham, I worry news of King Richard's ransom will drive him to precipitous action. But don't worry, I will keep a careful watch over you night and day—Sir Fulk must kill me and crush my faithful followers before you will become his bride."

Then, turning to other subjects, he spoke a little of his experiences in the Holy Land. He told her of her father's gallant deeds there and of his last moments. After two turns of the hour-glass, the abbess came in and respectfully suggested it was time for him to leave. He found Cnut on guard where he had left him.

"Anything suspicious?"

Cnut answered curtly. "Yes. The spies are here. Just after you went in, a man came from that house over there and went up to the gate to stare in fascination at its iron decorations. He didn't look like an art lover to me. Then he went back, and... don't look up now... he's peeping from an upper window. If we stand here for a bit, he may come out to see what's delaying you in this dark corner, in which case I can clout him with my axe, which will settle his prying."

"Better not," Cuthbert said. "If his body were found here, it would arouse his employer's suspicion. Right now, he hasn't much to report. Let's just slip quietly around this corner out of his sight."

They had barely walked a few yards when a man came up rapidly behind them and almost brushed them as he passed. He half-turned round and tried to catch sight of their faces. Cnut played the drunk, stretched out his foot in a fake stumble, and tripped the stranger into the gutter. The man staggered up with a fierce cry of anger, but Cnut stretched him out with a blow of his heavy fist.

"Meddling fool," he grumbled. "He won't have much to report to Sir Fulk this time either. If I thought he'd seen your face, he'd be lying in the sewer now with one half of his head looking at the other half."

The respectable looking burgher who hired the large house told the landlord's agent that he was opening a house of business for the sale of silks, and for articles from the Low Countries. The agent was pleased, especially as Master Nicholas offered a month's rent in advance. The mercer was a stranger to Worcester, which suited his purpose well—in his native Gloucester he had been charged with using false weights and had been condemned to lose his ears before fleeing to the security of Evesham forest.

He moved in the next day, with two stout serving-men and an apprentice boy; and from that time two sets of watchers observed without let up what passed on the opposite side of the square outside St. Anne's.

About half a mile off the road between Worcester and Evesham stood an empty grange whose owner had no further use for it. Becoming dilapidated, it was an ideal base for Cnut and ten men, after blocking up the hall window with hangings so that the light of their fire would not betray their presence at night.

The observers needed patience, for two months passed without any incident. But down the road at Evesham, matters were deteriorating. On six occasions the false earl's gamekeepers were set on by outlaws, and when they went under armed escort, the men-at-arms were ambushed and driven back. Gossip began to circulate and soon reached Sir Fulk's ears, stories about a tall, broad Saxon who had been their leader in times gone by, but who had been pardoned, and had, with a large number of his band, become a crusader.

Another story disturbed him even more: that this big outlaw deferred to another, a youth said to be of noble blood. Sir Fulk made enquiries and learned that this Cnut had been especially attached to the young Cuthbert de Lance, who had fought under the Earl of Evesham's banner.

Fulk began to feel uneasy. A man approaching forty and therefore over-anxious to make his mark before old age overtook him, he was tall, dark, with Norman features made starker by his part-Flemish origins. He held Saxons in utter contempt, and treated them as serfs solely created to till the land for the benefit of their Norman overlords. He was also, it has to be said, brave and feared nothing in the world, except the return of King Richard from captivity.

As soon as he was convinced that his rival was in the region, he knew that he had to do one of two things: kill Sir Cuthbert, or carry off Lady Margaret and force her to marry him—succeeding in both courses would be preferable. To achieve the first, he had to force his enemy out into the open and determined on a subterfuge by appealing to the young knight's reputed sense of duty and chivalry. And in so doing succeed in both courses, using the second to provoke the first.

The clearing rang with the sounds of the foresters about their daily tasks. The quiet, orderly bustle did not calm Cuthbert's rising anger as he listened to Cnut. The big Saxon and four of his followers had returned from Evesham, where they had collected some supplies, attired in the garb of simple yeomen to fit in. Cnut noticed a press of people all excitedly peering at something nailed on a door. "As I don't know one letter from another I asked one of the merchants what was written on the paper which caused such excitement."

"He turned to me and said, 'It is in the nature of a challenge from our present lord, Sir Fulk. He says that it has come to his ears that a Saxon serf, calling himself Cuthbert of Evesham, is lurking in the woods and consorting with outlaws and robbers. He challenges him to appear, saying that he will—although he would demean himself by so doing—condescend to meet him in the lists with sword and battle-axe, and to prove on his body the falseness of said Sir Cuthbert's claims.' The burgher seemed faintly puzzled."

"Go on," Cuthbert said in a tight voice. "Why the puzzlement?"

"He said, 'It's very strange that the earl should bother. There's gossip that before he sailed for England King Richard did give the rank and the domains of Evesham to Sir Cuthbert, the son of Dame Editha. I don't know if it's true or not, but it seems strange that such grace should have been given to one so young. But I know his father Sir Stephen de Lance was a brave Norman knight, and the mother is of good Saxon blood and descended from those who held Evesham before the arrival of the Normans.' My first impulse, to tear down the proclamation, stalled when I recalled the solemn promise to myself not to act rashly in future. So I came straight here to report the facts to you instead."

Cuthbert received the news with indignation.

"You did well, Cnut." His voice rose to a shout. "There's nothing I'd like better than to try my strength against this false traitor. He's a cunning foe, this Fulk. He reckons that if I appear he'll kill me and that if I do not appear, I'll be branded a coward, and my claims made a laughing stock. On the other hand, it may be a mere ruse to discover if I'm anywhere near. He's heard the local prattle and thinks this will draw me out."

Cuthbert pounded on Cnut's unyielding upper arm. "Yes, but Cnut, he's gone too far. Not so cunning, perhaps. Honest men will see in the challenge a sign that he thinks that my claims are just. Think of it—if I were, as he claims, a Saxon serf, you can be sure that he, a grand Norman, would never condescend to meet me in the lists as he proposes. I hope that the time will come when I may meet him in open combat, but for the moment I will bear his insult rather than upset the success of our plans. What is of far greater importance is the happiness and safety of Margaret, who, if anything happened to me, would certainly fall into his hands."

"It hurts deeply to let the bastard get away with it, though," Cnut grumbled, thoughtfully rubbing his arm where Cuthbert had landed his affectionate blow with surprising strength.

"Well, we won't. We'll send a reply, written by you… have you hurt your arm?"

"No. And I can't write either," Cnut pointed out.

"No, but I can. You ought to get that arm looked at. Now, let me mull this over."

After some thought, Cuthbert drew up an answer to the knight's proclamation as if the document were from the hand of Cnut.

"I, Cnut, a free Saxon and a leader of bowmen under King Richard in the Holy Land, do hereby declare the statements of Sir Fulk, miscalled the Earl of Evesham, to be false lies and slanderous. The earldom was, as Fulk well knows, granted to Sir Cuthbert, King Richard's true and faithful follower. When the time comes, Sir Cuthbert will doubtless be ready to prove his rights. But at present justice has no force in England, and until the coming of our good King Richard must remain in suspension. Until then, I support the title of Sir Cuthbert, and do hereby declare Sir Fulk a false and lying knight."

Two days following the posting of this declaration in Evesham, a lowly servant in the castle was brought to Cuthbert. He told of how he had slipped away in fear of his life and of Sir Fulk's towering rage. "When a report of the wording was brought to him he had the hapless page who informed him taken out and hanged," the man stammered. "All who work in the keep go in terror."

"The hornets' nest is stirred," Cuthbert murmured in satisfaction marred at the innocent pageboy's murder.

Soon after, the abbess sent Cuthbert a message, saying that she had received another missive from Sir Fulk, demanding in the king's name the instant surrender of Lady Margaret to his care, and that he would visit Worcester within the week to ensure compliance.

"There is no king in England. We must waste no time, Cnut. Ready the men."

That same night Cuthbert, Cnut, and forty archers stole, one by one, quietly into Worcester. They entered the town before the gates were shut, and so mingling with the citizens, they went unobserved. When it was quite dark they made their way stealthily to the square in which the convent stood and were admitted into the shop of Master Nicholas, the cloth mercer.

The large house, typically, had few ground-floor windows, only a large barrier lowered during the day to display wares, but its two upper overhanging floors had long casements running the whole width of the house. The "merchant" had laid up a hefty store of provisions, and the troop settled in comfortably for the wait, however long. When the men were settled Cnut returned to the disused grange with the ten men originally sent there.

On the third day Sir Fulk arrived amid a bustle and flurry with a number of knights and men-at-arms. His herald announced that the lord would spend the night at the town's main hostelry before continuing to his lands in the Welsh marches. Master Nicholas sent out a boy to test the air. On his return, the lad said that the citizens of Worcester, though somewhat surprised at this large complement, thought little more of it.

I imagine the abbess feels very differently, Cuthbert thought. *She must be terrified now my warning has come to bear evil fruit.*

* * *

"The men stand ready, my lord."

Sir Fulk regarded his castellan with a wolfish grin distorting his scarred face. "So now we smoke out this young cur who would fain rob me of the rights granted me by King John. He will ride on the end of my spear before I'm done. But prior to that, it's high time the Lady Margaret lose her virginity to the same weapon."

The first indication that the citizens of Worcester were in for an unusual night came at midnight.

An armed party fell on the townsmen guarding the main gate and took possession. At the same time those who had stayed at the hostelry with Sir Fulk suddenly mounted their horses and, with a great clatter, rode down the streets to the Convent of St. Anne. A squad on foot joined them, and some sixty in all suddenly gathered in front of the convent. With a thundering noise two sergeants knocked at the gates. When the grating opened Sir Fulk pushed forward. He glared at the partially visible crabby face of the janitor nun.

"Go at once to your abbess and order her to surrender Lady Margaret to me, by order of Prince John."

"You have no rights here, my lord," the nun said.

Sir Fulk stretched his neck until the nasal guard of his helm grated on the mesh. "If within the count of one hundred my order is not complied with I will have the gates broken down and take her for myself."

In only a few heartbeats a window opened above, and the abbess appeared.

"Rash man," she berated Sir Fulk. "I warn you against committing the sin of sacrilege. Neither the orders of Prince John nor of any other despot can override the rights of the Holy Church. Should you dare to use force in this convent you will be placed under the anathema of the Church. You and all who follow you will be excommunicated and the Church's spiritual terrors will be directed against you."

Sir Fulk stepped back and placed mailed fists on his hips. He looked up and his laugh came as a snarl. "I'm prepared to risk that, holy mother. So long as I am obeying the orders of my *king*, I don't give a damn fart for those of any foreign potentate, be he pontiff or emperor. The count I gave you has reached sixty, and unless within forty more Lady Margaret appears at the gate I will batter it down. Think yourself lucky that I haven't ordered my men to set light to it to smoke you out of your hole."

The abbess closed the window. As she did so the long row of casements in the mercer's house opposite flew open and a volley of sixty clothyard arrows sluiced into the group standing around the gate. Three men fell, killed outright, and shouts of rage and pain arose from many of the rest amid the carnage.

Furious at this surprise ambush, Sir Fulk turned and commanded those with him to attack the house from where the missiles had come. But even as he shouted, another flight of arrows, even more deadly accurate at such short range than the first, came like a horizontal rain of death through the dark. A knight called Harold, standing by the side of Sir Fulk, fell wounded, shot through the eye. Very many of the common men, undefended by mail, died as arrows pierced their quilted jerkins. An arrow even punched into Sir Fulk's chain mail and wounded him in the shoulder.

In vain the knight stormed and raged and ordered his men to advance. The suddenness of the assault seemed to his superstitious followers a direct answer from heaven to the words of the abbess. Their number was already seriously depleted, and those who were in any state to do so turned to run. They scattered through the city and made for the gate, which had earlier been seized by Sir Fulk's men.

Finding himself alone with only a handful of his knights and principal men-at-arms remaining, while the storm of arrows continued unabated, Fulk was forced to order the retreat. Uttering a string of fierce oaths describing the vengeance he would take, he turned his mount and followed the rout.

Chapter 22: A Foul Deed

Evesham, June 1193

Those who escaped from Worcester, did not do so unscathed. As Sir Fulk's tattered force rode helter-skelter along the Evesham road, a second ambush in the woods near a disused grange took them by surprise. From the dark an unknown number of archers shot at them and many fell there who had survived the square. When the roll was called back at the castle, thirty men were missing, while many others lay seriously wounded.

The noise of the tumult in the square of the convent aroused the whole of Worcester. Alarm bells were rung and the burghers, hastily arming themselves, poured into the streets. The picture was confusing in the extreme. Some twenty soldiers were lying dead or dying of arrow wounds in front of the convent gate. But of the rest of Sir Fulk and his troop, there was no sign.

The guards at the main gate had been overpowered and tied up in the watch room, but none of them knew anything about who had attacked them. And then to add to the mystery, the house of Master Nicholas was found deserted, with all its windows and the door wide open. A search revealed no goods of any kind, but many bales filled with dried leaves and tree bark. There were signs that a considerable number of men had been there, and although not knowing from where the archers could have come, the town's councillors concluded that those who attacked Sir Fulk must have hidden in the mercer's rented house.

At the discovery that the earl had brought his small army to attack the convent, public anger overflowed. A councillor questioned the abbess, but she could provide no further intelligence. She said that after retreating from the window she heard shouts and cries, and that almost immediately after the thugs in front hastily retreated.

The furious councillors sent a deputation to confront Prince John and demand damages for the injury his earl had done their town. The mayor and five worthies who made the long trip to London were kept waiting for five days before they were granted an audience with the man who already called himself King of England. Irritation at the insult of delaying them turned bluster into outrage, but the mayor barely spluttered his first words before the prince cut him short.

"I've heard about this matter," he said in a great rage. "I tell you now, leaders of your citizens, that I curse the people of Worcester. How dare they interfere and prevent my Earl of Evesham in carrying out my commands?"

The mayor took a sharp step backward as the lank-haired John stepped down and thrust his pointed nose into the mayor's alarmed face. Spittle flew from the prince's lips. He jabbed the mayor in the chest, rattling his chain of office. "In complying with *my* wishes, the good knight was attacked by men of *your* town and many of his company were slain."

"B-b-but, my lord, we don't know the men who did this—"

"So you pretend. Think you me an idiot to believe such a tale. I've a good mind to order the troop of Sir Charles Everest, which even now marches toward Evesham, to divert and sack Worcester as a punishment for its rebellion."

John paused, glared at the mayor, then swung on his heel and retook his high seat. He grabbed a deep breath and in a more reasonable tone added, "However, as I am willing to believe that you better class of burghers were ignorant of the doings of your rabble I'll be merciful, and merely fine you three thousand gold marks."

A threat of imprisonment dampened any further remonstrance. Sadly crestfallen at the unexpected result of their mission, the deputation returned to Worcester, where their report caused consternation. The arrival in the vicinity on the following day of

Sir Charles Everest, with five hundred of Prince John's mercenaries, further heightened the town's alarm. A palpable sense of panic reigned among the folk when Sir Fulk and his retinue, and several other barons of the prince's party also approached the town.

Worcester's walls were strong enough, and the town's guilds and council deliberated on matters of defense. The doves wanted to raise the fine immediately, while the hawks were greatly averse, especially as a letter had been received, signed "Cuthbert, Earl of Evesham," offering a century and a half of archers. The braver souls argued that with this help, they would repulse any assault, but clearer heads thought otherwise. While that might be true, they argued, since it was uncertain when King Richard would return, Prince John might soon be king in fact instead of pretense. When that happened, nothing would prevent his carrying Worcester by storm. Even in the meantime he could ruin their trade and inflict great suffering on everyone; better, therefore, to pay up now than to risk all these evils.

Lady Margaret had ensured the sisters kept her abreast of developments and she tried to be brave when she heard of Sir Fulk's fulminations. She rejoiced at what she thought of as the filthy Fleming's rebuff and guessed from whence had come the flights of arrows. *Cuthbert will rescue me.* A thrill ran through her very being at the thought of the young knight and earl. She had seen in his eyes how he thought her sheltered existence precluded any thoughts beyond sewing and lace-making, but when he'd visited his presence filled her heart and kindled a warm glow in her belly and loins.

The abbess came to her. "I have been informed of the council's deliberations, my Lady, but whatever the outcome, the convent is no longer a safe place for you. Thanks to Cuthbert—I can't yet think of my cousin's little boy as an earl—my plans are made. In fact I was ready to act two days before the prince's mercenary horde arrived to invest the walls or collect the money—and Sir Fulk's prize."

Margaret shuddered at the thought of the prize he coveted.

And so Margaret left the convent by a back postern gate late in the evening dressed as a countrywoman. Two of the sisters attended her, both similarly attired. In such garb, no one bothered stopping them for questioning at the postern gate leading to the small bridge which spanned the Severn. Her heart fluttered with anticipation as their footsteps clattered on the wooden strakes and she was hard-pressed to know whether the flight or the thought of seeing her betrothed again caused the disturbance. Close by on the other side of the crossing Sir Cuthbert, with a band of archers, stood in the shadows ready to escort them.

"My Lady—"

"Oh, Cuthbert…" She pressed close to his lithe body and stammered, "My Lord."

"No… Margaret. We have known each other too long for such formality, but no time now to renew familiarity."

With Margaret and the two nuns mounted on mules, they rode all night and arrived in the morning at a small convent five miles from the city of Hereford.

"Its mother superior came to her present position from St. Anne's and is known to the abbess," Cuthbert informed Margaret.

She stood with the mother at the door regretting Cuthbert's leave taking, with his promise that, as far as possible, he would watch over her and that she need never despair.

Sir Fulk and his men entered Worcester in the guise of conquerors and haughtily heard the apologies of the mayor, council, and guildsmen for the attack on him, for which the townspeople were not responsible. Sir Fulk tossed his head in disbelief, but it was a charade, for he knew exactly who the culprits were. The mayor presided over paying the fine, the principal portion in gold, the rest in bills signed by the leading merchants. "It has been impossible to collect such a sum in so short a time," the mayor apologized.

"See to the balance immediately. I give you a week, no more." He turned to his knight-commander "Time to renew my acquaintance with the Abbess of St. Anne's, but I think with a touch more tact this time."

He presented himself at the convent with only two squires in attendance and a royal summoner bearing "King" John's order for the delivery of Lady Margaret. The abbess met him at the gate, and spoke calmly in a cold tone.

"Finding that the holy walls of this convent are insufficient to restrain lawless men, and fearing that these might be tempted to acts of sacrilege which would bring down on them the wrath of the Church, I have sent her away. It would truly be wicked of me to place before them the temptation which would severely harm their souls."

Fulk's urbane expression folded in on itself. "Where has she gone?" he demanded, spitting with fury.

"I will not tell you," the lady abbess replied. "She's in good hands, and when King Richard returns, his ward will be sent to him at once."

In the heat of his ire, Sir Fulk wanted to call down his men-at-arms to ransack the buildings and precinct, if necessary tear down its walls. His restraint came only from his awareness that John needed to stay on the Pope's good side. Destruction of a convent in one of England's major towns would not help that.

Swallowing pride and rage in one lump, he turned away and a few hours later, together with his own men and a hundred of Sir Charles Everest's mercenaries, returned to his castle at Evesham. There, he sat and fumed at the failure—the double failure—of his plan. Neither girl nor forest rat were in his hands. *But then*, he thought, *there is always more than one way to skin a rat...*

As the resources of the greenwood—great though they were—were insufficient to support permanently a large body of men, the size of the brotherhood collected under the trees varied considerably. The Saxon franklins in the neighborhood—all hostile to Sir Fulk—did their best to provide food, but it was still necessary to scatter the force across a wide area to ease the problems of feeding so many men and animals. The main residents within a day of Evesham numbered about forty, and these, led by Cnut, were pleased to see their lord and his escort return.

"So now, Sir Cuthbert," the Saxon heartily greeted him, "how long before we storm Evesham and take back what's rightly yours?"

"All in good time, Cnut. Patience, my friend, brings its own rewards."

Two days after this took exchange, as Cuthbert sat at a simple meal in the forest, surrounded by Cnut and his followers, a young lad ran breathlessly into the small clearing. Cuthbert instantly recognized him as one of his mother's household. A cold fist clutched at his heart at the sight of the boy's face.

"What is it?" he shouted as he jumped to his feet.

"Terrible news, Master Cuthbert, terrible news…" the urchin exclaimed. "The wicked earl came down this morning, with fifty men, set fire to the house and all its buildings and stacks, and has carried off the lady, your mother, a prisoner to the castle."

"On what grounds?"

"On a charge, as he said, of helping traitors."

A cry of fury broke from Cnut and his men.

"That impostor," Cuthbert cried. "The snake will regret this outrage."

"I'll personally remove his lying tongue from his mouth and wave it in front of his eyes… before putting them out," Cnut promised.

"That, too, may have to wait, my friend. We can't take Evesham, but we can carry fire and sword around its walls. Call in all the band. We'll cut off all communication going in or out. If attacked by large forces, we'll retire to the wood and return to the walls as soon as the force is withdrawn. Heavily armored and armed men can't move fast enough to catch us, and if they do chase us, we know we'll pick them off one by one."

"What happened to patience?"

Flushed in his anger, Cuthbert snapped back, "Patience was yesterday's flavor. Vengeance mixed with caution is today's watchword."

As the brotherhood of outlaws assembled on the following morning, a distant horn sounded. Soon enough, sentries in advance of the gathering brought a herald to Cuthbert. He was young, not one of the experienced men accustomed to the role, and clearly expendable, Cuthbert thought. He was very nervous, too, and intoned his message hesitantly.

"I bring you, Sir Cuthbert... er, falsely calling yourself, hmm... Earl of Evesham, a m–message from Sir Fulk. The t–t–traitress, Dame Editha, your m–mother, is in his hands, and she has been found guilty of aiding and ab–a–abetting you in your war against Prince John, the Regent of this kingdom. For that offense she has been... condemned to die."

A cry of rage broke from the assembly. The young man coughed nervously, but doggedly continued.

"N–Noble Sir Fulk, being unwilling to take a woman's life, howsoever forfeited by the law, commands me to say, that if you deliver yourself to him by tomorrow at noon, Dame Editha will be set free." Further growls broke out all around. "But that if by the time the sundial points to noon you have not delivered yourself, she will be..."

"She will be...?" Cuthbert breathed.

"H–h–hanged above the battlements of the castle."

Cuthbert had gone as white as a newly laundered linen sheet, his lips pressed into a thin line. Still, he waved his hand to restrain the outlaws' fury.

"This boy is a herald and protected by the laws of chivalry. Whatever his message, it's none of his doing." He turned to the youngster. "Tell the false knight, your master, that he is a foul thug to visit on a woman the enmity he bears her son. Real men will detest him and know him for the pathetic coward he really is. The offer he makes me is as foul and villainous as himself. Nevertheless, I know he's capable of keeping his word when it suits him or amuses him to do so—tell

227

him that by noon I will be there. My mother is to leave the castle as I enter. Even though he may be gifted my death by this disgusting and deviant trick, he will be shunned like the feckless pariah dog he is." Cuthbert smiled thinly. "Can you remember that?"

The herald gulped, bowed, and left in the escort of two archers.

Cnut was transported by his fury and the archers were beside themselves. Cuthbert alone remained unnaturally calm. Moving away from the others, he paced slowly back and forth among the trees, analyzing the best course to be followed.

After a time, Cuthbert called Cnut to him. "A rope has saved us once, why not again," he began mysteriously. The two talked at length. Cnut went back to his men with a face less despairing than before, and sent off one to a franklin's holding near the forest edge to borrow a thick rope some fifty feet in length.

"Cheer up," Cuthbert told his men jovially. "We've been in dangerous straits before now and survived. Fulk the Fleming doesn't know the man he's dealing with, and we may yet trick the trickster."

It was about an hour before noon when some hundred and fifty bowmen, dressed in dark green jerkins, advanced in solid array on Evesham castle. On the battlements Sir Hubert of Gloucester, a fellow supporter of Prince John—there with twenty mounted men-at-arms—looked down in amusement. "Are these wood-cutters really thinking of attacking us?"

"They might as well think of scaling heaven," Sir Fulk said. "Evesham could resist a month's siege by a force well equipped for the purpose." He sighed, "If it weren't that so many good men are in the king's service, and that these villains shoot straight and hard, I'd open the gates and launch our force against them. We are two to one as strong as they, and our knights and mounted men-at-arms could alone scatter that rabble."

Its cruel outlines conspicuous on the battlements beside the two knights, a gallows had been erected.

The archers stopped a few hundred yards from the castle, and a young man barely out of his boyhood walked alone to the bank of the moat.

"Sir Fulk Fleming of Eresby, false knight and liar," he projected formally in a loud, clear voice, "I, Sir Cuthbert of Evesham, accuse you as a dishonored oath-breaker, and I challenge you to meet me here in the sight of your men and mine, and decide our quarrel as heaven may judge with sword and battle-axe."

"So, this callow pup is the mighty foe," Sir Fulk said with contempt. "Little more than another of Richard of Anjou's catamites."

Sir Hubert frowned. "He is indeed a boy."

Sir Fulk leaned against a merlon and shouted over the battlements. "It's too late for that, you hoodlum. I offered a challenge before, and you refused. You can't now claim what you were too frightened to accept then. The sun on the dial approaches noon. Unless you surrender yourself before it reaches the mark, I will keep my word, and the traitress, your mother, will swing from that beam."

He signed to two men-at-arms, who brought Dame Editha forward on the rampart and placed her so she was visible from below. Even from the heights, those gathered atop the wall heard the gathered Saxons sigh at the sight of the noble woman, descendant of thegns who had owned all the land before the Normans. To Sir Fulk's irritation, no sign of fear showed on her face as she firmly ordered her son to fall back.

"If this unknightly lord carries out his foul threats against me, let him do so. England will ring with the dastardly deed, and he will never dare show his face again where Englishmen gather. Let him do his worst. I am prepared to die."

A murmur rose from the knights and men-at-arms standing round Sir Fulk. Several of his companions had from the first, wild and reckless as they were, protested against this course, which smelt of dishonor. But when he assured them his intention was only to frighten Sir Cuthbert into surrender, and he had no intention of executing the lady, they had consented to take part in the charade. Now, at her fearless words, several were wavering again, among them Sir Hubert of Gloucester, who stepped forward.

"You know I'm your true comrade and the faithful servant of Pr… King John, but I'd rather that my name shouldn't be mixed up in such a squalid business, Fulk. I regret that I ever agreed to it. I beg you, by our long friendship, and for the sake of your own chivalry, to stop this theater. If the dame is guilty, as she well may be, of aiding her son's assaults on your soldiers, then try her properly, and doubtless the court will confiscate her estates. But tell her son that his mother's life isn't in danger, and that he's free to go without worrying that she'll be harmed."

"And if I should refuse to let my enemy escape when he's almost in my grasp what then?" Sir Fulk snapped.

"Then," said the knight, "I and my following will leave immediately, and will make clear to the foolish, but obviously brave young knight out there that Hubert of Gloucester has had no hand in this discreditable business."

Several other knights standing nearby murmured their agreement. "I refuse," Fulk ranted. "Go, then. I am master of my actions, and of this castle."

Without a further word. Sir Hubert turned and left the battlements. His men followed smartly.

Sir Fulk, lips twisted into a feral snarl, watched as Sir Hubert and his retinue crossed the lowered drawbridge. He curdled as the young whelp bowed courteously to the knight and raised his voice so all might hear.

"I always heard you spoken of gallantly, even though you side with a rebel prince, rather than with the King of England," the putrid little cunny said. "I'm happy you're no longer a part of this cheap farce. But no more talk. The sun's at noon, and I must surrender to my fate."

He bowed again, turned, and advanced to the castle gate. "Sir Fulk," he shouted up. "The hour's at hand. Let my mother go, whether she wants to or not. I give you my word that as she leaves I will enter."

Dame Editha tried to resist, but she saw that it would be useless. With a pale face she descended the steps, accompanied by three men-at-arms. She knew that any entreaty to Sir Fulk would be in vain, and with the courage of her race she mentally vowed to devote the rest of her life to vengeance for her son.

The gate opened and in a moment she found herself in her son's arms, sensing the tension beneath his chain mail. Behind her leered the faces of his executioners, all eager to do their lord's murder.

Chapter 23: Abducted!

June to July 1193

"Courage, mother," Cuthbert whispered in her ear after removing his helm. "We're not finished yet."

Cnut stepped forward, keeping a respectful pace behind, ready to offer his hand to Dame Editha. Finally, pushing her from him and into Cnut's care to be led to the group of waiting archers, Cuthbert crossed the drawbridge and passed under the gateway. The heavy portcullis fell after him in a rattle of chains. *Now, Cnut, keep to our plan.* Cnut would detail four men to take Dame Editha into the forest at all speed. Even as he entered the inner bailey he knew the rest of the advance band would string their bows and place a few arrows on the ground in front of them in readiness for instant use. He fervently hoped that no one on the battlements would observe their doings, more intent as they should be on his appearance inside the castle.

He glanced up with satisfaction to see every eye up there glued on the proceedings below them in the bailey, where Sir Fulk had taken his post with the captain of the mercenaries beside him, four of his knights, and the men-at-arms drawn up in order.

Fulk smiled sardonically as Cuthbert entered the wide area. "So, at last," he said, "this masquerade draws to its fitting end. You're in my power. You are a traitor to the king. You have attacked and slaughtered many of my friends. You are an outlaw. For any one of these offenses I could strike off your head."

Cuthbert squared up to his accuser and answered in a calm but firm voice. "I am no traitor to the king, King Richard. I refuse to accept your right to judge me. I can only be tried by my peers. As a knight of England and as rightful lord of this castle as ordered by

King Richard, I demand to be brought before a jury of my equals."

"I don't give a fig for rights or for juries," snapped Sir Fulk. "I have the royal order for your execution, and I should carry it out even if all the knights and barons of the realm objected."

Cuthbert, of course, knew every inch of the castle and, on checking his exact position, eyed the staircase climbing to the battlements a short distance behind a single row of armed men. He turned slowly to look all around to disguise his true intent. He took a step forward. "Fake and dishonest knight, I may die but I would rather suffer a thousand deaths than face a life as yours will be when this deed is known in England. But I'm not yet dead. For myself, I could pardon you, but for my mother—"

With a sudden movement he struck Sir Fulk full in the face with his mailed hand. All his strength went behind the blow.

Sir Fulk fell backward. Blood gushed from his nostrils. Before anyone could recover from their astonishment, Cuthbert burst through the line of men-at-arms, and ran up the narrow staircase as fast as his mail would allow. A score of Fulk's soldiers started in pursuit but Cuthbert gained the top well ahead, and without a moment's hesitation stepped into an embrasure between the merlons and sprang forward and outward. He vanished instantly from sight to a collective gasp.

Thirty feet below his silver-skinned form plunged into the water of the moat, and disappeared in a huge splash. He would have perished miserably, for in his heavy chain mail he was unable to swim a stroke, and the weight dragged him down into the mud forming the bed of the moat. A second splash came before the first had settled as Cnut, holding one end of the rope formed into a large noose, jumped in. Diving to the bottom, he grasped Cuthbert and deftly slipped the rope over his head and under his armpits. As soon as he had it secured, he gave two hard tugs and two archers on the bank began to haul it up, and in a minute Cuthbert was dragged to the bank.

By this time the battlements were crowded by men-at-arms. But as they began loading their crossbows the forest outlaws opened a volley fire that compelled their enemies to duck for shelter. Cuthbert lay on the bank, semi-conscious from the impact of his fall, and water poured from between the gaps in his plate. Cnut and three others at each limb swiftly scooped him up between them and carried him to the center of the outlaw band. Then, as a compact squad, they retreated rapidly toward the distant fringes of the forest before any in the castle could recover wits enough to launch any mounted knights after them.

Cuthbert quickly recovered, and soon felt able to walk. As he did so, the castle gates were thrown open, and men-at-arms sallied out. The archers started at a brisk run, several of them assisting him to hurry along. The rear ranks turned as they ran and let loose flights of arrows at the enemy, who weighed down by their mail barely gained on them.

"They won't chase us for long," Cuthbert said between hard fought for breaths.

"I wish I had your confidence," Cnut replied.

"His men are mercenaries intent on pay for greater matters than a local squabble. The officer in command will have no great stomach for this business. Soldiers-for-pay are hard to get, and Prince John will not be pleased to hear that a number of those whom he's purchased at such expense from foreign parts have been killed in a petty fray."

It seemed Cuthbert's assessment was correct, for after a short time the pursuit ceased. The archers fell back into the forest and soon made their way to its heart.

Here they found Dame Editha recovering from her appalling ordeal. She stayed with them for three days, in the shelter of a hurriedly built hut of tree branches. Her thanks for the deliverance of her son was endless, and when she left to stay with relatives in the south of Gloucestershire, son and mother were heartbroken at being parted again.

Cuthbert now began to worry about Margaret. He felt sure the setback he'd delivered the Fleming would goad him to further atrocity. Although the abbess had assured Cuthbert that Lady Margaret's retreat near Hereford was unlikely to be discovered, he was less hopeful. He knew how great a stake Sir Fulk had in the matter. "It wouldn't be difficult for him to find out through his agents her whereabouts."

Cnut grunted in frustration. "If he goes so near as a mile from the place, I'll have the illegitimate son of a tavern scrub strung up by his balls."

"My lord, we have news," said the constable, as he crossed the rush-strewn floor of the solar toward his master. Sir Fulk glanced up irritably from where he was seated nursing his painfully broken nose. The barber had tried to repair the damage done by the whelp's fist and nearly ended up strung from the very gallows intended for Sir Fulk's aggressor when the pain exceeded the Fleming's good nature.

"What is it?" he growled thickly through clots of scabby blood.

The constable explained that, convinced the abbess would have sent her charge to a religious house rather than to some Saxon franklin, he had checked out those within a few leagues' radius that looked likely for selection. It turned out that the convent in Worcester had a sister establishment near Hereford.

"Yes, yes, so what of it? Have you found the wretched woman yet?"

"I think we have, your excellency. My spies have found out from the country people around there that it was a matter of gossip that a young lady of rank has been admitted by the mother superior."

For the first time, Sir Fulk sat a little straighter and began to look interested. "I'll take a contingent myself to seize her. I don't fear excommunication from the Church for such an action, but the problem is Prince John. He's weak and wavering, at one time ready to defy the Pope's thunder, the next cringing before the spiritual authority."

"Might I suggest a ruse, sire, one that would give you the right to take the lady and be the knight in shining armor?"

* * *

The small convent at Bartestree, outside Hereford had settled down for the hour before Vespers, shortly after dark, when a violent banging at the door alarmed the mother superior. She listened as the sister on janitor duty opened the secure grille to hear a gruff voice.

"We are men of the forest, and we've come to carry the Lady Margaret of Evesham off to a secure hiding-place. The Earl of Evesham, Sir Fulk, has discovered her whereabouts, and will be here shortly. We need to remove her to safety before he arrives."

"Who gave you this authority?" the mother superior demanded, joining the janitor at the door. "I won't surrender her to anyone except the Abbess of St. Anne's. But if you have a written warrant from Sir Cuthbert, the rightful lord of Evesham, I will tell Lady Margaret and act as she says."

"We've no time for arguing," the rough voice growled. "Open the door now, or we'll break it down."

"Break it down?" cried the frightened janitor. "You're no outlaws, the men of the forest respect the Church."

The mother superior added her voice. "If you were who you claim to be you would have the authority in writing I mentioned. If you use force to make an entry, I warn you that excommunication will follow, and you will all be placed under the ban of the Church."

A thundering assault on the door's timbers answered her, which soon yielded to the blows. The sisters and novices ran shrieking through the corridors in blind panic, but the mother superior, made of sterner stuff, stood calmly awaiting in the entry hall.

"Where's the Lady Margaret?" the leader of the shabbily dressed gang of seeming outlaws, demanded.

"I shan't say anything," she said firmly. "Now leave this instant."

The man gestured impatiently, and several others piled in through the door to pass either side of their leader "We'll soon find out," he shouted. The men quickly seized some sisters, who let out terrified screams but refused to answer their torturers' questions.

In response to the sounds of distress, a door opened wide and the men looked up to see a young woman standing proudly in the opening. "If you're looking for the Lady Margaret of Evesham," she said calmly, "you have found her. Don't harm any of the sisters here. I'm in your power, and will go with you, but please don't add to your other sins that of violence against holy women."

The composure of the young girl, and her words, seemed to abash some of the men. They stopped tormenting the nuns, and their leader stepped forward and merely motioned to her to accompany them.

"Farewell, my child," the mother superior said. "God will deliver you from the power of these wicked men. Trust in Him, and keep up your courage. Wickedness will not be permitted to triumph. Be assured that the matter will be taken up with the Pope's legate and Prince John himself."

The men closed in around the now weeping girl and hurried her out from the convent. A litter awaited them outside, and in this they placed the young lady and, carried on the shoulders of four men, she started at a fast pace, surrounded closely by the rest of the band.

It was a dark night and the girl could not see the direction in which they were taking her, but she judged from the turn taken on leaving the convent, that it was toward Evesham. They had gone some miles, when she heard the unmistakable sound of horses trampling the road and a guard of armed men rode up.

For a moment Lady Margaret's heart gave a leap, thinking that she had been rescued by her friends. There was a loud and angry altercation, a clashing of swords, and a sound of shouting and cries outside the litter. Then it was dumped hard on the ground and she heard the clatter of her first captors hurrying away. She peered out to see horsemen surrounding the conveyance. Their commander dismounted, his face partly covered by his cloak.

"I'm very happy, Lady Margaret, to have to saved you from the power of these villains. Fortunately, word came to me that the outlaws in the forest were about to carry you off, and that they wouldn't even hesitate to desecrate the walls of the convent. Assembling my men-at-arms, I rode to your rescue at once, and I'm doubly happy to have saved you—first, as a gentleman, second, as being the man to whom our gracious prince has given you as his wife. I am Sir Fulk of Eresby, Earl of Evesham."

Lady Margaret leaned out of the litter from her ignoble position on the ground and sniffed loudly. "I thought I smelled your stench. Why am I not surprised, Sir Fulk? Why should I believe you? If, as you say, you have saved me from the outlaws, I demand that, as a knight and a gentleman, you return me at once to the convent from which I was taken by force."

"I can't do that," Sir Fulk replied smoothly. "Fortune placed you in my hands, and enabled me to carry out the commands of the prince. Therefore, though I would like to yield to your wishes and so earn your goodwill, my duty toward the prince commands me to make the most of the advantage which fate has thrown my way."

"Fate be blowed, Sir Fulk! You must think me a very silly little thing. Throwing a rough-looking sack over a retainer's badge does not turn a man into an outlaw of the forest. The robber in charge of your 'outlaws' was careless. He had the front of his jerkin open, and I saw the crest on his shirt underneath—yours."

"How very fanciful you are—"

"Enough, Sir Fulk," she interrupted him spiritedly. "You must do as you will. You tried before to carry me off, but failed, and now you've employed other tactics. I've also heard of what you did to Dame Editha, and frankly I would rather die than become your wife."

"Such endearments." The knight sneered. "I haven't the time to spend in idle chatter with you now. We shall have plenty of time at my castle."

Four days elapsed before Sir Fulk went to see the girl he had won by deceit. As he opened the door to the chamber in which she was locked, she burst into a peal of laughter, covering her mouth modestly as she did so.

"What is the cause of your merriment?" he asked harshly. "These bruises are honorably earned."

"Oh, I think not, sir knight. You forget. For many years this was my home and you haven't replaced all the serving girls. I've overheard them gossiping as they clean, chattering about how the handsome young Sir Cuthbert stroked your face."

"My dear, once we're married," Sir Fulk snarled, "you will keep a civil tongue in your head, or I'll have your head set in a scold's bridle—that will curb your merry nature, and keep you silent while I ride you like the mare you are."

And with that he swept from the room. He slammed the heavy oak door behind him so hard its stout timbers shivered.

"Foolish, girl," Lady Margaret said to herself.

It was two days after the kidnapping that the story of how Bartestree Convent had been attacked reached the forest, sparking anxious debates as to the course of action to be taken.

"Is there no way by which we might creep into this den, since we can't burst into it openly?" Cnut said furiously.

"It's ironic," Cuthbert mused, as much to himself as to those around him. "There is a secret way out. Sir Walter told me of it, reckoning that, if he never made it back from the Holy Land, I ought to know about its existence, since few beside himself did. A passage four hundred yards long leads to the little chapel standing in the hollow, and which, hidden among the trees, would be invisible to any besiegers."

"But if anyone inside can escape," Cnut asked, "why not enter by this way?"

"In the castle the entrance is closed by a very heavy slab under the high table in the hall. This is bolted down and is opened by touching a spring which withdraws the bolts and allows the stone to be raised. But it can't be operated from below. There are, as well, several massive doors in the passage, all of which are secured from the one side. So there's no way of getting in… but once we were in, we could easily carry off the lady through this passage."

Cnut then suggested an idea, which Cuthbert eagerly grasped. "If we were to entice the garrison to attack us in force, here in the depths of the forest, when the soldiers pour out to attack us, we could turn the tables by slipping in, and taking the stronghold."

"Cnut, you're a man of brain as well as brawn. It's the very idea, especially since Fulk's garrison has now been enlarged to about five hundred. That's many times more than he needs to hold Evesham, so that force is here for one purpose—to scour the forest and eradicate all the free members of our brotherhood." *He'll use most of his forces, leaving only a skeleton garrison in the castle.*

The plan matured in Cuthbert's mind. "At first we offer limited resistance, slowly falling back. Then, at a given signal, all but twenty of us retire quickly, and sweeping around, make for the castle. They won't suspect we've gone—in this thick wood it's difficult to tell whether twenty or two hundred are opposing you among the thickets. The twenty left behind must shoot thick and fast to make believe that their numbers are great. That's bound to lure the enemy on into the heart of the forest."

"We'll do the proud Norman yet," Cnut said. "I'd love to see his face close up when he finds us masters of his castle. What then will you do, Sir Cuthbert?"

"We can hold the castle for weeks," Cuthbert mused, "and every day is to our benefit. If we find ourselves forced to yield to superior numbers, we can at last retire through the secret passage, and must then scatter and each shift for himself until these bad days are past."

"What do we do if the drawbridge is up and the gate's closed?" Cnut suddenly thought.

"Ah, I have a plan for that." Cuthbert smiled.

Chapter 24: Under Siege

July to September 1193

Evesham castle's walls rang with the pandemonium of preparation. Most of the mercenaries were camped in tents outside the enclosure, for Evesham, large as it was, could hardly contain the four hundred extra men in addition to its usual garrison. The men-at-arms were provided with heavy axes to cut their way through the undergrowth. Some carried bundles of straw, to fire the wood. As summer now ruled and the prevailing breeze lay in the right direction, Sir Fulk hoped that the dry grass and bushes would catch and do more to clear the forest of the vermin infesting it than his men-at-arms.

Fierce hounds, trained to hunt and bring down deer, strained at the leashes held by their handlers. Fulk, his knights, sergeants, and squires were all on foot as they knew that horses were more of a liability in the fastness of the woods than an advantage.

When they reached the main ranges of the forest, a shower of arrows met the army, but at a distance these were more of a nuisance than a danger to men clad in mail. But as they came closer the shafts began to take effect on the foot soldiers' coarse and ill-made protection, although the finer armor of the knights still kept out the arrowheads. In the vanguard, Sir Fulk and his knights advanced cautiously among the trees, gradually pressing their invisible foes back. The hounds worked well at first, but were easy targets and bit by bit their barking lessened amid pained yelps.

Several futile attempts were made to set the forest alight, but in most cases the flames failed to take hold or the fire burnt out in a short time. However, Sir Fulk was pleased with the campaign's overall progress. The resistance was less severe than he had anticipated.

Several small huts and clearings in the forest which had been used by the outlaws, around which crops had been planted, were destroyed, and all seemed to promise well for the success of the enterprise.

In the mid-morning, after the army had trudged toward the distant forest, a heavy cart piled high with cut logs approached the castle gates. The few men of the garrison were enjoying a relaxed day without any expectation of trouble and paid no attention until it reached the moat. Then the warder, seeing its contents, lowered the drawbridge without question, raised the portcullis and opened the gates.

"Who's sent this timber?" he asked, as the man driving the oxen began to cross the bridge.

"The franklin of Hopeburn, excellency."

"Just as well," the warder remarked. "He's two months in arrears and a notice of arrest is due. He can thank the outlaws for not being in chains. Our lord's been too busy to concern himself. Take it to the wood-house."

The laden wagon crossed the drawbridge. As it passed under the great arch of the gateway it came to a sudden stop. With a blow of his ox goad Cnut leveled the warder to the ground and, cutting the ropes tethering the bullocks, drove the heavy beasts into the yard ahead. As he did so the pile of logs fell apart and twelve men armed with bow and pike leaped out. The soldiers lounging in the courtyard gave shouts of alarm and ran to grab their stacked arms. At first they were panic-stricken. But seeing how few were attacking them, they took heart and began to fight back in earnest.

The twelve outlaws were enough to form a solid wall in the narrow gatehouse passageway, six in front with long pikes pointed forward, the others standing slightly behind, firing arrows between their comrades' heads. The garrison fought well and, although losing several men, began to press the little band back. The assistant-warder tried lowering the portcullis but it landed on top of the wagon, which held it there, while its rear wheels blocked the gates from being shut.

The situation was beginning to look grim for Cnut and his men when, with the ringing war cry of *Deus vult*, Cuthbert and a hundred and fifty outlaws rushed across the drawbridge and burst in two streams either side of the stalled wagon into the bailey. Struck with terror at this sudden onslaught, the garrison fell back. The few pikemen dropped their unwieldy weapons and joined the assault with swords and maces. For a few minutes the skirmish was fierce. The outlaws laid about them with a gusto fueled by their loathing for the castle's usurping master.

The defenders, disheartened by the surprise, were swiftly cut down where they fought or, throwing down their arms, cried for quarter. Five men lay dead in their own spreading pools of blood and several more groaned in agony where they had fallen. One of Cnut's men went to a youth sitting on the ground feebly trying to hold in his intestines from a gaping axe wound and slipped his sword through the boy's throat to put him out of his misery.

The survivors speedily knelt before Cuthbert and pledged their arms to his cause. In any case, a few were part of Sir Walter's original retinue left to guard the castle in his absence and expressed themselves happy to see Evesham castle safely in possession of its rightful owner again. A team of the foresters removed the Trojan cart, raised the drawbridge, lowered the portcullis, and closed the gate. To the outside everything looked as before... with one important exception. Sir Fulk's flag was thrown down, and that of the late earl hoisted in its place. Cuthbert had not yet had the heraldic badge King Richard had granted him designed, and so had neither standard nor pennon emblazoned with it.

Leaving Cnut to supervise the disposal of the corpses, Cuthbert went to the chamber above the solar Fulk had imprisoned Margaret. She showed her joy at her deliverance by flinging both arms around his mailed neck and kissing his mouth, which effectively prevented him from saying much.

* * *

Sir Fulk felt no such affection. Words could not portray his stupefaction and rage when a soldier, who had managed to escape the castle at the time of its capture, came and told him the sorry tale. He would have done better to have run the other way. Speechless other than for incomprehensible spluttering, the fuming knight indicated eloquently enough to have the poor wretch strung up by his neck from the nearest tree and left to die slowly for being the bearer of bad news.

No one knew better than the evicted knight the strength of Evesham's curtain walls and the massive *donjon* inside, not to mention its very effective encircling wet moat. He knew that the stronghold was well provisioned because he had collected a large number of bullocks in order to feed all those extra mouths. The granaries were full and the three wells, one in the keep's lower level, never ran dry. With a groan Sir Fulk thought of the rich stores of French wines sitting in his cellars. Foaming with rage, he commandeered a nearby cottar's hut, camped his men around the walls, and prepared for a siege.

After much deliberation, it was agreed in the first instance to attack by filling up part of the moat and using scaling ladders. Meanwhile, those mercenaries familiar with big siege structures, were set to work to construct the engines of war.

Filling in the moat was slow, laborious, and dangerous for those ordered to the task. Huge wooden screens, fixed on wagons filled with sacks of earth, protected the men who had to push the carts to the edge of the moat. The sacks of stones and earth were then thrown in, and the machine pushed backward to get a fresh supply.

Wall-mounted catapults hurled large stones down, eventually weakening the screens, then crashing through to horribly maim or kill those beneath. Day by day the moat filled up across a width of twenty yards. As the wagons crawled closer to the walls, boiling pitch proved very effective, setting the screens on fire and scalding the workers. Hideous screams accompanied the sweetly sickening smell of roasting flesh. The defenders suffered from the mercenaries' extra-large *arbalest* crossbows, but their powerful and accurate longbows took a greater toll since a skilled archer fired up to twelve shafts to the *arbalestier's* two bolts.

After ten days, Fulk's knight-commander judged the landfill solid enough. Thirty strong ladders were distributed among three units of the mercenaries. When all was ready, horns sounded and the troops moved forward in *testudos*, covering each other with their shields so that no man's head or body was visible. Three of the great scale-covered "tortoises" advanced toward the castle. The air thrummed with the thwang and slap of the castle's catapults and mangonels, as they fired showers of stones and darts, breaking up the array of shields and killing many attackers. As soon as a gap appeared in a *testudo*, the archers poured in volleys of arrows.

But the mercenaries advanced steadily, established their footing beneath the castle wall, and prepared their ladders. Safe from the defenders' engines, they were still exposed to hand missiles, pitch, furnace-heated sand, and boiling water, which incapacitated many. Nevertheless, up went the ladders, and the first men began climbing, covering themselves as best as they could with their shields.

Cuthbert's troops dropped showers of boiling pitch and heated sand, which penetrated the mercenaries' mail and caused dreadful torment. Heavy rocks toppled over the battlements carried away men on the ladders to their screaming death or terrible injury. Other ladders, seized by poles with hooks, were pushed backward, with all the men clinging hopelessly onto them, down on those waiting below. For half-an-hour, encouraged by Sir Fulk, the soldiers fought gallantly, but at last they were compelled to retreat, having lost about a hundred men, without one soldier gaining a footing on the walls.

Inside the castle courage ran high. Although they believed that sooner or later the besiegers would break in, they had already been told by Cnut that there was a means of escape unknown to the enemy. This knowledge made for lighter hearts than would have been the case if the only reward for failure were to be the gallows.

On the twelfth day Cuthbert observed the appearance of the first giant siege engines. This monstrous structure consisted of two timber-framed towers on huge wheels, bridged at the top. Between the towers a massive iron-shod beam hung on iron chains. A team of straining men slowly edged the unwieldy contraption forward over the filled-in moat. On the upper story crossbowmen kept up a withering fire to prevent the defenders from using their missile throwers and to keep the archers' heads down. Below were those who worked the ram. Once in position, they began to swing the massive iron-shod tree trunk back and forth until it impacted against the lower stones of the wall.

On the following day giant catapults were brought into play, casting boulders at a corner in the wall, always the weakest spot in a castle's defenses. Day and night these thundered against the walls, while the ram repeated its ceaseless blows on the same spot, until the stone crumbled before it.

The garrison valiantly opposed their enemies' efforts. But each day showed the progress made by the besiegers. Their forces had been increased by at least a further hundred men under the standards of Stafford. Other towers, even larger than the first, now appeared, taller than the castle walls, equipped with drop-bridges. Soldiers in packed ranks, covered by their comrades still higher up, crossed the gap and leapt onto the walls.

As the besiegers gained a sound foothold in two places along the partly breached battlements, Cuthbert gave the signal to retreat to the donjon. The men of the forest fell back hastily, and were safely inside the massive keep before the enemy had mustered in sufficient numbers on the wall to interfere with the retreat. The castle's drawbridge was lowered, and soon the outer walls and baileys were back in Sir Fulk's possession.

The knowledge that the outlaw rabble could hold the keep against him as well as they had the walls tempered his sense of triumph. The donjon's walls were even thicker and, at over eighty feet, far higher and there were no windows other than arrow-slits below the third floor. The single doorway, solid and studded with iron, was the only way in.

Several efforts to assault and batter down the door were in vain. It had been strengthened by beams behind and by stones piled up against it. But it was not Cuthbert's intention to defend the keep.

"We could doubtless prolong the siege for some days, but this castle is mine and my lady's, and when the time comes—which it will—that we are again its owners, we don't want to live in a ruined heap. With just this brave small company, we've killed great numbers of the enemy, for little loss on our side, and we've held them at bay for a month. We've drawn all the Fleming's men inside the walls, so tonight we leave."

Shortly before midnight they all assembled in the hall. Two men pushed aside the mid-section of the great table and Cuthbert, with the knowledge given him by Sir Walter, operated the spring mechanism. The stone turned by means of a counterpoise to reveal a flight of steps. With rush torches to light the way, Cnut and a band of volunteers went first. Cuthbert followed, with Lady Margaret and the few women of the household staff, grateful to be away from Sir Fulk's hateful rule. The rest of the archers brought up the rear. The last of their number was a hugely muscled man, who single-handedly dragged the table section back in alignment before ducking under and down the steps, from where he swung the stone back into its place.

The passage was long and dreary, the walls were damp, and the massive doors so swollen by moisture that it was a struggle to open them. At last, however, they came out into the deserted friary through the carefully concealed tunnel exit.

Most of the archers had agreed to stay together and make their way to join the bands of outlaws in Sherwood Forest, where another returned from the Crusade nicknamed Robin the Hood was said to be fomenting revolt against Prince John. Cuthbert said farewell to his comrades. Cnut begged to accompany him.

"No, my good friend. Go with the others. After ensuring Margaret's safety I'm going in search of the king. I don't know what fortune has in store for me, so it's better I go alone. When I get back, I swear I'll get news to you and call you back to my side."

Cnut accepted this with sadness. "First, I shall guide you, Lady Margaret, the scullions, and maids to a nearby franklin's estate where they will find shelter and you might obtain transport."

"I shall take Lady Margaret with me and travel south to Sir Baldwin's estates where I hope to place her in my friend's care."

When the group arrived at the farmstead, the Saxon franklin took in the castle staff, promising to find them homes farther away from Evesham.

Cnut took his leave of Cuthbert to set off and catch up with his comrades on their northward march. The two clasped arms. "Don't forget me, Cuthbert."

"I won't. Cnut. I'll be back."

Dressed as a yeoman, with the Lady Margaret as his sister, he mounted a horse, with her behind him. Bidding a hearty goodbye to Cnut, and with thanks to the franklin who had aided them, they set off on their six-day journey.

Sir Baldwin received them with joy and immediately entered into the spirit of the thing. "I will say that we have a cousin of my wife's staying with her. We're off the beaten track here, so it shouldn't arouse the suspicion of anyone significant," he assured Cuthbert. "What are you going to do in the meantime?"

"If I remain in England I know that the false earl will move heaven and earth to capture me, which makes my presence here useless." Cuthbert sighed. "So I mean to return to Austria and trace the king's steps from the time he was captured. When I find out where he's held, I'll return and consult on the best steps to be taken."

"I approve of your determination, but I warn—no I beg—that

you take every precaution to avoid falling into the hands of either Archduke Leopold or the Emperor Henry. Think of it—if we can't discover King Richard's prison, how on earth would we ever find the one in which he confined a simple knight?"

A grin cheered Cuthbert's grim countenance. "Less of the simple, if you please."

Chapter 25: A King's Ransom

August 1193 to March 1194

On the following day, with many thanks to his host, Cuthbert started from the castle after a tender farewell to Lady Margaret. She hid badly the foreboding at his going and the tears ran down her cheeks. Cuthbert promised blithely that he would return and lead her back in triumph to her castle. Then he waved and rode for London.

In the apparel of a merchant, he took a tavern room near Cheapside. Here he remained quietly for some days absorbing the gossip. In London, as elsewhere, Prince John's greed and thievery had made him hateful to the people. The wish for the return of their king to free them from his brother's yoke was regularly stated in hushed voices. It seemed a good omen for his impending trip. He was preparing to leave for Brabant, when the sound of a lute and a familiar voice wafted up the rickety stairs to the room he shared with three other guests.

Somewhat startled, Cuthbert went down to the busy tavern room and, sure enough, he saw Blondel, seated in a corner entertaining the crowd. When the youth had finished his song, Cuthbert went up to the minstrel, his face wreathed in smiles. "What are you doing here?"

"Sir Cuthbert! Well met. What am I doing? Playing for my supper, pining for my patron, good King Richard, and keeping well out of the way of his dreadful brother, the Regent Prince of Hell."

Cuthbert confided his intentions, and Blondel instantly offered to go with him. "I'll be your passport," he said grandly. "Minstrels are like heralds, our persons are even regarded as sacred. The nobility of all Europe strives to gain our good will by offering hospitality and presents, all so that we'll relate in harmonious ballads their amazing deeds of derring-do. Belonging to no nation, we can pass freely where a knight is closely watched, perhaps stopped."

"The stumbling block in my plan is that if the locals don't want to tell, or can't reveal his whereabouts, I don't know if we'll ever find the prison holding him."

As Blondel returned his lute to its tough cloth bag, he smiled knowingly. "Ah, well that's where I'll also be of help. My voice can penetrate into places where we can't enter. I'll sing outside the walls of each prison we come to one of the songs which I wrote for him in Palestine. He knows my songs as well as myself. If I sing a verse known only to him and he hears it and follows with the next verse, we'll know."

"It sounds promising and we'll try it out, but if you're to be my passport, I'll have to dress and act as your serving man—I… I think I can manage that."

Keen to stay out of King Philip's domains, they sailed in a merchantman bound for the Netherlands. Blondel looked splendid in his rich attire of bright tunic, hose, and cloak that suited his high standing as a famous troubadour, while Cuthbert slogged along behind in drabs, carrying a long staff, a short sword, and Blondel's precious lute in its silken sack on his back.

They crossed to the Scheldt, and then journeyed along the Rhine as far as Mannheim, sometimes by boat, sometimes on foot. They were also well housed overnight, and were considered to more than repay their hosts by the songs which Blondel sang. At Mannheim they purchased two horses, and then struck east for Vienna. Their wandering was not without danger, for a large portion of this part of Europe had no settled government. Each petty baron in his own castle held only the faintest allegiance to any overlord, made war on his neighbors, blackmailed travelers in the name of taxation, and perpetually warred with the wealthy burghers of the towns. Immense forests covered the hills, which stretched for many leagues in all directions, infested by wolves, bears, and robbers. "Fortunately, my dear Cuthbert," said Blondel airily, "even brigands, men without pity or religion, hold minstrels in high esteem, so we've nothing to worry about." And so the young travelers entered the gloomy shades of the forest without fear.

They had not gone far when a number of desperate looking armed men barred their way.

"Oh good, look, lads, a singer," quipped the ruffian in charge. "The chief will be pleased."

In spite of Blondel's haughty protests, the outlaws surrounded the minstrel and his attendant, and hustled them off down a small track "I am a *trouveur*," Blondel said imperiously, "and as such I expect your courtesy."

"Our chief will be happy to see you. He loves his music."

Cuthbert followed the balladeer, hiding a grin at his friend's discomfort, but hoping nevertheless that the outlaw told the truth, which—as it turned out—he did. After half an hour's slow trudge, they came to a building which had formerly been a shrine, but which was now converted to the bandits' headquarters. The man who came forward to meet them, however, was clearly of noble breeding and wasted no time explaining his presence in the depths of the German forest.

"I am Sir Adelbert of Rotherheim, although you see me brought low. My castle and lands were stolen by my neighbor while I journeyed to the Holy Land with the emperor—that was Frederick Barbarossa, not his weak son, the fourth Henry. Our Crusade fell apart after Frederick's death, but I managed to reach Acre and then I struggled back to this." He waved his arms, indicating the realm that was now left to him.

"I petitioned the emperor to remove this traitorous baron, and I believe he did write, but Henry's power counts for nothing around here. The baron threw the royal proclamation into the fire, and with his fight against the Duke of Saxony, the emperor had weightier matters on hand than to set troops in motion to redress the grievances of a mere knight, and gave the matter no further thought. So, here you see me. But I'm sure," he continued, "I know your face, sir."

"It could well be, Sir Adelbert," Blondel replied, "for I was also in the Holy Land, in King Richard's retinue. Perhaps you saw me at one of his entertainments? My name is Blondel."

"I remember now," the knight said, a broad smile creasing his face. "It was at Acre that I first saw you and heard you play and sing, and if I remember rightly you can wield the sword as well as the lute."

"One can't always be playing and singing," Blondel quipped airily, "and since the place lacked other fun I was forced to do my best against the infidels."

Sir Adelbert had several times glanced at Cuthbert, and at last exclaimed, "I have it now. He's no serving man, sir minstrel, but that valiant young knight who so often rode near King Richard in battle."

"That's me, I'm Sir Cuthbert. Our stories match, Sir Adelbert. Like yourself, I'm disinherited. On my return to England I found my land and titles given me by the king in the hands of a minion of Prince John."

"Ah, hard times everywhere. Come, share our meal," the knight said. "In these woods there's no rank, and I've long dropped my knightly title, and shall not reassume it until I can pay off my score to the false Baron of Rotherheim, and take my place again in my castle."

The minstrel and Cuthbert were soon seated at the table with the knight and three of his principal companions. A huge venison pasty formed the main course of the feast, but hares and roasted game birds were also set out on the table, along with generous helpings of the local ale with its frothing head.

"So, what news have you of King Richard?" Sir Adelbert asked. "I heard that his ship sank in a terrible storm on the homeward voyage."

"There was a storm," Cuthbert said, "but we landed safely on the coast, and then split up into smaller parties. The king headed north, hoping to join his nephew first, and then his sister at the court of Saxony, but he never arrived. On the way he was seized and imprisoned by Leopold of Austria."

"Black treachery on the part of the archduke," Sir Adelbert growled. "And where is the king imprisoned?"

Blondel shrugged his shoulders eloquently, "That we don't know. We know that the emperor claimed him from the archduke, and that he is imprisoned in one of the royal fortresses; but which…?"

Cuthbert leaned forward and searched the German knight's face intently. "Sir Adelbert, since you are on his side, I'll tell you that the real reason for our journey is to discover the place where they have stuck him out of sight."

"He was a kind and noble master, and however long it takes me, I will find him," Blondel added forcefully.

"It is just possible," Sir Adelbert began thoughtfully, looking into the distance, "that I might be able to aid you."

Cuthbert reached out and grasped his host's wrist. "What, sir, what do you know? Please tell us."

"Don't get your hopes up. But I didn't connect at first, and even though we're very isolated here from Vienna, rumors do circulate. I heard of a noble taken in revolt against the archduke some months ago, but in whom the emperor also had an interest. Could this be King Richard? Since both our merry magnates each have a half, I would imagine they'll insist on his being held within easy reach of the other. That means you needn't be searching Styria, the Tyrol, Carinthia, or Salzburg. If he's anywhere it will be in Austria proper."

"Sir Adelbert, for your hospitality and for your advice, I swear that when we find the king and restore him to his rightful place," Cuthbert said passionately, "I will beg him to use his influence with his brother-in-law, the Duke of Saxony, to help restore your fortunes and again make you Baron of Rotherheim."

The two young men remained three days with the outlaws before continuing their quest across the patchwork of German and Austrian petty states. They stopped at many castles and noble houses where they were hospitably received—of course, Blondel was well known to many of the Austrian nobility, who had served in the Holy Land. They lingered for some time in Vienna in hope of finding some hard information on King Richard's whereabouts.

In his songs Blondel artfully introduced allusions to the captive monarch and to the mourning of all Christendom at the imprisonment of its champion. These ballads were not always well received, but in the main he found that a great many of the empire's nobles were indignant and ashamed at the conduct of Emperor Henry and Archduke Leopold.

The secret of Richard's prison place, however, was so well kept that they were unable to elicit any information. The best lead came from a baron who, through marriage, had a foot in both the camps of the emperor and his bitter enemy Henry Duke of Saxony and Bavaria. "My friends," he said, "the emperor will want him hidden in Austria, not Germany proper, but also not too far from his court at Bamberg, so I would look along the line of the Danube from here to Linz."

"That seems to agree with Sir Adelbert's advice," Cuthbert said to his companion later. "We must carry out our original plan, but at least we've narrowed down your singing venues."

Blondel agreed and, leaving Vienna, they wandered along the steep, hilly banks of the river for weeks, visiting one fortress after another. It was not always easy to get close enough to hope that the troubadour's voice might be heard inside, or an answer heard outside. More than once crossbow bolts flew at them from the walls when they failed to answer a sentinel's challenge.

In general, their routine involved wandering casually up to a castle, sitting down within earshot, opening their wallets, taking out food and then, having eaten and drunk, Blondel would produce his lute and sing, as if for his own pleasure. It needed, however, four visits to each castle before they could be sure that the captive was not there, for the song had to be sung on each side.

At the end of the fourth week of wandering, more than fifty miles west of Vienna, they hove in sight of a formidable castle of typically German *bergfried* type perched on top of a rocky hill, high above the Danube. This, a local informed them, was Dürnstein, and here, when singing outside its tall walls, a full rich baritone voice rang out with the second stanza of Blondel's song. With difficulty Blondel and Cuthbert restrained themselves from an extravagant exhibition of delight.

"Watch out, the men on the wall are looking at us suspiciously," Cuthbert managed finally. Blondel resumed singing, a final verse taken from a ballad of a knight who, having discovered the hiding place of his ladylove, prepares to free her from her oppressors and then treat her to pleasures which made Cuthbert blush. Then he packed his lute, and they started on their homeward journey.

There was no delay now. At times Blondel sang, but only when their food supplies ran out. On these occasions the minstrel received a handsome goblet or other valuable token of the owner's thanks, and the sale of this at the next town took them far on their way. "We must avoid France," Cuthbert said. "Philip's men will be on the watch to prevent any news of King Richard reaching England. We'll return through Brabant to sail for home."

As it turned out, he had reason to curse his sensible caution as a waste of valuable time. The king's greatest supporter, the co-regent, Longchamp, Bishop of Ely, sojurned in Normandy. They recrossed the sea, and found the warlike prelate at his cathedral in Rouen. The bishop was hugely relieved to have concrete information about Richard's prison. Within days, his news was published throughout England, and he announced it himself to the barons of Normandy and Anjou to stiffen their resolve against the encroachments of King Philip.

The certainty that the German emperor held Richard of England captive at Dürnstein caused a general stir of anger. The bishop's public embassy to the emperor received encouragement from every quarter, save the courts of Philip and Prince John. Now the matter was out in the open, Pope Celestine discreetly withdrew any support for the English regent and the emperor he had himself crowned. In fact, the open feelings of the empire's major nobility were made so apparent that Henry felt he could no longer refuse to discuss the surrender of his captive.

The emperor agreed to free Richard on the payment of a ransom of a hundred and fifty thousand marks, but insisted that he also be tried of the "many crimes of which he is accused." Found guilty, he would remain in prison; acquitted, he would be released.

The size of the ransom caused the people of England to shudder, but preparations were quickly made for collecting the sum. Queen Eleanor was unceasing in her efforts to raise the money for the release of her favorite son. The nobles contributed their jewels and silver; the people contributed goods, for coinage was barely used in England. Prince John placed every obstacle in the way of the collection, but enough barons threatened civil war that John's mercenaries muttered about not supporting him.

Eventually, Henry called a council at Worms before which King Richard was brought. Cuthbert and Blondel retraced their steps across the country to be there. The emperor enthroned himself on a raised dais and close in his company sat the great feudal dignitaries of the empire. Lesser barons and knights lined the side walls of the great hall.

When the doors opened and King Richard entered, the whole assembly, except the emperor, stood in respect. Although pale from his long confinement, Richard's proud air was in evidence, and the eyes that had flashed so fearlessly at the Saracens looked as sternly down the long lines of German barons. He wore his mustache with a short beard, and his curly hair closely cropped and topped by a velvet cap and gold coronet. A fur-lined scarlet robe fell over his coat of mail to complete his splendid presence.

Richard strode to his appointed place and turned majestically to the assembly. His ringing voice echoed through the hall. "Counts and lords of the Empire of Germany, I, Richard, King of England, Normandy, Aquitaine, and Anjou do not recognize your right to try me. I am a king, and can only be tried by my fellow monarchs and by the Pope, who is the head of Christendom. I might refuse to plead, refuse to take any part in this assembly, and appeal to the Pope, who alone has the power to punish kings."

The gathered host held onto the word "might."

"But I waive my rights and rely on the chivalry and decency of the lords of Germany. I've done no man wrong, and would appear as fearlessly before an assembly of peasants as before a gathering of nobles. Such faults as I may have, and none are without them, are not those with which I am charged. I've slain many men in anger, but none by duplicity. When Richard the Lionheart strikes, he strikes in the light of day. He leaves poison and treachery to his enemies, and I hurl back with indignation and scorn in the teeth of any who make the charges brought against me."

So saying he took his seat amid subdued but universal applause from the crowded hall. Cuthbert's soul rang with the sturdy rebuttal.

The trial then commenced. A cleric read out the list of charges, chief among them the murder of Conrad of Montferrat. The king himself refuted this in a few scornful words. The accusation that he, Richard of England, would stoop to poison a man whom he could have crushed in an instant, was too absurd to be seriously treated. His peers in judgment all agreed.

On the other major counts—of thwarting the plans of the Crusade by refusing to be bound by the decision of the other leaders, and of treating with the enemy by making a peace with Saladin injurious to the Christian cause—the king responded fiercely.

"I'm sure that no one here believes this idle tale. That I didn't always agree with the other leaders is true, but I call on everyone here to say whether, had they listened to me and followed my advice, the Crusade would not have had a different ending. Even after Phillip of

France had withdrawn, even after I had been deserted by Leopold of Austria, I led the troops of the crusaders from every danger and every difficulty to within sight of the walls of Jerusalem. If I had been supported with enthusiasm, Jerusalem would have been ours, but the apathy, the folly, and the weakness of the leaders brought ruin on the army. They thought less of conquering Jerusalem than of thwarting me. And I say that they—not I—sacrificed the success of the Crusade. As to the terms of peace, how were they made? I, with some fifty knights and a thousand followers alone remained in the Holy Land. Who else, I ask, under such circumstances, could have obtained any terms whatever from Saladin? It was the weight of my arm alone which saved Jaffa and Acre. If I had followed the example set by Austria and France, not one foot of the Holy Land would now remain in Christian hands."

The trial soon ended, and without any dissent his peers acquitted the King of England of all the charges brought against him. But the full amount of the ransom had not yet materialized, and the emperor insisted on remanding him in custody. At length, by prodigious exertions, half the amount claimed was collected, and pressured by the nobles of his own empire and the papal threat of excommunication, Henry consented to release Richard on receipt of half the ransom and his royal promise that the remainder should be made up.

"Have you heard of the treachery of the French king?" Cuthbert indignantly asked Blondel. "He's intrigued with Prince John to offer the emperor a greater sum than that asked for the ransom in order to keep the king behind bars in Germany."

"Fume not, Cuthbert. I shouldn't worry. Popular opinion is too strong."

He was right, and when the Pope threatened the excommunication of all the German and Austrian nobility the emperor, feeling that he would risk his throne if he refused, at last opened the prison gates on February 4, 1194 and let the king go free. Sir Cuthbert de Lance was one of the first to fall at Richard's feet, with Blondel jostling him a moment later and then Sir Baldwin. These three, plus three sergeants, were among the small entourage the emperor had permitted to accompany the king across Europe to take ship for England.

"How pleased I am to see you, my loyal friends," Richard boomed with outstretched arms.

"Many more await you in England, your Majesty," Cuthbert replied.

Horses had been arranged for the whole party, and without a moment's delay they started, even at the last moment worrying that Henry might change his mind. So, with fear on their heels, the royal retinue made no long stops on the way, riding almost all day and night, changing horses frequently—for everywhere the people received Richard with affection. In the lands governed by his brother-in-law, the Duke of Saxony, they were safe, but it was deemed worth the risk to save time by cutting through Philip's narrow northern domains to the Channel, where they arrived moments ahead of their oppressors.

As they were hastening toward Boulogne, news reached the party that a second embassy from John and Philip had caused wavering Henry to change his mind again. Anticipating their presence in his kingdom, Philip had sent a contingent of knights and men-at-arms to arrest his rival.

Almost flying from his saddle at the edge of Boulogne's dock side, where they were to abandon the horses, Sir Baldwin dashed through the night to find a ship to take them aboard and sail immediately. The others hurriedly dismounted, collected saddle packs and weapons and waited anxiously. Sir Baldwin seemed gone a long while. Cuthbert took out a small whetstone and honed the edge of his axe blade to calm his racing fears. A clatter of boots on cobbles announced the return of Sir Baldwin, who loomed out of the dark a moment later. "Sire!" he gasped breathlessly. "I've engaged a vessel. We must board this instant. From its deck I've seen a line of fast-moving torches. I fear Philip's double-dealing."

"Let them try to take me—"

260

"Your Majesty," Cuthbert cried out, "England needs you. You must go. The rest of us will hold them off."

They bundled the reluctant king aboard the cog, whose captain and sailors readied it for sea. Cuthbert, Blondel, Sir Baldwin, and the three sergeants ran back to the narrow waist where the curving mole of the port stuck out into the harbor and screeched to a halt just as a group of mounted men clattered onto the cobbled dock. Its surface proved too treacherous for horses and they swiftly dismounted. Unsheathing long swords, they sprang forward to engage the Englishmen.

Cuthbert wielded his long-handled battle-axe and strode toward the nearest man on his side. He took a mighty swing. The axe caught the other's sword blade with a loud ringing sound. His opponent shouted in anger and lunged under Cuthbert's guard. The young knight sidestepped the killing stroke and then brought the haft of his axe up under his foe's chin. The French knight staggered back, lost his footing on the wet stones and, with an anguished cry, toppled off the dock into the sea. The weight of his armor dragged him immediately under with a swirl of bubbles.

Philip's men allowed no time for recovery. Another knight engaged Cuthbert immediately and two more advanced, hindered only by the narrowness of the wharf at this point.

His shoulder bumped into someone and he was about to react when he saw Blondel from the corner of his eye. The minstrel gave an evil grin from under his helm's nose guard as he slashed at the second of Cuthbert's assailants. "Back up slowly, Sir Cuthbert. I think the ship's about to sail."

At that moment, Sir Baldwin disengaged and began to cover them as they all retreated, holding at bay the furious French soldiers who were unable to flank them because of the harbor waters close by on either side.

"I don't think we can all get safely on board," Cuthbert shouted. "You go now Sir Baldwin—jump up! Now you Blondel."

"I'm not leaving you—"

"For God's sake go! The king needs you."

Then he saved his breath to fight. Throwing down the axe and taking up his sword, he laid about him in large wide sweeps, which kept the Frenchmen on their toes. When it began to look as though Cuthbert would be soon overwhelmed, the leading three of those attacking him suddenly screamed in pain and fell, arrow shafts sticking out from their mail. A moment later two more collapsed, writhing in agonizing death throes.

"Cuthbert jump! Give me your hand," Blondel shouted. He whirled around, flung out his hand, and grasped the minstrel's before leaping for the departing ship's rail. Without help he would have shared a watery grave with the man he'd dispatched earlier. Thanks to three sailors on the vessel's complement, good archers all, they were saved and in a few moments the harbor disappeared into the dark night.

Prince John was at Rochester on the first day of March when he received a terse message from his ally in France. Philip simply said: "Look to yourself; the devil is loose." The following day the sails of Richard's ship were sighted off Dover. Thanks to his proximity, John made the port about the time the king landed and was the first to present himself. Cravenly, he fell to his knees.

"Oh, thank God, you're safely returned to us, dear broth—"

"Save it, you turd of a pariah dog!" Richard cut him short. "God knows where our father whelped you."

John became even more abject as he begged pardon for the injuries he had inflicted. As he gabbled on, a dark stain grew on the front of his hose, and a yellow pool began to spread around his knees. The sharp stink of the prince's urine suffused the sea air. King Richard waved him aside with a look of contempt.

"Go," he said, "and may I forget your injuries as speedily as you will forget my pardon."

Then the cavalcade rode on to London, where he was received with exuberant joy by his subjects.

* * *

With a clatter of hoofs Sir Fulk and some twenty of his knights rode out of Evesham castle, ahead of a troop of men-at-arms and a lumbering baggage train heaped with personal—mostly stolen—belongings.

"Farewell to this godforsaken place and all speed to France where King Philip awaits our services," spat the villainous knight, his breath pluming in the cold morning air. "Curse that cringing cur John who has lost me everything!" Having heard of King Richard's return, Sir Fulk bitterly accepted that he had lost all claim on Evesham castle, and was almost certainly at risk of arrest for backing Prince John.

Leaving the rest to follow, Sir Fulk and four of his most trusted men galloped south for the distant coastal port from which they would cross to France.

It was just where the highway was about to plunge into Evesham forest that Sir Fulk's charger suddenly reared with a snort of pain, a crossbow quarrel jutting from its breast, and threw him crashing to the sodden ground.

The other mounts came to a confused, skittering halt as the dying charger's legs thrashed helplessly and the dazed Sir Fulk scrabbled to regain his feet. Seeking the foes who had fired at him, he caught a movement in the dark fringe of the forest and gave a gasped curse.

Cuthbert stepped steadily into the open ground, dropped his crossbow, and advanced five paces toward the man who would have murdered his mother and stolen his betrothed.

Coming to a halt some twenty paces from the staring knight, he drew his longsword from its scabbard.

"The time has come, Sir Fulk, to face up to your evil doings. I will rid this land of you once and for all." Cuthbert spoke in a steely, measured tone.

Sir Fulk drew himself up to his full height and sneered, "The boy fancies himself a champion, but he's not worth a fight. See to him, men!"

There was an awkward silence, and then the four knights urged their horses to back-step. "Sire, the young man is surely owed a fair fight after all that's passed."

"Chivalry rules after all then? Ha!" the rattled Fleming jeered scornfully with a quick glance at his men. "So be it then."

Sir Fulk drew his sword and thrusting it before him strode belligerently toward silent Cuthbert.

"You arrogant little bastard. I'll make you pay for all the grief you've caused me. The little slut you wish to wed will never enjoy your puny cock. I'll take it off you and stuff it in your mouth before I split you end to end."

Powerful strides had taken him close to Cuthbert, who stood stock still, his young face tightening into a mask of fury, eyes full of glittering hate, until, fast as a whiplash, in a blur of movement he swung his sword in an unstoppable horizontal arc that caught Sir Fulk's mailed neck and tore through metal, sinew, and bone, and sent the head flying to disappear with a heavy thump into the forest undergrowth.

Sir Fulk's decapitated body stood frozen in mid-stride, sword raised in attack. Gouts of thick blood spurting skyward before it toppled sideways and hit the ground with a metallic crump.

Cuthbert stood trembling, even as the horsemen rode off.

King Richard's first orders dispossessed all John's minions from the castles and lands which had been taken from his loyal barons. Some resisted, but their fortresses were quickly stormed.

Dame Editha's refuge had remained undiscovered and mother and son were soon happily reunited. After sending a courier to Nottingham to contact Cnut and his merry men in Sherwood, and spending a few days sorting matters out at Evesham, he rode for Dorset to collect Lady Margaret from Sir Baldwin's care, where she had been safe and sound with the knight's wife.

She was now seventeen, and offered no objections to King Richard's command that she should at once marry the Earl of Evesham. By his order, the wedding took place at Westminster and the king himself gave away the bride. Cnut acted as Cuthbert's groomsman, while Father Francis officiated as server to the Bishop of London.

All of Evesham turned out to greet the newly wed couple. In the few weeks since his return to England, the young Earl of Evesham's retainers had worked hard to repair the damage Fulk's men had caused to the castle's fabric. The curtain wall still showed the marks of ram, ballista, and mangonel, but within the baileys everything looked spick and span. Great care had been taken over Cuthbert and Margaret's private apartments and once they were finally alone he took his wife in his arms.

"How many children shall we have?"

Margaret smiled happily. "Half a dozen of each, God willing."

"When shall we start?"

Her smile broadened. "How about now?"

As Dame Editha went off to make arrangements for the comfort of Father Francis, Cuthbert eagerly settled him on a window seat, uncaring of the pouring rain beyond the mullions of Erstwood Manor. He loved his castle, but he and Margaret loved the restored manor equally and enjoyed a break away from the bustle of Evesham. A distant crack of thunder signaled the approaching heart of the storm.

"Father, what do you wish to know about the Crusades?"

"Well, Cuthbert," said Father Francis, "to this day, my son, the Crusades have brought Europe little but woe. Can you tell me that anything has changed?"

"No, father." Cuthbert slowly shook his head sadly. "Nothing's changed in the last hundred years… and, do you know, I don't think things will change in Palestine for a thousand more."

Historical notes

Several of the places in which the story is set are fictional. Although the town of Evesham is real enough, there was never a Norman castle built there. Across the River Avon, however, the suburb of Bengeworth did have a castle.

Evesham is home to one of Europe's largest abbeys, founded by Bishop Egwin, an early Saxon convert to Christianity in the eighth century. After the conquest of 1066, a Norman knight built Bengeworth castle, which rivaled the abbey for income, so when some drunken knights trampled the abbey's graves, it provided the excuse to have the castle leveled—an example of the power of the Church in those days.

The Baron of Wortham is as fictitious as his stronghold, and the same goes for Sir Baldwin of Béthune. In fact the only real historical characters are King Richard I, his brother Prince John, King Philip of France, the German Emperor Henry IV, Pope Celestine III, Duke Henry III of Saxony, Archduke Leopold of Austria, the unfortunate Conrad of Montferrat, who did not end up succeeding King Guy (Lusignan) of Jerusalem, Longchamps, Isaac Comnenus, and the Ayubbid sultan, Saladin. Blondel may or may not have been a real character but lives the annals of romantic chivalry..

King Richard frequently removes gold chains from his neck as a form of payment to his loyal followers, or breaks up the links to distribute. In the early medieval period, coinage as a means of payment was almost unknown in England. Even in Europe coins were rare, usually of silver mined in Saxony (which is one reason the dukes of Saxony were powerful princes). The majority of trade took place through the exchange of goods of similar values.

However, the first notions of banking were beginning, with the Swabians (Swiss) and North Italians in the lead. The Jewish communities typically handled monetary transactions because they were allowed to charge interest (usury), which was illegal for Christians.

The basic silver coin in circulation was based on the Imperial Roman *denarius* (penny). Twelve *denarii* made a *solidus* (shilling, or *schilling* in old German), and 20 *solidii* became a *libra* (pound). The system was retained in use in Britain until the later 20th century; this explains why the pre-decimal notation for a penny was *d* for *denarius*. The *L* of *libra* was—and still is—written in old-fashioned style as £.

At the end of the 12th century as much as half of Europe was still covered in dense forest, although land-clearing was getting under way on an almost industrial scale. The forests made ideal hiding-places for those placed outside the law—outlaws. In England of the time, many outlaws were not criminals, merely unfortunate tenant farmers who had been thrown off their lands—usually Saxons who, after the Norman conquest, were regarded as little more than slaves by most Norman barons.

Saladin's popular image as a chivalrous and tolerant ruler is at odds with his massacre of all Christians when he attacked Gaza in December 1170 during his rise to power. On the other hand, as a strictly orthodox Sunni Muslim, he disobeyed his commander Nur ed-Din's orders to eradicate the Shi'a Muslims in Cairo and famously spared Jews and Christians when retaking Jerusalem from the crusaders in 1187. His relations with Richard the Lionheart are well attested to. Through a mix of extraordinary good luck and political skill, Saladin united the fractured Muslim world and made it possible for Islam to triumph over Christendom in the Holy Land.

During the Middle Ages, the term "Saracen" was used generally to cover all Muslims of whatever kind. It comes originally from the Latin *Sarakene*, or the people inhabiting the region around the town of Saraka, located in the northern Sinai between Egypt and Palestine, and which Cuthbert passes in the story in Chapter 14.

In Chapter 19 Cuthbert speaks of the "Swabian people." The southern part of the Duchy of Swabia later became northern Switzerland, always rebelliously independent of Austria.

Read an extract from:

Prologue: A Fatty Problem

Northern India, March 1857

On March 29, 1857, the burning heat of a late Indian afternoon was neither worse than the days before it, nor any better. The stifling humidity was energy-draining, and without even a hint of a cooling breeze, it left the native Hindu and Muslim infantrymen—the sepoys—drenched in their own sweat. This was Barrackpur, the British army's military station of the 34th Native Infantry, standing on the Bengal plain near Calcutta.

The oppressive heat seemed to suck all sound from the air and the base seemed very quiet; hardly anyone was outside. The handful of British officers lounged in the partial cool of their verandas while the native sepoys kept to their quarters in an attempt to avoid exertion.

Suddenly, the drowsy peace of the afternoon was shattered by loud shouts in a mixture of Hindi and English. At first it was hard to make out the meaning of the commotion, but one by one, sepoys came to the doorways of the regiment's barracks, overlooking the parade ground. They were greeted by the sight of a Hindu sepoy marching up and down the parade ground waving his loaded musket and calling on the men to mutiny, swearing that he would shoot the first European officer he saw. "Come out you blackguards," he yelled shrilly, "turn out all of you, the English are coming for us. Through biting these cartridges we shall all be made infidels!"

Most of the men stood and stared, fearful of doing anything, but one, with more presence of mind, slipped away and ran to find Lieutenant Baugh, the regimental adjutant, to tell him that Sepoy Mangal Pandey was in a "fearfully excited state." Baugh immediately called for his horse as he checked that all six chambers of his revolver were loaded with powder and ball, buckled on his sword, and galloped to the barrack lines.

Meanwhile, another sepoy had fetched Hewson, the English sergeant-major, who shouted commands to the native officer in command of the quarter-guard. "Jemadar Ishwari Prasad! Arrest that man immediately!"

"I cannot take the madman on my own, sir!" the jemadar, or noncommissioned officer, complained.

"Then turn out your guard, man!" Hewson shouted as he ran toward the offending soldier, who was still urging his fellow sepoys to mutiny at the top of his voice.

Mangal Pandey stopped ranting the moment he heard hoof-beats and ran to take up a position behind the quarter-guardhouse gun. As Lieutenant Baugh galloped onto the parade ground shouting, "Where is he?" Pandey took aim with his musket.

"For your life, sir, to the right." the sergeant-major shouted. "The damned sepoy's going to fire at you."

And Pandey did, as the adjutant rode at him. The sepoy missed Baugh, but the ball struck the horse and both rider and mount were brought down. Not allowing him time to reload the musket, Hewson charged at Pandey and the men locked in combat. The sepoy managed to free his weapon and landed a hefty blow to the sergeant's head, and Hewson went down, stunned.

Pandey continued to exhort the sepoys who had turned out to watch the proceedings to grab their arms, and although his comrades hesitated to join him, neither did they make any movement to arrest him. At great risk to his own safety only one sepoy tried restraining Pandey, who by now had reloaded his musket. Shaikh Paltu was threatened with violence by his fellow Indians and then forced to back off when they began throwing stones at him. As he did so, Jemadar Ishwari Prasad, brought out the armed guard, but instead of protecting their white officers, they began beating both men with their rifle butts.

Their situation began to look desperate, but at that moment General Hearsey, the regiment's commanding officer, galloped onto the parade ground with two other white officers, his son and a Major Ross. At a glance he saw what had occurred. He whipped out his pistol and aimed at the nearest sepoy of the guard. "Back off from the officers and arrest that man," he ordered the guards. "I'll shoot the first man who disobeys!"

When no one moved, he raised the pistol and took a bead on the nearest man's head. His officers sighted on two others. One by one, they replaced their muskets to arms and began walking to where Pandey still ranted. Seeing his cause lost, the sepoy turned his musket on himself and discharged its contents into his own body.

Two days later, the 19th Native Infantry based a hundred miles away at Baharampur was disbanded following similar—but worse—violence which had broken out over the use of the new Enfield musket cartridges, said to be greased with beef and pig fat, to which Hindu and Muslim sepoys alike objected.

On April 3 Mangal Pandey, who had only wounded himself, was hanged, and the same fate awaited Jemadar Ishwari Prasad for refusing to order the sepoys to assist the officers Pandey had attacked and for joining in their battering. The first rebel's name went down in history as the whites in India afterward used it as slang for the mutineers—the "pandies."

On May 6, the 34th Native Infantry was also disbanded as a collective punishment and only Shaikh Paltu came out of the business with his head held high. In recognition of his gallantry, General Hearsey promoted him to the rank of havildar, the native rank of sergeant.

The British and other Europeans scattered across the great swathes of the sub-continent fervently hoped that the example set by the execution of the ringleaders and the disbandment of the 19th and 34th would have a wholesome effect.

In this, they were to be sorely disappointed.

Time for blood to flow.

Chapter 1: Before the Storm

Northwest province, February 1857

Far away from Calcutta, under the spring sunshine the British cantonment of Sandynugghur looked bright, alive and glittering under the afternoon sun. Like other British garrisons in the Northwest province of India, it stood separate from the town, forming a suburb of its own. The camp consisted of the barracks and a *maidan*, or common, on which the Indian troops drilled and around which stood the military bungalows and those of the station's civil officers and few merchants who completed Sandynugghur's white population.

The timber bungalows were attractively built in a rustic style—some roofs thatched, others of stone slates or wooden shingles. All had wide verandas running right around them, with blinds in their openings made of thin slats of wood, known locally as tatties, which when let down gave shade and coolness to the rooms behind. About halfway along the sprawling line of bungalows, one of the larger houses belonged to James Warrener, a major in the 151st Bengal Native Infantry, and under the shade of its veranda two boys—of fifteen and sixteen—lolled idly in large reclining chairs. The books open on their laps suggested that they had been reading, but both were now eating bananas and talking to two young women, some three years their senior, who sat beside them.

Kate Warrener and her brothers Ned and Dick were entertaining Rose Hertford, their cousin. Born in India, the Warrener children had each gone to schools in England at age eight or nine. Their mother had sailed for England with Dick, the youngest, but fell ill and died soon after reaching home. Dick's passion for the sea had earned him a commission the year before as a midshipman in the Royal Navy.

His ship, the *Agamemnon*, lay at Calcutta and he had been given a month's leave to visit his father up-country.

"You'll really make yourselves ill if you eat so many bananas," Kate teased.

"I'm not that bothered about them," Ned replied languidly. "They're tasteless and I'd much prefer a good apple, but I need to do something and I'm too lazy to go on with this Hindi grammar. Anyway, how can I concentrate on work with you out here chattering?"

Kate bridled at her brother's words. "That's very good, Ned," she retorted, "when it's you who does all the talking. You ought to shut yourself in the study and not sit out here where you're bound to be interrupted."

"I've done three hours' steady work this morning, Kate; and that—in this climate—is as much as my brain will stand." He reached up and gingerly patted his mop of straw-colored hair. "In fact, it's started to boil."

In some bungalows the visitor walked from the garden, or compound as the colonial expatriates called them, directly into the dining room—a large, airy space with no carpet or mats on the polished floorboards. Apart from the simple dining table and chairs, the room was generally unfurnished, as it only saw use at meal times—the veranda acted as the bungalow's real living room. Young Dick stretched his wiry frame out in one of the comfortable cane chairs and yawned happily.

"Cover your mouth," Kate admonished her brother primly. She stood briefly to tug her own chair back from where the sun had reached under the veranda overhang. The cane or bamboo chairs of all shapes were cool, light, and easy to move to wherever the shade chased the sun's daily movement.

"I must get my fan." Cousin Rose barely tolerated the heat but she owned that Indian houses had some good points, particularly astonishing to a visitor from England that every bedroom had its own bathroom—an important adjunct in the tropical East. She crossed the dining room and disappeared into the drawing-room, off which the bedrooms opened. Across India the drawing-rooms were traditionally considered to be the special preserve of the family's ladies. The popular furnishings reminded them of home—light chintz chair-covers, patterned muslin curtains, and, most importantly, a piano.

Ned reached an arm back languidly and ran a fingernail with a rat-a-tat down the wooden louvres of the Venetian blind set into the French-doors behind him. The dining room had three of these double doors, each with a blind so that even when closed the air could pass freely.

Rose returned, fan in hand and paused in the doorway, head slightly cocked. In the quiet of the afternoon a comforting buzz of Hindi conversation reached them from around the corner. On the side not used by their employers, the veranda also acted as the servants' hall. In between tasks the domestics sat on their mats, mending clothes, talking, and dozing. The official servants' quarters were out by the stables, where they could cook and eat, but they usually preferred the veranda's cool freshness for sleeping. It also meant that they were close at hand when anyone called. At night they rolled themselves up in a thin cloth or blanket. Wrapped from head to toe, they looked like a row of mummies lined up against the wall.

Edward Warrener had returned from Westminster School in England with his sister and cousin Rose three months before. His father had sent for Kate, who had already completed her education and done two years in a ladies' finishing college, to look after his household, and invited Rose—the orphan child of his sister—to be her companion. Ned was going into the British-Indian army and the major thought his eldest son would be better off leaving school early and completing his education in India. This included learning the major native language of northern India from which Kate and Rose were distracting him.

"You know father says fluency in Hindi, at least, will give you a leg up in the army." Dick smiled as his words produced a mock scowl on his brother's face.

With barely a year between them, the boys were of similar physical build, Dick perhaps the slighter and more wiry, as suited a naval powder monkey expected to whip up and down ropes at the drop of a hat. Ned had an inch on Dick's height—a matter they argued over continuously—but the greatest distinction lay in their hair, Dick's the darker brown and curly, while Ned's topped his boiling brain in a straight, bleached flop.

The clopping tread of two horses came to the lazy group from along the road.

"Captains Dunlop and Manners," Dick said. "Bet you anything. Will either of you bet, girls?"

Neither replied, trying hard as they were not to appear too eager. Ned and Dick exchanged sly nods as the two horsemen rode up and proved Dick correct. As they dismounted they threw their reins to the *syces* who ran just behind their masters. The grooms were ever in readiness to take control of the horses whenever they dismounted.

"Good-morning, Miss Warrener. Good-morning, Miss Hertford," Captain Dunlop said breezily. "We've some interesting news for you."

"Really?" both girls said as one, as they shook hands with the two tall, good-looking and sun-bronzed officers.

"What is it?" Kate asked, but it was Manners who answered.

"A family of wild boars has come down from the hills and begun rampaging through the cultivated fields four miles away near Meanwerrie. So tomorrow morning there's going to be a pig-sticking." He added the last with a flourish and an inviting bow.

"You will come with us tomorrow to see the fun, won't you?" Dunlop gave both girls an eager appraisal.

"Oh yes," Kate said. "We'd love to, wouldn't we Rose?"

If Rose looked doubtful, she hid it well, Ned thought.

"Wonderful!" Dick shouted, "I'm in luck! I really wanted to see a wild boar hunt. Do you think the old man will let me have a spear?"

Ned gave his brother a sideways glance. "Hardly, Dick… last time you went out you fell off three times at some jumps only two feet wide. If you did that in front of a pig, he'd rip out your guts before you had time to say 'apple sauce.' Anyway, you'd almost certainly poke someone's ass with your spear."

Dick laughed. "I'm all right with a spear, thank you, and that was the first time I'd ever been on a horse. Are you going to hunt, Ned?"

"No way. I can ride well enough on a road, but you need to be a first-class horseman to gallop across this country, looking at the boar instead of where you're going… and carrying a spear in one hand."

"Do you think father will hunt?" Kate asked Captain Dunlop.

"I don't know, the major's a famous spearman…" he paused to glance up. "But he's here to speak for himself."

Major Warrener, a tall, fit-looking soldier in his early forties, still in day uniform, drove himself up in a small trap. Ned saw his father's usual expression of cheeriness and good temper clouded by some problem. As he pulled up his face looked serious. Then his brow cleared when he caught sight of the gathering.

"Ah, Dunlop, Manners, brought the news about the boar, eh?"

"You *will* take us with you?" Kate entreated.

"Oh yes, please uncle," Rose added in a fainter voice.

"Yes, yes, you can go. I'll drive you myself. There, I'm going to get out of this uniform—it's unusually hot for the time of year." He produced a cheroot from a cigar-case and shouted for a light. "Aglow!" An Indian servant ran up with a piece of red-hot charcoal held in a little pair of tongs.

"Sit down and make yourselves comfortable until I come back."

With their father suddenly absent, Ned sensed he and Dick were intruding and thought it best to leave the two young captains alone with Kate and Rose. They strolled to the stables, where Ned chatted with the *syces*, asking in which direction Meanwerrie lay. Like all English children raised in India, when the boys had left for an English school they had spoken Hindi fluently but then quickly forgotten it.

After three months' revising Ned found that it was all coming back. Apart from the remembered odd useful expletive, Dick had lost the skill altogether.

When they returned to the veranda the girls had gone indoors and their father was talking in hushed tones with his fellow officers. Major Warrener hesitated as the boys stepped up onto the boards.

"What is it, father?" Ned asked, struck with the grim expression on all their faces.

"Well, Ned, Dick, for some months past there have been all sorts of curious rumors running through the country. Chapatis have been sent around, and that's always an ominous sign."

Dick opened his eyes wide and gave his father a puzzled look. "Do you mean the chapatis we eat?"

"Yes, Dick. Nobody knows who circulates them, or the exact meaning of the signal, but it seems to be an equivalent for 'prepare' or 'make ready.' A chapati's quickly made and they're the bread eaten on a journey, and hence probably their significance. At any rate, these things have been circulated among the native troops all over the country. Strangers are known to have come and gone, and there's a generally uneasy, unsettled feeling among the troops."

"Is this to do with the new Enfield P53 rifle cartridges?" Ned asked, risking a sly glance at Dick to see if his brother had noted his knowledge.

"In part. A ridiculous rumor has spread among the sepoys that the new cartridges have been greased with pig's fat—if you heed Muslims—or cow fat, if you listen to the Hindus. They say that when they bite off the cartridges' paper ends before loading them their lips will be contaminated. I've just received news from Calcutta that the 19th native regiment at Baharampur has behaved mutinously over them, and it's feared the regiments at Barrackpur and Dum Dum may follow. The senior staff have a bad feeling that all the troops in Bengal are suspect."

Manners looked thoughtful and then tentatively added, "But we've no reason to think that the spirit of mutiny has spread to us in the northwest. Surely our own regiment can be relied on?"

"I hope so, Manners," the major replied, "but I wish that I'd let the girls stay on in England for another year—but who could foresee this? In fact, until this morning, although there's been a good deal of talk, we all hoped it would pass off without anything coming of it. If it spreads further it's impossible to say what may happen. All we can do is be watchful and avoid saying or doing anything that might offend the men's prejudices."

He turned to Dunlop. "We must explain to the native officers the absurdity of the greased cartridge story, and tell them to reassure the men. Can you think of anything else, Dunlop?"

"No, major. The regiment's always been well treated and the men seem to like us. We'll do our best to reassure them, but if there's any insubordination, I hope the colonel will read the riot act—kill the nonsense in the bud."

"Ah, here's the kitmagar, will you stay to tiffin?" the major asked, as his head servant approached the group and announced that luncheon was ready.

"Many thanks, major, but we're promised at the mess. How're you going to the pig-sticking tomorrow? I'm going to drive over, and send my horse on ahead, so I can give one of your boys a lift in my buggy."

"Thanks, Dunlop. That would suit us. I'll drive my trap, which can carry four of us, so if you can take Dick, that'll be fine."

With the two captains mounted and headed towards the officers' mess, the girls, Ned, and Dick came into the dining room, and the party sat down to the midday tiffin. The amount of food put on the Warreners' table would have killed the popular notion in England that colonials in India ate sparingly because of the heat. They not only ate well but, Ned often thought, they ate more than was good for them. A goodly proportion of liver disease suffered by the Anglo-Indians was due to the fact that—the appetite being artificially stimulated by hot and spicy food—people wolfed down more than they could reasonably digest.

Tiffin that day—as most days—consisted of several curries, with which were handed around with chutney and slivers of the dried fish (which strangers found intolerable) called Bombay Duck, cutlets, plantains sliced and fried, pomegranates, and watermelons.

In the morning Captain Dunlop called for Dick at six-thirty, although the time was by no means early for India, where everyone was up and about soon after daylight—the first morning hours before the heat fell like a damp blanket, were always the most pleasant of the whole day.

Kate and Rose were up, having eaten *chota hazaree*, the Indian equivalent of a light breakfast, and were ready when Dunlop drew up in his two-seater buggy. The major's horse-drawn trap was already at the door and, with everyone settled down, the party moved off.

Sandynugghur was situated in the Doab, the fertile tract of land lying between the two great rivers, the Ganges and Yamuna. The Doab was a kind place to plant life and the individual compounds were all well kept, with broad, shady trees and large shrubs covered by bright masses of flowers. They were well established, for Sandynugghur had been a station for many years, and under the hot climate, but with plenty of water, plant-growth was very rapid. The countryside around Sandynugghur was fairly flat, cut into small fields, divided by shallow irrigation ditches.

The major pointed out the deep watercourses with steep sides which here and there wound torturously through the fields to the nearest stream. "Those *nullahs* pose the greatest danger to hunters mounted on horseback," he said. "Often, you can't see them until you're on top of them."

They passed men working the fields wearing nothing more than a scanty loincloth, wielding their hoes among their springing crops. Women, wrapped up in the dark blue calico of their everyday costume, worked as hard as the men. The scattered villages, generally close to groves of trees, had mud-built huts, most of them flat-topped, but some thatched with rushes. Muslim villages invariably had at least one mosque, also mud-built but whitewashed and bright. Hindu villages usually, but not always, clustered around a temple.

As the Warreners enjoyed a refreshing breeze thanks to the pace of their carriages, they passed groves of sturdy trees, whose appearance at a distance looked very like ordinary English forest trees. To Kate, Rose said, "Only the few palms and many banana trees with those extraordinary wide leaves remind me that we're not in England—that, and the heat of course."

When Major Warrener and his passengers drew up at Meanwerrie a conglomeration of buggies had already parked. Ned counted eight men already on horseback, each carrying a boar-spear. The riders were mostly dressed in coats of the Norfolk jacket type, and knee-breeches with thick gaiters. The material of their clothes was a stronger version of the native khaki cloth, gray or brown in color. Some wore round hats and forage caps with bands of puggarees twisted around them.

A chorus of greeting met Dunlop and the Warreners.

Colonel Renwick, the regiment's commanding officer, welcomed them. "Well, young ladies, so you've come out to see the death of the boar?" He gave a hearty chuckle and then noticed that Major Warrener wasn't carrying a weapon. "You're not going to take a spear today? Think it's time to leave it to the youngsters, eh?"

"Where are the wild boars, Mrs. Renwick?" Kate asked the colonel's wife.

"Pigs, my dear, that's what we call them collectively, the father of the family is the boar, and his offspring are the squeakers. You see that clump of long grass and jungle right across the plain? That's where they are. They came out to feed before daybreak and just went back again. Is this the best place for seeing the hunt, Major Warrener?"

"There's a good view of the plain at the top of that rise, Mrs. Renwick, two hundred yards to the right."

The colonel's wife thanked him and set off with her party, including Rose and the young Warreners, and they walked in a chattering group to the indicated spot. The syces stood at the heads of the horses, and those who were taking part in the hunt cantered off toward the spot where the pigs lurked. They rode in a wide detour to approach the copse from the other side from where they would be able to drive the beasts out across the plain. Several native beaters waited patiently at some distance behind the clump, with a variety of mongrel village dogs, ready to spook the quarry.

The hunters took up positions on either side of the patch in readiness, while the villagers, whose rice fields the boars had ravaged, assembled on higher ground to get a better view. With late arrivals there were about a dozen horsemen with spears—three or four novices determined to pit their skill on the squeakers—the rest ready to race after the dangerous older beasts.

"Wild boar are extinct in England," so Ned—adopting the role of local expert—explained to the girls. "This is what you have to watch out for. At the start, a boar is as fast as a horse, very quick at turning and when cornered always attacks his pursuers. As he rushes past he can cut open a horse's leg or flank with a sweeping slash of his sharp tusk and—"

"If a rider's knocked to the ground, he's in deep boar pooh," Dick broke in with a dimple-wide grin.

Ned treated him to a scowl. "Yes, he's in trouble even if help arrives in time to distract the enraged animal. And heavy falls are common, too, what with the crisscrossing nullahs, boulders scattered over the ground..."

The girls followed his pointing finger to see a cluster of smaller rocks which would trip any unwary rider.

Dick cut off Ned's lecture. "Ah, they're off!"

Scarcely had the beaters, shouting at the top of their lungs, entered the patch of bush in which the prey lay hidden, than the pigs—a splendid boar and sow, and eight nearly full-grown squeakers—

darted out into the open. In a flash the horsemen were off in pursuit. The ground was deep and heavy, and the pigs at the first burst got away from the hunters. Making no attempt to stay together, they ran on divergent courses immediately after breaking cover. The old boar and sow kept across the plain—one bearing left, the other to the right. The squeakers ran in all directions—some at right angles to the line that their parents were taking. Their only desperate objective was to find cover of some kind.

With their hats pressed well down and their spears advanced with the point some two or three feet from the ground, the hunters kept up the chase. Some made after the boar, some after the sow, while some of the younger hands dashed off after the squeakers.

"I see Captain Dunlop after the boar, but who else is with him?" Kate asked eagerly.

Ned peered at the flurry of riders and murmured, "The young officer's Ensign Carpenter, then there's our regimental doctor and the other two I don't know—they're civilians."

For a short time they kept together, and then Dunlop and Carpenter drew ahead of the other three. The boar's stamina was extraordinary and his speed slowed only after a mile. Carpenter, mounted on a very fast Arab, drew three to four lengths ahead of Dunlop, guiding his horse toward the boar's left side so he could use the spear balanced in his right hand to advantage.

He was nearly up to him when the captain, who must have seen the beast's savage backward glance, shouted out at the top of his lungs. "Look out, Carpenter! He'll turn in a moment. Keep your horse well in hand."

A moment later the boar whipped around and turned viciously on Carpenter's Arab which, young and unfamiliar with hunting, started violently and swerved. Before the ensign could get him round, the boar was on him. Rose squealed in fright. In an instant the horse was on the ground, with a long gash along its flank Carpenter flew through the air and fell almost directly in the slavering boar's path.

"Oh, he'll be killed," Rose moaned. Even Kate looked alarmed.

"Look at Captain Dunlop," Dick said breathlessly.

Ned saw Dunlop, even as he shouted, veer to the left to head the boar off should it turn, and he was now so close that the snorting, snapping beast only had time to give Carpenter a swiping blow. The helpless onlookers saw a gout of blood fly up from his arm. Dunlop's spear then struck the boar's ribs, but only a glancing blow because his aim had been thrown by having to leap his horse over the fallen ensign.

In a split-second the boar twisted its sinewy body onto this new assailant.

"Dunlop's horse is a well trained hunter," Ned said and the proof of his exclamation came instantly as the horse easily avoided the vicious lunge, wheeled sharply on its hind legs, and sprang off at full speed. The boar swerved off again and continued its original line of flight, heading for a thick patch of jungle about a quarter of a mile distant.

The delay, however, proved fatal to the big hog's escape, for the doctor now brought up his horse with a rush and, with a well-aimed thrust, ran the boar through, completely pinning it to the earth.

A chorus of approval came from the watching party. Ned turned to his bother and the girls. "The honor will be divided between the doctor and the captain because Dunlop drew first blood while the doctor scored the actual kill."

The sow was more fortunate. She took a line across a part of the plain intersected by several nullahs. She, too, had received a wound, but one of the nullahs had thrown off several of her pursuers—one hunter was hurled over his mount's head and knocked unconscious. The sow made a sharp turn down into a deep, precipitous gully and got away. Three of the squeakers fell to the spears of the younger men and the rest escaped.

The kill happened only a short distance from the rise on which the Sandynugghur spectators watched, and the beaters soon tied the boar's legs together, slipped a pole through them, and six staggered under its weight as they carried the beast up to the colonel's wife for inspection.

"What a savage-looking brute it is!" Kate said. "Not a bit like a pig, with all those long bristles, and that sharp high back, and those tremendous tusks."

Ned smiled at Kate's enthusiasm, which made her cousin Rose blanch. "The tusks look like enormous razor-sharp scimitars." She shuddered. "See the terrible harm they can do." She pointed faintly at Ensign Carpenter as the doctor bound his arm where the boar had slashed through muscle from elbow to shoulder. As soon as the young officer was patched up, the doctor sent him home in a buggy, and the man who had stunned himself in his fall came to in a short time. The colonel and major jibed at the unsuccessful hunters for allowing half the game to get away.

"You ought not to grumble, colonel," Captain Manners said. "If we'd killed them all, we might not have had another run for months. As it is, we'll have some more sport next week."

This comment brought a glow to many cheeks, but Colonel Renwick dampened spirits. "Hmm, that's as may be, gentlemen, but the sow and her remaining squeakers may be spared a further chase if the sepoy situation worsens. But to look on the bright side we're still peaceful here in Sandynugghur.

The peace is illusory and what follows terrifying and bloody. Read more of the adventures of Ned and Dick Warrener in *A Storm of Peril*.

1884
Deep in the deserts of Sudan a crazed fanatic spawns violent bloodshed...

Available as ebook or paperback

As members of the British force engaged in a desperate bid to save heroic Gordon of Khartoum, besieged by the frenzied armies of the Mahdi, teenagers Edgar and Rupert Clinton, twin brothers divided by a woman's greed, unravel a past crime that threatens their futures.

Separated by events, Edgar and Rupert are thrown into their own desperate adventures as the conflict rages on – and both find Muslim allies willing to risk all to see them through.

In a hostile world of searing sun, sand and rocky wastes the two boys discover the wider meaning of what truly is a family.

1896
In the heart of the Sudan, the Mahdiya's despotic rule faces final retribution...

Available as ebook or paperback

As the British and Egyptian armies under General Kitchener mount a massive campaign to free Khartoum from the fanatic Dervish forces, one young man promises his dying mother to set out and seek the truth of his long-lost father's fate. Did he die in battle against the Mahdi's frenzied hordes in 1883? Did he escape and survive against all odds?

Sixteen-year-old Gregory Hilliard stakes his life on discovering the truth, helped by his loyal friend Zaki and two captains, the brothers Edgar and Rupert Clinton. Born and raised in Egypt, fluent in native languages, Gregory is pitched into the heat of war as interpreter for the British command, and through battle and peril unravels a tragic and life-changing mystery with its roots in faraway England.

1873
In the steamy jungle of West Africa the fierce Ashanti tribe seeks war...

Available as ebook or paperback

Orphaned at fifteen and with no money, Frank Hargate, too proud to accept help from others, determines to make his own way in the world.

Fatefully, his skills learned from a childhood hobby propel him into the adventure of a lifetime – an expedition that takes Frank from London to West Africa and will change him forever.

Among new friends and allies, he finds himself struggling against staggering odds to survive hostile nature, blood-thirsty tribes and savage war. From the horrors a young man with new aspirations is forged, who is determined to help others towards a better life for themselves.

1857
The terror of the Indian Uprising against British rule...

Available as ebook or paperback

As hell breaks loose, two teenage brothers, Ned and Dick Warrener, and their family are plunged into the maelstrom — hunted fugitives from appalling violence.

On their desperate trek through a mutinous country they must brave extreme perils if they are to survive. Only courage, cunning and sheer tenacity will see them through...

In this action-packed epic about a crucial moment in British colonial history, Ned and Dick are thrown into dangerous adventures that will turn them from boys into men.

Made in United States
North Haven, CT
13 July 2023

38985238R00163